IN THE END

KATI KIRSTEN

WYND AND RIVER
PRESS

First Edition September 2025

Interior Design by Stephanie Kirsten
Original Cover Design by Kaitlyn Kirsten
Cover Composition by GetCovers

Paperback: 979 – 8 – 9996161 – 2 – 8
Hardcover: 979 – 8 – 9996161 – 1 – 1
EBook: 979 – 8 – 9996161 – 0 – 4

TO GRAM,
For always pushing and believing in me.

NOTE FROM THE AUTHOR

IT'S BEEN A WILD RIDE FOR AMITY THORNE WITH ALL OF THE harrowing choices she's had to make along the way. Thank you so much for following her into the end. Your continued support means the world to me, and I hope you enjoy the epic conclusion of this story.

What some of you may not know is that the Fight for Survival Series is an allegory for life. We can't stop when one thing gets us down; we have to keep going. Even when all we see is darkness.

I'm happy to let you know that you've made it to the light.

CONTENT WARNINGS

In The End is the epic conclusion of a dark and twisty trilogy following characters that struggle with survival and morality. However, this book is intended for mature audiences and contains adult themes and potentially distressing content for some readers. Blood, character death/dying, death of a family member, foul language, flashbacks to trauma, grief, insinuation of sexual acts, intrusive thoughts, mental illness (depression, anxiety, PTSD), murder, neglect/abuse and death/murder of a child character, pain of an animal, systemic oppression, torture, violence, and war are presented on the page. As a reader that may be sensitive to these topics, only read if you feel safe in doing so, and get ready to follow Amity and Sarge to the end...

IN THE
END

12 YEARS AGO

THE PLANS FOR OUR HEADQUARTERS TO BE BUILT INTO Mt. Diablo have been approved. By this time next year, our quiet takeover will be deep seated in nature, hidden in plain sight. Thankfully, dear old daddy bought my pitch and I was able to finally weasel my way into his life.

Speaking of fathers...

"Madame," some nameless soldier—a friend of my father—calls over the radio. My father anointed him Sergeant Major of the new American Liberation Force; another of my ideas he feels the need to take credit for. "A gentleman named Paul Warin would like to see you."

Paul. It's been thirteen years since I've seen him. Thirteen years since I've seen our son. It was only a matter of time before he'd seek me out. I am, in fact, a well-known public figure now.

I wonder how Lucas is, how they're doing? Did Paul tell him wonderful stories of me? By now, he should be a strong young man. Soon he'll be capable of leading great armies and taking control of any situation thrown his way. Getting reacquainted will be necessary for the future.

"Bring him up."

I don't often get flutters in my chest, but the thought of seeing Paul leaves me almost giddy. Or maybe it's the fact that I'm powerful now. When Paul found me, I was a shadow of a human being, tossed aside like the garbage I was. Then again, Paul had been dealing with his own demons.

What a power couple we'll be; what a powerful *family* we'll be all together again.

"Ren." The man from my past is standing in the middle of my office now. *My* office.

"Paul," I answer back, a slight smirk playing at my lips. "How have you been?"

His face morphs into a painful expression. Or maybe it's anger. I've always been good at reading people, but not Paul. "What do you care?" he questions. "You left! What the hell are you doing here?"

I'm taken off guard. His temper had always been even. "Is that any way to greet your wife? You know why I'm here." I scoff. No more suffering. No more faults. We're going to make Humanity better. That's the goal.

"My wife?" He's shocked. "You left!" he repeats. "You left and never turned back."

Paul has completely ignored my plans. We used to talk about fixing the flaws of Humanity together. No poor, no different, no suffering. Everything—everyone—equal. And now, here he is, completely ignoring our dream.

I open my mouth to speak, but he cuts me off.

"Don't even argue. Janet is my wife. You are the ghost of my past," he scorns. "So what are you *really* doing? Combining the houses? It's one thing to talk about a future without flaws for our son, but it's another to completely take control of the very system that keeps us safe."

"Safe?" I cry, losing my composure momentarily. "That same

system that left me to starve? Left me to rot while my bitch of a mother got high? Left *you* an orphan to fend for yourself?"

Much to his consternation, he continues, wiping all emotion away. "These unresolved problems with your parents are exactly why you don't deserve to see Lucas after all this time. I've made my peace," he sneers. "And that's why *I'm* here. To come to an agreement."

Irritation surges through my veins. Fine the man I love has moved on with some trollop named Janet, but Lucas is *my* son. He is the one that will carry on the legacy after I'm gone. Forget Paul. I don't need him.

Taking a deep breath, I push forth with an even tone. "Why the hell not? He is still my son, isn't he? Or did Janet take some claim over him?" The way her name tastes in my mouth is like vomit sitting in the back of my throat.

"Pfft." Paul chuckles flippantly. "You don't deserve him because of what you've done. Sure, talk about change all you want. But you said you wanted to be different from your parents."

"I am different," I say. How could he think otherwise? I'm taking control like my father, sure, but at least I'm making a difference. What has *he* done?

"No," he derides. "You left for something better rather than making it. You're just like John. Hiding the parts you were disappointed in. And what, did you blackmail him for this cushy new position?"

The insinuation that I didn't earn every bit of this sends anger straight into my chest, rage filling it quickly. As if I'm not *making* things better currently. But I'm the Headmistress now. I need to make myself appear calm, even if I'm red hot and boiling on the inside. And Lord knows that Paul Warin gets under my skin. "I planned on seeing Lucas, yes. Once things died down a bit. I'm surprised he hasn't already asked to see me."

Paul is silent, his features stoic. His eyes are the eyes of my sweet Lucas, but they are troubled.

"What?" I question, squinting.

There's hardly any hesitation from Paul. "He believes you're dead."

"Excuse me?" This time it's harder to hold my composure. Fiery rage billows through every pore.

"You left us, Ren. You broke my heart. I wasn't going to give our son some sense of false hope that you'd return."

"So you told him I died?" I can't believe this. What a sick asshole. How could he do that to our son? My little Lucas.

"Oh, that's rich," he says. "Should I have told him the truth? That you couldn't handle how imperfect he was? That you craved control? He was just a kid, Ren. He needed guidance, and you tossed him aside like you were as a child."

His onslaught continues.

"I told him you moved to the East; that it was too far to see you. The Undoing... well..." His voice fades to almost nothing.

I back up until my backside rests against my desk. "How..."

"Take it as a blessing, Ren. At least he has a good reason to believe why you weren't around."

Paul wants me to see the bright side here. At first, I can't. But suddenly, my face morphs into a smile at the thought. This is great! Honestly, the best news I could receive. Lucas will be so excited to learn that I'm not dead. He'll be ecstatic to join the cause for some bonding time. My father and my son, together, taking on the flaws of Humanity. He'll come around. The same way I did. He won't blame me for searching for something better.

How wonderful! It is all I've ever wanted.

"What?" Paul's harsh tone tears me from my fantasy.

"Lucas will be so happy to reign by my side. To learn I'm alive."
All of the possibilities float through my head. Paul thought he was
delivering a Death blow, but he was wrong.

"You're not telling him," Paul says, calmly.

"Excuse me?" Death of a parent makes for a strong individual.
It's even better than I could have imagined. Lucas has to be perfect. Paul cannot keep him from me. I am his mother.

"He's a sixteen year old boy! He's already confused about
things. He doesn't need this."

"A boy needs his mother!" I screech, then chastise myself for
the outburst. Paul Warin does not deserve this power over me. No
man does. No man will.

"Then you wouldn't have left us behind like we meant nothing!" Paul is in my face, screaming. He takes a breath. "If you tell
Lucas anything about your identity, Ren, so help me God I will
kill him."

My throat tightens. "You wouldn't," I breathe, but I know he
means it. Paul is a straightforward man. He means what he says.

I feel the hotness of his breath on my face. "Watch me," he
seethes. "I won't let you ruin my son." He steps back, our eyes
holding onto each other, stuck in a battle of wills. "As long as my
heart is beating, I will take everything you want from this world,
believe me. Killing him would be merciful. So, give me your word."

An eternity of silence passes before I answer. "I won't tell Lucas
who I am."

Paul nods, his face still pulled into an uncomfortably pained
expression. He turns, ready to leave me just like I'd walked away
all those years ago. I guess I don't blame him.

But this new game, the thrill, is exciting to me. He may have the
upper hand now, but he will not keep it. Because in games I play,
I never lose.

Before Paul makes it to the door, I speak out. "I promise not to tell Lucas, though I still have big plans for him."

Paul doesn't fully turn around, but it's clear how rigid his body is. Adrenaline shoots through my very soul.

My next words are chosen carefully. "There will come a day where I will convince Lucas to kill you. And on that day, I will rejoice with my son."

CHAPTER ONE ○ AMITY

THE SOUNDS OF A HOSPITAL ROOM ARE NOT THE SOUNDS I wish to hear. I want to hear my father read me his poetry. Emma's sweet giggle. Grace's funny jokes. I want to hear my mother's voice again. But instead I'm stuck drowning in medicinal beeps and IV drips.

In my head, in my heart, my mother has only been gone a month or so. Grace just a bit more. But the doctors tell me it's been longer. Six years to be exact. They won't tell me where Emma is, though. Apparently she's not four. According to their timetable, a few months ago she turned ten. *How could I have lost so much of our life together?*

The doctors won't tell me where my father is, either. I don't get it. What happened to me? To them? Something doesn't feel right about all this, and instinctively my eyes search for the one they call Sarge. He's always here.

Laying on the love seat, the large, black beast watches over me. His golden eyes refuse to move from my direction. He doesn't lift his head, or blink. When I look at him, something flutters in my chest. His heart calls to mine in a way I'd never thought possible. I sit here in a hospital room, all broken, and yet I can somehow feel whole when Sarge is near.

They tell me he's mine; the best dog anyone can ask for. And it makes sense. He hasn't left this room for as long as I've been conscious. A dog potty station had to be added because he refuses to leave my side, even for that.

The truth is, I don't remember anything. I don't remember finding him in the woods, or my father letting me keep him. But when I look at Sarge, I believe it. We are tethered by a bond so unbreakable that the depth of it is unfathomable to the human mind. But it's not something you know in your head; it's something you feel in the deepest parts of your soul. And I felt it the second we locked eyes.

A commotion outside of my room pulls me from my thoughts. Pacing feet and the shuffle of something plasticky. Then a doctor—a voice I recognize—says, "You can't go in there!" before a tall, muscular man storms in, pulling back the curtain.

"Says who?" he answers with a roll of his eyes. His lips twitch as he focuses his gaze on me.

This is Luke Warin, or so they say. He's got a sharp and slanted nose, pronounced jawline, and gorgeous hazel eyes. But when I say that he's exasperating, I'm putting it mildly. He *rescued* me from the Reaver, I know that much. He's told me we were... something. Not friends, but... he won't be specific. He also told me that he'd take me to see Emma. So...

"Back again to lie to me?" My words are heavy, but the tone is playful. Making jokes at the expense of my fears has always been my default setting.

Luke brushes off the subtle jab. "Here to give you flowers." He pulls a stem of three beautiful, yellow marigolds from behind his back. The gesture is sweet, but my eyes subconsciously flick to the giant, elegant bouquet that sits across the room. Luke's eyes follow, his neck tensing slightly. "But I see you don't need any more." His knuckles tense around the plastic pot and I find myself in a weird state.

Normally I wouldn't care how someone felt about such trivial things, but something about Luke is calling to me, telling me to make it right. Whatever that means. "No." I blush. "But I much prefer the simplicity of yours." I peek up through my lashes to see a shocked expression, followed by a smirk.

In such a short time, I've truly grown to like the playful guise that Luke takes on in small snippets. Yet, every time I get a tumbling chest over it, I chastise myself. Luke is someone I can't trust... yet. My mind is feeble right now, but I'll be damned if I let him in.

Luke walks toward the extravagant bouquet and places the marigolds in front of it. "The three stems signify you, me, and Sarge," he whispers, barely audible. *Shit.*

Heat flushes in my cheeks. How is anyone supposed to keep distance after that? All of the most alluring things are dangerous. Maybe Luke should get the benefit of the doubt? *How could you, Amity? He's lied before. You know trust has to be earned.*

Luke turns, his hazels meeting my greys, and my face beats red once more. He holds the contact for a few but then pulls away to look at his watch. He's agitated when he returns his gaze. "So, I lied," he says.

Point proven. Of course. Panic settles in my chest and Sarge lifts his head from the love seat. Knowing he's with me, truly seeing me, helps me stay calm.

"I'm actually here to invite you to Axom and Charlotte's memorial tonight." The air changes harshly all at once with his words. Luke is no longer playful; there's no signature smirk anywhere close to his lips now. Only a deep-creased frown is present.

"The two that were with you that day?" I question. My brain is fuzzy, but the last couple of weeks are still tucked away in my mind. This memory in particular I've tried to bury, but Luke's words force me to dig it back up.

Two people—two *innocent* people—getting crushed by crumbling stone. I can't help but feel that their deaths are somehow my fault. It's hard to fight my body's natural reaction to numb itself.

Luke nods. "I'd like it if you were there beside me." The hopeful look in his eyes sends a twinge to my heart, and my face softens. Then:

"Mr. Baines, he can't keep storming in like this!" The doctor's shrill voice pierces through the room.

"I'll handle it, Morin," a deep, dignified voice answers back. Then it's not just Luke in here anymore. It's the one they call Mason, too.

Mason Baines has a round, benevolent face. His dirty blonde hair is perfectly tussled atop his head, and he has these magnificent blue pools where eyes should be. When he talks, it makes me feel ready to take on the day.

Apparently, he and I were friends as well. I'm more inclined to believe him. After all, he hasn't lied to me yet... as far as I know. So should I give him some leniency? No. I shouldn't, really. Now is not the time for friendships. I lost Grace, and then my mom. Who else could I possibly handle losing?

"Good morning, Amity." Mason smiles kindly at me. His plump lips pull back, his perfect teeth coming into view. His words cause visible disdain from Luke.

In the times this routine has played out, it's always a similar reaction. Luke bursts in, the doctors call Mason. Mason steps in to be the middleman, saying it's better him than getting the General involved. Luke makes a snide remark under his breath, and then they continue showing great disapproval of one another for the remainder of the event.

Forget dealing with my own history, I want to know theirs.

"Good morning." I nod. A small smile creeps onto my face. It's all I can muster up. "Luke was just inviting me to the memorial tonight?" I speak as though it's a question.

Mason subtly glares in Luke's direction. When his gaze returns to mine, it's as gentle as ever. "You really should be resting," he insists. His palm slides along the back of his neck. He's nervous. For some reason, he wants me to stay locked in this room. And just like that, I want to be everywhere but here.

"I think it would be better if I got up and moved around. Don't you agree, Luke?" Perhaps it would be good to learn more about my surroundings and those in it... not just the ones in this hospital ward.

Luke struggles to hide his smirk but is able to keep his face serious as Mason turns to him. "Whatever the lady wants," he agrees. He winks at me once Mason returns his eyes to mine. I stifle a giggle.

"Fine," Mason ultimately acquiesces. "You'll need something to wear. I'll send it to you. But for now, you need rest."

Mason pulls Luke out of the room before I have a chance to say anything more. No goodbye or anything. They don't get far before Luke starts to argue, though. "What's your problem?"

Mason lets out a loud sigh. "You know we're not supposed to see her."

"Well that's stupid," Luke retorts. "We should be helping her!"

"We are!" Mason shouts, a little too loud. "Just because you don't understand, doesn't mean you can break all of the rules."

Luke switches gears. "You sent her flowers?" His voice sounds angrier than it should be over some smelly plants.

"Believe it or not, it's common practice to send flowers as get well soon gifts."

Luke answers with a grunting snort. "You did this shit on purpose!"

If they're trying to make it so I don't hear, they're failing miserably. But then, it gets so quiet that I almost believe they've walked away.

Their hushed, whispery yells intrigue me. I've been terribly bored and desperate for answers. So, I sneak closer to the entrance. My bare feet barely make a noise as they touch the tiled floor. I go as far as the wires will allow.

"You have to look on the bright side," Mason whispers.

"What bright side, dipshit?" Luke spits back. "Amity can't stand me. Which is... fine." He gulps. "But she thinks I've lied to her. She won't trust me."

"You're grossly selfish," Mason replies. "Would you give her back all her pain simply so she *remembers* you?" What pain?

Luke utters something indistinguishable in return. My ears strain further.

Mason continues speaking. "She doesn't remember the Death or the torture. You know what that means? There's no pain. No emotional scar left behind." *What?*

Torture? Death?

CHAPTER TWO ○ AMITY

THE HUMAN PROTECTIVE SERVICE—WHICH IS WHO I'VE COME to know has taken me in—spares no expense for the memorials of their fallen soldiers. The young man and woman who had been with Luke as he rescued me are the first to be lost in a long time. There's no exception for memorializing them in the grandest way.

This is the first time I'll be up. The first time I'll be around people that aren't doctors. No hospital gowns, no wires, no isolation. Something deep inside me turns, the sensation leaving me sick to my stomach. Am I ready to face the world?

My mother wanted us to keep to the shadows; hide away, stay isolated. Exactly what Mason wants of me in this cell of a hospital room. So why do I feel it so deeply to get out? To put myself into the crowd?

Just then, Sarge moves. He makes his way from the love seat over to my bed, and he rests his chin on the soft sheets. His golden eyes make me feel safe. He's telling me it will be alright, that my decision is the right one. *Okay, Amity. You can face the world.*

One of the doctors had dropped off a box wrapped in a bow. They said I'd need to be ready for a grand ball of sorts. I've never been to one before, and I've been too nervous to even look in the box. But this is how they honor the dead here: host a great gala in remembrance of all they've done to celebrate their life and honor their death. It's admirable, I suppose, though, nerve-wracking nonetheless. How does everyone have such a good time with the reminder of Death plaguing the air?

Regardless, the one called Luke will be here soon. He'll come, and I'll accompany him for the night. Normally this would leave a feeling of disdain to settle in my chest, but perhaps there's more to him than I originally thought. Luke is convinced he was forced to lie to me, that he never intended to hurt me or do it of his own volition. Couple that with the fact that the *lie* in question is concerning my sweet little M and my mind is whirring with a tornado of all sorts of emotions.

Sarge backs up as I sling the sheets off my body but doesn't go far. The air is slightly cold on my now exposed legs. My body somehow carries me toward the box, Sarge heeling perfectly, tightly pressed against my side. I'm shaking from nerves as I stop in front of the full body mirror. I've not seen myself since I don't know when. The word *torture* swirls to the forefront of my brain. Is it really possible I was tortured? Maybe it's more sinister. *Did you do the torturing, Amity?*

My fingers tremor as I undo the buttons behind my back. Dressing in hospital garb is definitely not flattering. Before the cloth falls to the ground, I jerk my gangly frame away from the glass, startling Sarge. My heart races, yet I attempt to keep my breathing under control. I don't want to see my whole body exposed. Not yet. *Maybe put the dress on first, Amity. Then try.*

The box is untied and the dress is pulled out in a matter of seconds. Sarge sits patiently behind me while I study the garment. It's a long, silver dress with thin straps. I'm hesitant as I slide the fabric over my body, but it's silky against my skin.

There's never been a time where I've dressed up. Even when we were trying to project a higher status among the Slums, there was never anything this fancy in my closet.

Taking a deep breath, I try pooling all my courage. I need to look at myself, but I'm worried I won't recognize the person that stares back. Will she be covered in cuts and bruises? Will her eyes be devoid of light? Will she look... sad? After a few seconds, I reach my hand out to summon Sarge. If I'm going to take this next step, then maybe it will help if I've got someone solid by my side.

Sarge's tail wags in excitement as he nudges his face against my hip. My hands explore the soft fur of his head and his eyes close in appreciation. How can I not remember such a wonderful creature? I can only imagine that he helped me through my mother's death the first time. Now he'll be here to do it again...

We step forward as one toward the mirror, my heart beating wildly in my chest. This is it. One last breath escapes my lips before everything is suspended. My eyes scan over my body. I'm thin, sort of sickly looking. My grey eyes are dull, and my hair is slightly matted in the back. There are tiny circular scars—barely noticeable—covering my chest, shoulders, neck. *Could this be a small sign of a torturous path?*

It's not long of me studying the scars before my eyes catch on a deeply pigmented symbol on my right arm, just below my shoulder. It's a delicate, black mark on my otherwise clean skin. It's... beautiful.

"Signal blocking ink," a voice states from behind me. My body jumps in reaction to being startled. "Sorry," Luke says.

"What's it blocking?" I ask, ignoring my nervousness. As much as I want answers, I hate to admit that I'm just as equally terrified of what will come to light.

Luke stares at me with an intense gaze. It appears his own nervous look settles into his pupils as he says, "Your tracker."

Something deep within my gut screams that this information should hold more weight to me. *A tracker?* If it's being blocked, I can't imagine it came from the H.P.S.. I scan my memories for the eight hundredth time, trying to find a connection, but fail anew.

I open my mouth to ask more, but a different voice fills the air. "You look stunning." It's Mason. *Damn it. Left without answers, again.*

Sarge lets out a muffled gruff as Mason gets closer. Like a warning. Mason doesn't come any closer. *Hello? Is this a signal everyone knows?* Sarge is probably the only one I wholeheartedly trust in this place. And something about Mason has set him off.

"Thank you," I say. My face flushes with embarrassment when his eyes subtly scan my body.

Luke radiates intensity. "I was under the impression that Amity and I would be alone." Luke sighs. An odd emotion sweeps across my chest...

There's a feeling through the room that seems off. I can't quite put my finger on the animosity. I never could, but this is far worse than any of the other spats I've bore witness to.

"I had to bring Sarge his tie," Mason admits.

A quick glance in Sarge's direction shows his eyes holding the same wariness that's settled in mine. *Oh, how I wish he could talk.*

Mason hands the bow tie to Luke—a strange, out of place gesture. Luke asks if I'd prefer to do the honors myself. I nod and he steps forward. Listening for any trifle from Sarge, the room is quiet as Luke closes the distance. *Interesting.*

Our fingers touch when he places the bow tie in my hand, sending electricity shooting into my chest. *What the?* I ignore the feeling and awkwardly brush my hair behind my ear, turning away from him to deal with Sarge. I wish I understood what was happening. I wish I had at least *some* memory of the last six years.

Sarge smiles up at me, sitting tall and pretty, while I fasten the bow tie into his thick chest fur. He's a dapper gentleman next to me while I inspect us both in the mirror. The shimmery silk of the tie matches the silver of my dress. The sight calms me. Any unease that creeps into my heart is being combatted by Sarge's presence. *Perhaps tonight won't be so bad.*

I spin around and Sarge presses against me. The men gaze at me with the same expression. Only, Luke's eyes hold sorrow in them, too. But looking at him this time, an image shoots into my head, causing a sharp pain inside my skull. There's a man with a buzz cut standing in front of me. When I blink, he's gone. Replaced by Luke, who, I'm now realizing, has a similar style of hair. Or lack thereof. What was that? *Or rather, who?*

"You okay?" Luke is genuinely concerned.

"Should we get going?" I ask, innocently. I decided keeping this little vision to myself is best. At least until I figure out who's truly on my side. If everyone wants to keep my past from me, then I'll be damned if I openly share my present. *Is anyone here even trustworthy at all?*

Luke nods, not quite convinced with my display. Mason says he'll lead the way. There's no need to do an in-depth observation to see the pure and utter disdain this causes Luke. His body is tense; his gait is rigid.

Mason escorts, Sarge and I follow. Luke brings up the rear. His eyes soften a bit when I peek back at him. For now, I believe him about our past. Oddly enough, I do. And we want the same thing: to be alone.

Luke seems to know things, and by all things lucky, he wants me to know things, too. This means we have similar interests because I think I want to know everything he'll tell me. Perhaps it will be a lie, or perhaps that's just what Mason wants me to think.

But it's the best place to start.

Mason leads us through the medical ward and out into, what I gather, is H.P.S. Headquarters. Everything is hi-tech and clean, a stark contrast to the Slums of Western America. The pristine nature of the halls is vaguely familiar, but I can't place why. Never in a million years would I have guessed I'd see something this grand. I just wish my family were here to see it, too.

My hand finds Sarge's soft fur as we enter the grand ballroom. There's a large stage in the far right, refreshments along the back left, with what looks like a thousand people in between—and almost every single one of them is staring at us.

Anxiety pushing up into my chest, Sarge snakes his head around my hip, pressing himself closer. Mason is now to my side, with Sarge in between us, and Luke is slightly behind us to my left. Perhaps this was a mistake. Maybe Mason was right, I should be resting.

"General Favager will be happy to meet you," Mason shouts over the loud din of the room. "Shall we find him?" He holds out his hand, expecting me to take it. The question was asked, but I feel I don't really have a choice. I don't need to turn around to see the anger coming from Luke because it's already palpable from a distance.

"I..." I hesitate. "You think maybe Luke could take me for a drink first?" My words surprise me, but it's Mason's expression that shocks me even more. It's so subtle that I almost don't see it, but his eyes flash frustration and distrust. It's gone after a second or two, no trace it was there in the first place.

"No problem," he says, his smile not quite reaching his eyes. "I'll bring General Favager to the refreshments table." He walks away, but not before shooting a glare in Luke's direction. I pretend not to notice.

"Shall we?" My eyes flick to Luke's as I turn around. My palm is still buried in the thickness of Sarge's fur, but Luke's playful smirk offers me some semblance of confidence.

"Yes, please!"

It takes about two seconds to realize that my worries of a crowded room are for naught. The swarm of bodies parts and clears a path for me and Sarge as we walk. Perhaps it's Sarge who scares them. *Or maybe it's me...*

We get to the refreshments table quicker than anticipated. No one got in our way, no awkward shimmying past bodies had to ensue. Luke asks what I'm in the mood for. *Answers,* I think, but I tell him water because he's referring to a drink. As he fills my cup and hands it to me, I probe for what I'm really after.

"The people here must be scared of us to move out of the way like that."

Luke's body tenses, a tell-tale sign that I've broached a sensitive subject. "I think it's more because of how bad I must smell." He shrugs, not missing a beat. The normality of it throws me off guard, and my lip twitches with the hint of a small smile.

"I suppose that makes sense," I say. "You reek."

Luke turns to me now with a hint of adoration in his eyes. Then, it gets torn away and replaced with some other emotion I can't quite pinpoint. Sorrow? Maybe grief?

"What's wrong?" I question.

"This... reminds me of a conversation we've had before."

"About how smelly you are?" I'm slightly confused. What an odd thing to talk about.

Luke chuckles a sad sounding laugh. "Actually, yes."

The simplicity of this moment is bittersweet. Before Grace passed, and then my mother, I would have reveled in this type of normal. Yet, the thought of being close to anyone constricts my heart. What happened to make me change? If Luke is telling the truth, then I opened myself up to something more.

I know I should be finding answers about where my family is and what's happened to me, but maybe we can take a brief detour to learn about my mysterious past with this man.

"So you and I really were... something?" Luke may have lied to me before, but this particular tidbit appears to be backed up by the way he looks at me.

"Yes," he says, his face serious now. "M, I..." He reaches out his thick hand, gently brushing against my chest as he attempts to wipe the hair away, tucking it behind my ear.

My body jerks involuntarily, the contrast sending terrible shocks down my nervous system. My heart rate spikes, my breathing picks up, and Sarge is now in between Luke and I, blocking Luke's access to me with a snap of his teeth.

"I'm... I'm sorry," I respond. My visceral reaction to the contact has me confused, yet Luke's expression holds a hint of anger. At me? At the situation? "I don't know why I did that," I admit.

Is it possible that this is part of the remnants left behind from torture I can't remember? Will I be able to find answers? But, the better question might be, do I really want to know?

Luke opens his mouth to speak, but it's not his voice that enters my eardrums. It's Mason's. "Amity," he calls from somewhere behind me. Before I turn, Luke's tensed muscles catch my attention. Mason has somehow weaseled his way in... again.

I rotate to see Mason walking toward us accompanied by a tall man with slicked back hair. His shoulders are square, his body looks rigid, but his demeanor is quite relaxed.

"Bonjour. I'm Olivier Favager. The General of the Human Protective Service," the man says, authority oozing from every word.

Mason's eyes are smiling, the deep blue sparkling as if they were clusters of gemstones shimmering in the sun. The General is someone he admires. "Mr. Favager is the one who sent for your extraction!"

Oh, why? What does this man want from me? And why did I need rescuing anyway? It's all so confusing. Torture, trackers, extractions, lies. Even... *Death*. My head pounds with unanswered questions and distrust.

Luke's body heat is once again radiating from beside me. A sideways glance clues me in on how he's feeling. Something about what Mason has said doesn't sit right with him. *What else is new?* I mentally roll my eyes but put a notch in it for later.

"We're glad to have you here. Your recovery is going well, I take it?" The General's voice lilts in a way that simultaneously makes me cringe yet also empowers me.

"Y... yes," I say. "I thought tonight would be a good time to make an appearance. To pay my respects, of course."

"Of course, Miss Thorne. How admirable of you," he says.

The way he says my name—Miss Thorne—leaves my head reeling. There's no reasonable explanation I can formulate for this response. The only thing I know for certain is that my gut is screaming at me, telling me something isn't right. Sarge is pressing into me so hard I fear I might fall over. God knows my body is already struggling as it is.

The General is regarding me with a curious eye. Is he expecting a thank you? For me to grovel at his feet and kiss his shoes? How can I thank a man if I don't know what I'm thanking him for?

But I say, "I appreciate your kindness," anyway, because there's no reason to put myself on this man's bad side.

"You're very important to us, Miss Thorne," the General says. "It's good to see you're feeling better. Do have a good time." He nods and off he goes.

CHAPTER THREE ∘ AMITY

SARGE IS PRESSED TO ME WHILE I'M LEFT TRYING TO PROCESS my feelings. I've always told Emma never to ignore a gut feeling. But is it possible my brain is too damaged to distinguish anything these days?

"The fuck did you give him the credit for?" Luke seethes once the General is out of earshot.

Mason glares at him, looking around to make sure no one else has heard. But Luke's voice was so menacingly low that I barely heard it standing right next to him. "Keep your mouth shut, Warin," Mason warns. His voice isn't dark like Luke's, but it holds a similar command.

"Oh, that's right." Luke rolls his eyes. "I forgot this was Western America."

Before the tension of the conversation gets too thick, a voice in the crowd thankfully breaks it. "Amity!"

My whole body tenses in the struggle to find any recognition of this voice from my past. Unfortunately, there's nothing. I only recognize the voice from my last few weeks here.

I turn to find the one they call Lacy Barnett pushing her way through the crowd. Poor Sonya is trailing behind her, quietly apologizing for her girlfriend's rudeness. It makes me giggle.

"You look amazing!" Lacy says once she's closer. She puts her hands on my shoulders and keeps me at arm's length. "Absolutely stunning." I'm pulled in for a hug, and my body tenses once more.

Sarge offers his body weight against me, keeping his tail upright and wagging slightly. After a few minutes, he lets out a sharp crack of his teeth, and Lacy promptly pulls away.

"Sorry," she says, wiping her eye. "It's just…"

"It's alright," I mutter, casting my eyes down, brushing a loose strand of hair behind my ear. "You look great, too," I say after a few minutes of silence.

Lacy is wearing a tight pantsuit and blazer combo in a deep plum. She's stunning. Her black lob is perfectly styled, sitting just at her shoulders, and the matching purple of the tips accentuates her face. Her makeup is clean and crisp, leaving me to look tired and naked in comparison.

"Thanks!" She's glowing. "But don't forget about Sonya!"

Sonya is in a chic lilac dress that cascades down her body in different layers. A thin slit barely lets her right leg peek out. The light color of the gown complements the dark of Lacy's attire. On their own, they're beautiful, but together? They're to-die-for.

"It's okay, baby," Sonya says. "You're the only one they'll notice."

Lacy pulls her in close, hugging her tightly. "Are you kidding me?" she says with a smile. "You are the star of the show, always."

Their words are bittersweet. Anyone looking on would swoon at the love they have, but I don't feel such happiness. All I can think of is how hurt they'd be if one of them were ripped away by this shitty society we're in. Or… were in. Maybe things could be different now that we're here with the H.P.S.? *No Amity, you know that love is weakness.*

"Not to interrupt, but I actually think it's Sarge that steals the show," I say, hoping to stop the sappy displays.

Sarge sits proud, puffing out his chest. He's smug.

"Oh, yeah, little bro!" Lacy smiles. "You're killing it!"

Both Sonya and Lacy shower Sarge in pets. He's in dog heaven. I've never understood why Lacy calls Sarge "little bro", but that's on my list of things to find out. Perhaps Lacy and I were closer than I imagine.

The rest of the group makes introductions, but I'm not paying attention fully. Luke and Lacy are verbally sparring, and it's nice to see him so natural and not uptight like he is in my presence. *I wonder if he and I were ever like this...*

"Thank you all for making our acquaintance here at this Grand Memorial Ball." An MC quiets the crowd with his sultry voice. "Please let us have a moment of silence for our fallen."

The people of the crowd simultaneously downturn their heads, bowing in silent prayer. Sarge rests his cheek against my hip, nuzzling close. He can sense my growing anxiety before I pinpoint it myself. I don't know why it's here, but it is.

"Thank you, everyone," the MC says. "Now please remain silent while our General delivers his speech."

And just like that, my anxiety is tenfold. My gut is screaming at me, telling me I'm not going to like what's coming next. I couldn't possibly ignore it even if I tried. The thought leads me to Emma. Oh, how I wish she were here and we were far away from this place.

"Hello citizens," General Favager addresses. "Let us make this night a beautiful celebration as we honor those not here with us today. Axom Hoover and Charlotte Bouchard have paid the ultimate price for our cause. But they will *not* die in vain." The look of determination on his face, the darkening of his eyes, is something I've seen many times in the Slums of Western America. A certain desperation for vengeance; for blood. "Would you all please open a space for Miss Amity Thorne?"

Hearing my name sends a jolt of angst throughout every nerve ending, knocking me from my thoughts. The heat in my face makes it nearly unbearable to breathe. The crowd creates a bubble of space around me, somehow knowing who I am amongst the sea of people.

"Miss Thorne is the key to our success. She is the one to rally our people. She is our call to arms. Mr. Hoover and Miss Bouchard died getting her to us, and what a sweet sacrifice it is. The Guardianship *will* fall now that she is in our corner. Tonight, we celebrate, for those we have lost have left us with the greatest gift of all."

The crowd erupts with cheers. Everyone is shouting with joy, though no one dares come closer than the bubble for fear of a teeth battle with my four-legged companion.

My knees wobble, and I worry Sarge is the only reason I'm still upright. I didn't ask to be here, I don't even know what *here* truly means. I want to be with my family. I don't want to be the key. I don't want to be anything!

All at once my brain projects an image of an older man with kind eyes. *He tells me he doesn't know why people have decided I'm the key, but he knows there's a light inside of me.*

The memory is ripped from my head as fast as it was planted. I don't know the man's name, I don't recognize the pristine white of the backdrop, but the feelings building in my chest are all too familiar. The scene is surrounded with sadness and sorrow.

My teeth are clenched as I hit the ground, my hand finding a place on my skull to press away the pain. General Favager's voice carries through the hoard of bodies, seemingly getting closer and closer, yet still sounding miles from where I am. Someone calls to me, but I can't answer.

"Enjoy this night, for tomorrow brings not only a new day, but the dawn of a new era."

The clapping of hands is loud and harsh but soon dulls into the background. The beating of my heart and the bite of my hyperventilation drowns it out. I need to get out of here. "Sarge," I gasp. "Go."

My weak fingers grip his fur tightly and he braces himself to help me stand. With teeth barred, he releases a guttural snarl, daring anyone to get in his way. Every noise we make feels like it's a scream in the dead of night, but the truth is it's just a single drop in a massive ocean. The crowd tosses like waves, threatening to take me under. Thank goodness for Sarge. My lifesaver.

"Amity!" I hear my name again, but I'm unable to distinguish who's calling it. I don't want to be around anyone, anyway. I want to run.

Sarge and I collapse out into the hall and the cool ground beneath my knees offers a small slice of solace. Despite being in a thinly strapped dress, the heat is consuming me. Sarge is working hard to return me to reality. It's only a matter of time before Mason is behind me.

"What happened?" he asks.

"Give her a second," Luke seethes from somewhere nearby.

"I told you she shouldn't have left," Mason argues. This, I assume, is back at Luke.

"Or maybe she would've been fine if your jackass of a General didn't insinuate that she was responsible for the Death of those soldiers," Luke spits in return.

"Well of course it wasn't her, it was their shithead leader!" Mason shouts.

"Luke!" Lacy shouts. Out of the corner of my eye, Luke is lowering his fist back to his side, tightly pressing it in to keep it planted.

"Can you all just shut up!" I shout as loud as I can muster. "There's something going on here that no one is telling me, and I want to know what it is." I use Sarge's body to steady myself in a standing position. The whirling in my head makes it hard to focus. My limbs are weak.

The other members of the group turn, completely shocked that I've spoken. Mason is the first to open his mouth. "We really should be getting you..."

"No!" I stomp my foot like an errant teenager, slightly losing my balance. "I want to know, now."

The other two are silent, but I'm begging them to speak up. Yet it's Mason who replies again.

"Your heartrate is getting too high, you need..."

"Stop deciding that you know what I need." My foot slips again, but I catch myself on Sarge. The heat in my face is back, but its driving force is anger, not anxiety. "What I..." My voice stops working.

"Are you okay?" Lacy asks.

"I... need..." I speak the words, but the sentence isn't finished before the world around me is black, and the sensation of falling takes over.

"M!"

CHAPTER FOUR ○ LUKE

I LOOSEN MY TIE AS I OPEN THE DOOR TO MY POD, DIPPING MY head so I don't smack it off the ceiling. I walk slowly, casually sitting on the mattress, careful not to put all my weight onto the body that occupies it.

"Ack!" Sam cries, then giggles. His laughs are a needed melody tonight. Nothing with M seems to be going right.

"Oh, good," I say. "You're up!" I flip the switch and the light flickers on.

Sam covers his eyes with his hands—his real one, and the new skin modeled one that the Service gave him. If not for the robotic movements, I sometimes forget he only has one real arm. If only they had signal blocking ink when we needed it for Sam...

"I thought you were staying with your friends in Compound Two?" I question.

Sam and the other children in Mama June's care had been rescued by the Service while I saved M. Mama June is the fiery woman that risked her life daily to operate on the Tainted, giving them a chance at a better existence. I'll never be able to repay her for taking in Sam like she did.

"I wanted to be here when you got back." His small voice tugs at my heart. I've never wanted anything more than for M to get better. The M I know would absolutely adore Sam. But the Amity that's here now isn't ready for the connection.

"Luckily for you, I came back alone and I don't need the bed." I smirk, suggestiveness laced throughout my tone.

"One, yuck. Two, I know you can't fit two adults in here!"

"Well, you don't really need a lot of space if you're..."

"La la la la la..." Sam puts his fingers into his ears.

I chuckle from deep in my gut. "Alright, alright." I reel him in. "It's late. We better get to bed." I've been given special permission to have Sam stay with me. Not that I didn't give them a hard bargain. I sure as hell wasn't going to deny Sam what he wanted and staying in Compound Two was never an option. I need to be as close to M as possible.

So in order for our arrangement to work, Sam gets the bed and I'm stuck with the floor. It sure does wonders for my back.

The light is turned off again and as we lay in silence, I listen to Sam's breathing. It hasn't slowed yet, not evened out. Something is bothering him. "Sam?"

Sam knows what I'm asking. He's smart. He skips the "what" and goes right into the issue. "I miss Sarge." Ah. With the return of M, Sarge hasn't let her out of his sight. That leaves Sam to mourn his friend, just like I'm mourning Amity. Then, "So it didn't go well on the Amity front?"

I sigh. "It was better than any other night," I answer honestly. I leave out the part about her passing out from stress, or whatever. I stayed just long enough to know she was okay, but then I left for fear of my fist kissing Mason's face. "I'm sorry about Sarge. I'm sure he's dying to see you."

"Yeah..." Sam says, sighing.

"Hey," I speak softly. "You know the second I can get you to see him, I will." I hate that he has to miss Sarge. My secret dream is for all of us to be happy together, without the external pressures of Western America. But it seems no matter where we are, there are too many forces beyond our control that won't let it happen. Instead, I'm left with a broken dream and a crushed kid.

"Why do I have to wait?" Sam is confused. As much as I want to help him, we're both shit out of luck. Everything is a secret around here. And I'm none the wiser than a prisoner.

"I'm told it's because our presence might disrupt M's healing," I respond. Mason spews a lot of bullshit these days. Hell, just tonight he gave Favager credit for my extraction idea. But, seeing what happened to M after that speech, maybe she *does* need some time.

"You believe that?" Sam asks. He knows when I'm giving a diplomatic answer.

I sigh. "I don't really know what to believe."

o o o

SAM HEADS OFF to meet his friends before class. Normally I'd be on my way to M's room already, to do the usual routine of getting kicked out within minutes, but today I've decided to wait. She needs her rest, and it's always good to throw a curveball once in a while.

I've requested a meeting with Cateline Pierre, the smartest scientist in all of the H.P.S., and maybe even the world. Her inventions have given the Service the upper hand on everything, including the extraction mission, and I'm hoping she'll be able to help with M's healing.

Cateline has practically been begging for a meeting since she saw me fight Axom with the augmenting tech on. She wants to improve her algorithm. As it stands, it's an enhancement for the soldiers to give them an edge over their opponents. But like everything, it has its flaws.

Someone escorts me at 8:30. My Service clearance throughout the building is N.T.K.. Need to Know. This means I need someone with the highest clearance to take me most places. Personally, I think they have something to hide.

The Service has no doors, a juxtaposition for their clearly secretive practices. Sensors make it easy for the Service to identify people and if they belong where they're headed. Yet the deeper you get, the more obstacles you have to pass through. The truly restrictive areas are usually hidden by real doors and may even have guarded security. Cateline's working quarters are a good example of this.

My escort nods to the two Service members blocking the entrance. The men step aside and I continue, alone, through the door. The room is massive, yet surprisingly empty. The few tables in the forefront of the room have various equipment that I don't concentrate on too much. Behind them, black mat flooring extends up, surrounding the entirety of the wall.

Cateline is leaning over a small object, intensely focused. She doesn't lift her head until I'm right next to her.

"Aha!" she exclaims. "Mr. War... I mean... Luke." She smiles shyly.

Kudos to her for remembering my aversion to the formality. "Cateline." I nod.

"Thank you for coming," she says. "I've been looking forward to getting in your head."

"Good luck." I smirk, but really I couldn't be further from playful. "It takes a lot."

"It can be simple to do with the right tools." The gleam in her eye matches the playful façade I've put forth.

I highly doubt that lady, I think to myself. Ren had developed a way to see inside people's heads, and I found a way to shut it out. I'm able to compartmentalize even the nastiest of behaviors to not feel guilty. My brain is notorious for blocking everything.

"Come." She waves her hand for me to follow.

Cateline leads me toward the wide black mat. Her outstretched hand is in front of me when we stop. In it, a STARS device. Stabilizing Target and Range Simulator, or STARS, is a defensive advantage for those that wear it. It analyzes movement surrounding the wearer, giving them the ability to control their muscles in the special way they tell it to. The STARS requires knowledge of fighting, or at least quick thinking, without having to be physically trained in specific maneuvers.

I'll admit, it's a great idea. It levels the playing field for anyone that may want to volunteer for their cause here at the Service. But again—like everything—it has its weaknesses.

I place the STARS on my temple without question. It more than likely is already color matched to my skin due to the Chameleon Tech. Cateline is smiling when my gaze meets hers.

"Head to your place, please." She fans her hand outward in the desired direction.

There's a small mark in the center of the mat. My foot steps on it, and then I'm no longer alone. Different hologram bodies in a variety of different colors are now projected around me, all equidistant from me and each other. I spin around on my heel, returning my eyes to Cateline. "What's my objective?"

"Fight." She smiles.

The charged energy of the room excites me. The green body moves toward me first. It seems the others are staying in their place. Boo. One V One isn't excitable. So be it.

First, I'll have to decipher what type of fighter this AI is. More than likely, it's defensive. Though, who knows, Cateline could have made anything. Let's start with some light jabs.

Stepping forward, my right fist lifts, flying at half speed toward the face. At the last second, the AI shifts, sliding left. I do it again. The same result. The action brings me back to the first STARS experience I'd had with Axom. He is... *was* a very patterned fighter. Defensive rather than offensive. It's almost identical to the AI in front of me. My rage takes over me.

Axom deserved a better leader. One that didn't let the emotions of reuniting with someone get the better of them. Screw the light jabs. I go into full fight mode—swinging, kicking, and spinning my way into the next opponent.

It starts in, almost no time to prepare. Scrambling forward, I meet the putrid yellow-green one by catching its punch mid-swing. Twisting the arm, I complete a rear wrist lock on it, making it nearly immobile right from the beginning.

The first had been fairly easy to drop. The second one, while more offensive, was still just as effortless in stopping. This next one, a bright yellow, is already putting up more of a fight than its previous companions. This one retaliates every third throw. Still too patterned for my taste. But then, it clips me.

Fuck. The pressure against the side of my head pisses me off. Though, I only have myself to blame. I got lax. The fucker had thrown a fist at two, rather than three. I moved only as fast as I could, just barely making it, but not before the robotic knuckles scraped against my temples.

It's as if they're learning. I physically shake my head to restart fresh. This time, I circle behind the AI and bring it to the ground by launching onto its back. I don't release the chokehold until its limp.

In similar fashion, the next in line leaves no time before closing the distance. It doesn't immediately go in for a hit, but it expertly dodges and retaliates after mine.

This one is more experienced than the last, which had been better than the one before that. They've been getting more offensively smart with each new opponent. Color must have a correlation to skill. Which already makes this a fool's practice.

As the thought completes itself in my head, the remaining bodies run in circles around me while their colors muddle into a matching deep purple. Interesting.

The one in front of me morphs into the same shade just as quickly. Then, it promptly boots into an amazingly precise offensive maneuver, leaving me to dip, dive, and glide away from everything with very little time or energy to spare for my own attacks. Even with my mind controlling the STARS, the throws don't land. The AI is quick to pull away and continue its beating.

It's slowly backing me into a corner. If it succeeds, I may be toast. I could, in theory, use the wall to my advantage. But the timing would have to be perfect. Between the flying fists and kangaroo kicks, my focus is tied up in front of me. Out of my peripheral, I'm hoping to catch a glimpse of something that could help. There's nothing, though. It's just me, the mat, and the plum-colored bodies.

Wait. That's it! The AI in front of me continues its onslaught of attacks, and I bide my time, letting it back me up. Last second, just as we pass by the stoic fighters awaiting their turn, I dip low, spinning, slamming the body to my right up onto my shoulders. On the turn back to 360, the body slides with the momentum of the spin and I swing it like a baseball bat, taking out the one in front of me. Both of them crash to the mat and melt away like the previous ones.

The last of them starts in now, and I let it close some distance before I turn, running. It picks up speed behind me to catch up. Perfect.

The wall is directly in front of me, and a tilt of my head tells me the AI is basically at my heels now. I swear the fucker has a smile on its face despite not donning any facial features. That's when I launch into the wall, using it to push myself up and over the body barreling toward me. I land behind the AI, and in its moment of hesitation, I slam its head into the wall in front of us. Repeatedly. Voraciously. Letting all the built-up anger from the last few weeks out in a guttural scream, until the AI disintegrates like ash beneath my fingers.

My breathing is ragged when I turn to a wide-eyed scientist. Cateline's mouth hangs slightly open. Damn it, Warin, you've let the monster out.

But her words are not what I imagine. "That... was... amazing!" She's excited? "You have helped tremendously!"

"Helped?" I laugh. I knew I was coming for her to pick my brain, but I don't see how this could have helped her at all.

"Of course." She smiles. "The STARS collected your thoughts."

"My..." Oh... My voice fades, my lips forming an "o" shape without any noise. "You sly devil." I smirk.

Cateline blushes. "I've not had anyone beat that test before, Luke. This will help me analyze what makes you different."

A frown presents itself on my face. What makes me different? The intruding voice of my brain tells me it's the monster that lurks just below the surface. I push it away. "I've deduced that the STARS is only as good as the fighter it's attached to."

"Correct," Cateline agrees. "A fighter of sound brain will utilize the STARS in ways one can only dream about."

Cateline proceeds to share a story of a soldier they lost because he was not mentally stable and the STARS had taken his deeply disturbed intrusive thoughts and made them reality. His emotions had somehow pushed things too far. He ended up hurting his partner and quite literally tore himself apart. She dampened some of the effects of the STARS after that, but wants to improve without having consequences.

"It was brutal," she says, sighing. "The mind is fickle."

"That is exactly why Service training should involve critical thinking and problem solving in real world applications," I suggest. "If they focus only on physical training, the soldiers will fall short." It's surprising that no one has come to this conclusion yet. I'd bested Axom on the mat without any form of STARS on because he simply didn't have the capacity to analyze the situation. He was a skilled fighter indeed, yet his mind was his weakness.

Cateline regards me curiously. "Perhaps I will adjust the algorithm to analyze patterns, not just movement in general. I can give these soldiers an upper hand by letting them know the type of fighter they are up against." She touches her dainty fingers to her chin in thought. Then she smiles again, meeting my eye. "I'm glad to have met you," she says.

Compliments don't penetrate the tough exterior I've built up over the years. I wouldn't believe it anyway. Not even from Amity. Speaking of...

"What do we have in helping Amity recover her memories?" I ask, flipping the topic of conversation.

Cateline's face drops subtly. "Mr... Luke," she corrects. "We've done everything."

Tsk. Tsk. "Cateline," I say, dropping my voice low, leaning in close. The hitch of her breath clues me in on the power I hold. Gotcha. "You're telling me you haven't thought of anything else?

You? Cateline Pierre?" A smirk plays at my lips. It's harder to push the thoughts out of my head than expected. This is wrong, but I'd do anything for Amity.

Cateline's face flushes a pastel pink, and her eyes flutter in that way that most people's do when they're being flattered. "Luke," she breathes. "I'm not all that great with the biological side of things." Her words are tinged with double meaning.

"You're being humble," I state, pushing further. "I'm sure you could think of something." One more killer smile and I think it's secure.

Color rushes to her cheeks once more. "I will try," she breathes.

"Thank you," I say before walking out.

Once in the hall, I attempt to distance myself from who I just was in my mind. Sometimes we have to do things that make us questionable individuals. I've done it my whole life. It's easy for me to play on people's weaknesses because I'd learned from the best.

The thought of Ren sours my mood even more. So much so that I almost pass my escort in a rage. Fuck this slow ass. The only thing I want right now is to see M. Somehow that will make everything better. Maybe it's just my guilty conscience talking, which—relatively speaking—is a win, because until I met her, I didn't think I had one.

The escort leaves me once we're in the Commons, the central location that everyone has access to. It's a gigantic, circular room with a massive statue of the Service's emblem smack in the center. Resembling an angel, a *savior*, the individual with wings outstretched is nearly fifty feet tall. For being underground, it's quite impressive.

Above the statue is a faux dome skylight. Since we're underground, the Service projects an image of a beautiful blue sky. It emits UV rays, courtesy of Cateline Pierre's extravagant mind. Basically, it's the closest thing to a real window without actually being one. And since the weather is always sunny, the statue consistently has a heavenly glory about it as the rays peer down in a halo of gold.

The Commons is a meeting place for the Residential Ward. It's the location that connects all others.

So instead of veering left toward the sleeping pods, or right to the cafeteria, I keep straight. I'm on a mission to see M and nothing will stand in my way.

The Hospital Ward in and of itself is a mini version of the Commons. There's one central point with all the rooms spanning from there. It's a small place, what with all the advancements here. Yet, it's proven helpful—somewhat—in the odd case of M.

The light at the end of the tunnel-like hallway is as bright and harsh as ever. Only this time when I step over the threshold into the fluorescents, I find myself stuck. Literally.

A high-pitched siren blares, no doubt causing a ruckus for the six patients of the ward. The nurse behind the counter shakes her head as she lifts the phone to her ear.

"Unauthorized access," says a prerecorded voice. "Lucas Paul Warin."

Son of bitch! When I get my hands on that slimy weasel Mason Baines, I swear he'll be needing a room here if he survives. That lousy, no good, piece of...

"Luke." His voice fills my head when I absolutely do not want it to. The worst part is I still can't move. Which means I still can't see him. Or hurt him. Lucky Mason.

Even though I want to shout, I can't. I'm unable to move my mouth as well. How convenient. He's doubly lucky. For now.

His stocky frame rounds into my view. The cocky demeanor he

carries sends me overboard, but my body doesn't outwardly show it, because it can't. I've no doubt my face is red with rage, though. Explosive anger is building, scrambling to the surface, searching for release.

"I'm going to allow you to talk, but if you get loud, I'll shut you right back up," he cautions, as though I'm an errant toddler. Fuck this guy.

Mason waits a few seconds, like he's waiting for a confirmation, before realizing I can't fucking move. It takes another second before my mouth is able to open. "What the fuck is this?" The words sneak through my teeth in seething anger.

"Protocol," Mason snips.

"Bullshit!" I say louder than intended.

Mason widens his eyes in warning, tilting his head and lifting the button in his hand. "It is protocol," he reiterates. "As of yesterday."

"What could possibly be the reasoning for this?" I question. Every day that I spend here, the more I fear the Service and its leaders are like Western American and Ren. Or at the very least, they've got something big they're hiding, and M plays into it somehow. Why else would they go through all these hoops to keep her in the dark?

"I'm going to skip the formalities and jump right into it," Mason starts.

"Oh, please do," I goad, a tight expression on my face.

His body tenses, then relaxes as he says, "It's your fault, jackass. There. You happy?"

"My fault?" I stare at him in disbelief. Mostly because I still can't move my head to look away.

"Yes!" His voice is louder than before. "You knew you weren't allowed here and yet you argued with it every day; disobeying direct orders from your superior."

"My superior?" Ha! I laugh out loud at his joke. He really believes himself to be above me? Maybe in the Service, but never in matters where M is involved.

"She should have never known about the Memorial Ball!" He looks at me, a slight begging tone to his voice. "It's your fault she even left the safety of this hospital." There's something more to it than this. Favager was more than pleased to see M out and about. If this is Mason's doing, then I'll have to push his buttons.

"You mean the confines of this prison?" I spit, correcting him.

Mason takes a step back as if physically jolted by my words. "We're doing what's best for Amity," he says. "Unlike you, who seems to only do whatever it is that best suits yourself."

I open my mouth to speak again, but a sweet sound fills the air instead. M.

"I want to see him," she says.

"Amity," Mason starts, whirling around. "You need..."

"No!" The harsh bite of her words startles even me. It's clear the glower in her face is taking all her energy. "Stop telling me what I need. You don't know anything about me." She crosses her arms. Sarge sits quietly by her side, steadying her.

"You may not remember, but I do know you." Mason sighs. "And it might be hard to understand, but this is all for your safety..."

She scoffs. "If you're going to force me to stay in this prison cell of a hospital, then you're going to allow visitors."

Mason opens his mouth to speak but then shuts it. He casts his eyes away, battling with himself. I'd hate to have been M's father when she was a teen. Right now, she's developmentally in that stage, but thankfully there aren't any hormones to make it worse.

Somehow I'm able to keep myself quiet. Despite the rage

radiating with every pulse at the sight of Mason, I need to let M fight her battles on her own. She's always been headstrong. She just needs to learn her own power again.

In the midst of the showdown, a nurse scurries over to Mason. The look on his face is set with resignation.

After an intense whispering match, Mason's breath releases in another sigh. "Fine." M's shoulders drop with relief, but it's subtle. Mason doesn't notice, though he's already facing away from her. He walks close, knowing full well I can't do anything to hurt him. Coward. "Keep your mouth shut, Warin. Or I'll have no choice." He shoves past me before clicking the button to fully release my body. Fuckhead.

CHAPTER FIVE ○ REN

"DAMN IT!" MY FIST SLAMS AGAINST THE RICH MAHOGANY OF my desk.

Marcus Giles, my First Sergeant, is sitting uncomfortably in the furniture at our sky offices in the heavily fortified Capital of Western America. Now that Omphalos has been destroyed, and most of my patients are gone, the plan to save Humanity took the fast track to nowhere. I need to replenish my Exceptionals in the off chance the ones I had haven't survived. We were only able to get a few before the collapse. The Reserves are tempting, but that's still not enough. The time isn't right.

"The numbers for this week are as pathetic as that look on your face." The files fly from my hand, tossed away from me. Marcus sits up now.

"We will find them," he assures.

I scoff, causing him to flinch. The problem is nearly 95% of the Commoners we've tested so far are too much like that vile girl, Miss Thorne. Thanks to the scan of her brain, we're able to deem a person Tainted almost instantaneously. We can give them a score on how likely they are to change, but until we have a main facility where I can keep a close watch, we're stuck in the water. Besides, there have hardly been any new candidates.

"There are still plenty of other locations with non-Tainted individuals." Marcus won't stop. "Sure, the Exceptionals may be gone, but we can..." It's at this point he looks at me to find the scowl on my face. His voice fades into nothing.

"The ones we have should be safely secure under the shield, but unless we get to them soon, they'll starve straight into Death's arms." My eyebrows pull in at my words.

Marcus had projected the protective shield to save those on the inside of Omphalos when it started to fall. A safety protocol proven most worth it. However, there's been some unrest from the squads that lost their officer comrades.

"Are any of the Tainted good matches for subcopies?" Marcus questions in an attempt to distract me.

Are any of the Tainted good matches for subcopies? My inner bitch sneers. I admire Marcus' loyalty, but he damn sure gets on my nerves. Like a lost puppy.

"None," I spit. "Hence, the damn it."

Marcus recoils, cowering into himself again. He thinks he's being helpful, but the truth is, he's reminding me of the failure. I didn't come all this way, sacrificing everything, to fail.

Despite the lack of bodies to use, there is good in all of this. It's only a matter of time before my precious son will be back with me.

Not only is Miss Thorne's brain scan helping us weed out the rotten, it is also helping me find ample hosts for a little side plan to get my sweet Lucas out of her clutches. For those with a 96% or better brain match, they are physically reconstructed to resemble Miss Thorne, and the memories I have of hers are downloaded into what we're calling subcopies.

Since that little raid of Omphalos caused me to act in ways I hadn't originally intended, the new goal is that I get Lucas to fall in love with one of these other ones, thus convincing him to return to me. I held out hope that my other plans would work, but love is a stupid, fickle thing. He's my son, though, damn it, and if he's going to be dumb enough to fall, then I'm going to do my best to make sure it's with someone made more easily agreeable. Subcopies have proven useful in the past, so why not for this as well? Gah, the things a mother does for her child.

Along with that, we're also able to learn more about the human mind, which has always been an interest of mine. By implanting Miss Thorne's memories into other individuals, we will be able to study if experience affects people, or overall genetics. It's the age-old question: Nature or Nurture. And these studies will live on. At the very least, my name will go down in history somewhere.

"We still have more to test, Mistress," Marcus reassures, his eyes the size of saucers. "Hope is not yet lost."

Hope. The word is revolting. The last thing we want is hope. My fingers reach the bridge of my nose, pinching the irritation out of my brain. Marcus is extra insufferable lately since our little spat in the presence of that vile girl. He had questioned my motives, my decisions. As if being a protective mother is such a terrible thing.

"You are dismissed, Mr. Giles," I sigh.

His eyes hold the sad puppy look for a split second before he nods, removing himself from the room.

After a moment of silence, I reach for the Relay on my desk. Master Sergeant Dean Carovak is speaking a few moments later. "Yes, Headmistress?"

"Mr. Carovak," I greet. "How are you this morning?"

"The rubble is almost completely cleared from the East Wing, Madame," he answers, knowing I wasn't asking about him person-ally. Sometimes I fear I'd made a mistake promoting Marcus over Dean, but regret is not something I can afford. If I weren't saving

Sergeant Major for my son...

"And the unrest?" I question, not letting my mind wander. Marcus had been too cowardly to tell me, but the rigidness of the Force is beginning to wane. Those caught beneath the shield need to be freed, lest we only pull dead bodies from the cracked earth. The problem is that everything on top needs to be cleared away first.

"A few more lost it today, Madame," he answers. "I've heard from some of the other Masters dealing with unruly ranks as well." Crap.

The sigh slips past my lips before I can stop it, my forehead pressing against the side of my fist. The officers are losing faith in the plan. They are upset about the lost lives in Omphalos. The ones under the direct order of Mr. Carovak are acting out the worst. They are the ones assigned to clean up duty after all.

But they are stupid. Incapable of seeing the bigger picture. The longer they take, the more they risk those still alive at the bottom to suffer a terrible Death. They just have to push through the top layers to get through. They are weak.

"If it's not out of turn," Mr. Carovak starts, "may I offer some advice?"

Normally something like this would irritate me, but today it is miniscule compared to everything else that is going on. "Speak," I say, swirling my hand as if he were here, before returning my forehead to it.

"Perhaps, Madame," he begins, then stops to clear his throat. He's hesitant. "Perhaps you make a spectacle."

My head lifts as if this idea had popped into it on its own. That's it. That's exactly what needs to be done. Strike a bit of fear. "And who do you suggest?" I'm asking for the worst offender; the officer that will show the others exactly why they don't want to step out of line.

"I'll have a report to you by the end of day," he states.

"Thank you, Mr. Carovak," I say. "As always, it's been a plea-sure." The Relay clicks as our communication ceases. Then, Marcus is immediately on the line.

"Yes, Mistress?" His eager voice is sickening.

"Marcus," I say. "Get in here, I've got a plan."

o o o

MARCUS IS SPEAKING gingerly to Master Sergeant Dean Carovak as the A.L.F. officers shuffle nervously into formation. Marcus doesn't hold the same confidence that his inferior does and instead seems to shrink beside Dean. Damn it. I knew it was a mistake to choose Marcus Giles.

"Mr. Carovak," I say, stepping in. "Your men look restless."

Something familiar flashes in Dean's eye. Recognition? Yes. He understands I'm keeping Marcus from making a fool of himself in front of the watchful eyes of the low-ranking Force. They'll pick out any weakness and use it. I can appreciate that on a fundamental level, but not when it goes against my order. *My* order.

"They are," Mr. Carovak agrees. "Not only are we dealing with the same issues discussed previously, but my officers are also on edge about your surprise visit."

His expression gives nothing away as he mentions the word *surprise*. Every minute I spend talking to Dean, I realize what a fool I'd been to leave him as a Master Sergeant. But perhaps it's for the betterment of running his A class squad.

"Yes," the word slips from my lips. "Things will be rectified shortly." The sinister smile on my face is enough to make whispers scatter through the crowd. My eyes flick to the closest officer in line and he instantly tenses, looking blankly forward. This is going to be fun.

"Are you ready, Mistress?" Marcus asks.

A curt nod is all he receives from me. The small device he'd been holding is now pressed onto the space where my neck meets my chin. I step forward, shedding the two men beside me. The further they are behind, the less they'll shadow my authority.

"Hello everyone." My sinister voice is low, carrying beautifully over the crowd thanks to the amplifier under my chin. "Some of you may be wondering why I've made an impromptu visit."

The squirms of several members in the formation jolts my heart with excitement. Their discomfort, their fear—it sends pulses of energy through me. I love how, even with their training, they lose their discipline in my presence, shaking in their boots like leaves rustling in the wind.

"Would any of you like to guess?" The corner of my lip turns up in a playful smirk. I have always enjoyed a good game. The mischievous look in my eye can only truly be seen by those in the first few rows. The demonstration that's about to happen is long overdue, but it'll make for a good show. I'm glad the stakes are high. It's thrilling.

There is a good hundred men here. The twenty-five squad members under the direct leadership of Dean Carovak and three additional outside squads brought in as time ticked away. Those trapped below the surface of the collapsed mountain are running out of food and air as we speak. This is a waste of precious opportunity to save my Exceptionals, but it must be done.

Not-so-shockingly, no one speaks up. Why would they? Even if they know the reason I'm here, they wouldn't so much as dare to open their mouths. Perhaps they are *all* guilty?

"It appears a handful of your squad mates have been getting..." I pause to find the right word. "Rowdy," I finally decide on. "Some are refusing the order we so desperately need to uphold."

At this point, my legs have carried me closer to line one. The officers near the direct center are sweating bullets as I close the distance.

"How can we stop the Commoners from an uprising if we can't even keep control of ourselves?" My voice is faux woeful.

The man in front of me gulps. He's nearly shaking, as he should be. This officer may simply be nervous over my domineering presence. Or he's suddenly hyper-aware that he's my target.

Officer Harlow Jacobs. Recruited around the same time as my sweet Lucas. First in almost all the squads he's been assigned to, yet he's never shown interest in climbing the ranks. Though, he's a natural leader amongst his fellow officers I've heard. Hence why his increasing attitude toward authority is an issue. It's unfortunate such talent must be wasted, but that is the cost.

The special immobilizing device is in my hand and pressed against Mr. Jacobs' neck in a millisecond. Pulling him from formation and further from the crowd, I'm finally able to see the worried expressions on his comrades' faces.

"Mr. Jacobs," I say, "has been ousted as the worst offender of breaking order. And for that? He will pay."

Marcus and Dean step forward, each taking one arm of Mr. Jacobs when I release my immobilizing hold on him. His breathing climbs to a ragged state as some semblance of control resumes throughout his body. Fool. You don't need air where you're going.

"Anything you'd like to say?" I toy.

He shakes his head sharply. Mr. Jacobs has accepted defeat. Smart, yet an imbecile all the same.

"Very well."

Rope cuffs around Mr. Jacobs' wrists extend into taut lines held by Marcus on one side and Dean on the other. They need to keep their distance for what's about to happen.

I, too, step away. Not closer to the crowd, but further, so that Mr. Jacobs is in between. This way I'll be able to see the crowd's reaction as well.

Pulling yet another handy tool from my arsenal, the detonator is ready and waiting in my palm. After Lucas ran, I implanted every Force officer with a tracker, like my patients. One wrong move, one step toward somewhere they aren't supposed to be and *bang*.

I've only ever had to threaten this before. Thankfully, yet sadly, I've never had to use it. Until today.

The formation of officers is shifting like the waves of a sea in turmoil. This way, and that; churning with restless energy. Those who were unaware, or were willfully ignorant, can no longer hope for a different outcome now that the all-too-famous detonator is in my hand. The only thing that would make this better would be to have Lucas do the honors.

My brow pulls in at the slight souring of my mood. Lucas will be back soon. But not if I have a broken regime. The task at hand brings me back, separating myself from the sad mother persona. It's time.

"Let this be a reminder," I address the crowd. "Order and chaos cause destruction. To yourself, to others, to society as a whole." I've always loved a good monologue. Speeches about order are necessary to the rallying cause. "There will be no more disarray. For not only is it bad practice, but this complacency is also causing the Death of your brethren beneath this stone. Do not make Mr. Jacobs' death a poor one. Do not sully his passing. He is the cost today. Let this be the end."

My thumb presses the button it had so smoothly been caress-ing during the speech. Mr. Jacobs' body melts into itself, or so it appears. The tracker releases a specially formulated toxin into the bloodstream, heating the victim from the inside out. Mr. Jacobs' convulses and he pulls inward, trying to scratch the heat from under his skin.

After a few seconds, the blood in his veins turns black, and he combusts. The human body cannot sustain internal temperatures above 104 for very long. By 122, they've definitely shut down. This toxin shoots my officers up to 150.

The blast of guts and sludgy black blood isn't large. A five-foot radius is all that's left of Harlow Jacobs.

Just when I think we've settled things, a voice breaks from the sea of people. "He was a good man!" Someone pushes forward, racing their way to me. Mr. Carovak has him held steady in a sec-ond flat.

"You'll soon be wishing you'd kept your mouth shut, soldier," says Mr. Carovak through his teeth.

"Why? She'll kill me like she did Harlow? I'm not scared!" His eyes betray him as I get close. Such an insignificant rat. He has a point, though. Being able to play on everyone's weakness is what gives me the edge I need. I'm not so naïve to believe that all hu-mans are afraid of Death. Some souls are too far gone for that. So perhaps what happens next will help clear the air.

My voice is menacingly low yet amplified tenfold as those around hush to hear. I'm certain this young officer feels the icy chill of my breath as I say, "A good man is a quiet one. It's best you learn that lesson quickly."

Pulling clippers from my belt of many tools, I order Marcus and Dean to hold open the poor sap's mouth. His eyes are wide, tears soaking his cheeks. The onlooking officers are holding their breath as the nasty metal slams against his tongue. The pink flesh drops to the dirt and I kick it to the side with my heel.

"Clean this up," I order Mr. Carovak.

The soldier has pools of crimson streaming down his chin. His face is devoid of color. The audience behind him is trying to hold their stomachs. Some look away in fear, others keep their gaze for the same reason.

"Get back to work," Marcus shouts at the men. He turns to me with a smile. "This went well, yes?" he asks.

"Yes, Marcus," I answer with a smirk. "I think these children know exactly how to behave now."

CHAPTER SIX ○ AMITY

"FRESH AIR WOULD BE GOOD FOR HER," LACY ARGUES QUIETLY in the hallway. If she thinks I can't hear her, she's definitely mistaken. However, I don't catch Mason's response since his voice blends into the din of the hospital ward. "Oh, I'm sorry," she replies. "Are you a doctor?"

Somehow Lacy's face appears in my head as I picture what incredibly bitchy expression she has on. Admittedly, it makes me chuckle to myself.

Thankfully my fight for visitors had been granted, albeit hesitantly. But no one is giving me answers yet. I haven't been given permission to leave the room since the incident after the Memorial Ball. Lacy is currently arguing on my behalf.

"Sarge could use it, too," she states, probably pursing her lips with extra attitude.

At the sound of his name, Sarge repositions his head across my lap so his gaze is toward the door. Poor guy. He's the main reason I want to go outside. Sure, being away from all the hums, beeps, and hospital smells is a driving force, but really it's clear that Sarge is looking to run. He's tired of being trapped here, too.

Mason and Lacy continue their arguments for a few more minutes before shuffling into the room. Lacy had questioned why it mattered whether or not I could go outside, and Mason had mentioned something about it being complicated. They look at me like two parents who fought about how to handle their errant teen. I suppose that's nearly what they did. Though, I forget I'm not a teen anymore. I'm an adult.

"Lacy has convinced me that maybe some time outside will help you," Mason says, his voice faux apologetic. "But you have to allow a Serviceman to follow in case you pass out again."

Lacy's face is simultaneously smug and sorry. It's clear she's happy with the outcome of outside time, but not the unfortunate compromise. I, on the other hand, just want to get out of here. So, I nod.

"Let's go then," Lacy speaks, smiling. She lifts her arm, allowing me to hold on. Sarge happily trots beside us.

Though it would make more sense for the Serviceman to lead, he falls behind as Lacy forges ahead. My tired legs are barely able to keep up. It's been awhile since they've had to move anywhere beyond the confines of the hospital ward.

Eventually we pass a control room of sorts and come out through the mouth of a cave. The sunlight hits my eyes, causing them to clench into a squint. Sarge picks up his pace, excited, but then turns to look at me before he gets too far.

"Go," I say, nodding. "Run wild."

His tongue flops out of his mouth to the side and he hops in a way that pushes happiness into my bones. He's filled out considerably since my waking. Sarge has probably never eaten as good as he has being here. The thought splinters my heart. I'd count it a blessing I don't remember certain things. While I'm sad I've lost the good memories, it's clear I've lost the pain linked with the bad ones as well.

"He's happy," Lacy points out, snapping me back to the present.

"Yes," I affirm. My eyes find hers. "Thanks again for arguing on my behalf."

She smiles wide. "Of course." Her hand meets my shoulder. "I know how quickly the air underground can turn suffocating."

I smile back.

Lacy and I slowly walk the small trail that leads to a beautiful glass building. It's only half built, but the half that stands is stunning. I've never seen anything like it.

"What is this?" I ask, my mouth falling open.

"The Complex. It's beautiful," Lacy answers, her own sense of wonder tinged in her tone.

My eyebrows pull in. "What's it for?"

Lacy explains the point of the Complex. It's a place of escape; a resort. There are bars, sports courts, shops. I hadn't realized there were more citizens living under the Service's reign. I thought the structure I've been trapped in was it, but it turns out there are two Compounds below the surface of the water nearby that house thousands of individuals saved from the oppression of the Guardianship's regime.

"It's supposed to be even better than the original one," Lacy finishes.

"What happened to it?" I ask, wanting to know every detail of this place all of a sudden. There's so much I don't know. Not just about my own past, but about my current state as well.

Lacy shivers beside me, so subtly that I almost miss it. "Air attack."

The wind picks up, chilling me. *Air attack?* Sarge stops his running and watches me with concerned eyes. He takes long strides back to my side. My fingers instinctively trail through the soft fur of his head.

"Things are bad, then?" I question, my voice low. The General here had said as much. He also said I was somehow worth the sacrifice of their own people. I still can't imagine how I play a role in all of this, but if attacks are happening, then people are getting hurt. And if people are getting hurt, then it's basically another war.

"Unfortunately," Lacy nods, pursing her lips. She peers behind us casually, noting the Serviceman's location. Picking up on this, I send a knowing look toward Lacy.

"Sarge." I bend to him, making us eye level. "Can you do something for me?"

His eyes beam with happiness as I tell him to run and distract the Serviceman. Lacy and I chuckle as he loops around, pushing himself between the man's legs.

But we can't get distracted. Lacy is about to share forbidden information with me, and it's a piece of the puzzle I'm certain I'll need.

"I'm sure Mason is having that guard listen to us." She scoffs. "He's been acting so weird lately. Like, he's always been a little cuckoo, but there's something up."

I focus on holding my breathing steady. I knew we were being babysat, but I hadn't realized it was for more than a fainting spell.

"I honestly don't know what's going on and even telling you this little bit of information could lead to punishment. Mason is trying to keep you locked in the hospital ward, yet it seems the General has plans for you."

Before I can question anything, Lacy continues.

"You asked about the Complex? Well, the Reaver found out about this haven for people and she sent the air attack. Killed one-hundred-and-forty-six that day." Her eyes fall to the ground.

"How'd she find out? And why hasn't she sent another?" With

my last thought, my eyes search the sky and I shudder. If she knows about this place, why not try more?

"You," is all Lacy replies.

My face molds with confusion. The General has plans for me, yet I'm the one who sent the air attack? But, somehow, I'm also the reason another air attack hasn't been sent? The whirring of my head is going to overtake me. None of this makes sense.

"The General thinks you being here secures our safety, as for some reason, the Reaver wants you alive."

"Why me, though? What have I done?"

Lacy watches me with careful eyes, a worried expression settled on her face.

"What is it, Lacy? Please? Why am I here? Where is my family?" I plead with her, though unease creeps into my being without warning.

Do I even want to remember anything? Do I really want to know what happened? Maybe my brain is purposefully hiding things because the emptiness hurts less than the real stuff. Maybe it's actively combatting the memory serum to keep this dull ache instead. *Where is my family?*

Lacy opens her mouth to speak, but barking takes the place of her voice.

"Hey!" the Serviceman calls. "Present yourself!"

Lacy and I whip around to see a young woman stepping out from the bushes. Sarge barks, making his way to my side without taking his eyes from the girl.

She seems innocent enough, but something about her has set Sarge off. Is it possible that after everything that's happened, he's too distrustful of everyone? Or is this woman somehow the enemy?

The girl closes the distance, moving slowly toward the Serviceman. Her hands are up in surrender. Sarge is now quiet, but not relaxed.

The closer she gets, the more I'm able to make out her features. She's got choppy, chestnut locks, with an average round face. There's something familiar about her. I can't quite put my finger on what it is.

"What's your business here?" the Serviceman questions.

"Sarge," she cries. "Sarge, it's me!" The girl steps closer, but the Serviceman blocks the view.

"State your business. Now," he demands.

The woman's voice shakes. "I saw Sarge. I've been looking for him." She peers around the man's body to catch another glimpse at Sarge. "Oh! And her!" The woman points in our direction. "I know her!"

Lacy seems as surprised as I am. If I somehow crossed paths with this person before, I surely don't remember now. Why would she be searching for Sarge?

"Miss Thorne is not to see anyone. Please leave."

"Thorne?" The girl is confused. Genuinely. "That's... is that not Lacy?"

My face turns to find Lacy with a shocked countenance. "Do you know her?" I question.

"No," Lacy answers. "I don't think so."

Lacy steps toward the stranger now, trying to get a better look. The Serviceman is radioing for help. We've got two minutes before we're whisked away again. Sarge is still apprehensive, even more so the closer we get. His body is pressed closely to mine.

"What's your name?" Lacy calls to the girl, ignoring the Serviceman urging her to step back.

"You don't know who I am?" the woman gives Lacy a puzzled expression.

Being so close, I'm able to study her better. Lacy tilts her head, examining the same way I am. Out of the corner of my eye, I catch Lacy glance at me, then back to the woman in front of us. Under her breath she says, "She kinda looks like..."

The woman speaks again. "It's me. Amity."

CHAPTER SEVEN ○ LUKE

Mason is already waiting for me at the edge of the Residential Ward. I'm surprised he's let me in on the information at hand. Though, all he's told me is that they've captured someone in regard to the Guardianship and M.

I swiftly nod to him and he spins on his heel. I'm thankful there's no delay. The lack of knowledge is killing me. "What'dya got?" I ask.

"It's best you see for yourself." His eyes darken, though he keeps them forward.

The tone of his voice is enough to chill my bones. If Mason, of all people, has enlisted me for an opinion, it must be bad. Who could they possibly have in their possession?

Our trek through the different halls is silent the rest of the way. Though I'm itching for more briefing, I'm glad I don't have to keep up conversation with Mason. Soon enough I'll see what this is about.

Figures we'd get to the point in the facility where real doors are present. We stop near maroon French doors guarded by heavily armed Servicemen. Fuck. Who could it be? This much protection means they're dangerous; absolutely lethal. My initial thought is Ren's right-hand man or something.

Mason gives me a sideways glance, tilting his head in the direction of the doors. I step forward, noting that the guards focus past me to my *superior*. Fuck that guy. Both guards subtly nod to a cue I didn't see, and then step aside, opening the doors.

Who's beyond them? Nothing I would have imagined. Is it a terribly grizzly Force officer? A robot soldier sent to kill? Ren Keres herself? No. It's a girl.

She's chained to the floor by both her wrists and ankles. She's down on her knees, head dipped in surrender. Could she be an assassin? I don't think so. Ren never dabbled in that sort of training.

"What the hell is this?" I hiss, swinging to Mason. This is ridiculous.

Mason shakes his head in response. So I don't even deserve an answer now? But he walks past me, closing the distance toward the prisoner on the cold, cement ground. "Why don't you introduce yourself?" he says to the girl, lifting her chin with two fingers.

The girl's eyes widen when she sees me. Her breath hitches. "Luke," she whispers.

Suddenly I know what's going on. I may not know who this girl is, but I know who she's supposed to be. The grey eyes, the subtle droop of her nose, the plump lips. This is Amity. Or Ren's version of her.

My jaw tenses with irritation. Why? What game is Ren playing? She despises M, so why make another?

"Can we assume she has Amity's memories?" I ask Mason, not taking my eyes from the imposter.

"She's recognized the group without having to tell her, but whether that's from Amity's memory or some sick, messed up flash cards, we're not sure."

The girl stays silent, but her eyes are begging me. This could be M's twin; she has the same quiet longing in her eyes. And for a second, I wish she *were* M. But then the guilt takes over before morphing into anger. This person is not M. She's an imposter.

"Who else has she seen?" I question. Mason had mentioned "the group", which is a small portion of us now since Abby, Mason's sister, and Zach, Sonya's ex, have passed on.

Mason doesn't like to talk much about his sister's death, nor does he like talking about anything troublesome apparently. This conversation already seems to have pissed him off.

"Lacy," he says, pointedly. "Sarge, and Amity briefly."

"How is he?" the imposter speaks up, her pupils dilating in fear. "Sarge. Is he okay?" The worry in her eyes is palpable. And just like that, I can answer my own question. If she truly does have M's memories, she's scared and confused. "Why won't either of you tell me what's going on?"

"I'd argue she has the memories," I say, stepping further away and dropping my voice so the girl can't hear.

"What's your reasoning?" Mason inquires. His tone is full of condescension. Even still, after everything that's happened, he acts as though I'm some dumb asshole without a single working brain cell. It's a wonder I haven't already punched him in his stupid face.

"There's an emotional response connected to us," I answer. If Mason had spent two seconds talking with her, he could've figured it out on his own. Her worry of Sarge is the same worry that M has. If she'd learned about who we were through images, there wouldn't be such longing in her whispers. Well, perhaps there could be. But what purpose would Ren have for making someone look like M and not implanting the memories to match? Just to throw us off? There's got to be more to it than that. "Suppose there's a solid way to test?"

Mason's finger reaches his chin in thought. He's still refusing to
look in the direction of the girl, who is trying to get our attention.
My heart aches. She even *sounds* like Amity. "I'm not sure we'd
know for certain if the original memories are there, or if it's just
a recollection of the memories, if you understand what I mean."

Hm. I understand. If this girl was watching M's memories, she'd
have intimate knowledge of them, whilst still being her own individual. If anyone can figure this out, it would be Cateline. She
should meet our imposter right away. I explain to Mason the
importance of having her studied.

He regards me curiously. Then, he nods in agreement.

"In the meantime," I say, "can we unshackle her?" This Amity
has resigned to the quiet, finally. She's more likely straining to
hear us now. If I look back at her, I will lose all control. She's too
much like my M. Seeing her chained to the floor will release the
madman in me.

"It's a safety precaution," Mason argues, nervously glancing to
the guards by the door.

My teeth clench with disdain. "From what? Assume she'd react
like Amity. Amity is our friend." I speak as though I'm talking to
a two-year-old. Clear, short, simple.

"But *she's* not," Mason deadpans. Each moment here with him
is making it harder to contain the itching of my knuckles. Oh,
how they dream to make connection with his cheekbone.

"What are you so worried about?" I ask. "Does she have weapons
on her?" Mason's fear is unwarranted. Amity would never hurt
anyone. Not purposefully anyway. There's no reason to believe
this girl would either.

Mason is hesitant, like something bad is happening that he
doesn't want to tell me. Though, until we think of an adequate,
dangerous reason for Ren's game, we shouldn't treat her as a

prisoner.

"If she really does have Amity's memories, then she's confused and scared. Look at her," I prompt. Mason has refused to look in the girl's direction since the very beginning, but now he slowly tilts his head to gaze at her from the corner of his eye. "If we can't isolate them, I would hate for the real Amity to gain memories of us betraying her."

It seems I might finally be getting through to Mason. "Alright," he agrees after an eon. The guard is unlocking the shackles shortly after. "Could you give us a moment?" Mason asks the man.

The guard nods, and both of them exit the room, closing the door behind them.

"Thank you," the M imposter says, rubbing her wrists. The shy smile she gives me makes my heart flutter. She's similar to M. So similar it's eerie.

I nod curtly before flicking my gaze to Mason. "What's going on?"

"General Favager will not be happy about this." Mason's voice is cold and low.

"Favager won't be? Or you aren't?" I question. Mason has been acting weird ever since M woke up from her coma. He's been distant, yet annoyingly present at the same time. He's been taking Favager's side over everything despite the guy being a total dick.

"You act like you know everything here, but you are so far into the dark it's not even funny!" Mason spews. "Amity cannot know about her past."

The harshness of his tone sets me off. M is entitled to her own memories. And if this imposter can help us get them, why is Mason so against it? Or why is Favager?

"My past?" the imposter asks, but we both ignore her.

"Madame Keres is getting bolder," Mason continues. "She exploded one of our top undercover Amiteers and cut the tongue out of one of the lower-level ones."

"She cut out his tongue? Nice," I say, without thought.

"Luke!" the M imposter shouts, gasping.

"Shit, sorry. Yeah, no that's bad." Mason is watching me with an *are-you-fucking-kidding-me* look on his face. Ren is an evil bitch, but she sure knows how to hit a guy in the weakness if you know what I'm saying. Cutting out a guy's tongue? Sheesh.

"Listen, General Favager wants Amity out. He wants her in the forefront rallying the troops." Mason's voice is rushed, like he's trying to get everything out as fast as possible before *something* happens. What, I don't know. "The longer she stays in the hospital, the safer she is, and the less she has to endure."

Mason's eyes are begging me to understand. I do, sort of. I don't ever want to put M through more stress. She's seen enough for ten lifetimes already. But it begs the question: why doesn't Favager want her to know about her past? What is he trying to keep from her?

CHAPTER EIGHT ○ AMITY

SARGE IS SLEEPING SOUNDLY NEXT TO ME. HIS TIME OUTSIDE had been enough to wear him out. Me? Not so much. There are now a million more questions bouncing around in my head.

Who is the mysterious woman that claims to be me? She looks like me. She even remembers those that I don't. I admit, after a few dozen rounds of overthinking, I'm starting to believe that *I'm* the fake Amity.

Lacy was separated from me. I've been stuck in the hospital room since. If Sarge wasn't here with me, I fear I'd go insane.

We sit for a while, Sarge sleeping and me trying to make sense of things. I idly hope that Luke will come around. But time passes, and he doesn't.

When I'm about to lose hope on anyone coming to take me away from the craziness of my own mind, Sarge's eyes pop open and he lifts his head, peering toward the door.

My heart beats fast with excitement only to drop when it's not Luke standing in the entryway. "Did you enjoy your trip to the surface?" Mason questions. Does he genuinely care, or is he asking to be nice?

"A bit short," I reply. The woman who looks like me is on the forefront of my mind. Do I believe Mason will take the bait? No.

Mason is tighter-lipped than a mime.

"But nonetheless, it was good?"

I see through Mason's words. He knows what I want to hear, but he's moving on with the conversation. If he knew what Lacy had told me above ground, would he be so cautious to talk? Would he scold Lacy for recklessly sharing information?

I force a chuckle. "Honestly, the best part was seeing Sarge mark his territory so much." I smile down at my four-legged companion. His tongue rests at the tip of his mouth with subtle pants. "It's been his first time going outside in ages."

Mason's expression is unreadable when my eyes return to his after some silence. Is it sadness? No. Maybe. Empathy? Perhaps. Guilt?

"You want out of this hospital room, don't you?" he says.

My eyes widen. Really I want answers. Like where my family is for one, and who that woman is. But getting out of this prison of a hospital is a win in my book. I nod, vigorously.

"Let's see what we can do about that, shall we?" Mason smiles benevolently with hand extended. Sarge gets up, and I follow.

"Where are we going?" I ask while trudging past pod after pod for a while. The Residential Ward is bigger than I expected. One of these pods is Luke's.

"To your room," Mason says. The smile his face holds isn't heard in his voice. Like he's putting on a front for some reason. As the sentence leaves his lips, the long, seemingly never-ending vale of pod vines ends, and a thick, red rope crosses the room. Restricted access. This must be the area for the most important people of Headquarters. Luke never mentioned this part before. Only a pod.

"In there?" I question. I fear my worth is not in line with access to such an elite area. Lacy had mentioned the General believes the

Service is safe as long as I'm here, but I'm still not quite able to make sense of it.

"Of course," he says. "This is the VIP neighborhood."

Anxiety snakes its way throughout my chest. A thought crosses my mind, unwillingly. Am I placed in here because I'm truly important, or so that Mason can keep an eye on me? Something tells me it's the latter. Sarge presses close to me in hopes to slow my heartrate.

Mason leads us through a small hallway until it opens up into a massive mini-scale neighborhood. These tiny homes are plotted into a circle, with a large meeting area in the middle. Above us hangs a beautifully high ceiling, donning the same technology the center of Headquarters holds. This truly feels like we're outdoors in a close knit community in the suburbs. I can't remember a time when houses were this vibrant in Western America.

"Beautiful, isn't it?" Mason asks beside me.

"It's... amazing." My mouth is agape as I look at the stunningly beautiful landscapes and architecture. Couple that with the state of the art technology? Damn. It's clear why people are seeking refuge here. This is paradise. Well... at least if you're a VIP.

"The H.P.S. is hoping to get this to all Western Americans," Mason shares. Everyone getting a roof over their head? Wow. That's something. If the Service can pull it off, that would be a miracle. "The problem is," Mason starts anew, "they really don't have the space to house everyone. They're utilizing underwater bunkers right now. Or the much smaller pods here."

"I'm sure they're doing their best," is my reply. I try to act like this is new information for me and that Lacy hadn't already shared it. My hand holds onto Sarge tightly.

"We are," a new voice says, causing me to jolt with tension. General Favager snuck his way toward us and is now to the right of Mason. "But we need the Guardianship to fall." The General's words are charged. It leaves me feeling uneasy.

Mason's demeanor is completely different now that General Favager is standing over him. I once thought he looked up to the General, but it's almost as if our uneasiness is matched. Had I been so blind before?

"I'm sure it will," I say, hesitantly, hoping to avoid delving further into the conversation. Of course it doesn't work.

"Not without your help," the General says.

My mind is whirring with so many unanswered questions. My gut is screaming at me the way it used to when Force soldiers would pass by on the streets. Keep your head down, your mouth shut. Don't stand out, fade into the background. That's what I want to do now.

Sensing my trouble, Mason switches gears. "We must be getting to her room," he says. "Care to join us, General Favager?"

The General eyes Mason curiously, scrutinizing him with a sharp gaze. "I was only passing by," he says, bobbing his head. "There are pressing matters to attend to."

"Of course," Mason agrees, lowering his head in an awkward bow.

"Please, do make sure you are making our guest comfortable," the General states. "You know of the importance here." And with that, he's gone.

Mason's shoulder sag slightly when the General is out of sight. So it's not just me feeling uptight in his presence? He sighs. "Let me show you to your room."

We stroll through the homes, past the center meeting area. It's larger once actually being in it, like a park in the middle of a city. Despite the beauty, I can't seem to get my mind off of the General's words.

"What is it about me?" I ask, throwing Mason off. I don't want to be the center of attention. I don't want anyone's life to be in my hands. Especially not when my own life is up in the air at the moment. I sure as hell do not belong in the VIP neighborhood that we're currently ambling through.

Mason pauses for a moment, seemingly contemplating what he's going to say. The worry lines of his forehead are the only imperfections present. "You are the person that everyone identifies with," he finally says. "You could be their daughter, or sister. You could even be *them*."

I'm sure my eyes hold confusion. All this talk of revolution hurts my brain. There's nothing special about me. There never has been and there never will be. Sarge dips harder into me, nearly causing me to lose my balance.

Mason doesn't leave me any time to process or reply. Instead he drags me out of the middle area and into an empty lot. There's nothing but the innards of a room and a long tube extending toward the ceiling.

"This," he says, smiling, "is your room."

My eyes trail warily over the scene. I suppose I can, maybe, see it?

Mason chuckles, and I realize he's studying my face. "Your room requires a special design, so they have to build it from scratch."

"Is that tube a part of the design?" It's the one thing that sticks out, and the one thing not found present on any of the other tiny homes surrounding us.

"Yes," he answers. "That's the elevator."

My eyebrows shoot up in wonder, my chin lifting to raise my gaze subconsciously.

"You'll have access to the outside for Sarge," Mason explains. "All courtesy of General Favager," he adds at the end, almost like he has to.

My neck breaks to look at him. The smile plastered on his face is wide and inviting once our eyes meet. The General has thought of everything. "Anytime?" I question.

Sarge's tail wags at our words. My heart flutters at the thought of Sarge getting to be a normal dog.

"Well." Mason's eyes flash cold for a moment. "There will be an indicator on it. Green means you're safe, red means you're not permitted." He appears guilty at the restrictions, as if being told what to do and when to do it hasn't been my entire existence thus far, whether it be here with the H.P.S. or back in Western America with the Force.

I nod in understanding and Mason's smile returns to its full beauty.

"It should be ready tomorrow," he says.

My heart falls. Tomorrow. Going back to the hospital ward will be too much for my mind right now. It needs distraction. It needs answers. "Do I have to go back to that stifling hospital room?" I ask, quietly.

Mason is hesitant, clearly. It's moments like this that remind me that something is amiss here. They can try and distract me with a flashy, personally designed room, or tell me how special I am, but ultimately after everything that's happened, I believe there's still something they're trying to hide. And yet, for some reason, I don't believe Mason and the General are on the same page anymore. At least about something big. His attitude toward him today has shown that.

"I'll find something for you," is what he settles on after a few minutes. He reaches into his pocket, pulling out a device that looks similar to a Relay, yet different. Mostly only Force members and higher ups had been blessed with such advanced technology.

Is it the same here?

Within a few minutes, an officer comes to lead me and Sarge to the underwater bunkers. More specifically: Compound One.

We take the submarine to the entrance, where Lacy is awaiting our arrival. She nods to me, and I nod back as the Serviceman returns to his post from before. Lacy takes lead down the long hallways. Compound One is like a fancy, underwater hotel. Each room juts out from the central passageway, with doors every few feet.

"Thanks for volunteering to babysit me," I say to Lacy while she unlocks the door. This is my first time in the underwater bunkers, and I'm not really sure what I expected, but I don't think it was this.

"No problemo," Lacy answers, chucking her key on the counter. The room is simultaneously smaller, yet bigger, than I imagined whilst looking at it from the outside. To my surprise, there are windows, but it's the same technology that's used in Headquarters. Out Lacy's window is a beautiful green field, not the endlessly murky waters I know it to be. The H.P.S. has gone through great lengths to make people feel at ease.

The kitchen is tight, but functional, and it's an open shot to a cute living area of sorts. There's a small taper in the wall which leads to what appears is a bedroom. This is what I'd imagine for my home as well. The thought excites me.

At first I'd been upset I hadn't been given the option to choose between the Compounds, a pod, or the home currently being made for me. But after seeing the special accommodations for Sarge, I realize how it will be the best for us. *Maybe they aren't so bad after all?*

"Thoughts?" Lacy asks, catching me in study mode.

I open my mouth to speak, but an unfamiliar voice fills the

room instead. "Miss Lacy, Miss Lacy!" A rambunctious kid runs into the room, nearly tackling Lacy to the ground.

"Hey, turd. What are you still doing out?" She's smiling. Is this a brother? Someone of importance? Should I know them? Curse my brain for not being able to remember. "Amity?"

Lacy's voice is laced with concern. I must have zoned out. "Yeah?"

Her eyes are telling me she's curious about where I just was, but her mouth continues as if nothing happened, which I appreciate. "This is Jordan. He's one of the CROP kids here." *Crop?*

My eyebrow raises with confusion, but Lacy shakes her head in warning, as if to say *don't ask*. "Nice to meet you, Jordan," I say, bending to eye level. "I'm..."

"Amity Thorne." He cuts me off. "Sarge's mom."

At the sound of his name, Sarge's ears perk up, but he doesn't leave my side. His tail gently wags and the kid clearly wants to greet him. "Would you like to say hi?" I ask.

Jordan's eyes grow wide with excitement as he bobs his head up and down wildly.

Giving the release to Sarge, he runs toward the boy full force. Then, he stops and lays down, flopping his tongue out of his mouth.

Jordan giggles. "Sam is going to be so jealous." It is only now that I realize Jordan has one fake arm. It's a near identical match, and I wouldn't have recognized it if not for the slightly mechanical movements. It's robotic in nature, but very much humanized. *Poor kid.* I wonder what happened?

"Is Sam your brother?" I ask, snapping myself out of staring.

"Sort of," Jordan says, not taking his eyes from Sarge.

"Why don't you head back to the others?" Lacy suggests. "I'll stop by before bed to tuck you all in."

"But I don't wanna..." Jordan starts to argue, but a quick glare from Lacy shuts him up. "Okay. It's good to see you again, Sarge." He hugs Sarge's body tightly. "Nice to finally meet you, Miss Amity."

And just like that, Jordan is gone.

"Who was that?" I ask, trying to make sense of everything. Jordan seemed to know Sarge. Is this another person I've lost to the battle with my brain?

"One of the orphaned kids rescued from a farm in Western America. We call them CROP kids. Children Rescued from Outside Protection." Lacy chuckles, smiling. "They do really love their acronyms here."

Rescued from outside protection? What does that mean? And how does that tie into Jordan knowing Sarge? My mind races with all the possibilities it could come up with. They must have been in a bad situation if he had lost an arm. *Great, even more mysteries to solve.*

Lacy continues without the need for me to say anything. "I volunteer to watch them occasionally so Mama June can catch a break now and again."

"Mama June?" I question.

"Oh, right." She chuckles, ruefully. "She's technically their legal guardian."

How many CROP kids are there? My heart slivers a little. I can't think about that now; it'll drag me into a place I don't want to be. But with nothing else to discuss, Lacy and I settle back into silence. I hate the silence. My mind cannot wander.

"I don't want to be rude," I start. "But what happened to... ya know..." I'm alluding to Jordan's arm. Thankfully, Lacy understands immediately.

"His arm? Yeah. That's a signature for the CROP kids. All of them were operated on in Western America so that their tracker would be removed safely." Her eyes hold sorrow in them. "You were lucky and got the signal blocking tattoo instead." She points to the wisps of black peeking below the line of my sleeve. *Oh, yes.* Luke had mentioned a tracker before, but then we'd been interrupted.

My eyebrows fold. I have this in common with the CROP kids.

"Yes," Lacy says, pulling me from my thoughts. "They were once stuck in the program at Omphalos. And so were you." She eyes me carefully, waiting to see how this information fares.

Lacy doesn't know that I've been privy to a torturous path. I've been told I was rescued from Omphalos, but not why I was there in the first place. Sarge's body pushes against me for comfort. This is all too much right now. "Have you always wanted to work with kids?" I question in an attempt at keeping the intrusive thoughts at bay. "You seem to be a natural with them."

Lacy looks at me uncomfortably but keeps her smile. "A good friend of mine had always wanted to work with children. Doing so makes me feel closer to her in a way."

I try to think of the things I imagined myself doing, but I don't recall ever putting much weight on the matter. Living in Western America made everything seem like a forbidden fantasy. And suddenly, I'm jolted back to a time I'd had this exact same thought. Instead of staring at Lacy in a posh room, I'm sitting across from a young girl with bright blonde ringlet curls. *She's telling me she wants to find true love and work with children, and I want to be happy for her, but deep in my gut I feel the intense terror of wanting something you'll never get.*

"Huh," I say, shaking my head.

Lacy regards me with a curious eye. "What's up?"

"I think I also had a friend that wanted to work with children.

Though, I don't remember her much." I sigh. "I can't even place a name. But she had the most striking blue eyes I've ever seen."

Lacy's face folds into a sad expression. "Follow me," she says.

Sarge pushes himself into me as a sense of dread settles in my chest. Lacy leads us both deeper into her abode until we're front and center to a shrine of sorts. Surprisingly, one of the photos has the girl from my partial memory. Her piercing, icy blues are beautiful and bright. It appears Lacy and I have the same friend. But the thing that really catches my eye is the photo that's next to hers. It's a man with a buzz cut and an eyebrow scar. The man I've seen a few times in scattered images. In some of my dreams.

"Who's that?" I ask, unable to take my eyes away.

"That's Abby. Our friend that..."

I cut her off, stashing the name away. "No. Him." My finger lifts in the direction of the man. "I've seen him before."

Lacy is silent. For the first time ever, maybe. When I'm finally able to pull my gaze away from the photo, I turn to find tears in her eyes. "You remember Zach?"

"He's been in my mind lately," I admit. Zach. Abby. Hm. I wish I had more. I wish their names gave me more, but only echoes return from the void that is my mind. Those that once were there are just... gone.

"Zach and Abby were heroes," Lacy starts. "They sacrificed themselves for those they love."

"The true definition of selfless." A voice from behind startles me.

"Hey, baby," Lacy says, leaning into Sonya as she snakes her arms around her.

"Did you know them, too?" I ask, probing answers from Sonya. Does everyone here know them except for me? The thought makes me sad, and Sarge licks my palm.

"Zach I knew," Sonya answers, smiling. Though, it's a smile tinged with sadness. "Abby I didn't have the pleasure."

Do I ask what happened? My mind is hazy. I want to be able to connect the dots, to remember these people and what they've done. *Or do I?* Maybe it's a blessing to forget...

"Do you remember anything else about them?" Lacy asks.

Perhaps I'd zoned out for too long. I feel myself caught in the thousand yard stare. I shake my head.

"Would you like to know more?" Sonya asks, sweetly; softly.

Do I?

Lacy is uncomfortable, and the slight disdain of her gaze toward Sonya is clear.

"What?" Sonya questions, giving attitude right back to her love.

"Mason said we shouldn't tell her anything." Lacy's voice is a whisper.

Aha. So Mason *is* trying to keep things from me. I knew something was fishy here, but I still don't know why. Why would someone claiming to be my friend try and keep me from my past? Was I wrong in assuming he was not on the General's page?

Then it hits me. It hits me all at once, so fast, that I fear I may crack under the weight. It's for protection. Why else? If Mason truly is my friend, then he wants to keep things from me for my own sake. It's the only thing that fits. But if Mason isn't my friend at all, well. If *that's* the case, then I am back to knowing nothing at all.

"Guys," I stutter, quietly. Lacy and Sonya have been quietly arguing. Sarge lifts his head, wrapping his neck around my hip. I instinctively place my hand on the soft fur of his head. "Was Mason my friend also?"

Both Sonya and Lacy stare at me with confusion. But it's Lacy that speaks. "Yes, he was. Or is. He's always cared about you," she admits.

"Then I know he wants to keep things from me for my own protection," I say, addressing them both. "So, do I really want to know more about Zach and Abby?" My voice is quiet and scratchy. I don't like the sound of it as it passes my lips. I sound weak.

"Only you can decide," Sonya answers.

CHAPTER NINE ○ LUKE

MY BACK IS AGAINST THE COOL WALL, MY HANDS CLASPED IN front of my face, elbows balanced on my knees. I was summoned to Favager's office an hour ago, and I've been waiting not-so-patiently outside since.

I've resigned myself to sitting quietly, but only because one of the ten guards along the hallway here threatened to knock me out with his tranquilizer. Though, don't get me wrong, I did think about it. At least the time would have passed by quicker.

The large mahogany door scrapes open. "General Favager will see you now," the tallest guard closest to the entrance says. He steps aside, fanning his hand in the same direction as the office.

"Lovely," I say, hopping up from the floor.

Mason passes me on his way out, keeping his eyes down and away. Hm. I wonder what that's about.

The office is plush and earthy. Admittedly it's more my style than Ren's. Deep oak and natural greens. I take a full breath in, smelling the rich scent of coffee. Also a hint of liquor.

"Mr. Warin," Favager says as I step closer to the large desk. "Please, have a seat." He prompts me to take my place in one of the chairs that face him. I sink into the fabric.

"To what do I owe this... invitation," I say, not quite sure how to address all of this. Favager has never demanded my presence in his office. He had, through Mason, suggested I help with getting maps from my memory. Later, after M's extraction, I demanded certain terms be met for my stay here. But never, ever, has he wanted to speak to me at all. To be quite honest, I'm probably too much to deal with. Mason is much squishier.

"It's been some time since we've discussed things together," he says, his tone business-like. "It is my understanding you are... unenthused with our methods here." His choice of wording is interesting to me.

Unenthused? Yeah. I'm pissed. Everything here is ass-backwards. "I was simply under the impression we were trying to help Amity get her memories back, but recently it seems that we want to keep them away." My eyes are steady, watching Favager, scanning his face for any sign of whichever emotion might be aroused. I find nothing but stoic indifference.

"Mr. Warin, you're a man that admires bluntness, yes?" Favager leans forward with his question. I don't like when people get a read on me, but he's right. Why spend time beating around the bush?

"Yes, sir," I answer.

"Then let me be blunt." He presses his palms together in front of him, as if he were praying. His chin rests on his fingertips. "Miss Thorne *cannot* know about her sister's death."

My eyes pop open slightly with shock, but I recover quickly. "What do you mean?"

"I mean, Mr. Warin, that you may tell her anything you want. Help her try and remember her past if it pleases you. But if she somehow finds out that her blood is dead, there will be hell to pay." His eyes bore into me the way Ren's used to, but it's different. There's something colder here.

"But Mason said…"

He interrupts me. "Mr. Baines has been taken care of," he snaps. "Our goal here is for Miss Thorne to get better, simply without a certain tidbit of information."

"Why?" I blurt, before I can stop myself. "Who cares if she knows?"

A vein pokes out in Favager's neck as he tenses with irritation. "The loss of her sister caused her to go into hiding for a year. We don't have that luxury for time. It's all running out." He runs both hands through his hair. There's something unsettling about him right now. "I will deem when it's right. For now, if she becomes too restless, we will tell her that her sister is captured. We need that fiery spirit from before." His eyes aren't begging me, because he doesn't care whether or not I side with him. He's the General, and this is the plan. End of.

"I won't lie to her again," I say, standing from my seat, ready to take my leave, or defend my life. Either or.

"I'm not asking you to, Mr. Warin," he says. "I'm simply asking you to omit the truth."

Staring at him, I bite my tongue for the first time in my life. This man is delusional. Omission is still hurtful. It's a new way to justify the lies.

Favager speaks up again, sensing my trepidation. "You and I," he says, "we want the same thing."

I scoff, turning toward the large door, ready to leave this all behind.

Before I reach the exit, Favager stops me. "Mr. Warin?"

My teeth clench and I stretch my shoulders back to release some tension before speaking. "Yes?" I grate.

"For your cooperation, I've tasked Miss Pierre with a side project. Your little memory extraction idea. Hopefully she can fulfill both of our desires." His eyes darken as he speaks his last words. I slam into the door and get the hell away as fast as possible.

o o o

RAGE IS ONE hell of a drug. I don't know who to go to first, so I choose to focus on the rage in the old training section where I'd first worked with my extraction team. I should go find Mason and demand more answers from his dumb ass. Or maybe I should be talking to Cateline to see exactly what task she's been given. More than all of that, I really should go see M, but the truth is, I'm no good for any of that.

I hoped no one would be here, but when I exit the elevator, Thomas and Trevor are sparring in the middle of the training mat. Shit.

I've yet to face them since everything happened. They'd been on my team for rescuing M. Thankfully they were already out of Omphalos and at a safe distance when the collapse occurred. I haven't been able to look them in the eye and apologize for my shit leadership that day. Avoidance is a much easier tactic.

Before I can turn back to the elevator to find another outlet for my wrath, one of the brothers calls out to me. "Boss!"

I take a deep breath, closing my eyes and counting to five. All the rage I feel has to be buried, just like the shame of our mission. I whirl around with a smile on my face. "You know I'm not your leader anymore, right?" I chuckle, forcing an air of normalcy.

Thomas and Trevor have dropped their weapons on the mat and are walking toward me. They somehow look older since the last time I saw them. Fuck, Warin. When's the last time *you* looked in the mirror? You probably look older, too.

"How have you been?" Thomas asks as they approach.

"Yeah, we haven't really seen you much," Trevor adds.

I'm confused why they care. Do they intend to mock me? Pretend they care in order to make a fool of me? I'm a monster, and they know it. I see it in their eyes.

Shaking my head, I put on my smile again. "Busy," I say. "You know." I shrug. I'm trying to keep things vague. They don't need to know my business. They've already learned too much about me.

"How's Amity?" Thomas asks. His eyes show true concern. Yet, they weren't there when I was forced to lie to her. When she first came out of that pod and she didn't trust a single soul. They only saw her, and me I suppose, when they helped pull us from the rubble.

"She's getting better physically," I say, stepping from side to side. Any talk of this is keeping the rage at a steady boil. Physically she should have never been hurt. That's all my fault.

"That's good," Thomas comments, assuredly.

"We've heard she's having mental problems," Trevor says, cutting into the conversation.

"Trev!" Thomas scolds, elbowing Trevor in the side. "What the hell?"

"What?" His brother shrugs. "It's true!"

All of my energy goes into keeping my eyes from rolling. Her being physically hurt might be my fault, but her memory issues are the reason Ren will be burned alive by my hand. I'm starting to think Favager will be joining her. "Yeah," I answer, confirming the rumors. "She's got no memory of the last six years."

Thomas's gaze softens with understanding. He's a decently genuine guy. It's Trevor that lowers his voice and says, "Word is

General Favager is hoping to utilize her for..."

"Trevor!" Thomas cuts him off again, meeting my gaze with sympathy. He knows what poking the bear does. Whether the bear is me or Favager, I'm not sure.

Despite being the younger of the two, Thomas is the one constantly looking out for his more reckless older brother.

Though mention of Favager reignites my nearly forgotten anger. Of course there's an agenda. I just learned about it. Their General doesn't have *time* to let M grieve again. While I admit it was a long process, it's a special time that I was able to be there for her. She deserved the little slice of peace we had, even if we were never truly safe. The war of her mind was enough. And keeping all of this from her makes me the untrustworthy fool she already believes me to be.

"He's a general," I say, oozing nonchalance after a quick, five second countdown. "He wouldn't be where he is now without a plan."

Thomas and Trevor look at one another. "Yeah," they say in unison.

"You don't sound too sure," I say, pointedly. Is it possible that unrest lingers within the ranks of the Service? Are others not as thrilled with Favager's ideologies as he'd like me to believe?

"Thomas isn't happy as of late." Trevor nudges his younger brother. "Our next assignment is in Western America." With the lack of emotion from me, Trevor leans forward. "*Extended.*"

Thomas shakes his head, resigned to his over-sharing brother's tendencies.

The shock works its way into my expression, but only for a few seconds. Now I understand Thomas's apprehension. Sure, we had a mission in Western America a few months ago, but he lost some members of his team. And now they're getting shipped off for an extended period in the same hellhole they grew up in, the same place they lost people they cared about. It's triggering, sure, but it's a soldier's duty.

"So, you don't trust Favager these days?" I question Thomas. If I hear at least one other person admit they aren't happy with his ways, I'll chance Death to get M's full memory back.

"He must have his reasons," is all I get Thomas to reply. Fuck.

Trevor opens his mouth, yet it's not his voice that comes out. Dipshit Mason has arrived.

"Luke!" he shouts. "You were supposed to meet with Cateline."

Tension builds throughout my body, and I ignore Thomas and Trevor's uncomfortable gazes. They know my relationship with Mason is rickety.

"Oh," I grate. "Is *that* what I was supposed to do?" My hands are balled into fists at my thighs. Favager mentioned Cateline, but I didn't realize I was supposed to seek her out immediately. Hell, if I would've, there'd be too much expensive equipment destroyed right now.

The vein in Mason's neck bulges. "Just get to Cateline's," he spits, turning away before I make my retort.

After a few moments of silence, Trevor says, "We'll catch you on the flipside, Boss."

"Good luck," Thomas whispers, before heading back to the mat with his brother.

I watch them as they pick up their fighting routine, and a deep pit settles in my stomach. This is probably the last time I'll ever see them.

CHAPTER TEN ○ AMITY

SONYA AND LACY WEREN'T CONVINCED I WAS ALRIGHT. AND they are correct. I'm not. Sarge has pushed himself so far into my body, it's almost like we're one entity.

My legs shake as a Serviceman leads Sarge and I through the hallways of Headquarters. Mason had sent for me shortly after Lacy finished filling me in about my past with Zach and Abby.

We enter a room filled with monitors. There are beeps and hums in here that remind me of the hospital. Sarge guides me forward, despite the fact that my gaze is anywhere but. The monitors are showing horror films. I recognize the backdrop as Western America. I don't remember it being this terrible. Though, I suppose I don't recall a lot of things these days...

"Amity," Mason says with a smile, seemingly out of place amongst the darkness of the room. "Are you excited?"

I'm not sure what there is to be excited about. Unless my room has somehow been finished a day early, there's not much I've been expecting. I feebly nod my head.

"Come." He holds out his hand. "I've got a surprise."

Sarge watches Mason carefully but relaxes when I place my hand in his. I know Lacy told me that Mason cares about me, but Sarge's apprehension of him is alarming. His hand is cold, clammy. The emotion swirling my gut is unsettling, like I shouldn't be feeling his skin against mine. The strangeness has me thinking of Luke. Where is he? Has something happened to him?

Mason takes me to an opening in the ground, a pool. A submarine floats up. He helps me in, silently. Sarge jumps in after.

It's surprisingly spacious for what I imagine a submarine to be, yet with both Mason and Sarge, it's a bit too crowded. I'm slightly confused when the lid closes and no pilot joins us.

"You know how to drive this?" I can't hide the shock from my voice. I've no reason to suspect Mason wouldn't be able to, I just assumed he'd have someone else so he wouldn't have to multitask paying attention to me. *Though, Amity, there isn't anyone else here to be a distraction.*

"Of course!" His eyes light up with a smile.

My face flushes pink. Why am I getting the feeling there is more to this trip than there should be? Is this... a date?

The thought has Jeremy popping into my head. My ex-boyfriend. The one I turned away after my mother and Grace, my best friend, had died. I couldn't handle potentially losing him, too. It was easier to end things before they ended me. I'm still coming to terms with the fact that this wasn't just a few months ago, but *years*. What ever happened to us? Did I ever reconnect with him?

"You alright?" Mason is behind me now, and my shoulders tense.

"Yes," I say, more to convince myself than him.

He eyes me curiously. "Well, we're here." *What?*

My eyes widen. I'd zoned out the entire trip? Of course I did.

Mason steps up the ladder, screwing open the lid. He motions for me to join him. I do.

The ladder is tight for both of us to be on it, and our bodies are incredibly too close. Unfortunately, Sarge is forced to sit at the bottom, looking up. He whines.

When I make it to the top, the sun is bright in my eyes. The orange hues of its setting are beautiful. My mouth pops open in awe. The Complex can be seen from here; a big, glass beauty. Wide open fields surround it. The view is stunning.

"Beautiful, isn't it?"

When I look at Mason, he's watching me. My face flushes with embarrassment. I nod, not knowing what to say.

"This place isn't safe," he says, sighing.

I frown. "What do you mean?" Obviously I understand that safety is relative. With the Reaver still in power, those opposed to her regime are always in danger. The fact that the H.P.S. even formed is still a shock to me. The world had cast America out. But I suppose as our closest neighbor, maybe someone decided to come to our rescue. I can't imagine this place isn't safer than where we came from, though.

"Madame Keres knows this place exists," Mason answers.

His admission brings me back to my conversation with Lacy before the other Amity showed up. Lacy had mentioned an air attack. She'd also mentioned that I was the reason there hadn't been another one.

"I assumed," I speak, cautiously. I won't give Lacy away for telling me. What would happen to her if Mason found out they've gone behind his back on certain orders? Thankfully, I don't have to lie because I was there when the other Amity showed up. Who else would have sent something... or some*one* like that? It's not a far reach to believe the Reaver knows. If only I knew why my being here prevented more Death.

"Yes." He frowns. "Well, once the Guardianship falls, we'll be able to start rebuilding on their land, and ours."

I note the trepidation of his tone, so subtle it's barely there. I also note the fact that he claims the land here as his own, completely separating himself from Western America; his home. While Western America hasn't been homey in as long as I can remember, if it *ever* was, I still claim it as my place. It's where my family is. Or was... *ugh*. My head hurts.

Seeing where this conversation is headed, I decide to change the subject. He's going to push the fact that I'm the key, and right now, I'm not having it. "That sounds like an admirable plan," I deadpan. "How's the woman?" I ask.

I suppose if I want answers, I'm going to have to blatantly ask for them. Lacy told me Mason cares about me. If that's the case, I know a part of him doesn't want to keep things from me. I just need to push the buttons a little. And right now, I don't want to hear about how *special* I am, I want to know if my doppelgänger is alright.

Mason's jaw tenses and relaxes all within a millisecond. "She's with our top scientist at the moment."

The answer is vague. She's with a scientist? Not in the hospital like I was? "Sure," I say. "But how is she?"

"Haven't seen her since Luke met her. I don't know." His words are clipped, short. He's agitated, like my questions are pushing deep within his skin.

"Luke?" He allowed Luke to meet the other Amity? Is that why he hasn't been around? *He prefers the other one...* No. Right? He couldn't...

"Luke is working with our head scientist to see if the woman's memories are authentic." Mason's jaw tenses again as if giving me any tiny bit of information is painful. I push for more anyway.

"Could I maybe speak with her? I could learn about my past, maybe help connect some d..."

"No!" Mason snaps, cutting me off, causing me to flinch and

Sarge to jump up beneath us with a gnash of his teeth. "Sorry," Mason apologizes. "It's not safe."

He finally backs himself down the ladder, distancing himself from me physically as best as he can in this small space. I follow behind him, anger bubbling up through my veins. "Why wouldn't it be safe?" An exasperated sigh escapes my lips. It's hard to believe anything that anyone says. How do I know who to trust?

"Why would you want to speak with her anyway?" Mason questions, barely meeting my gaze.

Could he truly be this dense? He has to be going in circles in an attempt to throw me off. Is it hard to see the reason for wanting to pick her brain? "To learn about the missing time in my head!" I shout.

Mason takes a moment to process what I've said, then he shifts gears. His eyes soften into troubled pools of blue as he says, "Amity, I didn't want to tell you this... but you were tortured."

This, I knew. From that hushed conversation between him and Luke outside of my hospital room. Yet, why tell me now? After every step he's taken to stop me from learning my past, how does this fit in? "I've seen the scars," I admit.

"You knew?" He's hurt, which only serves to piss me off. I was the one who was tortured and he has the audacity to be upset about a bruised ego?

"Of course," I bark.

He blanches in response to the harshness, but probably also the information I've shared with him.

"I don't know exactly what happened, but..." My voice fades. Though I'm privy to the knowledge of my torture, I don't know the how or the why. *Did I deserve it?*

Sonya and Lacy gave me the choice of learning today. It made me sick, but it also gave me peace. It was *my* choice, *my* power. I want to come to terms with the unknown. Or at least be given the choice. I need to learn if I'm the monster I fear I was.

"See?" Mason pleads. "You don't want to know the pain. You can be at peace without knowing what you've gone through." His eyes are hopeful. Suddenly, his care for me is clear. But does he truly believe he's right? That *this* is the way to go about things?

The anger sweeps through me again, this time carrying me away. "You think because I don't remember being tortured that I'm not in pain?" The look on his face is surprise mixed with anguish. "I can't remember *anything* about my life! I don't have memories of Sarge, and I'm left in the dark about Emma and my father." I'm so exasperated, I don't think I'll be able to stop the flow of words.

Sarge is pressing his weight into me, attempting to keep me grounded, but it's failing. Mason is too stunned to speak, so I continue.

"There's a woman in there that thinks she's me. Everyone says I'm worth Death!" My anger reverberates off the walls of the small, enclosed space and surrounds us, but I don't stop. "I learn about this man I can't truly remember being dead, and a girl—your sister—also dead. And to me it sounds like neither of them deserved to die. So is it my fault?" My sanity is slipping through my fingertips by the minute. "Is that why you don't want to tell me? Is that what you're hiding from me?"

Mason is doing his best to keep a plain face, but it's dissolving.

My breathing is ragged from the shouting. My ears ring from the harsh clash of the screams quickly cut into silence.

Clearly Mason's mind is whirring. The cogs of his brain are turning. Perhaps he's wondering how I found out about Zach and Abby? The anger dissipates quickly at the thought of Lacy getting into trouble. I had let my emotions get the best of me and someone else is going to get hurt. They're going to... I don't...

The panic thankfully subsides with Mason's deep sigh. "What I can tell you is that we're currently looking for your father." *Looking?* Where could he be? Damn my mind! I don't know anything that's happened at all!

"And what about Emma?" I ask. "Where is she?"

"Once we find your father, he should be able to help you," he says. It's purposefully vague. Fucking politicians.

The anxiety creeping into my chest makes it hard to breathe. Something has happened to Emma and they don't want me to know. That has to be it, right? Why else? They mean to keep it from me, but why? Is she missing? Captured? My mouth runs dry and a scratchy gulp travels to the back of my throat. *Where is my sweet little M?*

I must've been quiet for too long because Mason speaks again. "I'm sorry I can't offer more for you."

"Can't, or won't?" I spit, my eyes glowering through my lashes. I'd take being angry over anxious any day, so I let the anger fill me once more.

Mason jolts at the sudden callousness, but recoups even faster as if it hadn't bothered him at all. "We are doing what we think is best. Can you trust that?"

His big, blue pools stare profoundly into my soul. *Can you trust it, Amity?* I don't know. I want to believe Lacy out of everyone right now, and she told me Mason cares about me. But him letting me overthink on all of this doesn't lend itself to that truth. I suspect something has happened to Emma, so why keep anything from me at all? Why keep me in the dark when I could possibly help?

But, for now, maybe it's best they believe they have my loyalty, despite not knowing where to place it wholeheartedly yet. Hopefully soon my father will be found so more answers will be presented to me.

I nod, hesitantly, scraping my fingers through Sarge's thick fur. He'd kept himself between the two of us this whole time.

"Good," Mason says, relaxing. "And speaking of good... there's a birthday celebration coming up." He smiles at the change of subject. "November eighth is right around the corner."

A sharp intake of breath heaves my chest. November eighth. My birthday. How old will I be? Surely not fifteen or sixteen like my brain wants to believe. But twenty-one? *Holy hell.*

I'll be twenty-one in a few days.

With everything that's been happening lately, keeping track of time has not been on my mind. I hadn't realized my birthday was so close. Am I ready for another celebration? Am I ready to be the center of attention?

"Are you alright?" Mason appears genuinely concerned. "I thought you'd enjoy something different for a change."

"Of course," I say, not totally meaning it. My fingers grip Sarge's fur again, snaking their way to his neck. "Thank you."

Mason seems relieved at my answer after the tenseness of the night. "It'll be fun," he swears. "Just wait and see."

CHAPTER ELEVEN ○ LUKE

A GUARD LEADS THE WAY TO CATELINE'S LAB. SHE'S ALREADY made a breakthrough only a few days after our start.

Cateline catches my eye. "Luke!" she cheers. "Good news."

Is this the moment she tells me we can get M's memories? I want to be hopeful, excited. But I know that M doesn't get her entire memory back—only the glorified version that Favager wants her to have. That bastard.

But can I really be mad? I haven't been able to stop warring with myself since our conversation. He's giving me what I want: an M that remembers me. An M that cares for me. And an M that exists without the pain of losing her sister. It's a dream I've always wanted for her, but still a fantasy nonetheless. She deserves her whole truth, even if it's painful.

"I've found a way to remove memories!"

Cateline is expecting me to be ecstatic. It's what I had asked her for, right? Before Favager put his presence where it doesn't belong. Now it feels criminal.

"Ahah..." she blushes, tucking the loose bangs behind her ear. The lack of emotion from me is making her nervous. "It's still new," she admits. "There are a few more tests I'd like to run."

Fuck. I shouldn't be so openly shitty right now. Who knows

what she reports back to Favager. That, and my father's incessant teachings on being a gentleman.

Counting to five, I plaster a smile on my face. "Whatever it takes," I say. "Could I help?" The honeyed tone of my voice causes bile to touch the back of my throat. I never could understand how my father was so altruistic. Sure, this is for M, but it's on their terms. I hate that.

Cateline eyes me curiously before smiling. "Of course."

The M imposter is sleeping soundly across the back of the room. Cateline whipped up a soundproof chamber for her. She's not bothered by the hustle and bustle of the lab. The girl rests, yet her eyes jerk beneath her lids; the sign of nightmares. It was always the first thing I watched for in M. It's crazy that her imposter would have the same telltale twitch.

A thought crosses my mind. A few, actually. I'm sure Cateline has thought of them herself, yet I feel compelled to ask regardless. "Are you able to isolate Amity's memories?" My gaze involuntarily flicks once more to the M imposter laying in the bed. She shouldn't have to bear the weight of M's nightmares, but she doesn't deserve to lose her own memories.

"I believe I can," Cateline shares. "You're going to help me confirm."

"Me?" My eyes widen slightly. I suppose there's nothing to lose. If I forget everything, I won't remember the pain, the bullshit. And maybe I could even fall in love with M all over again.

"You said whatever works, yes?" Her eyes hold a playful look. She truly loves science. Any challenge she takes head on, getting more determined the harder it becomes. If she can get M's memories back, I'll owe her my life. Even if she's only going to give her half of them.

I smirk. "I suppose I did say that."

"Come, come." She motions to the chair beside her lab table.

I sit. The monitor she's staring at reminds me of the Brain, the main database computer AI of the Guardianship's operations. My first thought is that it works in a similar way. Maybe recreating an artificial brain is how one can help remove memories.

Cateline places a tiny receptor on my temple. Then, her gaze returns to the monitor. Her eyes light up, utterly fascinated by whatever is on the screen.

"What is it?" I ask.

After a few seconds, she turns the screen and I see the same thing. My memories. It's one long strand of file, simple like clips in an editing software. Much simpler than I would have imagined my entire memory line to be. After five seconds, the line grows, showing a small thumbnail of me staring at Cateline behind the monitor. Oh! I see why she's excited. "It uploads as we go."

"Yes!" She's delighted with the outcome. "It had worked on me earlier, but I needed to see it on someone else to really solidify."

"You tried it on yourself?" I question. I suppose that makes sense. Yet with Favager backing this project, you'd think helpers would be lining the walls in here.

"Yes." She nods. "I even made a copy of my memories so people can study my work one day!"

Interesting. "But the test you're about to run on me, you couldn't do yourself?"

She shakes her head. "If I succeeded in extracting my own memories, I would run the risk of getting stuck in a loop of extraction."

Hm. Okay. Makes sense. I nod. "Let's do this then."

Cateline smiles. "First, I want to tell you a secret."

The stalling irks me. I want this to be over. The faster we test, the faster we remove M's memories. Sure, that means I have to keep secrets, but at least she'll remember me and stop giving me the cold shoulder.

"When I was younger," Cateline says, "I used to have this chemistry set. I'd take it everywhere with me. The other children would poke fun. I persevered, even then."

I resist the urge to roll my eyes. "You don't have to tell me what a nerd you've always been," I say, pushing forth an aloof attitude despite my growing irritation.

Cateline blushes. "No," she retorts. "But I do have to ask you a question."

This stalling truly is the biggest annoyance. I'm trying to keep the anger at bay. After all, Cateline is using up her time in a field she's not fully trained in to help get my M back. "Shoot," I say.

"Why did people poke fun at me when I was a child?" she asks.

The fuck? Why is she asking me to diagnose her childhood bullies? This is ridiculous. We should be doing the experiment and focusing on the task in front of us. "Your freakishly large brain?" I say, as if it were a question.

Cateline beams. "Yes!" she cheers. "It worked!"

"What worked?" The confusion on my face is clear. Did I guess correctly?

"I was made fun of for carrying a chemistry set." She smiles.

The downturn of my lips doesn't change, nor does the furrow of my brow. Has Cateline gone mad?

"You would know that if I hadn't spliced your memories." The gleam in her eye is bright.

Ahh. A smile breaks across my face. Now I see why she was so excited. It *is* thrilling stuff down at its core. But science only moderately intrigues me. M is the forefront of this for me, so I circle back to her. "Will Amity lose her memories from here?" I'm curious.

If we are replacing memories for her in the past, will it affect any of her future memories that are currently her past and her... present? What? Fuck I need sleep. This whole situation is a mess.

"I'm going to take the code of memories that belongs to Miss Thorne, and then I'll plug them into place in her brain," Cateline states. "Theoretically there will be a big gap that will align perfectly. The way yours is now." She points to the screen. On it, in my thread of memories, is a small blip where nothing resides. Shit. That means the girl in the room will have an empty space if we do the same to her...

We could leave the memories within her and let her go on believing she's someone else. Would that be any better? Fuck it. I don't know.

I keep this theory to myself and say, "Alright," though I'm a bit apprehensive. I've never really worried about things like this before. It's a feeling I'm not used to. But we're so close to getting M's memories back, and giving her *some* is better than none, right? Even if it means someone else suffers?

Cateline rests her hand on my shoulder, causing me to tense. "Luke," she assures. "Think of this like a computer. We're going to move one file and place it into the other folder. It should work. We'll test it soon."

Her voice is soft and reassuring, but there's still a deep pit in my stomach. No one has told M that we can do this. Will she even want her memories back? Will she still feel the lost time lingering? Deflated, I sigh to myself as more questions circle my brain. How will Cateline remove Emma's death? Is that really what's best for M?

Too many problems cause me to shove them into their own compartment to wither and die. I choose to ask one simple question instead.

"When will you extract the memories from the girl?" If I find this out, it tells me how much time I have to get more answers.

Before Cateline can respond, a noise draws my eyes away.

The M imposter is awake, pushing out of the chamber. Her eyes are asking the questions her lips haven't yet. Then, finally: "You want to remove my memories?"

The inquiry would suggest a certain level of fear, but this woman seems utterly confused instead. My mouth runs dry, not having an answer to give. Thankfully, Cateline steps forward.

"Yes," she agrees. "It is our goal to remove the memories that aren't yours and return them to their original host."

"You all keep telling me they aren't my memories, but how can you be sure?" This M is determined, like the one I've grown to love. She holds the same spirit that was somehow washed away from the original. I don't know how Ren did it, though if she had somehow given us this version of M first, it may have taken me a while to decipher that she was not the real one. That thought alone scares me more than anything ever has in my entire life.

But if this girl is like M, truly, wholeheartedly, then she will believe me. I close the distance, working my way toward her small space near the back of the room. Her shoulders are tall and square, no inclination of fear at all. "Look into those Amity memories you have about me. Have I ever lied? Have I ever shied away from giving you the brutal truth?"

She takes a moment to process my words, thinking about the weight of them. After a bit of silence, she finally shakes her head.

"Then please understand that's what this is. The brutal truth," I say, in the soothing voice I've only ever had for M. The words sour on my tongue, yet I continue. "You were once someone before Amity; before Ren Keres molded you into someone new."

The girl's grey eyes flick to mine. They're a slightly different shade than the real M's. She stares at me for a while, deciding if she wants to believe it or not. I feel for the girl, I do. She believes she's Amity, and we're trying to take that away. She has to battle with herself in the way that Amity would; she has to question everything she knows.

The M imposter lifts her hand to shake, forming some agreement. I place my hand in hers. "I believe you," she says. "I'll help you look deeper."

Fuck. I hate this. My heart is in the hands of a scientist and in the head of an imposter.

o   o   o

THE LAST FEW days have been a nonstop whirlwind of trials and tests. After this Amity had surprised us both, she became the pushiest of us. Cateline is all for more time, but with the help of the memory serum, this Amity is learning more and more about herself—her previous self—in snippets, and she wants out just as bad as I want my M back. Favager is also an ever-present shadow looming over us. He's not fully satisfied with his best scientist's timeline.

Cateline is fiddling with her machines. She's wary of trying on this Amity so soon. Some of our trials have shown resistance. Cateline has a theory that the people who are open to their thoughts being read are the easiest to dissect. Those that want their memories hidden? They're more challenging.

I blame myself. She was doing more tests on me but was looking for a less fresh memory. I want to say I was open to the idea, but it seems my brain had other plans. Some of my earlier memories—the ones of me in the Force—were darkened. I knew where they fell on the timeline, but my brain was fighting her system.

This has led her to a new worry. Is there something that will block M's? Will it cause us to lose our chance forever? Cateline won't go into details with me, but this Amity pleaded with Favager when he stopped by. Cateline no longer gets a choice.

Her worries are based in science, but not totally off. The M I know wouldn't open up willingly, but I've found there's a soft spot for the girl. She wants us to get inside, so I'll back her. There's nothing to really worry about at this point anyway, as Cateline has compromised with Favager and only agreed to peek inside her head for now.

"You remember what I told you?" I ask. This Amity is sitting on her bed. Cateline will be ready for us shortly.

"Keep my mind open," she says, rolling her eyes. It's made me wonder if the eye rolling transferred over, or if whoever this was before M had also done it.

"And?" I prompt.

"There's nothing to hide." She's annoyed with me, but only mildly. The small smile playing at her lips clues me into her mood. I hate to admit it, but spending time with this Amity has been nice. I've missed the banter, the ease. I've missed the way we were and the way we're supposed to be. It's wrong, I know, to be spending time here when I should be with the real M, but soon the right body and mind will be one again. I just have to keep one major secret...

"Are you ready?" Cateline appears in the doorway. She's not holding herself with the usual air of confidence, but I don't let it get to me. This *will* work. It has to. Whatever we find today will set the course for the rest of this goal.

The girl beside me nods her head and I offer my arm to her. We walk the few feet to Cateline's monitor, and I help her into the seat I'd been in so many times already.

This will all be new since we don't know what Ren has actually done. Anytime we've hooked the girl up before, her vitals didn't hold stable. Cateline has been working on that and is confident we can at least take a look inside. We need to find out if Ren left any remnants of who this girl was before, and if she did, how did she splice this time from M? What snippets is she remembering with the memory serum's help? Is it the ones from before? Or the ones during?

We can't formulate any plans on moving forward until we know more about the enigma of this girl. So, as scary as it may be, seeing her current memory thread is the best way to figure out the next route we need to take.

Cateline keeps her focus on the computer, refusing to look in our direction or make any direct eye contact. It's getting harder to ignore the air of uncertainty around her. I place all the wires and readers in the correct places on imposter Amity's body so that Cateline can focus on the monitor. Though she's aware she's not truly Amity, the girl unexplainably trusts me to be gentle with her. Cateline is still a stranger.

Once the final piece is in place, the data of memories pops onto the screen in one long file. The video feed of reels updates after five seconds.

"Off to a good start," I say, reassuring this Amity that she's doing great. Her vitals are normal, and she appears relaxed at first.

Yet her eyes jump to mine after one glance at Cateline and the distrust is clear. I can't see Cateline's face from where I'm standing. I opted to stand behind her for a view of the memories, and when my eyes flick to the screen, I catch a glimpse of what Cateline is seeing.

It's a long, blocked out spot of memory. Not the faded, blurry memories that the brain wants to keep hidden, but a definitive block of ashen black, like a box keeping its contents secure.

"What is it?" this Amity asks.

I wait for Cateline to give a response just the same.

"Looks like a... hm... what did they call them? A Trojan horse?" she finally says after a century of silence.

"A what?" I can't help the quick spit of my response.

Cateline chuckles, but it's out of place. "A Trojan horse? It's an old tale about hiding one's true intentions."

"What does that mean?" this Amity questions. She's more worked up than I imagined she would be.

Cateline is back to her usual, calm self. Questions to answer, tasks to do, a problem to solve. They put her in her element. "Why block memories unless you have something to hide?"

It takes me a moment to process her words, but less time to send out a response. "No, I don't think that's it," I say.

Both women whip their heads to stare at me with inquisitive eyes.

"How could you be so sure?" Cateline asks with her typical scientific curiosity.

"Well, we could just ask this Amity to tell us everything she remembers," I point out. "It would be time consuming and a bit subjective, but nonetheless doable. So I think this is more of a lock."

"Interesting. A way to keep us from gaining access." Cateline hums her approval to the theory.

While her trojan horse idea seems fitting, she doesn't know Ren like I do. Ren is deliberate, even when caught in a mistake. Ren has nothing to hide, but everything to lose. She's going to let us get so close, yet still be so far away. She's playing a damn game.

"Can you try removing them?" This Amity surprises us both, bringing me back to the present and Cateline out of her scientific thoughts.

"What?" I say at the same time Cateline speaks.

"There's too much unknown. We've only just got your vitals stable..."

"How can you know if you don't try?" this Amity counters. Stubborn as ever.

"We can try more tests... we can..." Cateline is cut off by a suddenly frantic Amity.

"And how long is that going to take?" she cries. "Days? Weeks?"

"Woah, woah, hey." I bend to get eye level with this Amity. My tone is soft again, something I can't help but do. "What's the sudden rush?"

Her eyes meet mine with water around their rims. Her full lip quivers. "I don't want to live like this anymore! I don't want to be someone I'm clearly not!" She's upset, but something is telling me to push further.

"Is that why you chose to give up the memories in the first place? You knew it wasn't you?" I question. We'd been taken aback at the lock on M's memories, we haven't even gotten past them yet to see if there's anything salvageable without them. Removal could mean dire consequences. Or it could mean salvation. But either way...

This Amity averts her gaze, avoiding my probing eyes.

"Why do you want to give up the memories?" I repeat, pulling her back into focus.

"I know how I... I mean... *she* feels about you." Her voice is low and scratchy, full of emotion. "And it's clear you care just as deeply." She flicks her gaze away again, brushing a stray lock of hair behind her ear—a motion M has done multiple times before. She meets my eye again. "I don't want to stand in the way of that. I want to go back to whomever I was before."

Oh. Guilt. She feels the guilt that M would. Interesting.

I guess I could see the intrigue for Ren to want to experiment on this. She'd always wondered—like many interested in the human mind and genetics—about the nature vs nurture debate that's been around for hundreds of years.

But could that truly be the motive? I wouldn't put it past her to do something simply for the sick of it. Though, she's been calculated in every endeavor up to this point, so it seems unlikely. Ren *has* always been a fan of killing two birds with one stone. It's more probable this aspect was a bonus for her. Fuck this.

"You really want to try this?" I bring myself back to the present, back to the terrified, yet strong Amity in front of me.

She nods.

"Then what are we waiting for?" Favager's baritone voice demands attention. It's out of place here in the lab.

Barely a second passes before Cateline jumps in. "Sir, I think we sh..."

Favager holds his hand up to silence her. "If this is what the girl wants, then we do it." He smiles at this Amity almost sweetly. "This isn't Western America."

For once I agree with the bastard. If this Amity feels the guilt that the real M does, she's already in her own personal hell, beating herself up, creating wars in her mind. Cateline sees reason, but she doesn't see the pain behind the girl's eyes. She doesn't see the absolute chaos in her brain.

Months ago, I couldn't stop M from marching herself right into Ren's arms. Her guilt was too strong, her moral compass begged her to take the place of those she felt she needed to protect. And I can't possibly begin to fathom that I understand it, but somehow there's a certain peace that settled in her eyes when she truly thought it would help. The best thing I can do now is give this

Amity her own little slice of that peace.

Cateline's mouth hangs open slightly, stunned. Her head shakes, inadvertently matched to her pleas. Still unable to let things go, she says, "But if we had more time, we could..."

"No," I say, sternly, cutting Cateline off and surprising both her and Favager. "I know the stubbornness of Amity Thorne, and she gets what she wants. Once her mind is set, that's it. Anything else would be torture." The words fall from my lips, and a piece of me—the harsh part buried deep inside that blames myself for M's predicament—melts away. I knew it back then, but M needed to go. She needed to do what she felt was right. And now, I will do everything I can to get her back. Which means, honoring this Amity's wishes.

Cateline stares in disbelief while Favager nods in approval. Resigned, Cateline wordlessly turns to the screen to work whatever magic she does.

This Amity catches my gaze, smiling. That peace is there in her slightly off-grey eyes.

My contentment doesn't last long. Favager has weaseled closer to me, his voice kept to a hushed level. "I see you've come around to the idea."

His head stays straight, as if he weren't speaking to me at all. Have I come around?

"This woman deserves a choice," I say, deliberate in my words. Everyone deserves a choice. Something he's taken from M. Hopefully this will help clear my character a little.

"You are still upset about Miss Thorne, then?" he asks, trying to confirm. Though, I suspect he already knows the answer.

"She deserves the truth. Or at least a choice in whether or not she wants to receive it," I say. Cateline is busy rifling through this Amity's memory thread. No one seems to be paying our conversation any mind.

"You need to think bigger, my boy," he replies. The moniker boils my blood, my fists clenching beside me. "The citizens of Western America deserve life. Should we not sacrifice the one to save the many?"

At this he turns to me, and the smug expression settled on his face has my knuckles itching. Could I get away with punching that square jaw of his?

"Amity is *not* a pawn!" I shout, louder than expected.

Cateline stops her fiddling yet doesn't dare turn to us directly. This Amity recoils, slouching her shoulders and dipping her head in a wince. The guards by the door lift their weapons but are stopped by Favager's quick hand.

"Should you ever change your mind, we could use someone with your spirit amidst our ranks." He places his hand on my shoulder before giving his final send-off to Cateline. Then he leaves without another word.

Fuck. This whole thing feels wrong. I know the cost of war. I know the unfair calls that have to be made. My father taught me that. Yet, it's not right when it comes to M. Isn't there a better way?

My mind is brought to reality as my hearing homes in on Cateline's mumbling. "No copy," she says under her breath. "Lockout."

I don't question what she's uttering, because somehow I know what she means. I tear my eyes from this Amity and study Cateline's face. Worry lines crease around her mouth and forehead. There's no way, as of now, to make a copy. The memory file is encrypted to stay in the body it was put into.

While I want to be hopeful, suddenly I'm apprehensive. This Amity wants to do a full removal, but I don't see how that could be possible with a lockout. If Ren blocked us from simply making a copy, she definitely has some sort of firewall to stop us from removing it as well. Or worse. What if it bugs the real M once they get reimplanted? A shudder rips through me.

"Wai..." I start but get nowhere.

Cateline has clipped the memory file and is cutting it out of this Amity's memory line.

In the same instant, I sweep my eyes over every inch of the girl. She smiles, seemingly not in pain for the first time in a long while. Her eyes are closed, but when she opens them, something is terribly wrong. Her pupils are quarter-sized, and growing more by the second.

"M..." I sigh, uncomfortable with being loud in case it makes it worse.

Her smile grows wider. "Thank you," she says. Yet her pupils are dilated to the point almost no grey is showing.

Then the black extends, covering any visible white and oozing from her eyes like sludge. Fuck!

"Cateline," I shout. "Stop!"

"Wha..." she turns to look at me, yet stops on her patient. "Oh no! Oh no!"

This Amity is still in blissful tranquility. Her smile is wide and steady. Her eyes, despite the black ooze, are relaxed. Not a crinkle to be seen.

I surge forward. Fuck this. She may have asked for us to try this, but she doesn't deserve to die.

"I dropped the memory file back in, but..." Cateline's voice fades into the background. I don't look at her. The panic is felt from here.

This Amity's vitals are still good, yet her temperature is rising quickly. It's like she's boiling alive and her body doesn't know it yet.

The black sludge covers more of this Amity's face now, and I pull her to my chest. "M," I whisper.

"Thank you," she breaths, repeating her phrase from earlier, tensing slightly as she hugs herself to me. Then her muscles relax, her smile is gone. And so is she.

My chest feels hollow, yet anger fills it quickly. Though, who or what I'm angry at isn't entirely clear.

She's dead. Gone. And with her, our luck of getting M's memories back. So yeah. That anger grips me, puts me in a chokehold, forces my arms to shove the lifeless body from my lap. I stand. "Damn it!" The rage threatens to completely overtake me. My foot connects to a cart holding medical equipment, sending instruments everywhere.

"Luke!" Cateline cries.

The guards outside the door are in here now, surveying the scene. I'm waiting for them to try and touch me, try and get near me. I'll fucking kill them when they do, I don't care. I don't want to turn and see the terror in Cateline's eyes. I don't want to see the motionless body on the floor. The surefire proof that I'm a monster. But I peek anyway.

Cateline's hand is held up to the guards, stopping their progression toward me. Her shoulders sag once she meets my eye. She slowly makes her way to me. "I am very sorry, Luke," she says, keeping her voice steady. "Sometimes experiments are not always met with favorable results."

I release the tension of my jaw, and the grip of my fingernails in my palms. Right. Experiment. Fucking Favager.

As fucked up as this whole situation is, I need to take a breath and remind myself that this is what the girl wanted. Hell, she even *thanked* me for it. I can't... no, I *won't* sully her last wish by being angry.

I offer Cateline a tight-lipped smile. "Of course," I acknowledge. "We did what we could."

She smiles, nodding. "Please," she begs. "Take the night and try to keep your mind off of this. There is still time to make it to your friend's party." Cateline's expression is endearing, but it quickly wipes from her face as my countenance morphs once more.

"Party?" My teeth grind.

"I..." she hesitates, stuttering. The guards behind her have put themselves in a defensive position again. "I thought it weird you wouldn't be there, but I know General Favager wants you here."

"What party?" I shout, questioning anyone who will answer me. That rage. The blinding red rage returns.

The guards have their hands on their guns, not sure whether they should pull them or stay where they're at. Cateline shrinks in front of me. "M... Miss Thorne's twenty f... first b... birthday..."

"Fuck!" I shoot toward the door, nearly sending Cateline to the ground, blasting past the guards as they run to help her.

I'm going to kill him. That two-faced, selfish, politician bastard! Mason did this on purpose. He wants me away from her. Or maybe it's Favager. He says he's okay with me telling M about her past, but maybe *he's* the one who's still tricking me.

The walls are mostly quiet except for the slapping of my feet against the ground. The thumping of my heart is even louder. Why didn't anyone tell me? They know how important M is to me, yet everyone kept the knowledge of her party a secret.

I've been busy lately, sure. Doing *actual* work to try and make her better, even if it's for only half of her memories. I'm not just sitting on my ass like the rest of them.

I turn the corner to the gathering hall shockingly quick. I'm surprised none of the door checkpoints have stopped me by now.

Lacy is about to pull open the doors, but she turns at the last second, her eyes connecting with mine. The handle slips from her hands, and her body squares itself to stop me from entering. Fuck her.

"Woah, big fella," she speaks, holding out her hands. "Slow down."

I'm barreling toward her, but she doesn't seem alarmed. She's slow and calm in hopes to get me there, too.

Well, it ain't happening. "Let me through," I demand, right atop her now. Her hands are on my chest.

"You're not going in there like this," she argues. "Don't ruin everyone's time because of your own shit." She glares at me, matching my own. Then, I take a deep breath and she removes her hands, relaxing with me. "What the hell is on your shirt?"

My gaze flicks down to the dark smudging on my grey t-shirt. Shit. The black ooze. I wave my hand, ignoring the question. I don't want to think about it now or the anger will return tenfold.

"Why didn't you tell me about M's party?" I redirect the conversation.

A harsh breath streams from Lacy's lungs. "I thought you knew," she remarks, pushing her chest out, standing tall. "Why would I suspect otherwise?"

"You should have checked!" I bark, before thinking.

"Oh no!" she chides. "Lucas Warin is a grown ass man. He can keep track of his *own* shit."

The rage covers the corners of my vision again, threatening to blind me completely. Why is everyone so infuriating? Fuck this! My body tenses in response.

Lacy shakes her head, dismissing my heated demeanor. "Maybe if you were more focused on Amity now rather than Amity of the past, you'd have known." The accusatory tone of her voice is enough to cut the rage, morphing it into shame. Is she right? Fuck.

No. Lacy knows nothing. I have to lie to Amity of the present. It's bothersome that she's okay doing it to one of her closest friends. But any chance we had of helping her get at least some of it back is gone...

"We don't have to worry about that now," I say, sympathy laced around each word. My hand instinctively reaches for the black on my shirt. Fuck this.

Lacy's eyes are questioning yet understanding settles in them quickly. Before she can respond, Mason flies from the ballroom, M dragged behind him with Sarge pressed to her side.

"Let's go," he says. "There's an emergency."

CHAPTER TWELVE ∘ AMITY

MASON FINALLY LET GO OF MY ARM ONCE LACY AND LUKE joined us. The sight of Luke had my heart racing even more than before. He came. I hadn't thought he would. As the night progressed, I figured maybe he simply didn't care.

But here he is, following behind with a glower that could put Satan to shame. His eyes are dark, and his shirt is stained with an inky black. His disheveled appearance is certainly something to question. It's crazy that my mind would put so much significance on him and his presence, especially with the impending emergency. Though, I'm starting to learn just how crazy the mind can be.

My hands instinctively search for Sarge when Mason stops unexpectedly, whipping around to halt all of us as well. Sarge's soft fur trails through my fingers as I wait for someone to speak.

"Why are we stopped?" Luke questions from somewhere behind me. "Isn't this an emergency?"

Mason's jaw tenses, and a flash of annoyance hits his eyes, but it's gone as he speaks. "Yes, we needed to get to a place where no one could hear us."

There's a pause from Mason, and the heat radiating from Luke is palpable. Thankfully, Lacy speaks, curbing Luke's anger for a bit longer.

"What's going on?" Her brow is pulled in, concern is etched across her face. I'm sure she's more upset that Sonya isn't here.

"Madame Keres has made contact," Mason answers, finally.

Luke lets out a huffy laugh. "Tell her to fuck off. Problem solved."

Lacy sighs. "What Luke means to say is, why pull us away from the festivities for that?" Lacy sends a sideways glance at Luke, warning him to behave.

The tenseness between everyone here is not helping the pounding of my heart. Sarge is nearly pressing me over at this point. I'm just as curious as anyone, though I'm more used to being kept in the dark as of late. But something about this situation has bile climbing into my throat, my gut doing flips.

The time it takes Mason to speak feels like an eternity, but it's only been a few seconds. "She said she'd..." he sighs, struggling to find the words. "She said she'd blow Amity up if she couldn't speak with you and her."

My eyes follow Mason's, wide with shock. He's staring at Luke. *So not just me, then*. Luke, too. But why?

Luke's fists are clenched tightly; his arms pressed rigidly to his body. The Reaver really gets under his skin. Yeah, she's a terrible leader, and she's threatened to blow me to pieces, but I have no knowledge of what she's done to him personally to elicit such a response. To all of them, really. And what has she done to me? Taken me to plant as a human explosive?

"So again," Luke finally says, gratingly. "Why did we stop?"

I've noticed when it comes to my safety, no one plays around. Especially not Luke. Though, I'm sure everyone has their own motivations for it.

"I figured Amity might need a moment to process," Mason replies, hissing through clenched teeth. Then, every pair of eyes are on me.

Sarge's fur is already clumped inside my fingers. His head is pressed closely to my stomach, creating a physical barrier from those around me. It helps a bit.

Do I need time to process? I should... I was just told that I would be blown up if we don't cooperate. Perhaps I should be more shook up than I am. But somewhere deep in my mind, I know she won't do that. I can't even begin to explain my thoughts to the others. Maybe I'm broken more than anyone could ever truly know. Instead of speaking, I shake my head, signaling that I'm fine to continue.

Mason watches me with worried eyes, but Luke's hastiness finally pushes him to move. The group travels down a few more corridors, the place eerily quiet.

That's until...

"Happy birthday to you, happy birthday to you! Happy birth..." The menacing sound of the Reaver's voice filters out into the hall as we get close to a room marked with strange symbols on the door. A video conference room. *This is really happening?* Sarge is huddled against me, hoping to keep the chill from my spine.

Mason passes the threshold first, then Lacy. Luke glances behind him and, upon seeing my hesitation, he steps back. "You can do this," he says, offering his hand.

He's right. Something in his eye tells me he knows she won't follow through on her threat, but she may reveal something here. Something about my past, or something about what we need to do in the future.

I plant my hand firmly in his and we enter the room.

A large screen takes up the whole back wall. The Reaver's face is projected onto it, making her large and more foreboding than she already is. I never liked when her dead eyes judged me through the television screens in Western America. That was only a little twenty-inch box. This looks nearly eight feet.

"Ahhh," the Reaver breathes. "There they are."

Her attitude is playful, it's oddly familiar. Yet something also bothers her. It's subtle, but was that a hint of disappointment? Anger? There's something that flashed in her pupils when she finally saw us enter. Something that I don't think I would've seen if she wasn't so large in front of us.

This knocks something loose in my skull. A partial memory. The same expression in otherwise expressionless eyes. *Some stupid commoner who opened her legs.*

Her voice pulls me back to the present. "I can't believe I didn't get an invite to the celebration." She frowns. "I do great party tricks."

Everyone's face more than likely matches my own. Confusion. Why has she called? Why now? Today? Is my birthday truly such a spectacle that she demanded to be a part of it?

Mason questions her on what she wants, but it's completely ignored. It isn't until Luke decides to speak that she responds.

"Why send the imposter?" he questions. My eyes flick to his strained face, but I don't move my body for fear of drawing attention to myself. *He wants to know about the girl?* My heart drops. Why does it bother me so much? I chew the side of my lip.

"She's a subcopy, dear. Get with the times, will you?" The Reaver's voice still holds its' playful timbre.

"I don't give a damn what you're calling her, Ren," Luke snaps. "Just tell me why."

His fingers tighten around mine as the heat of his anger picks up. And they tense even worse when the Reaver ignores him like she had with Mason, glancing at me instead. *Shit.*

"Don't look so confused, Miss Thorne," she says. "Don't you remember me?"

Of course she would go there. She's trying to toy with me. I think quickly. Letting her see weakness would be a mistake. As the thought finalizes in my head, an odd sense of déjà vu settles. "Should I?" I question, raising an eyebrow. Nothing gets a narcissist going more than making them realize they aren't important.

This visibly knocks her back, but only slightly. She's already done with me and is back on Luke. "Lucas, darling, the subcopies are gifts. Enjoy them." The evil in her eye makes my knees shake a bit. Sarge is thankfully acting as a brace. "Try not to kill them all, will you?" *Kill?*

"Gifts?" Mason is confused. Then he turns to Luke. "She's dead?"

Luke, ignoring Mason, questions the Reaver once more. "Copies?" He graciously points out that the Reaver has made it plural. Meaning multiple. We've only got one in our possession. Or... maybe none now? Is she really dead as the Reaver suggests?

She smirks. "Well, yes." She answers as if our confusion isn't warranted. "There are plenty more."

"What's the purpose?" Mason asks. "How many?"

The Reaver hesitates in answering, but she doesn't remove her eyes from Luke as she says, "As many as it takes, darling." Always cryptic.

"Goddamn it, Ren. Just tell us what you want!" Luke's anger is unmanageable. Before, he was agitated. But now rage billows off of him like smoke from a burning building. He releases my fingers, stepping closer to the screen.

Sarge and I step back reflexively. I want to sink further into the shadows and further away from this conflict.

It's at this point I become aware of General Favager's presence.

He must have snuck in at some point, when the Reaver was too focused on us.

"Do not use that tone with me." The Reaver tenses. "You are still my officer." The loudness brings me back to her. Her eyebrows raise.

"I should've listened to my father about you," is Luke's retort. *His dad?*

"You shouldn't waste time worrying about a dead man now. He's not here to interfere any longer." *Luke's dad is dead?* The Reaver throws off an air of casualness, as if this conversation is like any other small talk. Like she and Luke are the only two in the room.

What is happening?

"I figured he got killed long ago. He was a *true* leader." Luke says. "You never could handle competition, could you?" Luke is toying with her. There's a familiarity here. There's something, damn it! If only I could remember.

Luke was an officer, I must have known that. Right? Though I'm not all that shocked by it. But I can't help; I can't do shit but sit back and act like everything's fine. And we all know it's not.

The General is a statue, watching and listening without bringing any attention to himself. Yet, in the shadow of the wall, his grim expression is still clear as day.

Sarge licks my palm, nuzzling into my hand. A breath catches in my lungs as the conversation carries on.

The Reaver cackles. "Oh, you've always been such a silly boy."

She's under Luke's skin now. "You only know one part of me," he spits back at her.

"And you, me," she responds. "You see me only as you know me now, but I am *so* much more."

My head is reeling with confusion. Where do I fit into all of this? Luke and the Reaver are paying no mind to any of us in the room. They are locked into their own personal vendetta with each other and I'm so far into the dark about their past it's almost comical. This is ridiculous.

After a few seconds, the Reaver speaks again. This time with a different tone. "As for your father," she says. "He was killed only recently. Maybe ask your little *pet* all about that?" The smirk playing at her lips tugs her face to the side, wrinkling her skin. Her eyes dart to mine. *Me?* Surely I couldn't have been involved with Luke's father, right?

Luke's eyes jerk to meet me as well. They flit back to the demon on the wall quickly. "What do you mean?" he demands.

"You feel that, Miss Thorne?" the Reaver crows. "The guilt?" She cackles once more.

My mouth runs dry, my throat closes. There's nothing for me to say. I feel nothing. I feel... okay something. But I don't know why. I'm not sure what I've done. What I *could've* done.

Luke stares, trying to hold himself together. The waning of his control is enough to keep me from speaking.

"Keep your head, son." General Favager's deep tone travels between us.

"Your silence speaks volumes, dear," the Reaver retorts, ignoring everything else despite finally clocking the General's presence. I wish I could reach through the screen and rip out her vocal cords.

"Well?" Luke commands.

"I said ask your *pet*," the Reaver snaps, annoyed, her teeth clacking together.

"She doesn't have any memories!" Luke shouts. "You made sure of that."

"Are *you* sure of that?" The Reaver lifts a brow. "Have you asked?" Her voice lilts in a way that turns my stomach.

"She... no..." Luke's muscles ripple beneath his shirt. He turns to me. All the wrath he's had for the Reaver is now directed at me in a millisecond.

"Mr. Warin," General Favager says in warning.

"Do you know what she's talking about?" His voice is loud and harsh.

"I... I..." I'm trying to access long lost memories, but my mind draws a blank as per usual. My stuttering only serves to bolster Luke's anger.

"Luke!" Lacy cries. "She doesn't remember anything." She's trying to reason with him, but it's no use.

The Reaver laughs in the background, though it barely affects Luke at all. He's on me before I'm able to process what's transpiring.

"What do you know?" he interrogates.

Sarge's snarls are low. His body vibrating against mine is the only clue that it's happening.

"I... I didn't... I don't think..." I start but never finish. At first, there's nothing in my mind, but then a face molds itself in my memories, set off by the closeness of Luke's features. An older face with eyes that match the man in front of me. *Could this be his father? Is it true? Did I know him?*

"Don't play dumb with me," Luke chides, pulling me from what little clarity I may have gained. "You *do* know more than you're letting on." There's a distrust in his eyes that burns my flesh. *Damn it! Your expression must have given you away, Amity.*

The General is demanding Luke step down, but he won't dare move closer with Sarge's harsh growls growing louder.

My previously crumpled face twists with anger, ignoring the General myself. "You're projecting," I say, accusatorily. Luke's known more than anyone. He knows what's happened to me, to my family, and he's sitting back, keeping it from me, leaving me to fend for myself. I don't know anything at all, yet he's demanding I share some piece of my past that's missing from my memory. He's taking the Reaver's side.

"Fine," he says, glancing momentarily at the General before flitting his eyes back to me. "Emma is dead," he admits, as if the words are of no consequence whatsoever. He grips my shoulders tightly. "Now tell me what you know about my father."

My knees buckle.

Gasps meld into the background noise. From whom, I can't identify. Or why. They've known. They've *all* known.

"You've made a grave mistake," General Favager says before slipping out amidst the chaos.

"Get the hell off of her!" Mason chimes in at the same second, not acknowledging the General's threat. If Luke lets go, I'll collapse. Dead? *Emma's dead?*

There's no time to process anything before teeth are deep within Luke's flesh. "Aggghhh," he cries.

Lacy races to catch me as my body falls. No. *Surely he's lying, right?*

Sarge slashes at Luke, but he's resigned to the attack. He doesn't fight, or say anything, as Sarge pulls him away from me.

Emma. My little M. *No!* I refuse to believe that.

My body goes numb, my senses fade, until only the Reaver's evil cackle can be heard.

CHAPTER THIRTEEN ○ LUKE

SAM IS SITTING ON THE BED WHEN I RETURN TO THE POD IN A rush. Someone will no doubt be here to collect me and haul me away shortly. The anger flowing from me is so potent that I'm sure Sam can feel the heat from where he's at.

"What happened?" he asks, quickly noting my unsettled appearance. Sarge did a number on me. My shirt is torn, hanging loosely off my body. There's blood spattered across my skin. I'm treading the line between self-hatred and explosive rage.

"You need to leave," is all I say. It's hard to ignore the hurt expression on his face, but even worse is the slight tremble of his lip and the hidden fear in his eyes. Sam needs to go. Out of here. Anywhere that I'm not.

Once upon a time, I wanted to show him that I'm not a monster. But today I'm learning that the beast has been lurking in the shadows, waiting, watching for the perfect time to strike.

"Now, Sam." I repeat the order more sternly.

Sam gulps but doesn't move. "But... we could do this together." His voice cuts into my heart. "I could help you... maybe... I..."

"No!" I shout. "Leave!" My anger is climbing to new heights. I don't want Sam to see this side of me, but soon there will be no choice. The monster demands release.

"I can handle it!" he cries. "I'm a man. I can help you!"

"Damn it, Sam!" I shout, kicking the desk to my right with a loud crack. "I said get the hell out of here!"

His skeleton jumps from the mattress, my outburst of physical violence startling him. He's trying to be strong. He's trying to hold back tears that are on the verge of falling. Sam raises himself from the bed and rigidly walks past me to the door, carrying his head high, his shoulders square. His jaw is clenched tightly, his expression is flat and even.

He opens the door, but before stepping out, he looks me in the eye. He doesn't say a word. He leaves.

When the door clicks behind him, all hell breaks loose. My fists make contact with anything and everything they can. Shouts from deep within my soul push out into the stifling air of the pod. Fuck this, and fuck that. Fuck you, Mason. Fuck you, Ren. Favager, this place. But most importantly: fuck you, Warin.

My ass finds its way to the bed and my head falls to my hands. What have I done? How could I have done this to Amity? The anger melts into sadness. You're a monster, Warin, it's who you are.

I hurt her. I hurt the woman I love. That's it. It's true. I *am* a monster. I've done exactly what Ren wanted of me. The puppet master she is. I played right into her game.

M will never forgive me.

I'm not sure how much time passes like this, but eventually the expected happens. Servicemen break down my door and thrust me out.

I ignore the prickling beneath my skin as they lead me toward the control room. Their grip on me is too much for the monster within, but I dampen all feeling so I won't make anything worse. My knuckles itch for purchase on their arrogant faces.

We don't stop marching until I'm at the surface. The hidden

cave entrance is completely fixed, and all remnants of the massacre are gone. Last time I was here, Ren had sent an air strike. Innocent lives were lost. I remind myself it was the catalyst that led to M getting rescued, but even that doesn't lift my spirits much.

The burly Serviceman to my right shoves me past the threshold into the dirt. "Your Headquarters privilege has been revoked."

His voice is deep and monotonous. He refuses to look me in the eye.

"So I'm to stay out here?" I question. This is bullshit.

"Until General Favager decides what to do with you," he responds, this time catching my glare. There's disgust in his expression.

The Servicemen turn in unison, leaving me in the darkness of the cave. The gate shuts behind them.

"Fuck!" I shout, long and drawn out. I flop down, my back to the dirt. I deserve this. Really I deserve a cell, or worse. I'm actually surprised my sentence is this light right now.

The longer I lay, the more my anger builds. You'd think it would be the opposite, but no. The monster craves freedom.

Pushing up off the ground, I head to the moonlight at the mouth of the cave. The reflection of the Complex sparkles in the distance. I could go that way, but more than likely I'll run into guards. Can't imagine I'm even allowed there, anyway.

I've only ever spent time in the big, open field directly outside the entrance. Sarge and I used to run around to get away from the suffocating air of the underground. But further out, the trees grow denser, and from what I remember, there are trails and ponds to explore.

Who knows how long Favager will leave me out here, so I'll need to locate water and a good place for shelter. Survival in the wilderness isn't unfamiliar to me. I used to find it peaceful, but

the thought leaves me feeling lonely now. Back when I was by myself, there was nothing better. But being away from M and Sarge?
I've grown too accustomed to having company. Hell, even Sam
grew on me after a few days of roughing it together.

Shit. Sam. What's he going to think?

Fucking hell. You really made a mess of everything, didn't you,
Warin?

My eyes adjust to the lack of moonlight in the thickness of the
trees. I could be using my skills to track water, yet I simply don't
care enough to apply myself. Instead I walk aimlessly through,
killing time in the process. Sleep and I have never been on good
terms, so more than likely, I'll spend the night circling the same
trails over and over until my body collapses. But I need something
for my mind. My compartmentalization ability is missing right
now. Great fucking timing.

Minutes meld into hours, simultaneously passing like it's nothing yet also like it's in slow motion. The trees all look the same,
and the pathways merge, forming jumbled messes.

The sun crests the horizon before a small lake presents itself.
Falling to my knees, my cupped hands pool the water, greedily
slurping it to my mouth. My muscles ache with exhaustion, tense
with dehydration. I'm a walking nightmare.

When the water settles, I catch my face in the reflection. My
hair is growing back, but it's still a closer shave than I'd like. My
skin only has small pockets left of the burns that covered my body
a few months ago. I meet my hollow eyes and tense my jaw. You
fucking monster.

A scream rushes from my throat; my fist disturbs the smooth
surface of the lake. What am I doing here? I'm stuck feeling sorry
for myself instead of figuring out what's next. This is stupid. I slap
the water again.

"It's better with the ripples, anyway."

The rage cools slightly as a familiar frame plants down beside me, though I keep my eyes forward in the rippling reflection. I'd said the same thing to M last year.

After some silence, she speaks again. "The other is out there looking for you, so I figured that's probably what I should do, too."

It's at this point I peer up from the image and meet the eyes of a subcopy. I hadn't noticed in the imperfect surface of the water, but I see now. She's just another *gift* sent by Ren. I should've known the real M wouldn't come out here to find me. Even if they released their grasp on her, she simply doesn't trust me. Doesn't... love me. I hate myself for hoping.

Yet, while this subcopy looks like M, there's more confidence in the way she holds her shoulders, more life still clinging to the light of her eyes. I hate myself even more for not noticing right away.

"And you are?" I question, hoping to throw her off.

"Who I am and who I'm supposed to be are at odds right now," she admits, kicking the water lightly. "Though I know *you* are Lucas Warin."

"That I am," I say, scoffing. "Lucas Warin. Murderer, monster, and Grade A Asshole. Nice to meet you."

The subcopy chuckles. "You can be quite exasperating. But I'd argue those are all synonyms, and none of them *actually* mean Lucas Warin." She watches me carefully as I meet her eyes. In the early morning sun, the shade is nearly identical to those of the real M.

The lengths Ren will go to...

"You mentioned another?" I ask. Ren discussed more. Multiple, she'd said. I hadn't thought they were all coming at the same time, though. What's the point?

"Yeah." The girl nods. "She's a dumbass. Couldn't tell up from down." She laughs again.

"That's Amity," I agree, sighing out a small laugh. It took me almost a year of training before M understood cardinal directions. Good to know she didn't retain a single thing. I smirk at the ridiculousness. Then I glance toward the subcopy next to me. "So how'd you find me?"

There's something different about this one. She's clearly meant to be a perfect replica of my M, but somehow there's an obvious distinction. She is... but she isn't.

The girl slowly kicks her feet in the water. "The girl was given directions to a hole in the ground," she says. Her body shifts, and from her back pocket, she pulls a small, crinkled piece of paper. Her hand flops and I reach out to take the note.

Once unfolded, I see what she means. It's a perfect map of the area. X marks the spot of the hidden cave entrance of Headquarters. Ren knows if she gets too close with anything, the Service will retaliate. But they won't question anyone walking along their lands.

My eyes flick to the girl's again. "This explains how to find the H.P.S.. Not me," I say, chucking the paper into the water and watching it saturate and sink to the bottom.

"Yeah," the girl answers. "But I found it right as they were kicking you out." Her smile can be heard in her voice.

Shock momentarily changes my features. "You saw that?" I question, mock wincing at my embarrassment. The ease of the conversation reminds me of the first subcopy; reminds me of the shame I felt, like somehow this is a betrayal to the true Amity.

"I did, indeed," she retorts. "Been following you ever since." Her tone suggests this is of no consequence. Following me? What the fuck?

"Why'd you do that?" I ask, hoping to keep the monster within from stirring. I hate the idea of this person, this stranger, seeing me like that.

"I recognized you," she answers. "My brain told me to run to you." The confusion in her face is enough to catch my attention. She knows me, but she's not sure why. "Then I saw you all messed up and felt I should give you some space." She shrugs. "What'd they bounce you for, anyway?"

Her genuine curiosity has me reeling. This person has no idea about the mess we're currently in. It's been a long time since someone's been able to vex me in such a way. Ren made it nearly impossible for me to be affected by anything. But this? This is a whole new level I can't possibly hope to understand.

"What?" she questions, drawing me out of my thoughts.

"Uh... ha. Nothing," I say, my fingers massaging the back of my neck to relieve the growing headache. "I broke a rule," I tell her. "This is my purgatory in the meantime."

The subcopy laughs. "A rule? You broke a *single* rule?"

I scoff at the reminder. "It was a big, important one apparently." I haven't forgotten what I've done. I hurt Amity. But what I *had* forgotten is the reason I'd done it. And now, I have someone who could help me with that.

The girl is going off about being tired of rules and being told what to do. She'd escaped Ren somehow, following the other sub-copy that's out there, searching for the entrance to Headquarters. Hoping it would lead her to a better place. What a crock of shit. I cut her off, not caring much about her backstory.

"Yeah, yeah, it's truly shitty to have to follow orders," I agree. "But can I ask you something?"

"Shoot," she says, mildly annoyed with my interruption.

If this subcopy is anything like the last, she'll have knowledge of what happened to my father. So I ask, "Are you Amity?" She's different, but if she recognized me, there must be some of the original memories within her. The M I know would want to tell me about my father, but she'd be scared. The look on her face in that room with Ren was enough for me to conclude that. Whatever she'd seen inside her head must have been too much. But if this person isn't really Amity, then maybe she'll be more open to telling me.

"I'm not," she says, matter of fact. "Though, I think I'm supposed to be."

I push more, ignoring her commentary. "Do you have knowledge of my father?"

Her eyebrows pull in and she clicks her tongue, nervously. "Your... F... what?" She's uncomfortable, which means she knows something.

"Yeah, my father," I confirm. "Something happened to him, and you know what that is, don't you?" The monster awakens from within. My feet find purchase on the dirt, and I stand, towering over the girl.

She rises to put us on level ground, though she's still a head length below me. "Oh, you're going to try and intimidate me now?" The subcopy is pissed, yet also defensive. All I want to know is what happened to my father. Is that too much to ask? Do I not at least deserve that?

"Intimidate?" I laugh. "No." My face grows serious like the flip of a switch. "I don't need to waste time on intimidation when I've already thought of eight different ways to torture you."

A part of me, deep, deep down is yelling at me, begging me to not give in to the monster that Ren created. But it's hard to hear above the rush of anger and rapidly beating heart.

"You would never hurt Amity," she toys in an eerily similar way to the one and only Ren Keres.

I rush the girl, putting my face close to hers, digging my fingertips into her shoulders. "Except you're not Amity, you've made that clear. So whatever happens to you is inconsequential," I grit.

"Fine," she spits after a millennium staring into my eyes. "You want information on your father? How about this: he'd be *so* disappointed in you right now." An uncomfortable feeling jolts through my body, taking me by surprise.

"Hey! Let her go!" Fuck. Servicemen. Of course. The soldiers are rushing upon us now, yet I don't dare remove my gaze from the subcopy's.

She squints at me, leering. "Do it if you're gonna. They're closing in." My hands clam up, and my chest tightens.

Aggh! What the fuck is happening? My grip hardens.

The girl hides her grimace. "It's your move, Warin," she says through clenched teeth. "What's it gonna be?"

She looks so much like Amity it hurts, but the rage is too hard to contain. My knuckles are white and my body is tense. All of my muscles are cramping. Damn it. Fuck!

What the hell are you doing, Warin?

I shove the girl away from me and bolt in the opposite direction without looking back.

CHAPTER FOURTEEN ○ AMITY

MY MIND IS RACING TEN MILES A MINUTE. WHEN ALL I WANT TO do is sleep—to sink into a lifeless oblivion and temporarily numb this pain—my mind wants to force a different outcome.

What should be a glorious night is actually quite shit. Mason had tried to make my birthday salvageable by unveiling my completed room much later than expected. *At least you don't have to sleep in the hospital,* he'd said.

Too bad I won't be sleeping at all.

Sarge and I are walking the Residential Ward. The light on his elevator is red, which means outside isn't an option. But I'll be damned if I sit and let my mind take over, so this is the next best thing.

At first, we start our trek in the middle of the VIP residents. The mini park in the center is as close to the outside as we'll be getting. I stifle my laugh when Sarge lifts his leg to mark the silk bushes that line the walkway.

Once we've circled the spot twenty times, we venture into the normal residential area. You can only see the same shrubbery so many times. A small part of me shoots worry into my brain as we pass by the opening that separates us and them. *Will Mason come, demanding I return where I'm supposed to be? Will the General?*

Sarge pushes into me as always, instantly relaxing my muscles. My eyes meet his in the dim light, and for the first time since hearing about Emma, a small sense of peace settles in my chest.

Personally, I'm curious more than anything. Maybe I'm still in denial, but the thing that bothers me is why I was kept in the dark. What was the point?

Maybe deep down I knew something was wrong and now it's all clicking into place. I don't know. I assumed something bad happened since no answer was the default from everyone. We'll chalk it up to shock at the moment. The alternative is to acknowledge how detached from it all I am, and I'm not ready for that.

As Sarge and I weave through the stacks of residential pods, I wonder idly if I'll run into Luke. I still don't know which pod is his. And even though he kept Emma's death from me, something deep within me is calling to him. That's another thing I'll chalk up to shock. *Ugh.*

Who knows if he even wants to see me. The Reaver had all but spelled out that I'd done something to his father. And I *saw* him. There was a hint of a memory, and while I can't be 100% sure that the man I saw in my mind was Luke's father, I'd say it's probable. Those eyes are a damned mirror image. *Why do you even care, Amity?* Because I'm not a monster... am I? Shit.

When did my life become such a mess?

My thoughts are cut short when a young boy comes into my view. He's pacing around a column of pods. Though it's hard to see in the subdued light, the shadows of his face suggest something is bothering him.

There's almost no time between when the boy meets our gaze and Sarge takes off. At first, my heart pumps rapidly, worried that Sarge has perceived this boy as a danger. But then a wagging tail and happy smile from the boy in return eases my nerves.

"Sarge!" the boy calls, happily.

The tilt of my head happens involuntarily. Sarge knows this boy. My best friend immediately rolls onto his back, revealing his belly for rubs. The boy obliges, smiling wide.

I wish I could be as open as Sarge. A part of me wants to talk to the boy, while the other part wants to run the other way and not look back. That part of me crumbles in on itself, wanting to hide. The part still in survival mode.

Though, there isn't much time to act before the boy makes the decision for me. He doesn't stop petting Sarge, but he says, "And you must be Amity. You're even prettier than Luke described."

I blush, uncomfortable with the compliment. "Laying it on thick, huh?" I chuckle. "You know Luke?"

The boy's ears burn red. "I'm sorry," he says. His eyes widen, flicking to mine once he remembers the latter question. "Oh, yes! Luke is my friend."

This is interesting. "What are you doing out here?" I ask. I don't think he should be out here on his own. Granted, he's not much younger than me, though, so... wait. No. I'm 21. He's a young boy. Or looks like it. I'm an adult. Ouch.

"Luke and I..." the boy starts. "Well... he... I don't exactly know where he is."

Luke is missing? I keep my body from shuddering. He's probably off sulking somewhere. Sarge got him good. "He's a very exasperating man," I agree. "It's okay."

The boy nods in return. Sarge is now upright and accepting pets on his head. I realize I've not asked this boy his name.

"I'm sorry," I say. "I forgot to get your name?" It's been a while since I've had to make small talk. Making friends before Grace's death wasn't all that great. Now that she's gone, I can't fathom it. Imagine my surprise waking up in a hospital bed with a bunch of strangers around me claiming to be my friends. How'd that happen?

"Sam," the boy answers. Ah! This is the Sam that the boy from Lacy's room was talking about the other day. I study him, clocking the fake arm. CROP kid.

"Nice to meet you, Sam," I say.

He smiles up at me, but he's reluctant to move away from Sarge. I recognize the loneliness of his irises. Sarge was important to him somehow. And since he can't find Luke, and it appears something happened between them, he's as alone as I feel. Sarge is the only one that's ever-present.

"You have to go, don't you?" Sam asks, sighing. I'd been so focused on my inner battle that I hadn't realized my flighty behavior.

"No," I say with a smile, attempting to smooth things over. "I was going to ask if we could sit with you for a while?" Sam's eyes grow huge with excitement, yet he seems hesitant to accept. I'm beginning to realize sometimes it's nice having someone around to help keep your mind off of things. So I nudge a bit, saying, "Sarge has been lonely and could use the company."

This, of course, sends Sam over the edge. He nods with renewed vigor.

I close the distance and plop down beside them. Sarge's tail beats happily against the floor. Perhaps I should take note from him. While he's selective in who he trusts, he's as open as a field once he likes them. Maybe I could learn to open up, too. Maybe my mother's death doesn't have to mean staying closed off. Not this time, anyway.

"I'm sorry about your sister," Sam says to end the silence, keeping his eyes on Sarge. "And the whole memory loss thing."

Barely anyone has dared speak so openly about Emma since

Luke dropped the bomb. As much as Sam's words stab pain into my chest, they also make me feel seen; free.

He surprises me when he continues, saying, "I never met her, but I knew *of* her."

Was Sam somehow in the group with us? If so, why has he never been allowed to see me? "What do you mean?" I ask before I catch my tongue. Damn my curiosity.

"We both were in Omphalos," Sam replies. "I arrived shortly after her, but we weren't placed in any classes together."

Omphalos? She'd been taken by the Guardianship? Shit. Apparently, so was I. *Is that why they are looking for my father?* Shivers tense my muscles involuntarily.

"Everyone loved her," Sam admits, continuing without notice of my apprehension. "And I heard about you every so often as well."

"What about me?" I question. My palms grow wet with sweat. This isn't good. Emma is dead, so they say. And both of us were in Omphalos. The wayward thoughts keep pounding through. My father. Where is he? There's not many positive reasons for children to end up in the program at Omphalos. None where the parents are alive, anyway. "Was I there when you were there?"

Sarge shuffles to comfort me, leaving more distance between him and Sam. *Damn anxiety.*

Though Sam's mouth trembles a bit, he snaps out of his saddened mood at the realization of Sarge's motivation. "No," he answers. "Talk of you was hush hush in the school. I nearly made it to the end of my three months before I got caught. Then they threw me out."

Threw him out? My goodness. Because of me? *Of course, because of you, Amity. Everything is always your fault.* "What were you caught doing?" Though I'm curious about what happened with Sam, really I want to get more answers about me. This kid has given me more information about my past in the last few minutes than anyone has in the weeks I've been here. And to find out that both Emma and I were in Omphalos, but seemingly not at the same time? What does that even mean?

"I'd overheard some of my friends talking about how they'd joined the Amiteers."

The name jiggles a memory loose. The Reaver. She's mentioned them to me before. *Right?*

"They joined Force training a month before I could, and the Amiteers shortly after," Sam mentions. "I planned to do that, too. Like my friends. But you have to pass a test to make it into the Force. And the Headmistress found out about being a Thorne sympathizer. I'd been thrown out immediately. Tainted, she called it."

Tainted. That term jostles yet another memory. *Luke and I in the woods*, it seems. *He explains the meaning to me as we walk through the thick trunks.*

More. I have to know more. Memories are breaking loose left and right with Sam's help. It makes me feel more solid, less like a wisp. There are still so many things missing, but at least the pieces are starting to present themselves.

"What was the test?" I question. How had the Reaver been able to tell someone was sympathizing with me? With Emma? Surely there's not a specific test, right?

"They called it a MAP or something. They need to find weaknesses so you can overcome them. And, initially, I passed." Sam's voice grows a happy inflection talking about his success, but it fades quickly. "The problem was revealed *in* my weakness. That's when she found out about the Amiteers."

The guilt-riddled look on Sam's face is one I recognize all too well. He blames himself for outing the movement and outing his friends. It's a heavy burden to carry for someone so young.

"I shouldn't have even known about it." He shakes his head, frowning. "I was just so mad they left me out. I realize now there was a good reason that pre-recruits of the Force were not to be told."

Whatever it is about Sam, it's good, because yet another memory surfaces from the foggy haze. *I recognize a man from another snippet of memories. An A.L.F. officer with kind eyes. He tells me he's sorry for hiding something from me but they had to keep my memory clean.*

Realizing I've been quiet for too long, I nod to Sam in understanding. "That must have been difficult," I say. Maybe I'm just as lost in the world as he is, but perhaps getting to speak out loud and get this off his chest will help lessen the weight he's carrying.

He nods. "Anyway," Sam says, changing the subject, "I was ready to give up when Sarge and Luke pulled me from the river. And now I'm here, better than ever." His smile seems genuine, but this boy has been through hell because of me. I don't know how to fix that. I was a fool to think simply talking would be enough.

But I say, "That's good," and offer up a small smile. I *am* happy for him. A lot of the bad has been my fault, yet he's presenting me with a positive side. A good kid. I'm glad Luke found him. "Thanks for talking with me," I say.

This conversation with Sam has given me a much-needed reprieve. Despite its stressful content, I've hardly felt this free since I don't know when. Certainly not since I woke up here. My questions were answered honestly, not vaguely. It feels good to be a part of something.

But my brain keeps circling back to the age-old question: why keep Emma's fate from me to begin with?

Luke held his tongue, and as much as he believes he calls the shots, he's not the one in charge. I decide I won't wait to find out more. I'm going right to the one that can tell me everything.

"Will you be okay here? I've got something to do." Anybody out at this time is either someone on night shift, or the odd night owls like me that either can't sleep or don't want to. However, most congregate in the hangout spots, most of which children aren't allowed. In fact, Sam is the only child I've seen in Headquarters at all. Though I can only hope he's safe within these walls, unlike where he came from.

Sam nods again. "Bye, Sarge." He gives him a tight hug as we stand to leave. "It was nice to finally meet you, Amity!"

"Yeah," I agree. "You, too." I meet his smile with my own.

Sarge and I turn away. Guilt burrows into me at the thought of leaving Sam alone, but I need answers and I won't wait a second longer. I'm going to do what I should've done a long time ago.

CHAPTER FIFTEEN ∘ AMITY

MASON OPENS THE DOOR AND THE DARKNESS BENEATH HIS eyes suggests no sleep is present here, either. I don't let him process anything before I blurt, "Why didn't you tell me?"

Originally I planned on waking up the General, but my feet involuntarily carried me to the only other house I recognize.

The hurt that flashes amidst Mason's irises tells me I don't have to clarify. "I've been wondering that myself all night."

This irritates me. Like he's searching for pity. Sarge nudges himself beneath my hand and I clench my fingers into his fur as I ask, "What was the *original* reason you told yourself?"

It's awhile before he answers. When his sigh fades, he starts by saying, "At first it was to get you out of that facility. General Favager had his plans, but I agreed in wanting the innocence to stay with you a bit longer." His hand meets the back of his neck in a nervous tic. "I admit, it was selfish. I... I truly thought this was best."

Mason glances away, then back at me, then to Sarge once his neck snakes around my waist to keep me grounded. I meet Mason with silence and a dead look in my eyes. I'm not satisfied yet and he knows it.

"We all felt the loss of Emma last year, and I've since come to fully realize what it's like to lose a sister." His eyes drop to the ground, unable to meet mine. There's a subtle bounce in his stature. *Is he crying?*

The tension melts from my shoulders and Sarge pulls his head from my waist. I'm still mad, but at least it appears Mason was hurt; desperate. Riddled with grief. All things that make us do questionable things.

Should I be crying, too? My sister is dead. His sister is dead. The truth is, since the dust settled from the initial shock, I'm still finding all this hard to make sense of. I thought at first it was because deep down I knew Emma was gone all along. But the more I let my mind wander, the more I think it's because I simply won't believe it to be true. It's more than denial. My brain is stopping me, telling me something doesn't add up with it. It's a gut feeling. And for Emma's sake, I won't ignore it.

"What happened to her?" I ask, my voice a dry, crackling whisper. Mason glances at me with bloodshot eyes. "Your sister. Abby, right?"

Lacy had mentioned her death before. She's got a shrine of Abby in her room. But I stopped her before she could go into details.

Mason nods. "I failed her." He closes his eyes as if in pain. "I was supposed to keep her safe, yet I couldn't even save her from a simple infection."

His body shudders. *He blames himself?* Lacy had said she died a hero, like Zach, but after hearing about him, I didn't think I could stomach hers as well. I assumed everything was *my* fault. An infection is more of a tragic accident. No one to blame but this sick, twisted world that crushes anything soft, never letting it last. *Like Emma...*

"Oh, God!" he cries, glancing up. "I'm so sorry!"

My eyes instinctively meet Sarge. Emotions like this make me uncomfortable. If it makes me care, it makes me weak. Yet, to my surprise, I let Mason quietly release without much protest.

"I've spent all this time in denial," he admits. "I was envious of the fact you had no memory of your sister's death. I desperately wished I could be you, desperately wanted you to keep this aching pain out of your chest." His eyes meet mine, and the blue pools appear even deeper than normal surrounded by red. "I'm sorry, Amity," he says, his voice crackling. "Will you forgive me?"

I open my mouth to speak, but nothing comes out. How can I forgive him when he kept such an important thing from me? Even under orders, what kind of person... what kind of *friend*... would do that?

Thankfully I don't have to respond because a high-pitched ringing sounds from Mason's pocket. He takes the device out, slightly frowning at whatever is on the screen. Then, he puts a small circle on his temple that disappears with contact to his skin.

"Hello?" he says, his voice clear of all sadness. His face is scrunched with focus as he listens to a person I'm unable to hear. It's not long before his eyes grow wide, and a smile cracks his face in two. "Yes, sir. I'll get her briefed."

My eyes watch him curiously, but he's in no rush to share. I'm assuming the conversation has been about me, and despite the smile, I've weaved my fingers into Sarge's fur for comfort once more.

Mason plucks the small circle from his head and places it back on the device. Sliding it in his pocket, he finally speaks. "We've found your father. He's on his way."

o   o   o

MASON HAD WALKED me and Sarge back to my room. He'd begged me to get some rest, that my father wouldn't be here until morning. But now morning is here and my eyes are crusted over from the lack of sleep.

The mattress beneath me is hard and unforgiving, but I refuse to remove myself. Though my mind is all over the place, I *will* force my body to rest. If it's the only type of rest I get, then so be it.

My father is on his way. This news is a whirlwind. While I'm glad he's been found, it leaves my conversation with Sam all the more confusing. My curiosity is running rampant. I *need* to know what's happened to my family. How did we all end up like this?

Shortly after noon, my door creaks and a man walks into the room. Sarge stays quiet despite the intrusion. The man is covered in mud, caked on layers of filth. The scruff attached to his face blocks most of it, and yet I recognize him right away.

"Dad!"

I leap out of the bed and slam my body into his. Sarge follows happily behind, circling around us with wagging tail.

He hugs me as if he can't believe I'm real, as if I'll crumble and break if he lets go. "Oh, M. It *is* you," he says.

"Of course it is," I cry, tears soaking his dirty jacket. "Why wouldn't it be?"

The words hardly escape from my lips before I'm hit with a realization. Two years have passed. To me, it feels like just yesterday we were burying my mother outside of our house. And in my head, I've only been missing both of my parents for as long as I've been here. But to him? Who knows what he's been through?

My father scrunches his nose, lifting his arm. Glancing down at the dirt covering every inch of his clothes, he says, "Let me get cleaned up, then we'll talk."

Fifteen minutes later, Sarge and I are making it down the elevator as my father steps out of the bathroom freshly shaved and dressed. A guard had stopped last night, leaving behind a perfectly folded pair of clothes, a razor, and other specific shower necessities. At that point, they must have known how dirty he was. *Where did they find him?*

Is it a coincedence my father is here only *after* finding out about Emma?

"Well that's neat," he says, smiling. Now that he's got clean, silver hair, and less scruff, he looks more like the father I remember. Though, the wrinkles of his eyes are deeper, and the color of his skin is darker.

"Special just for Sarge." I smile down at my best friend. I'm so thankful he's been here for me. Now that Mason and I are sort of on the same page, I think my healing will come faster. And adding my father to the mix? Everything is almost right. *If only Emma were here, too.*

"Special, huh?" He's studying the room, the elevator, everything.

"What's the matter?" I ask, apprehensive. He's always scrutinizing.

"Nothing," he says, nonchalantly. "Had to be screened to confirm I was really your father." He laughs. "And you're getting special treatment. What a weird place."

Screened? For what? Proof? Then it dawns on me that the Reaver has been sending subcopies of me. Who knows who else she might use? Shivers shake my body compulsorily.

"I hear you're having memory issues?" Dad speaks in the way he always does, when he's not so subtly letting me know his ears are open to listen. He'd shut down after my mother's passing and I've not heard the tone in a while.

"So they tell me," I answer, covering the distance to the couch where he's now sitting.

My father is intuitive. He knows the subtleties of word choice, and he's an incredible people-reader. His slightly probing gaze reminds me of my childhood, when nothing would ever get by him no matter how many times I tried. So it doesn't surprise me when he says, "But that's all they've told you?" His eyebrow raises, begging for confirmation.

I nod, shuffling my body to account for Sarge cuddled into my lap. "To be fair, I *did* just find out about Emma."

At the sound of her name, my father's eyes dull. Shit. Maybe I shouldn't have said anything.

"I'm sorry," I say. A habit I'd recently—or not so recently—developed since my mother passed. Anytime I'd mention her, I'd immediately apologize for increasing his pain. All that angst comes running back to me at once.

"No," he says, sighing. "I've had a year to process this. You've had not even twenty-four hours. *I'm* sorry. I'm sorry for *many* things."

With that, all the tears I've held back, all the numbness I've felt, releases in a gush of sadness. Sarge encircles one side of me, while my father pulls me in for a tight hug. He holds me, keeping all of my broken pieces together, for a time I couldn't guess.

"It's not your fault," I say once finding my voice.

My father's chest deflates with a sigh. "I know you don't remember, but I left you both behind."

What? I lift myself out of his grasp, wiping my eyes. The questioning look on my face has him continuing.

"Emma had been captured, and you wanted to save her. I couldn't convince you otherwise." His eyes droop. The age around them is prominent now. He's a lot older than I remember. "Last second I ran in the opposite direction of you, hoping to distract the Force."

"You... what?" My dad, the rebel. I'm more or less in awe than filled with anger.

"It worked, actually." He chuckles, nervously. "But after a few days I tried to hunt you down. After a few months, I just..." He rests his palms on my cheeks. "I left you, M. I'm so sorry."

"I..." I stutter. "I'm not..."

"No," he says. "I told myself that maybe you'd made it to Creyke Point on your own. That I should check. But I left you."

Sarge's tongue flicks against my palm in my lap. My head falls, and my eyes meet his. I don't want to see my father like this. He blames himself. I suppose I see where I get it from. But I don't remember what happened. And as an outsider looking in, it seems he tried to sacrifice himself for someone he loved. That's the father I know, anyway.

"I wish you didn't feel this way," I say. "For all we know, you saved me."

His eyes soften. "I love you, M. I'm proud of you."

I avert my gaze. Love. I hate that word sometimes. If he didn't love me, he wouldn't feel this way. He'd be blissfully ignorant.

If he hadn't loved my mother, he'd have stayed the full man he was meant to be rather than the shell of one he became after her death. And suddenly, I can't keep the words from flowing out of my mouth. "It seems like love is a weakness in a world like ours."

"Where love exists, grief is inevitable," he agrees, not in the least perturbed by my lack of reciprocity.

"I'm almost thankful I don't remember anything. Losing mom and Emma is tough enough." I sigh, then chuckle to keep the pain at bay.

"M," he says, shifting to look in my eyes. "I wasn't there for you and Emma the way I should've been." Ugh. Here it is again. That sadness. It eats at me.

"It's not your fault, Dad," I say. "You were missing your love." This conversation is solidifying my ideologies. Love is a weakness. My father struggled to move on. It was all too much to be dealing with when your own survival wasn't even secure.

"Well." He sighs. "Yes, but you were grieving, too. And instead of being there for you and your sister, I started working behind the scenes to start a rebellion."

All at once, a memory stabs into my head. *My father, he's telling me we need to run.*

I don't say anything, though.

My father continues. "I admit, it was hard. Losing your mother and sister—and thinking I lost you, too—was a greater burden than any parent should have to bear. But I wouldn't change loving you for anything else in this world."

This brings a tear to my eye, but not because it's a sweet thing to hear. In truth, it makes me sad because I can't believe it. I wish I didn't have to play a part in my father's pain. Then I'm back in the woods in my mind, with who I now know is Zach. He's telling me something about loving Sonya. How it made him a better person? Shit. These memories are coming on more and more.

Perhaps there's some merit in this love thing, but my brain is too angered right now to believe it, so I move on.

"So what's next?" I ask. Right now I want someone else to take the lead. My mind has been racing for as long as I can remember, and it's tired.

"Well." My father pulls me back in, resting his chin on my head. "We start getting answers."

CHAPTER SIXTEEN ∘ LUKE

THE VEIN IN MASON'S NECK IS BULGING. IT'S ALL I CAN FOCUS on as he scolds me like my father used to. That thought alone is enough to cause rage to build up in my chest, but the argument here is that I get my freedom in Headquarters revoked permanently and I'm sure an outward burst of anger would to push Mason to agree.

"Are you even listening?"

Mason peers at me expectantly before I nod. "Yes," I hiss.

"Then pay attention. General Favager wants you removed from Headquarters forever, but I'm trying to talk him into limited access."

"He can't do that," I argue. My stipulation for giving information and service was that I be close to M. If Favager has any honorable bone in his body, he won't betray the agreement. Though, I suppose I betrayed his request first. Fuck. This is that *hell to pay* he mentioned.

"He can and he will unless I present an argument in your favor."

My eyebrows are practically touching. This is all bullshit. The worst part is, I'm not any closer to figuring out what happened to my father. On top of that, I'll probably never be allowed near the subcopies again. And the kicker is that I probably also lose M as well. How did this get so convoluted? Damn it, Warin. You really know how to screw things up, don't you?

If only I could focus on the conversation at hand. Too much of my energy is going into keeping myself calm. My eyes scan the space that Mason retires to every night. The VIP rooms are larger, and more like tiny homes, than the one room pod everyone else receives. I repeat again: this is all bullshit.

"Dear God, Luke, would you at least *act* like you're sorry?"

My eyes tumble in my skull as my attention returns to the conversation. "Yes, yes. Terribly sorry." Sarcasm drips from my tone.

"You're doing yourself no favors," he replies, sighing.

"Then why am I even here?" I question. Mason hates me as much as I can't stand him. It's our mutual love of Amity that keeps us in forced proximity. But if my freedom hinges on his argument, then I'm finding it strange as to why I haven't been sent away already.

Mason stares at me, dumfounded, responding in a tired voice. "Because I'd been clouded in my judgement to follow General Favager's orders before." His face is tightly wound, and suddenly my interest in this conversation is renewed. Mason? Doubting himself? Hell yeah.

"What do you mean?" I ask, sitting up straight with a smirk.

"Jesus Christ," he utters to himself, casting his eyes away and rubbing the back of his neck. "We shouldn't have kept Emma's death from Amity."

"Oh, you don't say?" I blurt without thinking.

Mason's lips tense with disapproval. "Could you stop being a piece of shit for two minutes?" He eyes me questioningly.

I huff, nodding. He's right, I may be enjoying this a bit too much. Mason continues.

He cries about how Favager wanted to keep M's head as clear as possible. How there were plans for her to be a figurehead. I know all of this. It's still stupid. "General Favager believed we could replicate her drive for saving Emma. And I believed it best for... more... personal reasons. But we were wrong."

Favager's plans had been made clear. He didn't have *time* to let M grieve again. But Mason admitting that he was wrong? This is news to me.

My eyebrow raises. "So this time you want to make sure you're judgement free?"

He nods. "If it were up to me, I'd have sent you away the second you set foot on our camp a year and a half ago." His voice is monotone, but his eyes are playful.

My mouth pops open to respond, but I never get to. Instead, a small knock on the door has Mason's face contorting with confusion before he grabs the knob.

My expectations were unclear, but M being the one waiting in the doorway hadn't crossed my mind. My heart stops. Sarge is pressed to her, though I'd be more worried if he wasn't. What does surprise me, however, is the man standing next to them.

Mason slides aside, waving his hand in invitation, and they all shuffle into the room. I could never fit this many people inside the pod...

M refuses to meet my eye. And why wouldn't she? I'd acted carelessly toward her. That subcopy was right. My father *would* be disappointed. Fuck.

"I want to speak with the subcopies," M demands. "The Reaver mentioned more." Her fingers are woven into Sarge's fur, but other than that, her body is held with confidence. For once, though, I can't keep my focus on her. My gaze inadvertently flicks to the man acting as her shadow behind her.

His demeanor is calm, yet protective. He's sitting back, yet keeping close. His eyes hold wisdom that flows from the wrinkles of his lids. His nose has a familiar hook to it. Where do I know this man from? He's oddly familiar.

Wait. This is Mark Thorne, Amity's father.

"I don't think you'll be allowed," is all Mason responds with.

M's eyes roll, and mine flick back to her father's, who is watching everything around him silently. What's he thinking?

"Who makes these rules?" M cries. She takes a deep breath, starting again more calmly this time. "Never mind. Everything has been so secretive here. It's no wonder I'm subconsciously blocked." Her arms flail with frustration.

Mason's brow furrows.

M continues with her monologue. "I've had more memories break loose in the last twenty-four hours than I have since you brought me here. Do you know why?" She pauses for dramatic effect. "It's because I've *talked*. I've been semi free to speak."

"You didn't alert anyone of your recent breakthroughs," Mason says. It's meant to be a scold, but the way he says it, it comes out more like he's concerned. I make note of the subtle change in Mark's expression. He's familiar with the disguised tone.

"It's only snippets here or there," she answers, retreating into herself for a moment. Then her confidence returns. "I want to speak to them."

"I..." Mason starts, hesitating. "They..."

"Oh, come on!" M shouts. "Are you taking the General's side on this?" She scoffs. "Typical. I already know about Emma, so what's the big deal? I want to know more." Her grip has tightened in Sarge's fur. He doesn't seem to mind.

The mention of Emma has Mason turning green. He feels guilty enough as is. But then he blurts, "Luke violated the subcopies." That motherfu...

"Excuse me?" M questions.

Fuck. "Sub*copy*," I correct, noting I'm only on the hook for manhandling the one a bit too hard. But I let her go, didn't I? They don't care about that.

M's expression sends a harpoon through my heart. Her father is still studying the situation at large and our interactions quietly. Like my father used to do. His silence is unnerving.

I shoot a glare in Mason's direction before returning to M. "Not sexually if that's what you're thinking."

This is the first she's looked at me, truly, since entering the room. "Any sort of violating is uncalled for! Gah! This is so off-topic."

Mason chimes in now, though I'd rather him lose his voice permanently. "We were in the middle of discussing Luke's potential loss of access in Headquarters before you showed up."

"What did you do? Shit. Never mind, I don't want to know." Amity mumbles to herself, raking her hands through her own hair, tensing at the roots. Her eyes meet mine again. "*Why* did you do it?"

Why did I do it? Hm. "I thought I could get information on my father," I admit.

Her face softens momentarily, then scrunches again. "See? How does it feel to not have the information you're looking for?"

"That's not the same thing, Amity," Mason says.

"Are you defending him?" M questions. "When I want information, everyone stands around, tongue-tied. When anyone *else* wants it? They just go around *violating* people, whatever the hell that means. Ugh!" M's famous eyeroll presents itself.

Mason starts blubbering once more, going on about how it was Favager's decision. I speak over him, arguing that Favager doesn't care about her knowing her past, so what's the problem? M's shrill voice is added to the mix as well, unwilling to hear either of us. Then:

"May I step in?" Mark says from behind M. I want to be pissed off, but I can't. We're all a bunch of shitheads right now.

"Please," Mason replies after a deep breath. "And may I say what a fan I am?"

Okay. Now I'm pissed off.

M's mouth tightens to physically keep herself from speaking again.

"Call Olivier," is all Mark says. "No use arguing. Take this up with him." Mark's jaw tenses, almost unnoticeably.

The three of us have no objections and next thing you know, we're all waiting outside Favager's damned office.

The guards in the hallway keep their shoulders straight, chests puffed, and eyes forward. Though, the nearly silent murmurs amongst them are clear. How is it that I've been let back in? How was I ever once a powerful soldier? No wonder Axom and Charlotte were lost.

My knuckles turn white. I could kick everyone's ass here, but what would that get me? I'm already in deep shit for stupid reasons. I've got a target on my back.

I jerk in the direction of physical contact; a small, cool hand lightly touching my shoulder. It's easier for my body to relax once I realize it's M.

Sarge is plastered to her side as always. He's regarding me cautiously. But it's M's greys that keep drawing my attention. There's concern in them.

"You alright?" she asks, softly.

Her father and Mason have been deep in conversation since we started our trek here, so this question goes unnoticed by both of them.

"These people piss me off," I say after a hesitating scoff.

M chuckles lightly, amused with my discomfort. "Who *doesn't* piss you off?" she questions, though I think it's rhetorical.

"Good point," I smirk. I've missed her. "Just so you know, Mason made it sound worse than it was. That subcopy thing." Fuck, ew. Even as I say it, it sounds like I'm making excuses. "Not that what I did was by any means okay, but I... well. Fucking hell." This is harder than I thought.

She'd been smiling, but her face grows serious; solemn. "You don't need to apologize to me, but you should apologize to whomever it was that you may have hurt."

Our eyes hold each other's gaze for a long while. I have never deserved her. I nod. "Of course," I say.

"Now it's my turn." She tucks the hair behind her ear, nervously glancing away. "I..." she stutters. "I... I know you think I've done something to your father. I want to talk to the subcopies so maybe it jostles a memory."

My lips downturn. She's nervous, uncomfortable. Her fingers are immersed into Sarge's neck fur as if it's her lifeline. Fuck. This is all my doing. I shouldn't have been so harsh to her.

"Look, you don't..." I start to say yet never get to finish. Favager is ready to see us.

Everyone shuffles into the office of the man somehow responsible for the future. M, Sarge, and her father file in first. Mason next. I follow last. Through the bodies, I see Favager's jaw is already ticking with irritation. His eyes blaze with fiery anger the second I'm clear in his view.

"Thank you for seeing us, General Favager," Mason says, attempting to break the tension. Kiss ass has always been his first language.

"Turning down a request from our guest of honor would make

me a poor host," Favager says, focusing his gaze on M. His face is devoid of all emotion.

Though M's expression isn't in my line of sight, I watch her carefully. Her body is rigid with nervousness. It's only a matter of time before her fingers find Sarge in the expected anxious tic. "Y... yes," she says. "Thank you, sir. I'd like to talk with the sub-copies." A few seconds pass before she adds, "Oh, and request that Luke is cleared of any transgressions."

Favager's jaw grinds with a click of his tongue. "I'm not normally in the habit of negotiation," he replies.

Not a beat passes before M's sharp attitude cuts in. "Well maybe you should reconsider since you quite literally kept my sister's death from me. I'd say you owe me one."

Her fists ball at her sides, pulling away from Sarge defiantly. I don't think I've ever witnessed such sass from her before. This is definitely a result of her memory loss. She's full of teen angst. Though, I *am* surprised it had been directed at a superior. Good, though. Fuck him.

"Sir," she includes, her fingers fumbling to Sarge as she backpedals.

Favager stands now, causing M to sink into herself slightly.

I step forward, stopping Mason before he's able to "rescue" M. She has to do this on her own. He subtly glances back at me and I shake my head in warning. M needs to learn her own strength again.

"Your lack of knowledge on the subject was the tradeoff for the success of our goal here at the Service," Favager argues. "I thought we were *all* in agreement on that." His eyes sweep through the group, melting Mason in his place, but he doesn't linger. He returns his concentration to M quickly. "Do you understand what sacrifice is?"

Words bubble up on my tongue but die out when I bite it. This guy may be in charge, but he's out of touch. M is the very definition of sacrifice. Her self-preservation is non-existent if it means she can help someone. Maybe she doesn't fully understand that about herself anymore, but it's not any less true. Hell, she wouldn't even be in this situation if she hadn't sacrificed her own freedom.

"Sacrifice insinuates I had a choice," M finally spits back. Mason, Mark, and I are completely silent. Mason can't believe what's happening, but M's father looks on with a sense of pride. As he should.

Favager's knuckles tense against the wood of his desk, until he relaxes and circles to the front. He folds his hands in his lap, leaning so his ass is resting against the top. "You'd like to speak with the subcopies, then?"

"And clear Luke of his wrongdoings, yes," M confirms to him with a nod of her head.

Favager and Amity stare at each other in a battle of wills.

And like an idiot, Mason opens his big fat mouth.

"What's the harm, sir?"

Favager doesn't answer, and doesn't take his angry eyes from M. Her fingers are gripping Sarge in a white-knuckled fist, but she's holding her own quite well. Yet Mason is forever the dumbass...

"Sir, I just think..."

"No," Favager snaps. "You *don't* think. The Human Protective Service had a specific plan—in which *you* agreed upon—and it hinges on the fact that this girl is ready to move hell and high water to save her own flesh and blood. Tell me why I shouldn't wipe her memory again for your duplicitous promise."

Favager's voice is loud and commanding, completely overshadowing M's gasp at his latest threat. I hadn't minded when he was giving it back to Mason, but then he continues, and the anger in my chest starts to boil.

"And *you*," he says, redirecting to me. "You are a fool for breaking the one rule there was. Treachery. You could have been a perfect member to our team, but your aversion to authority is not welcome here."

"Fuck you," I grit, before I'm able to stop myself.

This erupts everyone in the room. The volume is deafening as Favager slings curses my way, setting M off in a defiant rage. Mason attempts to argue for both of us, and at this point, I scream at the top of my lungs because it feels good to let it out. This whole thing is bullshit!

"I will have you all thrown in a cell for treason!" Favager grates.

But it's Mark who surprises me when he finally speaks. His voice somehow rises above all of us when he shouts, "Enough!"

Favager is outright irate with the blatant disrespect. Yet he stays quiet, as do the rest of us.

After a few seconds of silence, Mark nods his approval. "It's clear Amity is important," he says. "Not just to the two of you, but to the H.P.S. at large." He glances between me and Mason before meeting the gaze of the crazed General. Mason and I both nod our heads, actually in agreement for once.

Mark is diplomatic. I wonder if that's a quality he learned from working with Mason's father, or if that's why they'd connected to begin with.

"Glad that's settled," he says. "Now I say you all cut the shit and start listening to my daughter."

I don't quite know, but I think Mason's jaw hits the floor.

"Your problems simply do not matter in the grand scheme. Plans change. Get over it. You want her to be a figurehead? You want to use *my* family's name for your rebellion? Then you better start respecting those that carry it."

Fuck. Okay. Mark Thorne is my hero.

The tension of the room is so thick it almost weighs me down. Mark doesn't shy away from Favager's scrutiny. M's eyes nervously bounce back and forth between her father and the man who had threatened to wipe her memory again.

Favager exhales a long sigh before speaking. "What do you suppose we do?" His jaw is wound tight.

Mark simply fans his hand to allow his daughter the floor.

She glances around nervously once more, but then removes her hand from Sarge's fur, squaring her shoulders. "I will do what you ask of me—be what you need—but only if you allow me to learn my truth," she demands. "The *whole* truth."

CHAPTER SEVENTEEN ○ AMITY

THE HALLWAYS FILL WITH THE THUMPING OF OUR SHOES AND the subtle clack of Sarge's nails. After what my dad pulled, a guard is escorting us to Cateline's lab. Who knew he could be so badass? How'd I forget that Thorne's are sharp?

I'd convinced the General to pardon Luke, but I promised I'd see the subcopies alone. Luke wasn't thrilled, but at least he's allowed to stay in his pod. My thoughts flit to the boy. Sam. He had been so worried about his friend. If nothing else, at least Luke can stay in Headquarters for him.

Nervous butterflies flutter through my stomach. *Are you ready to face yourself, Amity?* I know they'll trust me right away. They don't have Sarge, but I do. And Sarge wholeheartedly trusts me, which means they'll base their assessment off that. I know, because I would.

We reach the door to the lab fairly quickly. "Luke and I will wait out here," Mason says, slowing. "You have twenty minutes. If Cateline thinks they can handle more, she'll let you stay. Less, and she'll kick you out early."

It's bullshit that Cateline Pierre can dictate how long I spend in there, but I guess it's her lab and, for now, I let it go. Gaining my memory back is going to be a long process, and if Cateline is going to be a part of it, I'll have to deal with her every time I want to see them.

Luke has been silent through all of this, clearly tense from everything going on and the lack of control it leaves him with. I don't need my memories of him to understand that.

But right now, he can wait. He and Mason can discuss whatever. It's a punishment for them both.

I may have defended them to the General, but they're still on my shit list for now. They lied to me. I won't soon forget that.

"I know my limits," I point out before turning to my father. He's been a silent observer ever since he'd put the General in his place. "You coming?"

My father nods. "I'll be right behind you."

I don't question Sarge. Wherever I am, he is. No doubt.

We slowly enter the lab. It's clinical, like the hospital, yet there are makeshift rooms across the back wall that are infinitely homier. The subcopies occupy the two rooms. Woah. Seeing two of me is trippy.

They're separate from each other, and us. The walls between them are opaque, but it's crystal-clear glass front. For observation, I'm told. It's only clear to us.

The knowledge that these human beings are being treated like lab rats irks me. Something like this seems only possible in Western America, yet maybe the filth is spread here as well. My brain recalls the General's bulging eyes as he threatened to wipe my memories again. I shake my head, ridding it of that thought quickly.

My brain is having a hard time processing the visions. It's like I'm watching two separate movies of myself doing different activities. One is reading, maybe writing. The other one? That one is sitting in the middle of the floor. The sight jolts a memory loose. *I'm in a room that feels like a prison. I'm stuck, left to my own devices. I sit in the middle of the floor.*

Cateline steps closer, snapping me out of my memory. Her eyes squint slightly in study. But I can barely focus on the words she's saying. The second subcopy is taking too much of my attention. "If there is anything you'd like to know, please, don't hesitate to ask."

I throw a flippant smile her way, thankful that my father quickly takes her attention with questions.

It's clear Cateline enjoys science. Her whole life is engrossed by it. The sound of her voice as she explains to my dad what she's been working on proves it. Growing up, my father's interview skills truly got under my skin. But presently, I'm grateful to have a father that asks all the right questions.

No one notices when I slip away toward the subcopy sitting in the middle of the floor. What it is about her, I couldn't even begin to guess, but I'm drawn to her. She's like the other one, but... different somehow. The aura around her? The way she's holding herself, maybe. Something. And the question that comes to my mind is why? Does she have a purpose? Or is she a mistake?

Is it possible for a powerful woman such as the Reaver to make mistakes? At one point, I figured the answer was no. But listening to Sam talk about Emma in that facility, I truly believe if anything were a mistake, it would be her death. But the nagging doesn't stop. Does she *make* mistakes?

The woman in the middle of the floor has eyes devoid of light, yet a full twinkle all the same. Even as Sarge and I get closer, her focus is seemingly on nothing as she stares blankly forward. If anything should get the attention of the subcopies, it would be Sarge. Yet, as we push through the door, there's no immediate reaction like I'm anticipating.

"Hello," I say calmly, hoping to grab her attention.

The woman takes a few moments to bring her mind to the present. She wears the inner workings of her brain on the outside somehow. When she looks up, her eyes get a full, bright light to them at the sight of Sarge. There, that's more like it.

My sense of triumph is cut short when something strange happens. The woman stares blankly again for a moment, then violently shakes her head. "Sorry," she rasps. Her voice holds pain, like she's straining. "I know he's not mine." Her eyes remain tightly closed.

"You..." I stutter. "Y... you know?"

How could she know that if she's supposed to be me? I'd met the first subcopy. I saw her with my own eyes. It wasn't just that she *looked* like me that was the eerie part. It was that she truly believed she *was* me. She'd been drawn to Sarge.

"I've been fighting this other person in my head since the Reaver put her in there," the subcopy says. "This other person must be you." She peeks an eye open to catch a glimpse of me but closes it fast. "You sure do have a lot of intrusive thoughts."

I laugh. Not because it's funny, but because it's the only thing my brain can deduce doing in such an awkward situation. Sarge plants himself next to me, awaiting my fingers in his fur. Thankful, I do it.

"I'm assuming you're here to get your memories back?" the woman says.

"I'm here to talk, actually," I admit. "I suppose you know a great deal about me, but I know nothing about you." The cogs of my brain start turning. If I can get her to open up, she may be our best bet into learning the Reaver's plans. Forget my memories, something is causing this person to fight them. So what is it? And is it on purpose?

Upon hearing my words, the subcopy chuckles. "You and Luke are oddly similar," she says. *Luke?* "But I don't remember my name. Or anything else for that matter. Trust me, I've tried."

Sadness burrows deep in my bones. Sure, I can't remember the last six years of my life, but at least I remember my own name. Who I am. "I'm sorry," I say. It's a habit, really.

"Yeah," she sighs. "I know." She pauses a second, then starts a new thought. "Your guilt is really weighing me down, man. I don't know how you live like this."

Sarge nudges my palm to keep me grounded. "My guilt?"

I know what I feel guilty of right now. And growing up, I suppose there were some things I regret. But how much could I possibly have from the last six years? What have I done?

"You wear this shit like lead boots," she snorts. Then, her face scrunches up with a wince. "I'm slipping," she admits. "I need a moment."

Before I'm able to say anything, Cateline knocks impatiently on the door before entering. The motion of her hands on her hips reminds me of my mother. I don't like it.

"Miss Thorne, it's time to go."

Cateline is looking at me, but the woman in the middle of the floor is the one that answers. "Where are we going?"

CHAPTER EIGHTEEN ○ LUKE

"It's been twenty minutes." My leg is rapidly bouncing to expel energy and keep calm.

"And?" Mason questions. "Afraid she might hurt them?" His accusatory look sends anger straight through me, but I bury it by counting down from five. "She's dealing with herself," he argues. "She's fine."

"Yeah," I agree. "She's dealing with herself. That's exactly what worries me." It's comments like this that remind me how little Mason knows about her. M can face a lot of things, but *she* is her own worst enemy. Who knows what's going on in there.

Thankfully I don't have to wonder for long. Mark exits first, followed by M and Sarge. Cateline brings up the rear, and the guards close the door behind her. Mason is the first to speak.

"Did you gain any more memories?"

"Only a small snippet that made no sense," M admits. The drop of her tone leads me to believe there's something more, but she leaves it at that.

"Was that enough?" her father asks.

M's eyes dart around, catching mine for a few seconds with a telling glance before returning her gaze to her father. "For now," she says, offering a meek smile. Something happened in there. It's written all over her face.

"Alright then," Mason says. "I guess we're free for the time being then." He turns, smiling widely at M. "Would you care to join me for dinner?"

M inadvertently glances my way again and it's the only thing keeping my anger in check. I may be on thin ice around here, but Mason knows how to get under my skin. I guess I shouldn't be angry, though. Was I ever truly worthy of M the way Mason is?

He's annoying, and somewhat narrowminded, but he's not a monster. Not like I am.

I open my mouth to speak, but Mark steps forward. "A... actually, Mason, I was hoping you and I could discuss your father and his plans. Have you implemented any of his practices here since becoming right hand man to Olivier?"

Mason blushes a subtle pink. "Oh, I..." His arm lifts as his palm meets the back of his neck. "Sure," he says. "Let's head to my room. Catch you later, Amity."

Before they head off and turn the corner, Mark looks back, winking at M. Did he...?

"Aha... well," Cateline says, nervously. "If that is all, I'm going to get back to my studies. Enjoy this night." Cateline swiftly turns to enter her lab once more, and then it's just Amity and me left. Well, and the guards.

Time stands still, and we both stare at each other in awkward silence.

"Would you..." I start at the same time she speaks.

"Are you..." She stops, giggling nervously. She looks away, pushing her hair behind her ear. "You go."

The sound of her giggle stops my heart. She's the reason I know I'm alive after all this time; that I know Ren didn't succeed in taking away all of my Humanity. I smirk. "I was going to ask if you wanted some dinner." It sounds pitiful coming from me in comparison to the *benevolent Mason*, but there's not much to do about it.

M chuckles again, sending another jolt to my heart. "Dinner. Yes," she says. Then she adds, more serious, "Are dogs allowed in the cafeteria?"

Now it's my turn to laugh. "I promise you; Sarge is allowed *everywhere*."

We fall into a steady pace through the halls. "Oh yeah?" She reaches down, tapping Sarge on the head. His tail wags happily.

"Definitely," I answer, recalling Mason's words a few months prior. "Everyone loves the dog."

Her shoulders bounce with another chuckle. "Only the dog?" she questions, feigning naivety.

A sideways glance has me gazing into wide saucers of grey. M peers up through her lashes with a mischievous grin. My foot malfunctions, causing me to nearly trip over myself. There's something I hadn't considered ever seeing again: Playful Amity. Despite the news, despite the trouble she's gone through here, somehow her memory wipe has led her to retain some of her playfulness. She still has the ability to let go. It took her a while to learn that with me. And I with her.

Yes, everyone loves her, too. How could they not? She's strong, brave, selfless. Beautiful. Favager knows it. It's why she's a perfect face for the rebellion.

I smirk, saying, "Well, I may be biased, but people definitely love me around here." Confidence exudes from every pore, though my words are utterly false.

M nods. "Of course, of course." Her lips twitch with a tiny, hidden smile.

The hall opens up and we're finally in the center of H.P.S.

Headquarters. M studies the winged guardian in the middle, closing her eyes and quietly mumbling to herself as we pass. Sarge cozies up next to her, raising his head to wrap around her waist. She glances down, meeting his eyes and smiling. I wonder what that's about.

The cafeteria is right off the central circle so there's not much time to ponder. It's crowded this time of night, though it's whisper quiet thanks to its design. The tables are inlaid into the ground which helps dampen the sound.

Most anyone in a pod has no choice but to eat here if they want to be social. I, however, have never cared much for other's company and usually take my meals back to my room where Sam and I can be ourselves without the watchful eyes of others. It's ten times worse now since being kicked out.

As M, Sarge, and I travel through the various tables, the room's focus shifts to us. The waiters traipsing through avoid our path. We're three odd balls standing out. Conversations cease as everyone stops their chattering to watch. The deeper we get, the closer we make it to the food, the more eerie it gets. M's shoulders sag a bit, and her grip on Sarge's fur gets tighter. I pretend not to notice her apprehension.

"What can I say?" I smirk, nudging her. "Everyone loves me."

Her hand finds its way to her mouth, covering her smile. She breathes out a tiny laugh. Ah, so beautiful. Her eyes flick to mine.

"Oh, yes. I almost forgot." She chuckles. "I'm with the most beloved man in the H.P.S."

I've missed her. This.

Us.

The crowd slowly builds back to its dull whispers, eventually growing bored with us. M is much less tense as Sarge jumps excitedly around her making his plate.

This dingy mess hall has never been so bright. M has a certain glow about her, like the haze I'd seen from her memories when she looked at me. Oh. I hadn't realized how empty I've been feeling lately. Not until I've somehow been filled up again.

"What?"

M pulls me from my thoughts. I've been caught staring. Oops. "Oh, nothing," I say. "Just admiring Sarge."

"He *is* a looker," she agrees.

We pick a table off to the left that's more secluded. The tables are smaller and less packed together the further from the middle you go. A much more intimate choice than the giant feasting table that's the centerpiece, or even any of the standard six-seaters.

With Sarge's size, a two-seater table is out, but that's alright. I wouldn't want it any other way.

The plush seating sinks beneath my weight, and M and I break into laughter almost immediately when Sarge gobbles his plate before we're even settled. This is much better than the last time I stayed in here. When I met my team... fuck.

Damn intrusive thoughts.

The meal carries on quietly; awkwardly. My voice is lost somewhere and I can't find any words either. It's been so long since we've been in each other's company like this.

M slides her plate away, leaning back and resting a hand on her stomach. She releases a contented breath. "That was good."

I've never been one for fabricated meals, but they've grown on me since it's the only option here. I'd prefer real, but even real can't compete with the densely packed vitamins and nutrients of this lab created shit. Though, the taste is just a little bit off.

When you grow up the way M has, food like this is probably a feast fit for royalty. "Definitely," I agree, smiling. I don't want anything to ruin this.

Yet M's face falls and I'm concerned it's already too late some-how.

"So..." she says, her voice trailing off into the din of the cafete-ria.

What the fuck is happening? I thought this was going well. What went wrong? Has she remembered something terrible?

"What's the matter?" I question, unable to take the unknown any longer.

M hesitates, looking to Sarge for strength. Then she meets my eye. "I need to discuss something with you."

"Is that why you agreed to dinner with me?" Anger builds in my chest, pushing out the question before I'm able to filter. Of course. I shouldn't have thought M wanted to spend time with me just for the sake of it. You're an idiot, Warin.

"Well, no," she replies. "Though I admit it's hard to know who to trust around here." M chuckles nervously. "But I also wanted to apologize about your father. We'd been interrupted earlier."

My father? Did she get some information from the subcopies? Do I even want to know? I thought I did, but now I don't know. I can stomach a lot of things, but I'm not too sure about this any-more.

I need to approach it carefully. "Did the subcopies help you?"

"Well, uhm. No," she admits. "But I have a theory."

"About my father?" Shit, Warin. That was too fast. Take a sec-ond next time.

"What? Oh, no," she says. "I think I met your father at some point, but that's all I saw, I swear. As soon as I get something, I'll tell you." Her eyes hold sincerity, but I already know her words are true.

A few seconds pass and I nudge her. "So, what's your theory?" M is lost in her mind.

"Oh!" She smacks her forehead lightly. "Right. I didn't know who to really talk this through with. My father is a good option, but I know you've had first-hand experience with the subcopies."

Where is this going? I don't like it. My nails are digging half-moons into my palms. The way she said *first-hand experience* was like a slap in the face.

"Did you notice anything strange about them? Or, maybe, the one in particular?"

Okay. Not so bad. She's not asking about the moment at the lake. Oh! The moment at the lake! That subcopy had been so different. M must have noticed, too.

"The one, yeah," I state. "She was like you, but not like the others."

"Yes!" Amity cheers to herself. "She's our in for why the Reaver is doing this. I *know* it!"

Seeing her so sure of herself is sexy. She's always been headstrong. It's good to see that conviction for her beliefs has returned, even if the last time she'd used her power was to convince me to let her walk into the Reaver's trap. Eh. That stunt her father pulled against Favager was the nudge she needed.

I carefully listen as she goes on about her theory. She's hesitant to tell Favager, or anyone else, in case they decide to hurt her. Reasoning with her is hard, since our trust isn't fully there, but I explain that Favager has already approved memory extraction experimentation, so telling him might be the best bet.

At this, she surprises me by saying, "I don't know that I really want my memories back."

"What?" I question. "Why?" After her arguments for the truth with Favager, how could she not want her memories back? Does she not care about our past? About her past with Sarge, even? How could she be okay without the knowledge of what she's done?

M takes a second to think about her answer. "I'm looking for the truth," she argues. "I don't think my memories are necessarily synonymous with that. And having the non-emotional buffer is helping me stay afloat."

"You're missing out on so much!" I cry, too enthusiastic for my liking. Fucking impulsive ass.

M distances herself from me, and Sarge nestles as much as he can in between her and I, putting himself across her lap. Fucking hell. "Did you even listen to me?" she grunts. "What am I missing? My ten-year-old sister's death? Did anyone care about that before?" She rolls her eyes. "You know, I thought you'd be the right person to open up to, but maybe I was wrong."

Fucking hell. Shit, shit. Make this better, Warin. You're losing her. "I... no. Amity, please. I just, you..." Word vomit. Lovely choice.

She stands, pushing her hands onto the table to lean in. "You know, Mason lied to me about her death, but at least he seemed to have a good reason. What was in it for you?"

Mason fucking Baines. His name raises my blood pressure. "Really, M? He's a snarky fuck who does whatever he pleases, and yet you think *he's* the good one here?" Damn it, Warin! Just stop!

She rolls her eyes. "At least he'd understand my aversion to my past! We *both* lost our sisters. Do you have any idea what that feels like?"

My body shoots up to meet her face to face above the table. "Actually, I do. Are you forgetting I lost my family, as well?" I pull back, immediately ashamed at my choice of words. My jaw is taut. Stupid, Warin.

M's mouth pops open with a gasp. Then her hand finds her temple, rubbing it softly. "I'm trying here, Luke. Maybe you and I just played a game of love to avoid our real problems. Clearly you're expecting someone I simply am not." She signals for Sarge to follow her as she turns away without another word. Sarge is the one who looks back quickly before they exit the cafeteria.

Fuck. I need to leave right now or this mess hall is about to get a lot messier.

○ ○ ○

THERE'S A BLARING knock on my pod door at the ass crack of dawn. I roll out of bed, rub the hangover from my eyes, and fling the door open. "What the fu..."

My mouth snaps shut at the sight of a Serviceman. "General Favager expects you shortly." He spins to descend the pod tower and that's that. Damn it.

Thankfully Sam is staying in Compound Two with his friends. I quickly get dressed. Is there time for a shower? No. I've no doubt I look like shit. What's this about anyway? I admit, I partook in a bit too much of the hard stuff last night, but I kept my cool. I think...

The Serviceman is waiting for me at the edge of the Residential Ward. He'll be my escort to Favager's hallway. We pass very few others in the halls and all I can think is: am I being led to the gallows?

If this is my final day here with the Service, would it really be all that bad? I wouldn't ever have to see Mason fucking Baines again. I'd miss Lacy and Sonya, but they're always off doing their own thing anyway. Amity... well. I blew it there. Every chance I get, I somehow squander it. She probably never wants to see me again.

There's no waiting in the hallway outside Favager's office this time. Instead, the guards immediately open it and I'm shuffled through. It takes me a moment to process what's happening, but even then, my sluggish brain still can't make it out.

Mason, Lacy, Sonya, Cateline, Mark, and M are here.

"Welcome, Mr. Warin," Favager greets me cooly. "This is the first official meeting of the Amiteers lead group. Please, have a seat." He fans his hand to the small crowd in front of him, urging me to take my place.

I keep my head forward, ignoring the worried glances of my peers. Though she's in my peripheral, I especially keep from glancing in M's direction.

When my ass hits the seat, Favager continues. "Before I hand the floor over to Miss Thorne, I'd like to say how thrilled I am that despite what she's learned about her past, she has agreed to move forward with our plans for this rebellion." His dark eyes meet M's. "Miss Thorne, thank you. I knew I sensed something in you. I know you'll do great things." He smiles a wicked smile that rubs me the wrong way. An early meeting after a long night of drinking is really not the way I want to be spending my time. Ugh. Favager passes the meeting off to M, and she moves herself to the front, standing to his left.

"Welcome, all," she says. "I've been discussing things at length with General Favager all morning and we've come to an agreement about where we're going to go moving forward."

It's odd to see her standing without Sarge, but he's lying, relaxed, at the foot of the chair she left empty. She's not nervous, then.

"All of you are special to me or the cause in some irreplaceable way, and we've assigned each and every one of you a job for this team."

Special. Pfft. To her? How could I be? I must fall into that latter category. I'm somehow special *for the cause*. I could barf right now. I choke down the bile as she continues. Damn she's sexy. All leader-like. Fuck.

"Mason is in charge of communications," she says. He's been doing this since he got here, so nothing really changes there. Whoopty freaking do. "Lacy and Sonya are optics. Basically, they're going to make sure I look good for the people. They'll decide what propaganda goes out."

"You always look good, girl," Lacy says, hyping her up. M returns her comment with a small nod and smile.

"Dad, you'll be our staff writer." She winks at him and he smiles, nodding back. "These are all important roles because I need time to finish something on home base. General Favager has been gracious in giving me time to find the answers I'm looking for. Once that's complete, we'll rework things."

My head is hazy and my vision is cloudy. I smell like a damn liquor store. But the disregard is clear when M scans over my face, skipping right past it to lock eyes with Cateline.

"Cateline and Luke are in charge of memory research and transplants on the subcopies. However, there is one that appears to be fighting my memories, and she will be off limits. Luke knows the one, he will fill you in, Miss Pierre." Did she somehow change her mind and want her memories back? No. This has to be something Favager pushed for. Why?

"Wait... fighting your memories?" Mason asks, cutting in. "How could that be possible?"

"I'm not really sure, but these are the answers I'm hoping to find out," M replies. "Now, I kn..."

"She may have found the flaw." All eyes are directed toward me in a second. Shit, I guess I interrupted. Well, whatever. "Before Amity had left for Omphalos, I'd warned her about certain flaws to pick up on in order to persevere through certain tests. It's possible the girl has found a way out of the memory implantation somehow." Stranger things have happened, right?

Cateline looks as though she wants to speak but doesn't want to respond because I was the person who'd presented the argument. Mason is thinking, Mark is studying, listening. Favager seems utterly bored. Lacy and Sonya have been canoodling in the back since Mason started asking questions, but they perk up now. I'm going to be sick.

"Do we have theories as to why they were sent here?" Sonya asks. It's a valid question. One that still doesn't really have an answer.

"The Reaver wouldn't respond when asked, just said they were *gifts*," Lacy relays to her wife and the group.

Mason argues. "Does it matter the why if we're able to get memories from them?" Amity tenses at his words, but I ignore it as best I can. She *definitely* hasn't changed her mind since our dinner.

I recall what the one subcopy had said by the lake. She escaped with the other, so she's not the one meant to be here. One gift at a time for someone... but does it matter who? Or why?

"There might be something in the memories that can help us figure it out," M states. "That's the whole point of this."

"This subcopy, she was... different, as Amity says. She admitted she wasn't Amity, but she *did* have her knowledge." Remembering the calculation on her face as she shot her insult at me is enough to send rage billowing through every synapse of my brain. She wasn't the Amity I knew, but only *that* Amity has knowledge of the way my father affects me. I never wanted to disappoint him again, not after going against his pleas in the Force. Not after my attempted patricide.

"Like all things scientific, proof must be obtained to support our theories." Cateline's lip twitches in a way that suggests she's deep in thought. *So she decided to speak after all. I suppose we'll be working together for the foreseeable future, which means whether we like it or not, we'll have to speak.* "We should still look into her brain, if we can..."

"No," M cuts Cateline off. "This particular subcoby will not be a part of your experimentation, and that is final."

"But Miss Thorne," Cateline starts. *The subtle flinch of M's muscles tells me I'm not the only one with an aversion to the formality.* "You have tasked us with a very important job; we could use her as our control. She may be an integral part..."

"Kindly, Miss Pierre," M hisses, "you need to stay in your lane." *Everyone in the room is but a spectator to this battle of the minds.*

Damn.

Cateline blubbers. "I..." she stutters. "Miss Thorne, I did not..."

M cuts her off for a third time. "I know what you want, but you will stick to the assignment given. And you will get permission from the subcopy before you do. They are human beings, not lab rats."

"Yes, of course," Cateline agrees.

"Anything else, Miss Thorne?" Favager steps in now.

"I believe that's all."

"Are you sure?" Mason asks, butting in where he doesn't need to.

M nods. "Respect the name, remember?" She smiles, a gleam in her eye.

Mark looks at his daughter with proud eyes. *Mine hold something different, however. I have never been so turned on in my life.*

CHAPTER NINETEEN ○ AMITY

THE DAYS HAVE MELDED INTO WEEKS. SOON, IT'LL BE MONTHS. The holidays are right around the corner and the General is growing impatient, but, thankfully, he's staying within the boundary. My father has been meeting with him weekly to go over propaganda which, unfortunately I've had to learn. Lacy and Sonya doll me up and pose me for photos. But that's hardly anything. I haven't been asked to do much more than that so the focus can be my truth.

I've honestly kept myself out of the science behind all of this and have been trying to dissect Two's brain in my own way. Two is what we're calling whoever's body and soul is fighting against my memories. I admit, Cateline's machines could be useful, but I hated the way she overstepped me in that meeting. I bet she's expecting me to come crawling to her. It's okay. It's nice having a friend that's similar to me.

I've visited with Two every day and today is no exception. We've found it's easier for her to fight my memories if she's looking at me. Lacy had visited a few times, Mason and Luke, too. Even my father. And though I was always there with them, my memories beat out Two's efforts because it was all too much for her to deny.

"Amity?" Two asks.

"Yeah?" I must have zoned out as usual. Two has gotten used to it, especially lately.

"I'm sorry," she says. "Knowing what I know, I shouldn't have brought it up."

Two is referring to Emma. Believe it or not, my sister has stayed out of most conversation. Either people are too scared to upset me, or they're too uncomfortable with the situation. Regardless of the why, Two is the first person to mention her in weeks.

It's not like Emma hasn't been on my mind. She's there when I close my eyes at night, and she occupies my deep thoughts during the day. I think I'm torturing myself with the images, and I probably deserve it. I've been too scared to ask for anything more than surface level details. Scared what it means and what it might do to me.

"You know more than I do," I admit with a shrug, instinctively reaching my fingers to Sarge. He's wrapped around me with his head pressed to my lap. Most of him has to stay hidden to help keep Two from slipping into Amity.

Two closes her eyes. She does it to disconnect the visual senses and only focus on the flow of her very being. She's gotten better with it, but my guess is that the guilt of asking about Emma is a trigger for my memories. We've learned certain emotions react similarly to the way seeing people from my past does.

"Can I tell you something?" I ask.

Two's eyes pop open, the relief in them clear. She nods.

"I don't believe Emma is dead." There. I said it. For the first time ever, I've said what my gut has been telling me all along. Out loud. The reason I haven't wanted to go into too many details about her "so called" death.

Two is quiet for a few minutes, contemplating what to say. Her mouth bounces open, then closed, then open again. Still, no words come out.

Sarge snuggles closer to me, quelling my growing nerves. I shouldn't have said it. But the truth is, I needed to. I couldn't keep it in any longer. No one wants to talk about her and Two finally gave me the opening my soul has been searching for.

Everyone tells me Emma is dead. They say I saw it. Her body is laid to rest at my family's house in Burns. Deep in my chest, though, something catches. It doesn't make sense. And maybe that's just Death. Maybe it's not meant to make sense...

"She's dead," Two finally says. "You watched it happen."

"So I've heard." It takes everything in me not to roll my eyes. My fingers tangle tightly into Sarge's fur. "It doesn't add up."

"If you had your memories, it would." She's adamant, yet sincere. She's probably right, too.

"Yeah, well I don't!" My voice is raised with mild irritation and hidden anger. Sarge immediately sits up, licking my face. Two might be speaking rationally, but I still refuse to believe it. Surely I'd feel if my little M was gone?

Two closes her eyes for a minute, smoothing her features, then starts anew. "Would you like me to describe these scenes to you?" Her voice is kind. It reminds me of someone. A distant outline of... a friend?

This time it's my turn to close my eyes. Can I handle this? Do I want to?

"No," I say. I don't want my brain clouded with *emotion*. "But taking all the information you know about the Reaver, can you at least see it from my perspective?"

Two doesn't answer, she awaits a continued explanation. I don't know that I have one, but she has access to all of the Reaver memories she's told me about, and more. I was kept hostage, a plaything for her, and she didn't kill me. But Emma was there first. Emma isn't like me. She's good.

Being an outsider looking in, can Two see how that Death wouldn't make sense?

"Like, you take away the visual response to help keep your brain in check. So, maybe it's the same thing?" I say it like a question, theorizing out loud. "I don't know. Like my brain saw something and filled in the only thing it could make sense of at the time."

"Why would it be fake?" Two spits without a pause.

"Why *wouldn't* it be?" I counter, equally fast. "The Reaver puts her mission above all else, right?"

Two is uncomfortable, but eventually she nods.

"Then why would she kill someone so important to her plan? It just... doesn't make sense." I release a tired exhale. This is stupid, but she *has* to see it. "Not having the visual proof is keeping my mind clear."

"Amity, there's more to it than..."

Sarge barks, interrupting Two. Our heads whip around to find Luke at the door. I turn back to Two, barely acknowledging Luke.

"What were you saying?" I watch her expectantly.

She sighs. "I'm sorry about your sister," is all she says. She leans forward, resting a hand on mine. "Truly."

The icy chill of a familiar emotion sweeps through me. My hand jerks away.

"Sorry." She casts her eyes down.

"What just happened?" Luke questions. Sarge has pressed himself firmly to my side.

Two is speechless. "I..." she starts. "It's..."

I know what this is. Fear. Two shared with me during our first few days together that the Reaver implanted emotion readers in her fingertips. In *all* of their fingertips.

Two glances at the soft pads of her fingers and she recounts her knowledge to someone else this time. "Mine is fear," she finishes telling Luke.

"What?" Luke says from behind me. "Did you know about this?" He questions me now, placing himself on the floor beside us. He's upset because they could have been experimenting this whole time had they known. Whatever.

I nod, ignoring the tense of his knuckles and the flare of his nostrils.

"I'm... not sure why she did it. I'm not even sure if the other copies are aware of their own abilities. But I can read fear." Her eyes lock with mine and I give an encouraging nod. Despite everything, I want to trust Luke. He's been distant since our dinner, but I don't blame him. We've each got our own things to deal with.

"You've known this all along?" Luke asks, pulling Two's eyes from me.

Two gets a playful gleam in her eye. It's out of place within the somber context of our conversation. "You react with anger to hide your fears. It's why you felt the way you did by the lake." An impish smile twitches across her lips.

Both Luke and I blanch at the mention of Luke's misdeed. But Two is unperturbed. She continues.

"Amity's fears typically trigger a guilt response. Mason hides his behind superiority. Lacy behind humor, Dr. Pierre needs proof to combat it..."

"I'm sorry," Luke apologizes, stopping Two's list of collected fears. "Again," he adds. His mood changes give me whiplash sometimes.

"It's not your fault," Two assures. "I think I'm programmed to drive out fears. That doesn't seem to be Amity specific. Even when I'm... me... it happens."

My brain doesn't stop my tongue before I blurt, "So what do I fear?" I'd never asked her to dive into it because she seemed un-comfortable. Simply bringing someone's fear to the surface makes sense, but I didn't realize she was analyzing them, too. They both look at me like I've sprung five heads. "You said *typically*." I shrug. Sarge shimmies into position, sensing the shift.

The silence stretches between the four of us for a long time. Then Two finally responds.

"You fear the truth."

CHAPTER TWENTY ○ REN

DESPITE GOING OVER ONE-HUNDRED MILES PER HOUR, THE
O-Train isn't fast enough. Seconds wouldn't be fast enough. Hell,
milliseconds wouldn't even be. It's been entirely too long since
Omphalos crumbled. Entirely too long for those not frozen in the
Reserves to have survived. Yet today we'll see the damage because
Master Sergeant Dean Carovak and his team have finally broken
the earth.

Marcus steps out before me, reaching his hand up to steady me.
I don't acknowledge him, instead I push past his outstretched arm
and descend the staircase without a single glance back.

Mr. Carovak is already waiting. Behind him is a singular squad
of about ten other Master Sergeants. As the distance closes, he
nods. "Welcome, Headmistress," he says. "I've sent everyone to
their barracks. Those of us here will assist in any way needed
should we encounter tough terrain."

The suggestiveness of his tone as he says *tough terrain* leads me
to think he believes there will be plenty of dead bodies. Thankfully he'd thought ahead to send the others away. Something like this
can only be trusted with the top of the Force. The majority can't
know how far of a setback we've taken in this mission.

We all shuffle toward the opening my men have cleared. I ignore the slight huff of breath from Marcus behind me when I take Mr. Carovak's hand, allowing him to lead me into the rubble.

The oldest Exceptionals had clear instructions: get to the Reserves if we don't get to them first.

There were not enough open spaces for everyone, so inevitably the casualties will be high. Who of those among the perished is what we are about to learn.

The new catacombs of Omphalos are dusty and debris filled. Old blood spatters the crumbled walls, and the acrid stench of decay pollutes the air. Quiet hacks escape from a weakling's throat here or there. Especially once we stumble upon a body nearly picked apart.

Cannibalism. Hm.

Wind whistles through the echoey halls as we descend further. Creaking ceilings above us cause whispered murmurs to sweep through the group. *Is it safe?* they ask, *this whole thing is going to collapse.*

Bitches.

The center is what we're after. I've left it up to Marcus to catalogue the dead, so I've not been paying attention, nor do I care much about the others behind me. I'll only pay attention once I get to the pot of gold; my treasure. The Exceptionals.

The air is chilled this deep below the surface. It's been a while since my body has shaken with anticipation. I blame the brisk temperature when Mr. Carovak asks if I'm alright, and I appreciate him nodding despite knowing it's a farce. We're almost upon the room. Marcus says something behind me, but I ignore him.

The Reserves door is cracked open. My throat is dry. One-hundred Reserve pods total. Twenty-two used prior to collapse and seventy-eight available with over three hundred Exceptionals ranging in age from a few months old to mid-twenties needing space to survive. Those odds are shit.

We haven't been able to catalogue who had been taken by that Service my sweet Lucas allowed in the day of the collapse. My heart stammers at the thought of my Exceptionals dying beneath this cold crust, but I can't stand the alternative. If any of my Exceptionals have been taken, that's too much to bear. Knowing they may currently be growing more and more Tainted is horrific.

Mr. Carovak gives his men the signal to wait, allowing him, Marcus, and me to move forward on our own.

The whispers of the officers behind me carry clearly. *What's so important about the Reserves? There's a lot of our kind down here, don't they matter?*

They are all idiots unable to see the bigger picture. Selfish imbeciles. I would make an example out of those with questioning whimpers, but my Exceptionals are what matter most in this moment.

I'm the first to enter the room. The smell of Death sucker punches my nostrils. Now, in the room dense with putrescence, it's clear. I have lost so much.

The men to either side of me cannot see me fall. "Leave," I order.

"B... but Mistress..." Marcus begins, unable to help himself.

I whirl around, bloodshot eyes wide and menacing. "Do not question me!" I yell. "Leave at once!"

Dean Carovak grabs at Marcus and they disappear quickly out the door.

A sob claws its way from somewhere deep, and my teeth bite into my knuckles to stifle it. My heart skips. The room is ice, it's long and full, it's a tragic masterpiece. Bodies are huddled in piles with not a single heartbeat to spare. The pods are upright, lined ten by ten, and I've not considered until now how cold and lifeless those inside them appear.

I watch my step, careful to not disturb the dead. Faces I recognize, faces I've worked with, faces I lo... no. They are faces. Exceptional faces, but that is the past.

We will recoup this loss. We will. For the sake of Humanity.

No one dares enter while I study. I look over each individual pod, checking names. The story here is still unclear, but it seems younger Exceptionals were prioritized for the Reserves. Though this is good for many reasons, it's not great for refilling our birthing rooms. We need great stock to produce more Exceptionals. And now the majority of my stock is spread out dead on the floor.

I keep my shuddering to a minimum, yet my entire being ignites when I find myself amidst the original twenty-two members of the Reserves. A glaring token of the past, and a hopeful glimpse at the future. It is within these pods I am reminded why I'm here and what's to come.

That vile girl. It's *always* her. Everything decent so far has been tainted by her presence. My Exceptionals, my system, my son.

My sweet Lucas was set to come back, he was going to rule by my side. Hell, I even kept his father's other spawn in my Reserves for him. My eyes meet her through the frosty glass. Lily. Ick. She's got the likeness of her birth giver. Sickening. The things a mother will do for her son. My head shakes.

It wouldn't be so bad if the girl weren't nearly perfect. It pains me to admit it, but she's an Exceptional through and through. How, with her progeny, I couldn't explain. Still, she's forced into stasis because of her situation. Because it's too dangerous to risk her in the program. Like another young Exceptional here...

All because Miss Thorne had to come along. All because she had to cause this chaos and destruction, sticking her nose where it doesn't belong.

Miss Thorne is a flaw. A pesky bug. I would have wiped her existence out long ago if it weren't for those hooks she has in my sweet boy.

Oh.

A smile weaves itself across my face. Standing in the center of these pods, seeing my contingency, is enough. That's it! A new plan hatches in my brain while surrounded by my nameless soldiers. If subcopies won't lure my son away from her clutches, we'll try a different approach.

"Boys!" I shout. "Carry these out, will you? There's much to do."

CHAPTER TWENTY-ONE ○ AMITY

MY HEAD SHOOTS OFF THE BED IN ONE SWIFT MOTION JUST AS Sarge's tongue connects to my cheek. Hot, sticky sweat clings to my skin.

As quickly as I can, I'm out of bed, cleaned up, dressed, and walking into Cateline's lab. Two is waiting for me expectantly. Her face falls when she sees the dark circles under my eyes.

"I told you it was a bad idea," she chastises.

"You also told me I fear the *truth*," I say, spinning into a sitting position, slumped into an oversized bean bag chair in the corner of the room. Sarge settles in next to me. "This time I lost Sarge..." *and Luke...* I keep the second part to myself, my fingers gripping Sarge's fur more firmly than before. His eyes flick to mine with an apologetic gaze.

I asked Two to draw out my fears. If I'm going to persevere, I need to confront them. How could I possibly be the face of a revolution if I'm caught in this in-between? It's not like I'm not used to cursed nightmares lately, anyway. But Two said I fear the truth despite it being the main thing I'm after. The truth is what I'd hoped to see—not these demented scenes torturing me with the loss of those I love.

While my goal is to remain distant from my memories, that

hasn't stopped me from seeking the truth. I'm not convinced the two are synonymous and I need to know why.

Two silently stares at me. Then says, "You know the *real* reason you turned yourself in?"

I shake my head. When it's not too hard for her, Two tells me about the parts of my past that I ask for and adds in her own knowledge. Like confirming Emma is Exceptional, further proving her death doesn't make sense. And that I'd ended up at the facility because I turned myself in. She'd originally said it was because the Reaver was going to kill more innocents.

"Because you hoped it would save Luke and Sarge from being targeted and dragged into the messes you somehow find yourself in," she says. "You thought yourself a monster, and deep down you felt you belonged there."

I want to roll my eyes but resist the urge. I don't need her to tell me how guilt eats at me. It always has. I hadn't realized how much it affected me until I lost my mother. Somehow everything feels like my responsibility, my fault; my weight to bear. "Why are you telling me this?" I question.

Two huffs a breath that scatters the hair from her forehead. "Because as much as you fear the truth, you also fear losing what you love. And in some cases, like Emma, those fears collide."

I tear my eyes away from Two's begging ones. "I just..." My voice fades. "I don't think they do."

"But you *do* fear it," she argues. "Whether or not you believe it to be true." Then, with a sharp intake of breath, she winces. Two looks pained as she tries to dissect her own true life from the one she was given.

My throat dries. "Everything okay?"

I pretend it hasn't been getting worse the past few days. I pretend my mind has been playing tricks on me. The alternative makes my stomach tumble nervously.

"It's getting harder to separate myself from you," Two admits. "I think... ack..." She presses her palms to her temples. "I think it's because I've been fighting it. We're melding into one person now."

The nerves I've been holding at bay push past my barriers and Sarge snuggles closer. "What do you mean?"

I'm pushing off the inevitable. My hope was that Two wouldn't have to be experimented on, but even if she's not a part of the damned memory shit Luke and Cateline are working toward, it seems she'll need *something*. A medical doctor won't cut it. We need a scientist.

Two takes a few seconds to calm her mind. "It feels like instead of pushing someone out, I'm just denying certain things. I can't... ugh... I can't explain." She winces through clenched teeth. "Like there used to be a clear line between you and me, but now that line is blurry and two is becoming one. Not quite me... but... but not quite you either."

I grab her hand despite knowing the fear that will rip through me. I shudder past the emotion. "I wish there was something we could do."

Guilt stabs into my chest. The truth is, there *is* something. I could allow Cateline to look inside her head.

Time passes slowly as Two gathers herself. *Or does it?*

Next thing I know, Luke's voice is breaking the silence. "Am I interrupting?"

My head swivels to where he stands in the doorway, his eyes holding a hint of amusement. There's a small smirk plastered on his face, but nothing about it seems real. That means bad news.

If Sarge could get any closer to me, he would. He tries as Two invites Luke to sit with us.

"To what do we owe this pleasure?" she inquires. Her voice is strained, her features taut. Does she get the same vibe from Luke? Or is she simply still in pain?

Luke takes no time diving right in when he says, "The other subcopy has passed during memory extraction." He avoids my eyes, keeping them on Two instead. A heavy stone drops deep into the pit of my stomach.

I've kept myself from getting close to the other. Sure, she was me, but that's precisely why I stayed away. Adding to her plate wasn't an option.

When I found out how the first one passed, I begged them not to let it happen to the second. But now it was a whole scientific experiment beyond getting my memories. This was something potentially important for the future. I just happened to be patient zero. The only thing giving me solace with it is that they were both consenting individuals that willingly chose to accept this experimentation and they knew the risks.

With this one dying without a success, I'm left wondering what's next. Will more subcopies appear out of thin air like the last time? Will this be the end? Does the Reaver know that Two escaped?

Fear needles into my heart, prickling my scalp and leaving my hair to stand on end. I quickly release the connection between Two and I, then grip Sarge even harder.

"Two," I say. "I've got to speak with Luke for a few. I'll be right back."

She nods, and Sarge and I climb out of the seat, leaving the room with Luke behind us.

"Why did you come in to tell us that?" I interrogate immediately once we're out of earshot. Though I've been kept updated briefly, I specifically requested that Two stay out of it. Especially any Death. She's strong, sure, but my mind is making her fragile.

"We got closer to the memory extraction this time," Luke answers. His weight is shifting from side to side.

"So?" My fists rest against my hips, and my foot taps steadily on the ground. Sarge's head and neck wrap around the front of me, creating a barrier between my body and the man in my view.

"So," Luke hesitates, "we'd like your approval to continue experimentation."

A response shoots from my lips before I can stop it. "You didn't care about my opinion before." My arms fold across my chest now. He's insinuating something I don't want, and arguing is my first line of defense. Only someone as guilt riddled as me could poke others in theirs. I told him I didn't want my memories back and he judged me, yelled at me.

"Wasn't it your idea?" His jaw tenses, but after a few seconds, he relaxes. "We thought you knew the risks," he says. "We're doing this to get your memories back and to hopefully avoid anyone dealing with this in the future. These are groundbreaking studies."

"Ugh," I groan. "You sound like Mason." Luke's face momentarily shifts into outrage. Before he says anything, though, I forge on. "Groundbreaking or not, you really thought people dying wouldn't mean something to me?" I snap. "Do you even know me as well as you say?"

Luke's face blanches, flinching with the harshness of my words. "I..."

My chest flares as I cut him off. "Are you on their side *for* me? Or because you want whoever I was before back?"

This conversation is tiring. I still don't want my memories. It's like our dinner all over again. Luke is stuck in the past with the ghost of who I used to be, and Cateline is demanding we look to the future with these studies. Damn it for putting them together. Sarge leans into me and I welcome the weight against my thigh.

"Well, obviously for you," Luke argues, rolling his eyes. "And consent was gained. We didn't do anything they didn't accept."

Obviously. "Everyone thinks they're doing what's best for me without actually checking." My eyes tumble in my head, matching Luke. Not treating people like lab rats is hardly something to pride ourselves on. It's standard decency. So how could Luke think that Death wouldn't matter to me?

Luke scoffs. "Would you even know what was best for yourself? You're developmentally *fifteen*."

My blood boils. He's being such a... ugh! Such an asshole since our dinner gone wrong. "I don't need you to tell me anything!" I shout, though I hate to admit it sounds childish.

"I know that," Luke says, clearly regretting his choice of words. "I've always known that." His voice is broken. He doesn't get to be hurt, though. He's not flipping this around.

"Then you should understand what you're asking of me is too much." I swiftly turn from Luke, entering Two's room again. She's the only one left. I won't let them take her.

Do I really need my memories? Sure, remembering Sarge would be great, and clearly there's a whole history between me and Luke. At first, I thought I needed my memories to function. But the more I think about it, the more it seems they were a heavy burden. Now I realize it might be a blessing in disguise.

Are my memories equal to the Death? Should this research really be all this important?

"Hi," I say, smiling, pushing the negative emotions as far away from my voice as possible. Two is sitting up in her chair.

"Hi." She smiles back. "Everything alright?"

I've never been a good liar. I'd always told Emma that the truth would prevail. Though sometimes, omission means safety. It means keeping the peace. I think this is one of those times. Yet

Two is perceptive, so before I say anything, she opens her mouth to speak once more.

"They want to experiment on me." She sighs.

Damn facial expressions. "Yes," I admit, since I have no other choice.

"It's only logical," she says to herself. "That's what we're here for, right?" Her slate grey eyes flick to mine.

"I won't let them," I spit, hopefully assuring her. Changing the subject, I ask, "How's your head?" *Perhaps removing the memories would be good for her?* No, Amity. You will *not* let her die.

"It's alright." She shifts uncomfortably. "I wish I could remember my own name."

I chuckle to lighten the mood. "I know the feeling," I say. "But Two is a nice one."

Two smiles, though it doesn't reach her eyes. I hate it. She doesn't deserve this. She deserves a life. A real one. Not one weighed down by my bullshit. Not one where she loses herself.

Am I really keeping Two away from the experiments for her own good? Or is it for me? I'd just cursed Luke out for the same thing, but maybe it was all a projection. My palms moisten with sweat and Sarge nudges closer. If I'm being honest with myself, I think it's both. Once the subcopies are gone, once Two has served her *purpose*, I'll be back at the beck and call of General Favager. I'll be his patsy. Two is the only one protecting me from that right now.

But I don't want Two to die either. And maybe Luke is right. Could it work this time? They're close. Or so they think. What if they're not? What if I send her to her death?

"Does it hurt?" Two asks.

I'm pulled out of my rapid thoughts. "What?"

Two clarifies, "Does having blanks in your memory hurt?"

Does it hurt? Hm. No, it's empty. Black and dark. There's nothing where something should be, but I guess it doesn't hurt. It's aggravating as hell, and somehow also peaceful, but definitely not painful in the traditional sense. There's also the added benefit of seeing your situation from a new perspective, one not skewed by experiences.

"No," I reply. Then, adding quickly at the end, "Does having memories that aren't yours hurt?" I can't believe I've never asked her this before. Maybe I *am* selfish. I've only been caring about myself.

Two grimaces. "It's busy. There are too many voices in my head." The look on my face urges her to explain. Thankfully she does.

"I have my memories. I lost my mother, and I have a younger sister. But then everything is gone and suddenly my sister's name is Emma, but that doesn't seem right. And she's dead? But I don't know why. And if I focus on it for too long, I lose myself."

My heart cries for Two. As much as having no memory has caused issues for me, I couldn't imagine having the wrong ones. The separation process pops into my head, unwelcomed. *Could it work this time?*

My head splits the same as my heart. A part of me wants to try, while the other part attempts to bury such thoughts. Shit. If she were going to do it, it would have to be her choice. I won't accept her doing it on my behalf. I won't force her to do it. She must choose it herself. Here goes... "Would you want to separate my memory from yours?"

"What?" Her eyes widen with surprise. "You could do that?"

"Well," I start. "That's what they want to experiment with."

"Oh, right." She shakes her head. "And Death is a side effect."

"Yes," I confirm. I hate this so much. "From my understanding, it's difficult and risky." My voice is even, monotonous. I can't help it. It's the only way to stop myself from breaking, but she needs to know everything before she decides.

Two gulps, but her mouth stays tightly shut, her features smooth.

"The original memories you lost may not return in full either," I add. I know how this goes all too well. Though having nothing seems better than being forced to house someone else's. I realize I've been doing to Two what everyone else has done to me. I want to make it right. Giving her the choice is important.

Two studies me with sad eyes, remaining silent.

"Think about it," I say, resting my hand on hers, letting the fear of her death fully overtake me. "You don't have to, but if you want to try, then maybe this time it will work. You wouldn't have to be someone else anymore."

"I'll do it," Two says, no hesitation in her voice.

My eyes flick to hers. No fear, unlike mine. "Are you sure?" I'm shocked. Surely, she should take more time to think, right? "You could take some time."

"No," she states. "I'll do it."

A tight-lipped smile finds its way to my face. If she dies, it's on me. But perhaps there are fates worse than Death.

CHAPTER TWENTY-TWO ○ AMITY

"UPON FURTHER INVESTIGATION, I DO NOT BELIEVE THIS TO be a viable transplant," Cateline says, shattering my world as if it's nothing. She's been examining Two the past few days and has finally called a meeting. Luke is here, watching me with a hooded gaze. Two is sitting quietly. I've refused to do anything but stand completely still for fear of collapsing. Sarge can only do so much with keeping me upright.

"What happened?" My voice finally makes an appearance. Sarge's hot tongue licks my palm, and my fingers snake their way into his fur without much thought.

Cateline gives a sideways glance to Luke, and he opens his mouth to speak. "The mix of Two's memories with yours is causing her to become a new person. We couldn't implant these into you without risking the same."

I ignore the bloom of anxiousness by tightening my fists. Two's getting worse. She's not been herself. She's not me, but not her. It's not fair!

Screw this. It's my time to be angry. "I don't give a shit about my memories!" I cry. "Two is in pain and she's losing herself. Can you simply *remove* them?" My eyes dance back and forth between Luke and Cateline. I've never cared about their experiments being successful. I want my truth, but Two has made me realize I still want to be a stranger to it. It's giving me a perspective I fear I'd been blind to before. So forget about me. This is all for Two.

"I would strongly advise against it," Cateline warns. "There isn't a lot of salvageable memory of her own leftover."

Damn it! Damn it! "She won't be in pain, though!" I argue, speaking from experience. An empty brain is better. It *has* to be.

"We don't know what will happen," Cateline answers honestly, but I hate her for it. "She may grow to be scared and confused. She may be a whole new person."

"But at least she'll be alive!" I cry. "At least..." My head falls and Sarge pushes himself up to lick my tears away. I don't want to break down. I don't want to be weak in front of these people. I want... I don't know what I want. I... ugh!

"Please try to remove them anyway," Two says, jolting me from my episode. *Did I hear that correctly?* I'd been so deep in the moment that I forgot she could speak for herself. "I can't live like this much longer," she argues. "I'm losing myself. So, what's the harm?"

Her tone of voice is disheartening. She's basically sending herself to the slaughterhouse. I guess I can't blame her...

Everyone looks to me for an answer.

"You heard them," I say, directing myself to Two. "You might not even be yourself at the end of it."

Two says nothing, but her eyes beat their sadness into me. Finally, I nod, and Two offers a meek smile.

"I just ask that I do it in my room with Amity," Two requests. "Alone."

Cateline glances to Luke once more, then nods, returning her gaze to her patient. "Alright, let's set it up."

"Wait, right now?" I panic, Sarge pressing himself into me.

Luke attempts to reach me, but Sarge snaps his teeth before he makes contact. He sighs. "The longer we wait, the harder it will be."

"It will be fine," Two says, placing her hand on me. Luke huffs, clearly upset that Sarge didn't offer her the same arrangement. The fear creeps from her fingertips, leeching into the very fibers of my being.

"Okay..." I say. "Let's do it."

Everything is ready an hour later. Cateline modified her setup so she could be out of the room and away from us.

Luke warned me that subcopies bleed out of their eyes when they're about to die. Some sort of thick sludge. He called it a gruesome overload and shutdown. So that's what I have to watch for. Great.

I've opted for not holding Two's hand, but she doesn't seem to mind. Though she's the one who drives the fear to the surface, I don't need her feeling scared for me the way that I am for her. Instead, my fingers snake through Sarge's fur as per usual. He blinks up at me with golden eyes filled with understanding.

"We're about to begin," Cateline says before closing the door.

Then it's only us in here.

"So this is really happening?" Two says, as if this is something she's been looking forward to for months.

"Yep," I say, forcing a smile. Unease surrounds me, but if Two notices, she doesn't react.

It takes five minutes before she takes a sharp breath, holding air in her lungs to dull whatever invisible pain is weaving its way through her.

"You okay?" I ask, nervous to know the answer. My brain fights itself on how to feel. It's my fault, her death is on my conscience, it's her choice, the Reaver did this, life is what it is. It's all true, and none of it is.

"I'm sorry, Amity," Two says, wincing.

This guilt must be from the part of her that contains me, and I'm mentally screaming at myself for making her this way. She's apologizing for something that clearly isn't her fault. I choose not to argue. I know when someone tries to tell me something isn't my fault, I double down on myself, unable to believe them. I won't do that to her.

"It's alright," I say. "It needs to be done."

"No," she says through clenched teeth. "I should've told you sooner."

The apprehension burrows deep within my soul, causing Sarge to nearly knock me over with his weight. "Told me what?"

"Her son." Two coughs, breathless, with eyes clenched.

"Excuse me?"

"The Reaver..." she says. "Her son... is the... answer."

"Her... son?"

My eyes pinch closed. A memory stabs into my brain, shocking me to the core. No, that's not the memory itself, *it's the man beside me with his prod. The Reaver shouts at me. "Where is my son?" she screams.*

Oh my goodness! Her son!

Two is right. The Reaver thinks I know where her son is, and gauging from the crazed look in her eye, her son is a sore spot for her. Good. I hope she's suffering.

This is the answer. If she doesn't want me to take what's hers, she'll have to give me back what's mine.

My eyes pop open excitedly. "Two," I say, rushed. "Who is..." My voice fades to nothing.

Two's eyes are closed, yet a black sludge is crowning the corners. Her brain is melting, just like Luke warned.

"Two, your..." I can't. "Your eyes."

My hand reaches out on reflex to take hers.

Two's eyes open and settle on my face now. There's not a single drop of white in them. They're black holes in her otherwise beautiful face. She's smiling. Despite my rising fears, she couldn't appear happier.

"You're... dying..." My voice is small and whispery, yet somehow too loud.

"There is no pain," Two assures. "Only bliss."

A sob chokes me, stuck in the back of my throat. I hold it there as to not disturb her peace.

"I'm going to miss you, Sarge," she says, reaching out to my friend, sliding her fingers through his fur the way that I do. The sludge drops from her eyes like slow tears. "But at least I'll be with my mother and Emma. Zach, too."

My throat closes as my fingers clench hers. It's not the bleeding eyes, or the gruesome Death that gets me. It's not even that she's basically me if I were to die. No.

It's the fact that she truly believes she will find solace with my mother and Emma in these last moments of her life. More of my memories must have been hidden somehow.

I wish it were me in her place. I know there's only emptiness on the other side because it's not really her family she's reuniting with. Though I'm sure my mother and Zach would be thrilled to have her anyway.

All of them...

CHAPTER TWENTY-THREE ∘ AMITY

SARGE AND I LEFT, HEADING TO OUR ROOM AS SOON AS TWO took her last breath. Not only was Death already imprinted deeply in my mind, but her last words to me were also swirling around in my head unchecked. I needed out of there as fast as possible.

So, I've been sitting in the middle of the room, trying to channel Two's energy and my lost memories, constantly combatting the haunting images of a gruesome overload. But the key to proving that Emma's alive is to find the Reaver's son, which means swallowing the sadness before it swallows me.

Funny how I'd been so certain on keeping my memories at a distance and now I'd give anything to have them. What a shit irony.

How much time passes, I couldn't say. But a few knocks on the door clue me in that someone has decided it's been long enough.

"Come in," I say, not moving from my spot on the floor. I don't want to see anyone, but I imagine I won't have much of a choice.

I expect to find Mason entering—hell, maybe even the General—but am surprised to open my eyes to Luke. He looks like shit. Though I've only seen him mad or completely hollow since our botched conversation at dinner, sometimes I remember the guy that brought me flowers in my hospital room. And other times I get a wisp of a familiar memory of how he was *before*.

"M," he says. "Mity... Amity." He's choosy when it comes to my nickname since I'd yelled about it. At first, I'd been happy, but now it leaves me with an unexplainable empty feeling. I ignore the unreasonable pang of a stupid emotion.

"Lucas," I say, mocking him.

The name makes him wince and I instantly feel heavy. "I want to apologize," he continues. My eyebrows pull in with confusion. "I'm sorry I pushed so hard to get your memories back. Maybe Two would be alive if I'd given up on trying to save the past and focused on the present instead."

His tone is soft; he seems genuinely heartfelt in his apology. Which is why his neck nearly breaks when he turns to me as I say, "No."

Sarge has placed himself nearly on top of me.

"No?" Luke questions.

My brain pulsates with annoyance. "Two hadn't been herself. And it was getting worse extremely fast. She was in pain." That's the truth. Two made the decision to try, and now she's at peace. *Right?* I'll repeat it over and over until it becomes true.

"I'm..." he stutters, speechless. "I... don't know what to say to that." The expression on his face is worrisome. Would I be acting differently with my memories intact?

"So don't say anything," I reply, quickly. "I don't need words."

I'll never let him know how broken I am. How I just lost a piece of me and how bogged down I feel with the heavy burden of a resistance. The responsibility is too much, but it's the only way the Reaver will fall, and I *need* her to fall. Because she's either the cold-hearted bitch that murdered my sister, or she's the only one who knows where to find her.

"Well, I need to say this," Luke starts. Not that it means much, but I can't ever place a time where he'd been this nervous. His lack of comfort with it means he's not used to this either. "Listen, you were right all those nights ago at dinner," Luke admits. "You have to do what makes you happy *now*. Even if it's not in line with the past." The feeling that stabs into my chest is incomprehensible. Damn it. I told him I didn't need words. "Besides," he adds, "friendship isn't a zone, it's a standard. It means I've got your back no matter what." He offers a meek smile.

I remember this. I'd said it to him. Sometime, somewhere. My heart swells in a baffling way.

"Thank you," I say.

Maybe I did need words.

o   o   o

WE'RE IN THE General's office not too long after sunrise. I should've known he'd expect more from me now that the sub-copies are gone. Luke is pacing, killing time for things to start. Mason is too busy asking if I'm alright. We're still waiting on the rest of the team.

When Lacy and Sonya arrive, they bombard me with soft hugs and kind words. The only one that leaves me alone is my father. Even Cateline expresses her condolences.

Clearly the person these guys know would have been more affected by Two's death. But I won't let them in. It's not important anymore. I'm not sure whether it's good or bad that I'm numb to it now. I'm not sure it matters either.

I've got a purpose; something to focus on. Two's death can't slow me down. It needs to mean something. It *all* needs to mean something.

"I'm fine," I assure for the eighth time, a bite to my words I hadn't intended. Glancing around the room, I meet the eyes of everyone on my team.

"Good to hear it," spouts the General as he enters, marching himself to his seat. "Have you thought about how best to serve the cause?"

Jump right in, I guess? I'm the one he's looking to, which has me simultaneously shrinking into myself and blooming an unfamiliar sense of pride in my chest. I don't want to be here, but I'm going to do this for Two, for Emma, for anyone else that can't fight for themselves.

"I suppose the first question is can we expect more subcopies?" My eyes scan the room to find Luke. The Reaver had mentioned as many as it takes. I'm wondering if Luke believes more are on the way. We never did dissect what her goal was.

Luke stutters, seemingly unprepared for me to ask him questions. "Uh, hm. Well, Ren said there were *plenty more*."

"Do you plan on toiling with that witch's *toys* forever?" The General asks, pulling my attention back to him. My being in the lead was all a façade. "I was hopeful my star rebel would be ready to do more than get lost in the past. It is the present we are hoping to change, is it not? You cannot film propaganda forever." His fingers twiddle in front of him as he releases a tired gruff.

Sarge stands from my feet to nudge my palm. *Toys?*

"There's another angle to consider," I admit, after way too long of a silence. I'm not sure I want to share the information, but it seems I have no choice.

"Please," the General says, bowing his head in invitation for me to continue. Ignoring the curious eyes boring into me from the rest of my team, I gather all my strength, ready to state my case.

"Two mentioned the Reaver's son. Do we know who that is?"

There's a steely determination in my tone. The General's eyes widen, his fingers tighten, and his shoulders tense. His face remains impassive. I spin around. "Anyone?"

Mason is the first to speak, of course. "Hm," he thinks aloud. "Throughout our extensive files, no son is mentioned."

Our. There it is again. He's pairing himself with *this place*. My chest is heavy.

Lacy and Sonya are talking amongst themselves, unable to believe the Reaver actually procreated with someone.

Luke chimes in, though I'm much more interested in the conversation the girls are having. "Ren never said anything to me." Then: "Are you sure Two wasn't... crazy?" He hesitates on the final word, knowing that it may upset me.

Sarge snaps in his direction, reading my emotions. "No," I proclaim. "It was real."

No one questions how I could be so sure. Thankfully they're learning.

It's Cateline's turn to speak. She argues she never saw anything when attempting to rifle through the previous subcopies. "They've also never mentioned such a thing, so could it truly be that important?"

My eyes ignite, piercing into her with hot anger.

My father steps in before my building frustration explodes. "Could we look through the files here?" he asks, his eyes passing by me and going directly to General Favager. "It could be beneficial to have a fresh set of eyes."

The General has been oddly quiet and ridiculously tense. He releases pressure in his muscles with a deep breath. "There is no need," he says, flippantly. "Mr. Baines is correct. There is no record of any spawn."

"We could look anyway," I say, arguing for my father. "Just in case."

The General tenses again, and my eyes flick to my father in a quick message.

"Is there something to hide?" my father questions, pressing.

Everyone in the room is silent, awaiting General Favager's response. Is the Service hiding something? Does the General know who the Reaver's son is?

"Miss Thorne," he says, changing subjects. "I'd like to see you more involved in the war effort. Like we discussed."

My jaw drops with a gasp. He wants more than propaganda. He wants a *true* leader. Someone who's willing to get in and get their hands dirty. He's told me the numbers, the amount of people still too scared to fight. He needs someone on the ground convincing them. I don't think I'm ready for that. I'd bought myself some time with the subcopies, but I need more. "I'm trying, sir," I argue. "Two said the Reaver's son is the answer."

He takes a deep breath, mulling over my words.

I scoff. "Why do you need people on your side, anyway? Don't you have an army? Just take the Reaver out already! She was there when I was rescued for fucks' sake!" My hand rushes to my mouth. *Did I say that?*

With eyes wide and teeth clenched, the General pushes up from his desk, staring into my soul. "That's right. I *rescued* you. And you will not speak out of turn again. As I have explained to you before, we need to know that there will not be counter resistance. We cannot risk falling further into ruin and losing more innocent lives. Believe it or not, there are still people within Western America that stand behind their shepherd." Spit flies from his lips. There's a thick vein poking out of his neck. He has mentioned that the current numbers suggest a third civil war will break out if we aren't careful. I've never understood, but I don't see how I can. It doesn't make sense how anyone could still be backing the Reaver.

"Please, just give us until the new year," I beg. I hate it. Why should I have to plead for this? To *him*?

General Favager's lip twitches with contempt. "We negotiated for you to spend time with your little side project. Time is of the essence. Time is something we cannot afford."

Something overtakes me, and I speak before I realize my mouth should have stayed shut. "Please," I implore. "Just 'til the new year. Then I'll have a better plan. One you'll love." The words fall out like garbage from a broken trash bag. This is stupid. *You're acting like a child, Amity.*

The General's jaw tenses, as do my fingers in Sarge's fur. I prepare myself for another round of arguments but am surprised when General Favager snaps, "Fine," at me. Then he adds, "But you will not use Service resources for this silly nonsense about a son. And you will make yourself available for the *extra* propaganda as I require of you."

"But..."

I don't get far at all. "That is my offer. Take it or leave it," he says. His body leans closer to mine, and through his teeth he says, "I recommend you take it."

A sigh escapes my lips. "Yes, sir."

Ugh. What ever happened to respecting the name?

This is becoming a mess.

CHAPTER TWENTY-FOUR ∘ AMITY

I DON'T BUY THIS BULLSHIT WITH THE GENERAL. HE'S HIDING something. Thankfully I know just the expert to help.

One week is all my father needed to carry out the mission I gave him. His digging skills have always been unmatched. Unfortunately, goody-good Mason hopped back into the General's pocket, more than likely scared of his outburst with me. He's refused to help us go behind his back. I haven't seen him much since. Both Luke and my father assured me they were with me until the end, so it's just us in on this now. I will bring Lacy and Sonya in when I know a bit more. But, like myself, they've been busy with the near-constant propaganda images the General has demanded I do.

My father has asked us to meet him on the surface. Why there, I can't say, but Sarge and I are the last to arrive.

"Her son is a well-guarded secret, I'll tell you that," my father says once Sarge and I close the distance. The light wind feels good against my clammy skin. Having access to the fresh air is something I won't ever take for granted. I can't imagine being stuck under the ground forever.

"Does that mean you didn't find anything?" Luke asks, his brow furrowed.

Pfft. He doesn't know my father. He's damn good at sleuthing. "He found something," I say, but my father's face has me falter at the last second. "You did find something, right?" Sarge cuddles closer to me, and the once-refreshing wind chills me to the bone instead.

My father sighs. "If we had access to the files here, I might be able to get you more, but..." He pauses for dramatic effect. "There's a source we could find in Western America."

"Then let's go," I blurt. Damn. I didn't mean to say that out loud. There needed to be better planning here. Something that would *actually* convince them.

"What?" my father questions.

"Why not write a letter for fucks sake!" Luke interjects.

My head swirls with a mix of too many emotions. "A letter?" I sigh. "That could take months. We need answers now. And if we can't use the files here, then this is our only option." I try to keep the desperation from slipping through. I might have failed.

"M," my father says, "Luke is right."

I suppose I knew everything would lead to this. Western America is where everything started, and it only makes sense that it would be calling us back to end it. It wasn't something that made itself clear until this very moment. "We should go back. Being here isn't serving us anymore." I've started in already, I've no choice now but to push full force.

Something isn't right here at Creyke Point. I don't know who to trust, and my little M might be out there somewhere, waiting for me to rescue her. No one seems to care about anything but the optics of a rebellion. What's that going to do? There's real potential here to stop the Reaver if we find her son.

My father's voice snaps me back to reality. "I know losing Two has been rough, but we can't up and leave." How dare my father say that.

A lump forms in the back of my throat, cutting off words. I don't even know what I'd say if I *could* speak. My fingers ball at my sides, and Sarge inches closer, nudging his nose into my fist.

"You don't remember it, but things have gotten worse there," Luke says, filling the silence I've created. "This place serves you by giving you somewhere to sleep, and as many meals as you can eat." His eyes are begging me to understand despite his tone.

And then my voice finds its way from the labyrinth of my knotted-up emotions. "Ugh!" I cry. Or something similar, but more guttural and less coherent.

My outburst stuns both my father and Luke, but Sarge stands watch so no one gets close. They keep their mouths shut. They simply wait for me to get my bearings again.

The world out here is peaceful, and seemingly far away from any problems. Standing in this field, it's almost like I could pretend we're not in the midst of a rebellion. Like this is all... normal. Cool air fills my nose with a deep breath. *Nothing* is normal. And it can't be if we don't figure this out.

"Listen," I start once my composure is more solid. "Everyone thinks I'm the key in all of this." I pause and a sigh escapes my lips while I search my brain for the correct words. Sarge pushes his body into me further, giving me the strength to continue. "But did anyone ask me what I wanted? No! You all sat around and projected what you *thought* I did."

My father's eyes dim a bit, but I can't stop now. Luke opens his mouth to say something, yet I press on before he can.

"Sure, I'm the key to the rebellion somehow. I may even be the key to the safety of the Service in some way. But the Reaver's son is the key to her downfall and the answer we've been waiting for." A surge of power spreads through me. I've never felt so in control of those around me. It's like they're hanging on every word, pulled forward by the promise of more. My soul hums with the strength, and Sarge even stands a bit taller and away from me, as if he's listening in awe, too. "You can ask me to think it over, you can tell me I'm being irrational over Two's death, but the fact is, the more you think about it, the more it will make sense." My shoulders square a bit at their stunned silence. "I will only wait so long before I'll do it myself."

My eyes dart back and forth between my father and Luke. My father isn't silent for long before saying, "I left you once. I will not make that mistake again." He nods, and I nod back, trying not to break into the biggest smile imaginable.

Luke is still studying me when I focus on him. There's a glimmer of an unfamiliar emotion in his eyes. A twitch of his lips and he says, "As stubborn as always," with a smirk.

My chest deflates with relief. "Alright," I say, reaching my fingers back to Sarge. "Then it's settled. We've got to fine tune things. Obviously, the General is our biggest obstacle..."

Shit. All of this sounded so great a few minutes ago. I completely forgot the General won't just let me off the hook for his rebellion plans. The wind picks up again, rustling my hair and raising bumps on my skin.

"Speaking of..." my father says.

Luke snaps to him. "What now?"

"Journalism was my first love." My father smiles seditiously, raising an eyebrow to me. The reference has me smiling, despite the sadness and uncertainty surrounding it. My mother used to tell my father she was the other woman when it came to his job. They always said it with a smile, though. They had me believing in true love, until one day my mother was gone. "You know Senator John Collins wife?"

Luke's body stiffens at the mention of his name. My father notices but ignores it. John Collins is the man who is credited with the merging of the Houses and the American Liberation Force. He is the reason the Reaver is in power. Sure, I'm not all that pleased with the man myself, but Luke's reaction is certainly confusing. What could the senator's wife have to do with any of this?

"Her maiden name?" my father continues. "Favager. She's Olivier's sister. Or she was." His eyes droop. "I think revenge is a motive here. His niece is not recorded to be dead, as far as I know."

"Your dad is cool as hell," Luke says aloud, but quietly to me. Not quietly enough, though.

My father chuckles. "Thank you, son," he says. "Baines was a nice guy and a big help, but his kid is getting lost in the politics here. I think everyone needs a kick in the ass. We'll need more people on our side."

"Great," I utter. "So, we've got two enemies?"

There's too much at play here. The H.P.S. has unclear intentions, but I suppose I can't place blame. I want to avenge Emma as well, if she really is dead. But what does that mean for the rebellion? For all the innocent people caught in the middle? Is it all just a smokescreen until they get what they want and then their promises fall apart?

"The enemy of my enemy is my friend," my father speaks. "We'll have to figure out who the bigger enemy is and not forget about the other."

After a bit more discussion, Luke leaves us to meet with Sam.

"Yes?" I say, once it's just me and my father. Well, and Sarge too. But he's quiet enough and won't share any secrets. And he's not expecting anything of me.

My father, however, is giving me that look.

He doesn't waste a second. "While we figure out what we're doing here, I can only hope you'll use the time to grieve." His tone is commanding yet understanding. He's in fatherly advice mode.

My eyes roll out of habit. "I'm fine." I think I've said this phrase too much lately.

"It's not always straightforward or linear." He pauses. "Take it from an expert."

Shit. Why'd he have to go there? My voice is small. "Things are better this way," I admit.

A deep breath releases from his nose, and he offers a sympathetic smile. "M," he says, placing his hands on my shoulders. "Don't hide all of your feelings because it's painful. Emotions are what prove we're alive."

He studies my face. I want to believe him. Maybe he's right. But grieving won't get me anywhere. Finding the Reaver's son will. "Yes," I agree, finally, "but I can't let it hold me back. There are more pressing things than grief."

CHAPTER TWENTY-FIVE ∘ LUKE

I FIND MYSELF LEAVING SAM ASLEEP IN THE BED AND HEADING to M. Something's been bothering me since our meeting earlier. I'd filled her father in on everything John Collins related. His relation to Ren, what she did to him. Mark will do his job of connecting it all somehow. I've no doubt he's hunched over his notes in his pod right this second despite it being two in the morning.

Stepping up to M's door has me hesitating for a moment. Can I truly believe she's still plagued by insomnia after all her terrors were erased?

There's not much time to question it because the door unlocks and I'm left looking like a dumbass with my fist in the air.

"I was wondering if you'd ever grow a pair and knock." She smiles at me, but it doesn't quite reach her stunning grey eyes.

Sarge must have alerted her of my presence. Damn smart-ass dog. I'm tired, but the smirk finds its way to my face naturally. "You're more than welcome to see my *pair* if you have doubts."

Her eyes hold a playful look as she steps aside, gesturing for me to enter. I do.

"What brings you here?" she questions. "It couldn't possibly be to show off your assets." She chuckles. She's not annoyed like I first thought she'd be. She's genuinely curious. That, in and of itself, helps my shoulders relax.

It's been a while since I've seen her playful side. Our plagued dinner all those nights ago still haunts me. It's why I almost decide to make up some story about coming here so I won't ruin it again. But I need to know, so I ask, "Why do you want this so bad?"

The M I knew before wanted revenge, but this is something different entirely. She's running, but not away from something like her father thinks. She's running toward something. After it. Trying desperately for it. There's only one thing she'd do that for.

Her eyes widen slightly, but then she covers the surprise. She's smart, she knows what I'm asking about. It's one of the many reasons I lov... well. It doesn't matter.

"I just... I think... No. I know it's..." She's stuttering helplessly, searching that brain of hers for something that'll make sense. Her fingers are locked into Sarge's fur. She's trying to hide it but is failing miserably. The nervous person in front of me is a far-cry from the confident leader that convinced us earlier.

"You're either trying to protect someone somehow, or you're trying to save someone," I state the fact. She may not have her memories, and she may be acting differently all around, but this much I know. It's who she is deep at her core. Lost experience won't take that away. There's someone she feels responsible for.

Her eyes are saucers. No hiding her emotions now.

"So, what did you remember?" I question. Or who? That's what I should've asked. Is there someone else out there she loves? Someone she found while we were apart? My knuckles tense against my thighs. If she tells me there's someone else, I'll lose it, I'll...

"Nothing," she says, looking away.

The filter of my brain slips. "Don't lie to me!" My voice raises a decibel or two. The anger always slithers out without warning. There wasn't even a chance to count this time.

Sarge places himself between us like a physical barrier.

"I'm not lying," she says, meeting my eye. Her jaw is tight. Great. Now I've pissed her off. Good job, Warin, you fuck.

"Then tell me," I plead, softening my voice. I know I told her it didn't matter, that our past was the past, but I can't lose her. Even if it's just as friends, I need her in my life.

She sighs, weighing her options. Then: "I don't think Emma is dead." She slumps to the ground, sitting crisscross on the floor with Sarge still in between us.

What? Why would she think that?

I get that she doesn't have those memories anymore, but she's smarter than this. She has to understand my dilemma here. Though I often try to block the image, it still creeps into my mind most days. Amity, screaming in the middle of Omphalos, holding a limp Emma. There's no other explanation. I carried her tiny, lifeless body hundreds of miles to bury her.

I suppose I've taken too long being silent, or maybe my damned face gave away too many emotions, because M sighs again before continuing. "This is why I only told Two about it." She rolls her eyes. "If the Reaver is able to make other women look like me, is it not possible she'd made another girl look like Emma?"

My brow furrows. The direction of her thoughts is dangerous. "Don't go down that road," I warn. I want this to be true, for her sake. But there's too much at stake. Too much of her soul on the line if it's not.

"It's possible though, right?" The hope in her eyes is not lost on me.

Only a monster would squander it. I hesitate, not wanting to piss her off, but not wanting to entertain the idea. My mouth opens, then closes again. Everything I say is usually the wrong thing, but I settle on: "I feel I would've known something."

"Things have changed since you were there." She rolls her eyes in classic Amity fashion for the third time now. This isn't good. The sudden surge of anger throws me off guard. "There are a lot of things you didn't know."

My jaw tenses, the vein of my neck bulging. I count to five and my body relaxes once more. I can't escalate her *or* these thoughts. My ass finds purchase on the ground, deciding that being closer to her level will somehow help. "This is a slippery slope for you to fall down," I start, my eyes silently begging her. "I understand the want for it to be true, but I saw how broken you were after her death, and I had to see it again when you learned what happened. I don't want to see it a third time."

I realize how selfish this sounds, but it makes sense; it's logical. There should be no argument, even if she wants to. Hope is dangerous. Hope is what keeps us in situations we shouldn't be in long past their expiration date. The hope that change is coming, the hope that if you pray hard enough it may come true. I've seen it plenty of times before in the Force from officers and commoners alike. It's why I hate myself so much for being hopeful about the memory extraction. We'd all taken it too far. Now look where we are...

And yet, as if I'd said nothing at all: "If only I could look at her body again," M says, completely ignoring my heart to heart. "I was in shock then, perhaps I missed the subtle differences of her face. Maybe I..."

"M!" I shout, interrupting her. "This is madness!" Is this why she wants to go back? To excavate and investigate? Shit.

Her nostrils flare, and she squares her shoulders. "No. Think about it. Why would she waste the potential? Even *if* it was all some elaborate scheme to get her son back, why would she throw away a good candidate? Why?" Her eyes pin me in place with her daggered glare. "For me? I won't believe that."

Her palm slaps the ground, and Sarge lowers himself, nudging to get beneath her hand. She's refusing to look in my direction and I take the few moments to study her side profile. The subtle dip of her nose, the plumpness of her lips. She's beautiful, and she's hurting.

The anger is driving her. I can't help but feel I've rubbed off on her somehow. She should be in the acceptance stage, but with the loss of her memories, she's regressed further into denial. What am I supposed to do?

M continues her rambling. Two confirmed Emma's importance. "She's an Exceptional, my exact opposite. So why kill her and not me?" She's trying to work things out in her head, and maybe it's best I let her do that. I can be a sounding board, right? "If I were the Reaver, I'd do *both*. I'd go for my son but also keep the Exceptional. And this is the way for that to happen."

She's begging to be heard. She wants this theory of hers to be validated. Can I do that? The devastation that followed Emma's death was too much for her. She cannot go through it again. But I'll have to do something, or I'll risk losing her in an entirely different way.

I sigh. "Did you plan on mentioning this to your father?" Not my original thought, but sometimes my brain doesn't really communicate well.

M's mouth turns down. "Not yet."

"Good," I say. "Don't. I'll help you look into this, but don't you dare break his heart all over again by giving him false hope."

Her face falls and her lips quiver slightly. "I..." she says, but her voice fades. Her red-rimmed eyes meet mine again. "I didn't think about that." Sarge snuggles into her lap, and she welcomes it.

I hate seeing her like this. But I'd hate to see her even worse if this theory turns out to be false and her father has to go through his grief again, too. The guilt would feel extra heavy for her then.

"If only we could get into the files here," she says, staring off as if I'm not in the room. Her tears are gone, her sniffles far away. She's back to being that determined spitfire.

"What?"

Her gaze flicks to me once more; her fingers slowly stroke Sarge's fur. "Don't you think General Favager had been a tad jumpy?" she asks. M wants to gather as much information as she can before curating a plan to present to Favager. Her father can only do so much without Service resources. Honestly, I'm surprised he got what he did with what little access he has.

"Yes," I agree. She knows we feel the same. Her father believes Favager was hiding his connection to all of this, but I don't know. M feels he wasn't acting right about Ren's son. I think both have merit, though none of it makes sense. But then, Ren having a son makes the least sense of all, so if I'm going to believe in that, I guess I really have no reason to think anything is impossible. Including, maybe, an Emma subcopy...

The only good thing about all of this is the fact that Mason Baines is as far as humanly possible from us.

She interrupts my thoughts when she asks, "Can you sneak in?"

The look in her eyes makes my heart flutter. I hate to disappoint her. "With my reputation around here? Pfft."

"Shit," she says. "I forgot." Sarge comes to the rescue and puts his chin into her palm.

Wait. That's it! "Sarge!" He looks up at me with happy eyes while M stares at me with confusion. "Sarge has the same clearance as Mason!"

Her eyes widen and she swallows hard. "What?"

"I told you, everyone loves the dog," I mutter, rolling my eyes.

o o o

"Do you really think this will work?" M's soft voice asks from the couch.

Will this work? I have no idea. We've been planning for the last week, and though Sarge is the smartest dog I know, there's still too much left up to chance.

I rest my hand on M's leg covered in a cozy blanket. She's been acting sick the last few days as to not raise suspicion for why Sarge is out on his own. "Fifty, fifty?" I say it like a question, smirking.

She playfully smacks my hand away. "It better, because I'm tired of being sick, and I'm tired of doing nothing." Her tone is more playful than the content.

"At least you play sick beautifully," I argue.

The first day Sarge was out roaming around, a Serviceman came to ask if everything was alright. M quickly pretended she was frightfully ill and had ordered Sarge to get some much-needed exercise. It took everything in me not to break out in a fit of laughter. Ever since then, she's been cooped up in her room receiving sick packages every day.

"Yeah," she says, reaching to grab a hot cup of tea from the side table. "I suppose I could get used to the pampering, too." She smiles and wraps her hands around the warm ceramic, sniffing in the scent of the herbs.

She's stunning, even in ratty old pajamas and messy hair.

"And you're sure Cateline won't turn on us?" Her eyes pop open again and she sets the teacup down once she takes a small sip.

Cateline is a loose end I wasn't expecting to have. We needed a device that would be able to retrieve the files on its own given Sarge's lack of opposable thumbs. After arguing for hours, M finally agreed to let me talk to Cateline. Surprisingly, she was on our side.

She spent a few days tinkering with an idea and then integrated her design into a collar for Sarge. All he has to do is press it to the correct spot and it should wirelessly extract the files we need completely undetected. Cateline Pierre is truly a genius.

But can she be trusted? Who knows. She agreed Favager is growing rather impatient for odd reasons. She didn't like the things she was being forced to do anymore.

I suck in a breath through my teeth. "Well, we won't have much longer before we find out, so..." I shrug, portraying nonchalance. If Cateline decides to turn us in, we're all screwed. But there's not much we can do about it now. She was a necessary addition to the plan. It was either that or somehow teach Sarge how to type.

M shakes her head. "This is wild."

Outlandish? Yes. But the most fun I've had in a while? Also yes. The only thing that could potentially ruin it were if...

A knock on the door pulls me from my thoughts, and M glances nervously at me from under her blanket. Sarge can't knock, so someone else is out there. Shit.

"I'll get it," I say, pushing myself up from the couch. Maybe Cateline really did turn us in. One hand reaches for the knob while the other rests on the weapon in my waistline. If we're busted, I won't go down without a fight.

Through a small crack in the door, I glance to see who could possibly be here. "Fuck," I utter under my breath, annoyed. I roll on the ball of my heel and walk back to the couch.

"Who is it?" M whispers, the blanket pulled up to just below her widened eyes.

I roll mine, slumping onto the couch at her feet.

"Well hello to you, too," Mason mumbles as he pushes through the entrance. M visibly melts beside me.

The door clicks behind him, and I roll my eyes again—clearly a bad habit I've formed. It's been so nice not having Mason around, yet here he is once again. I should've known. All good things must end.

"Oh," M says, "Mason. Don't come too close." She puts her fingers up in a cross and hides her face behind her knees. A fake cough and it almost breaks me.

"I had heard you were sick, but I thought maybe you'd be better by now," Mason says, his brow furrowing. Oh, for the love of...

I hold in my groan while M says, "Yeah, it's not fun." She's pinching her nose subtly with her knees to sound congested. This time, I can't hold in the laugh, but I recover by fake coughing and concealing my mouth with my hand to hide the smile.

Mason glances between us both. "Alright, well," he starts. "I wanted to check in on you. Cateline said you needed this computer, but she didn't want to get sick, so I offered."

He sets the laptop on the small dining table. I hadn't even realized he was holding it. This is good. This is reassurance that Cateline is on our side.

M realizes it, too. "Yes," she says, sighing with relief. "I've been so bored all cooped up in here. I wanted something to do." Her voice is so innocent. I don't know how she does it.

If Mason is skeptical, he's not showing it. Though, he does ask about Sarge. "I heard he's been all over lately."

When M opens her mouth to respond, a scratch at the door halts any previous answer she may have given. A shit-eating grin splits across her face. "He's right outside," she says.

I practically leap from my seat on the couch to let him in. He strolls happily through the threshold, wagging his tail. He doesn't stop to greet Mason or even acknowledge me. Sarge traipses straight to where M is sitting and hops right into her lap, soaking her in slobbery kisses.

In the commotion, Mason scoots closer to me by the door. "You and Amity are growing close again I see," he says, watching the view of M's sweet giggles like I am.

My brain takes in the words, trying to find any secret meaning or hidden malice. Sure, maybe we are. Despite the lack of memories and my dickish ways. I shrug. "Maybe," I say, non-committal.

Mason's gaze turns to me, and there's something in his eyes that I can't quite read. He doesn't say a word; he just nods and off he goes.

Weird.

After a few minutes—and a check to make sure Mason isn't outside waiting—I run to Sarge to retrieve the collar. M sits up, Sarge still in her lap.

"This is it," she says, excitement exuding from her. "I can't watch." She covers her eyes with her hands but then slides her fingers slightly to peek through.

I chuckle, turning to open the computer. The screen boots on immediately. There's a small pad on the left beneath the keyboard with a little x marked on it. Okay, I guess I set it here?

Once the collar touches the pad, files start popping up, down-loading, and storing themselves within the computer. He did it!

I whirl around to M. "Sarge did it!" I cheer. "We got what we need!"

A proud mama smile covers M's face as she pulls Sarge closer to her. "Yes! We did it!"

And just like that, I fall in love with Amity Thorne all over again.

CHAPTER TWENTY-SIX ○ AMITY

"I'VE GOT SOMETHING TO TELL YOU," I SAY AS SOON AS SARGE and I cross the threshold into Lacy's cabin in Compound One. Sweat drips down my neck. My chest aches with the weight of secrets. I need to lighten the load.

Time is dragging. Since Luke somehow pulled off teaching Sarge thievery, my father has been combing through extensive files, but he doesn't know what he's looking for. I've kept my promise and not told my father about my Emma theory, but I bet we'd be in Western America right now if he knew that his youngest daughter might be alive. He said it himself: he'd made that mistake once before.

Thankfully Lacy and Sonya have been filling up my time whenever General Favager hasn't monopolized it. Campaigns this, and preparations that. Memorizing scripts to rally those around us. What a waste when the *true* answer to the rebellion's success is the very thing we're not getting help with. If all the resources, the time, was being pumped into a search, we'd have her son already. We'd have the Reaver's head.

And that's why I need Lacy's ear. I just need to *talk*. I want to know that what I'm doing is the right thing. Bringing Mason into this would be beneficial to us, though he's kept his distance lately.

I can't talk to Luke about it because he hates Mason. Not that it matters anyway. I haven't even had the chance to ask him. Our schedules aren't lining up all that much since our successful heist.

"Me too!" Lacy cries, excitement bubbling through her.

Sarge leans into me. What could she possibly be this energized about? "You first." I ignore the worry that's latched onto my heart. In past experience, excitement often leads to disappointment.

"Sonya and I are engaged!" Lacy shares.

"Oh." I intend for my tone to be filled with enthusiasm, but my heart hurts and I think she's stupid for connecting herself to someone like this. Their relationship as it stands is already a lot for me to process. Tethering yourself for life to someone in our world? No way. I can't imagine.

Lacy's face falls, but only for a moment. "I'm sorry," she says. "I forgot about your memory issues for a second."

Excuse me? Sarge taps his toes on the ground, trying to gain my attention so I'll push my hand through his fur. "Present me would be happy?" Shit. "Not that I'm not happy for you... just... I... It's..." I'm groveling and my fingers do, in fact, trail through familiar, soft fur which pauses the clacking against the hardwood.

Lacy smiles. "You think I'm foolish." Okay, not the response I thought. She has always been an enigma; a passionate, amazing, mystery of a woman. *That* much I know to be true.

"Maybe a little." I offer a small smile in return, putting my thumb and forefinger together in sign.

A chuckle escapes from Lacy. "I'd like to think if you had your memories, you'd understand a bit more. But honestly, you'd probably still have the same reaction." At this, she laughs. Quiet, at first, then loud. It's contagious.

Sarge leaps around us as we both fall into laughter.

I hadn't realized how empty I've felt without my friend Grace. I miss her. I wish she didn't have to be gone. But it's amazing when you stop and think how time keeps ticking, how hearts mend. The hole in my chest just got a little bit more filled in.

Lacy trails a finger beneath her eye, wiping away joy-filled tears. "You've gotten yourself into some pretty sticky situations when it comes to love," she points out, once the laughter fully subsides. "You don't choose who you love, you can only choose whether to accept it easily or not."

Sarge has laid beside us, and I instinctively run my fingers through his fur once more. The good mood of the last few minutes is wavering now. "Do you truly believe that?" I question.

Is love uncontrollable? Surely not. Familial love, maybe. That's a part of you somehow. But romantic? No. After my mother and Grace, I let go of Jeremey; of the idea of a love-filled future. I *chose* to push everyone out.

And I chose to let them back in, apparently. Foolishly enough. It has to be a choice. Though, it's possible that without my memories I'm a bit naïve.

"I really do," Lacy shares. "Some things are set in stone from the moment our heart beats for the first time."

"Sounds like something Abby would say," I point out, dismissively.

Lacy's eyes widen.

"What?" I question, anxiety skyrocketing. All I said was that it sounded like something Abby would spew to us, how is that.... Oh. "Is that something she would say?" I question, for confirmation. My eyebrows pull in. I don't know why I felt the need to say it. I don't know how I could possibly know it would be an Abby saying unless...

"Yes!" Lacy smiles, a complete juxtaposition from how I'm feeling. Heat pools beneath my flesh. "She said it to both of us one night while keeping watch over our camp. You were arguing about fate."

I... I remembered. But... not. It was subconscious, like the knowledge was there, but I didn't have to search for it. What does this mean? My palms grow sweaty. Too many different thoughts swirl around in my head, making it hard to concentrate on what Lacy is saying.

Gaining my memories back would help with finding out who the Reaver's son is. It would help me defeat her and save everyone from a future with her as their leader. But what if I lose my objectivity? What if I somehow miss out on the clues I should've picked up on in the first place?

"What's the matter?" Lacy asks, tearing me from my rapid thoughts.

"I..." No. I won't tell her about Emma. But I do need her advice on our plan. "I don't know how, but... we're planning on going back."

The next several minutes are spent explaining everything that's been going on. From our secret meeting after General Favager, to the successful heist of H.P.S. files. I also apologize profusely for not telling her sooner. We talk about the revenge theory, and how Mason is still in the dark about all of this as well.

When I've finished, Lacy says, "I'm in." Then she takes a second and adds, "I'll have to get married first, but after that I'm ready!"

Lacy is backing me like it's nothing. Like nothing could possibly be more clear. "You'd go with us after getting married?" It's unbelievable. Who knows what lies in wait for us there.

"We've been through one adventure before, what's another?"

"You're..." *Going to feel on edge to keep Sonya safe,* is what I want to say. I don't necessarily want them to go either. If something happens to them, I'd... I can't think about it. "It's reckless," I admit. Not just for her, or Sonya. For everyone.

"As cautious as you are, you seem to invite recklessness." She laughs. "We're going. Sonya and I can have a proper Western America honeymoon."

Lacy is even more stubborn than I tend to be. Though I want to strangle her right now for demanding she go with me, it also fills me up. I smile at her, reaching for her hand. It's not hard to see why I let her in. I miss Grace so much. It's not fair that she's not here; that she's been gone longer than I remember. Grace would have loved Lacy, and vice versa.

"Would you come with me to tell Mason?" I ask, gently squeezing her fingers in mine.

Why am I so nervous? Probably because I'm going behind my father and Luke—potentially risking our plan—for a weak reason I can't even quite place yet. I've been telling myself it's because he knows the General the best out of all of us. There's not much time left to present a plan that General Favager will agree to that gives us the freedom to explore my theory without him knowing. If Mason can help formulate something, knowing how the General is, then everyone gets what they want.

But if Mason turns his back like he did on me before, if he decides to tell the General my intentions don't align with his, then it will be the end. I'll be stuck as a pawn in what feels like a never-ending game.

Lacy nods, offering me assurance with her smile. "Of course," she says. "Let's go."

It's not long until Mason finds us. I'd asked him to meet in the center of H.P.S. headquarters, under the statue of Fortana. She's the protector of the Service, embodying strength and good fortune. Her wings extend the length of the room and every time I pass, I make sure to say some words to her.

And that's basically all I've been doing while we've waited. Lacy took the time to explain to me that Mason and I are friends; that he cares about me and will understand. But something is telling me it's not true.

"Odd choice for a meeting, don't you think?" Mason questions as he gets closer.

"There's comfort in Fortana's shadow," I admit. What I'm not saying is that I'm seeking her protection and guidance, no matter how ridiculous it seems. Sarge is sitting alert at my feet. Somehow, one protector isn't enough right now.

"I've got to say, I was surprised when you summoned me," he says, rubbing the back of his neck with his palm. "You've definitely piqued my curiosity."

My fingers rake through Sarge's fur, the words get stuck in my throat. I don't understand the nerves. Something deep within me is worried. Worried Mason will reject the plan, tell me I'm crazy, talk me out of it. Like he's done before. Right? *Has he done that before?*

"I..." My voice fades before it ever really projects. "Well."

Fuck! This is embarrassing. Lacy's reassuring grasp has one of my hands, and Sarge occupies the other. What an odd sight this must be for the occasional passerby. A heap of flesh and nerves below the tough and strong symbol of the exact opposite.

"Well, aha," I repeat, stammering nervously. Lacy tightens her grip, and the words that slip from my lips are not something I expect. "Uh... Lacy and Sonya are getting married!"

Shit. Why did I say that?

Mason is momentarily shocked, but he shares his congratulations. Meanwhile, Lacy removes her hand to lightly smack my arm.

"Wha..." She makes a disapproving groan sound. "No. Well, yes.

But we're going to Western America," Lacy states. She shoots me a sideways glare and I offer her an apologetic shrug in return. Sarge leans over to give her a single kiss, which helps to ease the tension.

Mason's eyes widen. Not slightly—not like usual when he's trying to hide his true feelings. No. This isn't his political demeanor. This is him. And he's shocked. "You..." he stutters. "You... you're what? Why would you want to get married there?"

Lacy scoffs. "What? No, you dingus. That's not why we're going!" She presses her fingers to her skull in agitation. "J'y crois pas," she utters beneath her breath, shaking her head.

Gathering my courage, I find the strength to push forward. "I need to find the Reaver's son and the only source we found is somewhere hidden there," I say. "So we're going."

My one hand is an iron grip on Lacy's once more, and the other tightens into Sarge's scruff. Mason is going to unleash. Warning bells are sounding throughout my skull.

"You couldn't *possibly* think this is a good idea," he says, accusatorily. "And marriage? Right now?"

Heat reddens my cheeks. "It's not about good or bad," I argue, unable to bite my tongue. "It's the only option we have. And who are you, her father?" Woah. I hadn't planned for the attitude.

Before Mason opens his mouth to debate further, Lacy interjects. "Amity is certain this is what needs to happen, and I'm with her." She smiles, pulling me closer and linking arms. "And yes. I'm getting married. Deal with it."

Tears spring to my eyes, unwelcome. It's been too long since I've had a friend like Grace. Wiping the water from my face, I return my gaze to Mason. "My father and Luke are also on board," I say. "I'd like it if you were, too."

Maybe it's some unknown emotion swirling to the forefront of my brain, or maybe it's my father's warning that we need more people on our side, but I do want Mason in on this. I can't explain it, but it's been empty without him. Besides, his clearance gains us access to anything and everything in Headquarters if he'll help...

Mason's hand finds the back of his neck again. A long sigh escapes him. "The two of you, sheesh," he says, chuckling to himself and shaking his head. "What is it you need from me?" he asks, his political mask back in place. "I never wanted to step foot in that god-forsaken country ever again." His body tenses with the words.

In my haste to prove my theory correct, I'd overlooked the fact that Mason lost his entire life—his family—while there. Here at H.P.S. Headquarters, he can reinvent himself; become new. If he goes back to Western America, he'd have to confront the same demons I will. Only mine are dampened from the memory loss.

Hesitation swirls in my gut, but I'm not asking him to go with me. I've just asked him to be on board with the idea. "I need a plan the General will love," I request. "Oh, and get me a call with the Reaver if you can," I add at the last second. An interesting idea has popped into my head.

o o o

A FEW DAYS later and Mason calls for me.

"Good news?" I ask, walking to meet him beneath Fortana. Sarge keeps his body relaxed and his tail wags lazily as we approach. I'm inclined to believe Mason is in an okay mood, which means success. *Hopefully.*

"We're lucky enough to gain access to Madame Keres for a short time," Mason confirms. "Be smart in getting whatever it is you're looking for." His warning is unmistakable. General Favager doesn't know.

I'm fairly certain this falls under *service resources*, which it was made clear we're not to use. The fact that Mason delivered means he's on our side. *My* side. A sigh of relief escapes me.

Then Mason speaks again. "There's something else. The H.P.S. is utilizing land to the east of the Rockies in Western America."

Disbelief scatters across my features. That land is considered uninhabitable since the Undoing—the cataclysmic natural disaster that changed the landscape *and* the trajectory of everyone's lives. Expeditions were scheduled, but after the fourth group of explorers went missing with no contact, they closed the land off. Then the war broke out, and everyone seemingly forgot that our map used to be a lot wider.

Mason continues. "General Favager has been wanting to send you to the camps there as a figurehead. At first, I told him you weren't ready, and then you asked for time here. But this may be your ticket out."

"Ticket out of where?" Shit.

Luke.

Whirling around, my father and Luke come into view. I'd been so focused with Mason, I forgot we were in the middle of Head-quarters where others can hear us. See us.

"Uh..." Fuck. It's been too long since I've seen Luke. The slight flutter in my chest at being so close has nerves jumbling in my stomach. Sarge licks my palm, and I swear it sizzles against the heat of my skin. *Why am I like this?* Ugh. "Well, uhm. Mason was telling me about the Undoing land," I say, chuckling nervously like an idiot. "The Service is apparently using that space for rebels."

Neither my father nor Luke show surprise. Damn. They know. They must have seen it in the files.

"Oh," I say, speaking my realization aloud. "You already...

knew... that. Ha." I'm a bumbling fool. Why does being around Luke disarm me like this? I don't like it.

My father offers an understanding smile. "We were on our way to tell you," he says.

Mason chimes back in now. "Good! Everyone is thinking the same thing."

"He knows?" Luke questions before I'm able to process. Out of my peripheral, he's staring at me intensely. Sarge vibrates against my leg as he releases a low growl, ready to strike if necessary.

"Of course," I hiss, ignoring the expression on Luke's face. But my head is whirring. I couldn't ask before with the interruption, but now I ask, "What would I be doing?"

My mouth dries. The General wants me to convince people to join our cause. I don't want to be responsible for anyone. Being present, showing the rebels I'm ready to drop it all for them like I had for Emma, sure. Makes sense. But the pressure weighs on me. Sarge's fur is soft in my hands. Focusing on that, it keeps the drowning thoughts from pulling me under.

What if they see me as a fraud? What if we lose our chance at finding the Reaver's son? What if we simply *lose*?

"I think it's as straightforward as making an appearance," Mason assures. "Selling them propaganda."

"It's never as straightforward as that!" Luke spits, allowing his anger to take over.

My father holds up a hand to steady Luke, warning him to simmer.

Sarge is pushing into me with his whole weight, and I'm putting all of my energy into keeping us both upright. Thankfully I'm close enough to Fortana to utilize her.

Mason closes his eyes for a moment, taking a deep breath before speaking. "Most people have identified with Amity from last year and the propaganda sent out. They are fighting for her justice, as well as Emma's. But also, any past, present, or future families like them."

"The Amiteers," I say, to no one in particular. All at once it makes sense why the General wants me. I thought he created the rebellion, needed a face for it, and took mine. But the truth is, *I* created it. Not on purpose, but my actions led to a snowball effect, and now here we are. It started with *me*.

"Yes," Mason continues. "They sympathize with the Thorne story. The people of the H.P.S. believe in justice for all. It's their creed: pour notre justice." Hm. For the justice of us. I've grown extremely familiar with this saying. "The Amiteers embody that, but it's not necessarily a sense of justice that drives them. It's Amity's courage and bravery in the face of evil that has spoken to them."

My father adds, "Seeing her in the thick of it again would raise spirits, further encouraging the rebels."

Mason nods. "Right. General Favager believes it will help pave the way to success."

It may help, but the Reaver's son is who we need. "There's only one person that will secure a win. And it's not me," I say.

"This is your ticket to find him," Mason says, his blue eyes begging me to understand. "Mold your plan around it." They soften when I nod. "Alright, you ready?"

Mason watches me expectantly, and it takes me longer than I'd like to admit to realize what he's asking. "Oh, right. Yes." I almost forgot what we're actually doing here.

"Where are you kids headed?" my father probes.

Mason tells him we've got a date with the devil.

"You didn't tell me you were trying to contact Ren," Luke whispers so only my ears hear it. It's the first thing he's said since his outburst, which is unusual. "You haven't told me a lot of things, apparently." His jaw tenses.

I shrug. "Didn't realize I had to report to you," I say, then mentally smack myself. *Why are you pushing him away, Amity?*

His muscles tighten for a few seconds. Five. That's all.

I've seen such control before on only one other. And I'm about to face her again.

Shit. Maybe talking to Luke would've been smart. My father, too. They know more about interrogation and the subject than I do. Maybe Luke is right... I'm acting like a kid again. Damn memory.

"You want information?" my father confirms.

I nod. He thinks it's about her child, but really I want to know about his. Maybe the Reaver will give me a clue as to whether I'm right about Emma being alive. With the integration of memories without my knowledge, I'm worried I won't have a solid hold on my theory for much longer. The only good thing that could come from this, though, is hopefully my knowledge of who this son is makes itself known.

"You're going to ask about her son?" Luke questions, irritated.

"Not directly," I answer. I learned a few things over the years from my father. We can't ask her about her son; we need to ask about her life. See how she reacts, what she tries to hide. She'll give clues indirectly.

My father puts in his two cents again. "Asking directly would put her on the defensive, and alert her of our plans," he clarifies. "You have to be strategic."

Sweat pools in places I wish it wouldn't. "Do you have a few?" I ask. "I could use your help." This should've been the plan all along. *Damn it, Amity. You're being stupid.*

My father nods immediately, physically unable to turn down

the chance at a juicy interview. Luke keeps his face plain, giving nothing away. His eyes say everything I need to know, though. That unfamiliar sizzle in my chest rises at the power I feel. I'm in charge. A smile slowly spreads across my face. "Let's do this."

With the adrenaline shot still burning in my veins, it's eons before the Reaver's smug face is plastered against the back wall of a large empty room in the middle of Headquarters. Her hair is perfectly tucked at her shoulders like always, her eyes alight with a teasing glee. She's definitely ready to play.

"To what do I owe this unexpected correspondence?" she asks, her lips molded into an impish smirk. It's familiar in a way I can't quite put my finger on.

"We were getting lonely," I toy. "Wanted a little chat." My teeth clack together with the final letter.

"I could imagine loneliness is inevitable for your kind," she surmises. "You were offered help, you know." Her eyes darken.

Pfft. My attitude moves to the tip of my tongue. "Imprisonment is what you call *help*?" I question. The others have sunk into the background. Even Sarge, who is pressed against the back of my legs, feels far away. It's just the Reaver and I here.

"Might I remind you," she snaps, not missing a beat, "that *you* came to *me*, my dear."

Ugh. Fuck this. How can I redirect the conversation to her and keep it there? We'll get nowhere if I let my teenaged angst carry us.

"You make it seem like I had a choice," I scoff, rolling my eyes.

The Reaver keeps her smirk, studying me. "Everyone has a choice," she lilts.

"Yeah," I spit. "The *illusion* of one, maybe."

She's silent now. Her pupils dart around subtly, studying the others in the room over me. She breathes in deeply before continuing. "In our short time together, I'd learned a lot about you," she toys.

"Avoiding the truth, are we?" My brow raises in curiosity. I have to get under her skin somehow.

"You never could hold your tongue, could you?" She speaks as though this is a confirmation for her, and the vein of her forehead makes an appearance for a few seconds. "You think you'd show more respect to the person whose *choice* allowed you to live."

At this, a laugh rushes past my lips. "What life is this?" I argue. "What life do you think it is for the *commoners* you despise so much?" Madame Keres is a menace masquerading as a savior. "Do you truly believe your *choices* have been admirable?"

The Reaver huffs, or something resembling one. "There is hardly room for regret in this life." An unfamiliar emotion sweeps across her pupils.

Is this my way in?

From what little memory I've gained, it seems she was looking for her son, and I was the one who knew where to find him. But she has my memories. So the question is, is she still looking? And how did she lose him in the first place?

"Then tell me, *Madame*," I sneer. "What is there *room* for, as you put it?" Sarge is still behind my legs, but the pressure isn't as much now. I take a step forward, puffing my chest in defiance.

The Reaver is bored. She sighs, picking something from her sharp teeth. "Are you finished?" she questions. "If anyone should like to share their regret, perhaps you could tell me about *your* choices."

Fuck. Sarge pushes into the back of my legs again, and I sag into him slightly.

"Better yet," she continues, flipping her hand through the air. "Perhaps I'll share them *for* you. Wouldn't that be fun?"

"We have very different definitions of fun," I mutter.

"You claim to be on the right side, but you're selfish," she spits, ignoring my comment. "You don't care about anyone; you only care about yourself. *That's* what I've learned about you, that's..."

Her voice fades as my mind disconnects. I can't help the sharp intake of breath at her words. Sarge moves closer, but it doesn't stop my brain from ripping into a memory. *The Reaver's breath is hot on my ear as she whispers, "You're a selfish little girl deep down."*

A shiver rips through my spine as I'm brought back to reality. "Struck a nerve, did I?" The Reaver questions, smirking. I have no idea what else she's said.

"N... no," I stutter. "I..." How did this get derailed so quickly?

"Enough, Ren," Luke says from behind me. *Great, now I'm weak.*

"Oh, please," she scoffs, dismissing him. "This one is many things, but she's not fragile. She. Doesn't. Need. You." The Reaver annunciates every word perfectly. The audible gasp from Luke behind me is enough to get me to peek. His face is getting a deeper shade of red the longer we stand here.

"Fuck you," Luke spits.

"Always with the curses," she says. "I don't have all day, so how about you tell me what this is really about? Would you like more information about your favorite subcopy, by chance?" Her pupils dance with amusement. I want to throw up and jump through the screen to stab her in the eyes all at once.

"I..." Fuck, I didn't expect this. Everything's all turned around.

"This is why I thought you'd be more grateful," she derides. "You know how easy it is to lose. How many times do you have to go through it before you learn?"

What can I say? The words clog in my throat, choking me. I didn't want to think of Two like this. It was easy for me to forget that she was a creation of the Reaver. But now, it's clear she was created on purpose to get close to me, to make me lose all over again.

"What am I supposed to learn? I already know you're a deranged bitch. Killing more people isn't going to change anything." *Insulting her won't either, Amity.*

"Careful, my dear," she says. "It's best you stay on my good side. I could've killed your friends that day you stormed my precious Omphalos, but I didn't. Don't tempt me." The Reaver's eyes darken once more, as does her voice.

When I should bite my tongue, I find my attitude ripping through. "I may not remember everything from the past, but I remember some. You blamed me for what happened with my sister. That's denial. You're not gracious, you're delusional." My tone is patronizing, and I realize how juvenile I sound, yet that doesn't stop me from toying with her further. "You don't want to take any responsibility because that would mean *you're* the problem with society, not the rest of us."

The Reaver chuckles as my insults bounce right off her thick skin. "Actions have consequences, my dear. Yet another thing you haven't learned." She smirks. "Such a child."

"I'd think you'd care more," I scoff. "About children, I mean. But you just can't seem to keep them with you, can you?" I goad. "Everyone leaves you. You can't be *that* gracious." The children of the facility rebelled against her, and perhaps that's how she lost her child as well. There's no reason to believe that's what happened, but the feeling in my chest is strong, though unclear. She was abandoned. I have to play on that.

Her eyes burn with a sense of amusement tinged with something much darker, more sinister. "Your choices have led to nothing but chaos. And still you live," she spits. "I let you plague this earth, Tainted beyond repair. *My* choice to do so has not benefitted our community. *That* is gracious," she sneers. Her eyes flick to the others behind me, like she's telling everyone what a mistake I am. When her gaze returns, she continues. "But since you've still not had enough, I will continue to take, and take, until there is *nothing* left."

My mouth pops open in shock. Her sudden change from playful to angry is like the flip of a switch.

"I will not rest until I have desecrated your very essence. First your sister, then your memories, and now your precious subcopy friend." She laughs. "How does it feel to always be one step behind? To lose again at my hand?"

My blood boils. How dare she? Fuck. *Take a deep breath, Amity. Focus.* This is the pinnacle of the argument. She's heightened, which means this is when she'll slip. I just have to get under her skin, somehow. Disarm her further, in a way she won't be expecting.

Unfortunately, that means I may have to break a promise...

"Except Emma isn't gone, is she?" I question.

The gasps behind me don't pull my eyes from the Reaver. Luke can handle them. This is for me and the evil bitch in front of me.

Her mood once again flips, giving me whiplash. She chuckles. "Oh, dear." She mock wipes a tear from her eye. "Has your memory evaded you again?" These sudden changes of emotion are setting me off balance, but my father's words are busting through my skull. *You have to be strategic.* I push on, ignoring the anger flowing through my veins.

"Where is she?" My gaze is steady. Mouth smooth, determined.

When the Reaver comes to terms with the fact that I'm utterly serious, her face grows dark. Yet, nothing draws from her lips.

"Your silence speaks volumes, Ren." My eyes are molded daggers; my words are a bullet to the chest. I've got her.

The Reaver scoffs. "She's gone," she spits, jumping out of her silence in an attempt to cover her tracks. "Cold and lifeless since your little stunt last year."

"Is she?" I question. My voice has never been so full of malice. "Because if you want your son, you'll give me Emma."

Shit! I didn't mean to say that. There's nothing about this that was strategic. My knees buckle slightly, but Sarge is here to catch me.

The Reaver's eyes flare, then settle. Her features mold back into their playful, relaxed state. Fuck. What have I done? "I know you, stupid girl. You wouldn't trade one for the other."

The screen goes dark and my mind races through a million possibilities. Her son isn't just someone I know. It's someone I'm *close* to. Someone I feel responsible for.

Quickly, I turn to my father. "Tell me everything you know."

CHAPTER TWENTY-SEVEN ∘ LUKE

SAM IS TOYING WITH SOMETHING ON THE BED WHEN I FINALLY
return. I couldn't risk coming right away for fear of my temper
getting the best of me. But now I'm not sure how long Sam has
been waiting.

"How'd it go?" he says, looking up as I enter the pod.

M had pulled us all aside after our conversation with Ren. She
is certain the kid is someone she knows. I'm pissed she broke her
promise and told her father about Emma, and I was hoping to
keep her in check about everything Ren said. It was all a game, I'm
sure. All some sick, twisted, bullshit to trip us up and torture us.
Somehow it became gang-up-on-Warin time.

Sam's optimism and continued support is precisely why I've
been shutting him out, too. Sounds backwards, I know, but I don't
deserve his kindness. Somehow it makes me feel even more mon-
ster-ish if I accept it. But worse than that, I knew if I showed up
after whatever the hell happened earlier with M, it would have
made things worse.

"Not good," I answer honestly, slumping onto the floor with my
back against the door.

His brow furrows at my words. "What happened?"

I really don't want to talk about it, yet I can't help but feel that

Sam needs this. I don't know why. So I say, "Amity has some senseless ideas and I went too far trying to bring her back to reality."

"What's her idea?" he asks immediately.

Gah. Damn kids. I haven't told him anything about what's been
going on. Only the absolutely necessary things. My heart clenches
in a way that makes me wince. I never wanted to tell him about
the Western America plan. I've been hoping M would change her
mind, or somehow abandon the idea because of new, better information. Yet here we are. That's what I get for letting hope in.
Fuck.

"She wants to go back to Western America."

Sam's sharp intake of breath sends shivers through me. The
rigidity of his posture is clear. We're both acutely aware of the
atrocities that happen on that damned soil. "She does?" he asks,
carefully. "Why?"

I contemplate revealing M's true intentions. Now that the cat's
out of the bag to everyone else, there's no harm in sharing it further. Fuck it. "Amity believes that her sister, Emma, is still alive.
And she believes we can get her if we get to Re... I mean... the
Headmistress's son."

His eyes are wide. "That's..." he starts. "That's a lot," is what he
settles on. His forefinger and thumb meet his chin in thought.
His brow furrows deep. "A son?"

"Yeah." I sigh. It really is a lot. And if I'm being honest, talking
to someone about it feels good.

Sam surprises me with his next question. "You don't want to
go?"

"No, of course not! It's a dangerous waste in my opinion." Being
there for M is about the only thing that makes it worthwhile. But
deciding to go back to that hell hole on a whim? No.

After a silent moment stretches between us in an awkward way,

I glance in Sam's direction. His lips are downturned and tense, the way they do when his thoughts are so deep that they're sucking him in.

When he notices me watching, he snaps out of it. "That doesn't sound like you at all," he points out.

"Whatever," I grumble, twisting away from him. Exhaustion is suddenly too present in me to deal with his questions. He's just a kid. What does he know? Why did I think talking would help, anyway?

"No," Sam states, finite. My head snaps to him. "You can't push me away like this whenever you're mad. And you've been avoiding Amity, too." His confidence is admirable, yet surprising, and a little annoying; inconvenient. He stares me down until I nod my head in resignation. "You tried so hard to get Amity's memories back. Why don't you go get them from the source?"

My mouth pops open to argue, but then my brows pull together as the thought settles in my brain. Sam doesn't know that I gave up on that endeavor. That in the process of trying to regain M's past, I was losing her in the present. But he continues.

"You don't back down from a challenge. You embrace it, head on. And you *don't* give up. At least, not the Luke that I know." His fist slams into the palm of his hand to drive the point home and an unfamiliar feeling bubbles into my chest. I actually have to hold back my laughter. Sam's a great kid. One I'm definitely undeserving of knowing.

And he's also right.

"When did you become such a hard ass?" I question, a smirk rolling onto my face.

"I guess it rubbed off on me, somewhere," he says, chuckling.

"Well, I'm glad it did," I say after a few minutes of laughter. "You're pretty smart, you know that?"

"Yeah, of course." Sam smiles. "You're just late to the party."

Sam and I spend the rest of the day together, keeping ourselves occupied with various activities until I'm summoned into a meeting. At least this go around, there's a pep in my step.

Sam has given me a renewed sense of self. There's no reason I can't be here for present M, while also getting back to the original goal. She may not want the memories now, but perhaps in the future she might. I know I've told her friendship is all I need, but if there's even a sliver of a chance she'll want to remember our past, I'm going to take it.

My mood only falters slightly when my eyes finally meet M's across the round table. I'm momentarily reminded of all the things I've done to hurt her. But now we're going to fix it. Like Sam said. I can't keep pushing her away and expecting everything to be okay.

"I'm sure everyone's minds are still bursting from earlier," Mason starts the second Lacy plops herself at the table. "But the question remains. Does everyone still want to go to Western America?"

M jumps in right away "Why wouldn't we?" she questions, confused. Her concern is palpable.

Of course M still wants to go. What a dumb question to ask. And now I have a good reason to go as well. Sam is definitely onto something. M's memories should be hidden in the Brain. If we go straight to the source, we could pull them from there. With all the subcopies gone, and no reason to believe any more are coming, this is the best option. Well, it's something at least. But Mark steps in before I can.

"It couldn't hurt to still go. If M believes the son is the Reaver's downfall, then I want to be there when she breaks." Mark's pain shoots across the table. He's kept any mention of his youngest daughter out of it. Yet, the curiosity is there, hidden beneath every word. The what if. I know that pain well.

"Is there a rush?" Lacy questions. Why is she here? Would she even be going with us? She's got a life here now. A stunning girlfriend, a fulfilling job working with the other kids in Mama June's custody. Would she throw all of that away to follow us into hell once again?

"General Favager only granted me until the new year," M reminds everyone. "He's been impatient with me sitting around for a while now."

The General. My eyes find M's at the mention of him. We know what Mason doesn't. Favager is driven by revenge, and M is simply a pawn in his game. He can get what he wants by using her. Fuck that guy, though. He's been sitting on his ass, too.

"Then let's not keep him waiting," Lacy replies. Shit. So she *is* willing to throw it all away.

"And what happens if Madame Keres' son is someone close to us? What then? Do we come back to get them?" Mason questions. He's playing devil's advocate which is usually my job. And though I dislike him with every fiber of my being, he brings up a good point that I'd been too distracted to think about. We have no plan for what we'll do when we actually find Ren's son. *If* we do.

"I've been thinking about that," M admits. "It's someone close to me, I'm sure of it. Which means they'd be in Western America already. Because you guys are the only ones I'm close to here."

As always, M is reaching. Like she's trying to put a square peg in a round hole, but she's doing it with all her might.

"Luke, you've been awfully quiet." M's voice is small, but her words speak loudly to me as they pull me from my thoughts. She wants to hear my opinion. Even after everything that's happened.

Here goes... "I know what you believe, but it's possible she's playing on your sense of responsibility to others. You would sacrifice yourself for almost anyone." It's true. M is not the selfish commoner Ren painted her to be. She's the most selfless human being I know. She doesn't care about her own heartbreak, as long as it means she could save others. It's one of the many things I love about her. Fuck. I shake my head to empty the thoughts, pushing myself back on track. "But I still think it's worth it to get your memory back. At least we can go straight to the place they're being held in this case." I shrug.

Mason's shrill tone cuts in, pulling me from M, but not before catching the shock that litters her face. "This is ten times more dangerous than it was ever supposed to be. You were finding *a source*. Now you're talking about storming the devil's lair!" Mason is exasperated. Good. This is better than expected. Yet I can't help but feel I've somehow disappointed M. I should look into it further. Her theories I mean. Maybe if I spoke to Ren alone, I could get a better read. It may also help me gain my own information about her lost memories.

But if M is right, that means someone close to her is actually related to that evil witch. This thought leaves a strange taste in my mouth.

The conversation has continued on without me, and Mason's voice pulls me into the present once more. "General Favager is adamant on M's appearance with the rebels. You won't even need a truly solid plan for him to send you over there. But you may be detained if what you're trying isn't discreet. You may be able to get away with a loose plan here, but you need a more solid form once back in Hell."

Screw Favager and his rules.

"My goal was always to see if Emma is alive. I just kept it to myself." Her eyes flare in a quick glance in my direction. "Whatever that entails, I'm doing." M's timbre is solid. She's not backing down. Stubborn as ever.

"Sonya and I will join you," Lacy mentions. "After the wedding," she adds, like a reminder.

Wedding? What wedding? Have they discussed this before? Have I truly been this far gone from M—from everyone—lately that I don't know any of what's happening with them?

"You really don't..." M says but gets cut off by Lacy.

"No. No. Another chance at potentially saving Emma? I'm in. I was in before, and now more than ever. What else are friends for?" M smiles meekly at Lacy.

Suddenly my good mood from earlier is soured. Lacy and Sonya's ceremony is apparently in a few days. I'll have to talk to Ren as soon as possible. That means asking for a favor from my least favorite person.

"So it's settled." Mason sighs. "We'll leave the day after the wedding."

CHAPTER TWENTY-EIGHT ∘ LUKE

WE'RE ALL SET TO BREAK GROUND IN THE UNDOING LAND THE day after tomorrow. Favager is ecstatic about M's *plan* to be the figurehead, like Mason said he would. M really laid it on thick for him, though, and he ate it all up.

I press the button in front of me, ringing Ren another time. The call fails once again, but I immediately send out another signal. By the eighth time, someone finally picks up. He's a scrawny, meek man. Buff by normal standards, yet his countenance proves him weak.

"Marcus," I say, flashing him a smirk. "Look at you, moving up the ladder now that I'm gone."

Marcus Giles shrivels into himself. His cheeks turn pink. He clears his throat before eliciting a response. "Mr. Warin." He nods, formally. "What an unexpected surprise."

His words are carefully chosen. Marcus's disdain for me has always been clear. It's seemed to triple since my *unexpected* departure from the Force.

"I need to speak with Ren," I say, using my commander voice. There was a time when I was his superior.

"She's not taking any meetings right now," is all he has to say.

"You and I both know that she'll take a meeting for me. So run that sorry little excuse she calls a First Sergeant to her office and retrieve her. I won't stop calling until you do."

I hang up, but not before noticing the flash of contempt on Marcus's face. He knows he's not the favorite and never has been. Poor guy. But it's his own damn fault for following so blindly. It will only disappoint.

I'll give him ten minutes. If I don't hear from Ren by then, I'll start my onslaught of calls over again. Thankfully Mason has given me a private room all afternoon. I don't know what's up with him, but he was completely unquestioning.

Just as I'm about to start calling, Ren's face pops onto the large screen. "Hello, my dear," she says. "Have you finally decided to come back to your people?"

The question makes me sick. Ren has always believed that I'm a monster like her. A perfect copy, plucked right from... wait. No. No. Definitely not. Keep your cool, Warin.

"My people?" I spit, projecting my anger. "I'm not a monster." If I'm going to get answers, I'll need to get under her skin. I've always been good at that. But now, I have a secret weapon: the STARS that Cateline built specifically for me a few months ago. It has lie detecting capabilities. Stronger than anything the Force has... or had. Who knows now.

"Of course not, my dear," she says, smirk forming. "What can I do for you, then?" Her eyes are ever-probing. Ren is the type to constantly read you. It's why I've had to gain impeccable control over my emotions. Anger is all she's ever seen from me. But there's only been one person better at it than I am, and I'm looking at her.

"I want answers, Ren," I say, grinding my teeth at her name.

Ren hates that I call her that. She hides it well, though. "Don't we all," she replies with a smirk. My stomach twists.

"Why take her memories?" I ask, ignoring Ren's comment. We'll need to jump right in if we're going to get anywhere. While Ren adores games, she respects straightforwardness.

"Why not?" she replies, not missing a beat. "There was a Tainted individual I couldn't crack, and I was trying something new."

The buzzer for the lie goes off in my head. Interesting. Though I suppose it's not a new practice for her. She's used it before. "Admitting a fault in your system?" I question. "I'm impressed."

"Well, you know," she starts, twisting her hand in a signal of boredom, "the Organic Approach was always the first plan, not the only one."

"Yes, of course," I reply. She's referring to the Impetus Method. Unlike the Organic Approach, the Impetus Method is forceful. If she can't convince those around her to do her bidding of their own volition, she'll make them do it through other various ways. The most surprising thing about Ren is her determination on getting others to choose the path she believes is the right one before forcing their hand. Everything in Omphalos was designed with that in mind.

Shit. She'd made it extremely known that M should have learned by now. That means everything leading up to this has something to do with where she wants M to go. Like a certain trajectory is expected. Damn it, Warin. You're an idiot for not thinking of this sooner. Keep your cool, get back on track. "You used memory draining once before, though. With John Collins. That senator, right?"

Ren's expression changes immediately at the mention of his name, but her stoic disposition is recovered within a few seconds. "You looked at the files," she says, sounding impressed.

"I did," I admit. "Which means I know it's not new, and that you had a very personal goal attached." There's a fine line between game and truth. While Ren makes everything a game, there's always a motive.

She's silent for a moment, then her eyes meet mine. They're searching me, figuring out the best method to play. I hate her. Finally, she speaks. "The memories of your little pet have served me well," she sneers. "We're excelling in our search for Exceptionals."

I note the change of her pronouns. M's memories have served *her* well, but *they* are excelling with their search. Half-truths tied together to try and misdirect me. It's funny she thinks I haven't learned her ways after all this time. As if I'm not the one she taught extensively to be just like her.

"You were my greatest achievement," she says, changing the subject like she's read my mind. "So smart. So strong."

No buzzer goes off in my head, which means she wholeheartedly believes it. Yet it curdles my blood. "Don't take someone else's credit," I spit. "It's unbecoming."

Ren scoffs. "And who is it you credit for that unyielding strength?" Her eyebrow raises in question.

"My father," I answer, without question. It's but a second before anger overtakes me without warning. "I almost killed him for you. I almost threw away my Humanity to make you proud." Anger surges through me, and the words don't stop either. "And *then* you take the only woman I've ever lo... just... fuck off." I don't realize the tears streaming down my face until they're puddling at my chin. What the fuck?

Her eyes open in shock, like I've ripped away all that strength she claimed I have, but they soften quickly. "Lucas," she says, her voice more comforting than I've ever heard. Her mouth opens once more to lecture, but then it closes and she clears her throat. When she speaks again, the tenderness is no longer present. "There is still time to make me proud."

Ren's face is plain, no sign of her momentary lapse in control. The feelings muddying my chest are heavy. I don't understand any of this and it's making me angry.

"You have already taken enough from me," I deride. "You will not take any more."

"Oh, please," she says, scoffing. "You have no idea of the things I've given you. Everything is yours if you would leave that vile girl behind!" There's a moment where her subtle gasp surprises me.

"Amity?" I question. "That's who this is about?" This is it. I've known M played a part in all of this, but the why is not anything anyone could have imagined. It's because of *me*.

Ren is back to her usual self, pretending as though she didn't just hand me the biggest piece of the puzzle she could. "Apparently so, my dear," Ren replies, sighing. She's bored of this, the same old thing. "I want this to be ours. I want you by my side as we mold Humanity into a better future. Don't you see?" A begging Ren? That's not normal. Unease creeps into the corners of my brain, pushing any possible anger out. "Besides, that pesky *General* you've chosen to align with isn't all he's cracked up to be either."

She wants me back. She wants me back? What's going on?

Ren wants me, but I've gotten myself tangled in the Tainted world. It all clicks into place.

All of this, everything, has been a means of control. Emma, Nan, the memory wiping, the subcopies. It all leads to one hopeful goal: the demise of M and me.

And the worst part? I've been terrible to M. I've been pushing her away, claiming it's for her, but it was me letting everything around us get the best of me. I've been exactly what Ren was hoping for. But this only makes sense if what's been hiding in the dark recesses of my mind is true.

I'm her son.

CHAPTER TWENTY-NINE ∘ AMITY

SARGE AND I ARE SITTING IN THE CENTER OF THE FLOOR OF OUR room. For some reason it's comforting to me. Not because of its connection to Two, though it feels familiar somehow.

My father left a few hours ago. We'd been discussing plans and going over the information we have on the Reaver's son. I'm positive he's someone I care about. Positive he's someone important.

Yet I'm missing something. Hence why I'm sitting in the middle of the floor with Sarge pressed across my legs for comfort. I'm hoping to let my mind wander its way to the answer.

I don't know how many hours pass, but I'm interrupted when Sarge lifts his head and lets out a single alert bark. Someone is here.

A sharp knock cracks at the door before I reach it. When I open it, Luke is there, and he looks like absolute shit. *What the hell has he been up to?*

"Luke," I breathe. We've been on somewhat rocky shores lately. And even though I should be mad at him for picking up the whole memory thing again, I can't explain the strange flutter in my chest whenever he's around. "Are you alright?"

He pushes past me, barging into the room. "In all honesty?" he says, gripping his hair. "No. I'm not."

Luke plops himself on the couch and finally meets my eye. His hazels to my greys. I'm speechless. For many reasons.

Then he shoots up, ushering me and Sarge into the elevator that leads to the surface. Only once we're out into the cool breeze does he continue.

"I think..." he hesitates. "I think I might be who you're looking for."

"What do you mean?" I ask cautiously, afraid of where his mind is leading him. Afraid of where *mine* is leading *me*. Sarge scoots closer, and I glance down at him, hopeful to hide my worried expression from the man in front of me.

Luke is silent for a while, and when it becomes unbearable, I wrench my eyes back to his. They're wide saucers, watching me. "I don't want to believe it," he says, "but I think I'm Ren Keres' son."

His words blast my mind at full speed. The wind is knocked from my lungs and my knees hit the ground. Sarge catches me before I'm sucked into a memory so strong, it's like I'm ripped into the past with it.

The Reaver is standing before me, smug as can be, yet internally I'm screaming. I'm unable to process what she's told me. Her son. I know him, and it's... unbelievable.

But could it really be Luke? Damn memories only giving me bits and pieces.

I realize I've been silent for entirely too long. Luke is in front of me, hands placed on my shoulders to keep me from completely melting into the dirt. When did he get here? "Are you sure?" I ask him. "How could that be?" My brow furrows in thought.

He studies my face, concern etched across his own. Then he takes a breath and answers more calmly than I would. "Hear me out. I've driven myself nuts. It's... not something I want to believe, but the evidence... well... it's overwhelming." His eyes are begging me to fight him on it. To tell him he's wrong before he even gets into whatever evidence he thinks he found. But I nod, and he dives right in.

He explains how his father had told him his mother passed away, and about his aversion to Luke joining the Force. The Reaver's special treatment of him. The way we'd escaped last year. His father's dying wish to look up John Collins.

"John Collins?" I question, pausing him in his argument. "The senator?"

Luke nods. "Ren's father was John Collins. She wiped his memory, and instead of learning to cultivate the relationship from scratch, she grew impatient and angry. She killed him."

Interesting. The Reaver's dirty laundry. Does the General know? The Reaver is his niece. Not by blood, but marriage. But how does this pertain to Luke? "Why are you telling me this?" I ask.

"It's the piece we've been missing. Her obsession with you."

I'm jolted into another memory. *I'm begging the Reaver to kill me, but she tells me she can't. That* he'll *never forgive her. That I'll have to be a shell of myself so* he *will leave on his own.*

"It only makes sense if I *am* her son," Luke argues, pulling me from the past. "Everything she's done was to get us apart. Even the memory wiping. She thought I'd be like her, that I'd leave." Luke is hysterical, or at least, the version of it that only he can be. "You're my everything, M. Friends, or more, or less. It doesn't matter. I'm not like her. I'm not." Luke is frantic now. Like he's trying to convince himself of the words spewing from his lips more so than me. News of this magnitude is enough to unwind even the strongest of knots.

"Okay," I say. "It's okay." I hold out my hands as if somehow it will steady him. But his face screws up in anguish and he shakes his head. The setting sun casts shadows over his troubled expression.

"I lost my family. My father is dead, and I have no idea where my own sister is... I..." His voice cracks and so does my heart. His hazel eyes meet mine once more. "You're my only family. And I've been really shitty lately, but I'm with you to the end. If you think Emma is alive, I'm here for it. I'm sorry I doubted you. I'll be here in any way you need. A shoulder if it's not true, a cheerleader if it is."

The hollowness of his tone reminds me of my own. It's guilt. He's feeling guilty; responsible.

I study Luke's face again, and he speaks before I'm able to. "Before you ask, we have a different mother." He smiles, but it's sad looking. "I don't know about my stepmom either."

"I'm sorry," I say, feeling foolish for not putting aside my selfishness during Luke's despair. Perhaps the Reaver was right on one thing at least.

"I realize how disturbed you must feel at not truly knowing Emma is gone. In some way, knowing makes it easier. Not knowing about Janet and Lily has admittedly been something I've been burying for a long time."

Something deep within me tells me that Luke has never been this open. But is he truly the Reaver's son? Does this change anything?

Sarge pushes himself closer to me, as if it were possible to merge himself with my body. I imagine looking at this scene as an outsider, imagine the mess we must look like. Both Luke and I are slumped in the middle of an open field with Sarge melted in between us. Life has been so ridiculous lately that I actually want to laugh.

So I do.

Sarge glances up at me with a curious eye, and Luke stares at me with confusion, like I've finally lost my mind. And maybe I have. But then everything grows contagious, and suddenly Luke joins in and Sarge leaps up from my lap with excitement, wagging his tail happily.

A few minutes of bliss pass. A few minutes of laughter and happiness. Then we pull ourselves back to reality. "I'm sorry," I say, wiping the tears from my eyes and throwing my arm around Sarge. "I don't know what came over me."

Luke smiles, then it slowly fades away like the sun. But after a few seconds, the smirk plasters itself to his face. "You enjoy laughing at my pain?"

At first, I'm worried. But the tone of his voice is playful. Of the many sides I've come to see, Playful Luke is my favorite and is the one that hides away the most. "If you can't laugh," I say, "it would just be one more thing that the Guardianship has taken away."

His face grows serious in an instant. "You're damn right. And it won't be taking anything else."

I nod and ask Luke to take a nighttime walk. I could use a snack and some exercise to clear my head. Now that the sun is down, there's a chill to the air and it helps keep me grounded.

Luke agrees, and we're silent as we traipse around the surface, but I like it. It leads my mind in splintering directions as we return inside. All of this is too much. What are we going to do? When the dust settles, what's left for us?

I inadvertently made a comment, a trade. I told the Reaver she'd get her son if she gave my little M back. And she was right in her response. How could I sacrifice either of them?

"Are you excited about the wedding?" Luke questions after an eternity of awkward silence. Now that we're back inside, it would be weird to not speak at all.

Right. Lacy and Sonya's wedding. I chuckle to myself. How crazy these last couple of months have been, and how hectic the next few will be.

A wedding! In the middle of all of this.

"Sure," I admit. "Could be a nice change from the usual shit around here."

We circle around the fake center of the VIP section for a while, then hit the café for a late-night dessert. Luke actually does a decent job of keeping my mind off what's to come.

It isn't until we're headed back to the Residential Ward that I ask, "Do we tell anyone else?" Is there any benefit to everyone knowing Luke's revelation? I'm not even truly sure it's the truth yet.

Luke's face drops in thought. "Maybe we keep it a secret until we're sure."

"Even from my dad?" I question. He may be best to break the news to first. With his stolen files, he may be able to make a different connection.

"You're in charge," he says, shrugging. "You decide."

My chest flares with the newly familiar power that builds when I realize how much influence I have. We walk a bit more in silence until we come upon Luke's pod.

"Aren't I supposed to walk *you* back home?" He smirks, causing my heart to flip over a few times.

I chuckle. "I've got something I have to take care of, so today I'll be walking you," I say. "Besides, Sam could get a few minutes with Sarge." I shrug.

"You think we'll all fit?" He laughs. "Yeah, right!"

Luke gets Sam from his pod and we sit, enjoying each other's company for a few. But there's something on my mind, and it's time I do something about it.

After our goodbyes, Sarge and I make our way to Mason's room. It's late, and I hadn't considered that until now, yet he opens the door, rubbing the sleep from his eyes. "Amity!" he says. "Is everything alright?"

I nod. "Yes," I say. "Do you think you could get some people here?"

CHAPTER THIRTY ∘ AMITY

THE TIME HAS PASSED WAY TOO QUICKLY. TOMORROW WE LEAVE and head back to Western America. Back to the hellhole we all tried so hard to escape from.

Am I ready to lead? Am I capable of being who everyone needs me to be? I never asked for this. I happened to be the catalyst in an explosion building long before me. That's a lot to live up to.

But tonight, it doesn't matter. Why?

Because tonight we celebrate.

Everyone in the Human Protective Service is buzzing with excitement, though I don't quite understand it myself. Lacy and Sonya's wedding is the first one in a long time. And while the ceremony itself will be intimate with only a few dozen people, the after-party reception will have a few thousand.

A dazzling gown has been sent to my room, with a matching bowtie for Sarge. Its texture reminds me of the one I wore to the celebration of life for Axom and Charlotte during my first couple of weeks here. Silky and soft.

The dress hangs off my shoulders, draping down my body and opening at one thigh, splitting to show off my right leg. My hair is situated plainly, standing out as odd against the backdrop of such a stunning gown. My shoes are simple ballet flats, unable to be seen beneath the train of the dress unless I push them out through the slit. When everything is done with my outfit, I tighten the bowtie to Sarge.

Luke will be here soon to accompany me and Sarge to the ceremony. Last night when I'd left him, I asked Mason if he could locate and retrieve Janet and Lily Warin like he'd worked out for my father. I'm hoping to surprise Luke with the knowledge of their safety.

And then I spent the better half of the night watching the recording of the conversation I'd had with the Reaver, wondering if there was any hidden message within her words to suggest that Luke is her son. Maybe I'm reaching, but when she discusses her graciousness on letting me live, her eyes flick to whomever was behind me. Like she wasn't actually talking to me. I hadn't realized it in the moment, but it makes sense if what Luke says is true.

Heavy knocks thump my door, startling me from my thoughts. I quickly make my way to the entrance, Sarge at my heels. The urgency is not something Luke would do. I'm not sure who I expect it to be, but the General is not them. My eyebrows fold in confusion while unease clouds my brain.

"Miss Thorne," he greets. "You look lovely."

"G... General..." I stammer. "Thank you. To what do I owe this pleasure?" While it's been far and few that the General speaks to me without others present, each time it causes my heart to hammer loudly in my ears.

"I wanted to check in before everyone gets carried away with the joys of celebration," he says. "May I come in?"

His tone suggests he's not truly asking. I shift to the side and fan my hand into the sitting area. My quiet glare reaches Sarge once he lets out a low growl as the General passes.

"Is this in regard to our trip?" I ask. The General stands in the middle of the room, towering over everything. He's a fish out of water decked out in his ceremonial dress. My room has never looked so grungy and plain.

"Indeed," he confirms. "I'd like to be certain you're understanding of the assignment."

"Of course," I agree. "I'm to bring hope to the rebels by showing them I've not given up." Mason shared the General's idea, and I simply flipped it into a plan that benefitted *both* of us.

The General nods. "And how do you propose to do such a thing?" His eyebrows raise in questioning.

"I..." I stutter. "I... repeat the propaganda we've gone over. I know if I just show my face... they'll..."

"Let's not shuffle around," he says, cutting me off. "I'm aware of your side quest to find the progeny of evil." The General's tone is full of malice. "If such a creature exists, it should be driven out of hiding."

My lips turn down with anger. "A son," I say. "A human being. And the key to Madame Keres' downfall." How could the General speak so harshly about another living soul? *About Luke?*

The General's eyes darken with a familiar anger. "The *key* to that evil witch's downfall is keeping our troops bolstered, which you will do. We will locate the spawn. This *son* you speak of will be snuffed out of existence."

I can't help my sharp intake of breath. If the General finds out what we know, Luke is in danger. My tongue is sharp as I say, "What do you mean *snuffed out*?" Apprehension prickles my scalp.

"No offspring of that evil woman should plague this earth. All traces of her must be extinguished."

An involuntary gasp escapes my lungs. "You're going to kill an innocent person because of their DNA?" I question. The words spill out of me without any filter. "Sounds very Reaverish of you." The General has always rubbed me the wrong way and, after finding out his connection to the Reaver, any tiny bit of trust I had was suffocated. But this? This is worse than even I considered.

"Miss Thorne, you are not well-equipped on the intricacies of war." He dismisses me.

I know I should be quiet. I should shut my mouth and let it be, but that teenage angst presses forward without much thought. "I suppose not," I reply. "But I am well equipped on the intricacies of revenge." My arms cross my chest. "Pour Notre Justice, right?" I ask. "Or have you spun that phrase, too?"

Do I have a Death wish? I don't know. Thankfully we'll be away from the General's prying eyes soon. Who would've thought we'd actually be safer in Western America?

The General steps forward with intent but quickly stops in his tracks after a sharp crack of teeth from Sarge. "You will tell me the source you intended on seeking, and you will keep to your duties as figurehead of the rebellion." Then he adds, "Be thankful I'm letting everyone go with you."

His fists are tightly closed by his sides. The Reaver had said something like this to me, too, and it's something I don't want to take a chance on. I grit my teeth and swallow my disgust, eventually resigning to the powerlessness. "Yes, sir."

The General stares at me, then nods, a smug smile snaking to his face. Just in time for more knocks on the door. My shoulders tense at the sound, and I hope the General doesn't pick up on my uneasiness.

We shuffle to the entryway. Sarge keeps himself in between me and the General as a physical buffer. Not that I need it to stay as far away as I can.

General Favager turns to me before rotating the knob. "Do

have a good time," he says.

The door opens and Luke's eyes meet mine before flipping to the towering man in front of me.

"Mr. Warin," the General says, nodding. "Have a wonderful evening." Then he's gone. And with him, Luke's control.

"What the fuck was that?" he questions the second the General is out of earshot. "Are you alright?" He's in front of me in an instant. Sarge is pressed against the back of my legs, keeping me upright.

I nod, but my eyes can't focus and my mouth is dry. We're not safe anywhere we go. And that leads me to one of two things. Either Mason is a two-timing snake who hasn't kept his mouth shut about anything, or there are ears everywhere. Maybe both.

My body shivers involuntarily with the realization. But it can't get to me now. Lacy and Sonya deserve a day filled with happiness. We can stress about this later.

Luke eyes me warily, not convinced in the slightest that things are okay. But then his jaw ticks and he's a new person. Smiling, as if nothing in the world could bring him down. "Shall we head out, then?" He props his elbow out to me, waiting patiently for me to wrap around it.

Luke and I make idle chit chat along the way. It's not far at all to the ceremony. It's set to take place in the center hub of Headquarters, underneath the statue of Fortana. Guards stand at each entryway, and groups crowd to see the spectacle.

"'Scuse us," Luke says, which is all it takes. They turn, noticing Sarge, and the crowd parts. A pathway is cleared for us.

The guard at the opening nods to me, removing the barrier. As we pass, he pats Sarge on the head. It's a small thing, but it makes me smile.

Finally through the commotion, the full scene comes into view.

Beneath Fortana, Lacy is waiting patiently, shifting her weight from side to side. Beautifully ornate chairs are set into the center circle. Those near the back and middle are filled already. No one I recognize except for the CROP kids.

Sam notices us first and bolts over immediately, his face lighting up. Sarge bounces happily, and it isn't long before the full stampede of CROP kids come. They crowd Sarge, hoping to get their chance at saying hello and petting him.

"You kids get over here!" an older woman in a beautiful lilac dress standing by the seating yells. Her southern accent is thick. "Leave that poor dog alone!" The kids round up, sighing and groaning, and head back to her like the flip of the switch with the exception of Sam. A somewhat familiar ache settles deep within me.

"Who's that?" I whisper to Luke as we continue toward Lacy.

"You too, Sam," he nods, and Sam protests but not for long. He says his goodbye to Sarge and off he goes to join the rest of his group. "Mama June," Luke says once Sam is gone. "She's the kids' legal guardian here."

"All of them?" I say, a pit forming in my gut. A vague sense of knowing tumbles into my brain. Lacy mentioned her, I think. My eyes travel to Mama June's direction once more. She reminds me of someone.

Luke nods.

"Hey, wait up!"

The both of us turn to find Mason trotting our way. He's in a standard suit, like Luke, yet he doesn't look out of place in the same way. His blue eyes are killer amidst the black backdrop of his outfit.

"You look lovely," he says, catching up. Luke tenses beneath my palms.

The heat flushes my face and I look away from Mason, tucking my hair behind my ear. Before I'm able to reply, Luke mutters, "Thanks," in my place, smirking at Mason, who purses his lips in reply. I stifle a chuckle.

"It's actually Sarge that's catching all the attention," I argue, trying to keep the peace for Lacy and Sonya's special day. These boys belong in Mama June's care. A scoff escapes beneath my breath, and my eyes roll.

"He is quite the sight," Mason agrees. "He's going to look great in the photos." His white teeth are blindingly bright as his lips pull back in a smile. *Mason couldn't possibly be against us, right?*

Photos? Ugh. I'll get through this for Lacy, but if I'm being honest, my stomach is full of knots. The General's threat, the love in the air, the fact that I haven't seen my father yet. Everything is heavy, overwhelming.

The sickly stench of happiness leaves me breathless, as if I'm drowning. I let the General get to me, fill every wounded crack with despair. I'm a black hole in the otherwise bright occasion. I hate it.

"Amity!" Lacy cries once we're closer, nervous energy radiating off her for the first time ever. She hides it well. "Little bro!"

Her make-up is immaculate, and she pulls me in for a hug, holding me away from her face so I don't mess it up. She's stunning in her white suit. It hugs her body, showing off every beautiful curve she's blessed with.

"Wow," I say as she pulls away. "Just... wow." I offer her a smile, despite my own worries.

Lacy is beaming. "Thanks," she replies. "I could say the same thing about you. I mean." She holds me at arm's length, giving me the look of approval while scanning her eyes up and down my outfit. "If I wasn't getting married today..."

"Lacy!" I playfully smack her arm. She chuckles.

The sound around us goes up a decibel as more people filter in. "Are you excited?" Luke questions, and he and Lacy start their own conversation about the future. Mason is off networking. My fingers look for Sarge as my mind wanders a bit.

My father still isn't here.

Scanning the sea of people filtering to their seats, I realize I'm the only one in a deep wine color, while the rest of the guests are in a pale purple shade. *Why must they always make me stand out?*

"You okay?" Luke whispers, causing me to jump.

My eyes rake to his, and the concern in them causes my heart to flip. I nod, letting him lead me to our seats.

By the time we're asked to stand for Sonya to make her appearance, I'm a ball of nerves. My father should definitely be here by now, yet he's nowhere to be found. I will my mind to focus, to pick up the details of Sonya's gorgeous black dress as she slides down the aisle, of Lacy's expression as she watches her future bride waltz toward her. I want to get lost in the music and the mood, yet it's getting increasingly harder to breathe.

Don't make a scene, Amity. My breathing picks up, and Sarge steps back, pushing me against Luke's rigid body behind me. The mix of emotions is almost too much to bear. Sarge is hoping my senses will fade if I'm smushed between the two of them, but it feels too late. If only I could let it out, allow the emotion to overtake me, but I can't. I won't. Not right now.

Luke's hand snakes around my hip and holds me steady to him, and my knuckles clamp into Sarge's fur. We're all connected. Whether I want it or not, all of us are connected in a dangerous way. The General knows it, and his threat from early drowns out everything else.

Where is my father? Did he hurt him? Is he okay? General Favager wouldn't do that today of all days, would he?

Yes he would. Of course he would. He outright admitted he would kill the Reaver's son simply because of who his mother is. This is not okay. *Nothing* is okay.

"M?" Luke says, putting his finger to my chin and physically moving me so I'm forced to look at him.

Coming to reality, my head whips around, noticing everyone else is leaving the center of Headquarters, making their way to the reception room. *I missed the entire ceremony?*

"What's going on?" Luke questions, demanding an answer.

The words roll up but die on my tongue. I can't tell him. I can't open up until we're far from here, where I can be sure that no one is listening in.

Mason is lingering on the perimeter, watching us with a worried expression. I glance from him back to the man in front of me, and then back to Mason again when I catch movement.

My shoulders relax and nearly all the tension in my body eases. My father walks up to Mason, speaking to him as if nothing out of the ordinary is happening.

"Nothing," I say to Luke immediately. "Let's get to the party."

The waves of people sloshing about in the reception room makes my heart beat faster. The walls are tight and it's hard to breathe. But my father is okay. At least physically. I search the room but fall short on locating him again.

"You going to be okay here if I go get a drink?" Luke asks as we circle the edge of the dance floor.

"Of course," I reply, though I'm not entirely sure I will be. "I've got Sarge."

Luke nods and disappears into the thousands of others that are pushing to the border of where Lacy and Sonya will present their first dance. I can't believe I missed their ceremony.

Lacy is married!

To distract myself from the buzzing of the crowd, and the nervousness of not having eyes on my father once again, I note the décor around the room. A ton of greenery flows from every possible place, all wrapped in beautiful royal purple ribbons, garnished with lilac accents.

A memory stabs my skull and I'm in a house with bright green plants. *The air is somehow fresher, and despite the sad aura that surrounds the scene, there's a sense of comfort. Nan.*

Immeasurable sorrow sweeps through me, and Sarge's paws find my shoulders. I hug him to me. Nan.

I remember now. Her memories flood into me, unwillingly. She gave her life for us to get away. She gave her life for *me*.

And love. She believed in love. I glance at Lacy and Sonya, who are now twirling on the dance floor together. Maybe that's why my mind is choosing this moment to remember Nan. Looking at them, I may be able to believe there is strength in love. Nan knew it, my father told me as much. Sure, it could be a weakness, but it could also make you stronger than you ever thought possible.

It's in Lacy's body language when Sonya is near, and it's mirrored back in Sonya's eyes. It's the way my father looked at my mother. Even despite the war, they held their own little haven of peace together.

And look at me. My love for Emma trumping every rational thought, making me move hell and high water to somehow get the chance to save her. *If she's alive to save...*

My arms cling to Sarge as if my entire life will fall apart if I don't. Something tells me I've spent a long time hiding away, shutting people out, when the truth is, I should've been listening to them, opening up. There's strength to be found. There's courage in putting your heart out there. If I'm going to get to Emma, and take down the Reaver, I'm going to have to start here.

"Excuse me, sir. May I cut in?"

My gaze flips to the source of the voice. Luke's eyes are focused on Sarge. I chuckle quietly, my heart doing somersaults.

Sarge removes himself from my shoulders, taking a few steps back in response, and Luke raises his hand, holding it for me to take.

A sideways glance has me catching Sarge's tongue flopping out of his mouth in a lopsided smile. His body language is happy and relaxed as it usually is where safety is of no concern, like he's telling me this is my chance to open up, to live a little.

I stare through my lashes, gently placing my fingers in Luke's palm. My skin ignites as his grip tightens, pulling me closer, and reaching his other hand around to my waist. Partygoers are filling the empty spaces of the dance floor to join Lacy and Sonya.

My cheeks burn, and I keep my face down. Really, I should look at him. He's been through enough lately. He just found out his mother is the person who may have killed my sister. That has to be awkward, if nothing else.

Though, to be fair, it's a lot for me as well. And yet, like every other time we're together, he's completely relaxed with me. My greys flick to his hazels. They're studying me, watching me apprehensively.

"You look beautiful," Luke says. The steadiness of his voice does not match that of his body. His tone is cautious, but his movements are secure. "I didn't tell you that earlier."

"I tend to think Sarge is the real showstopper," I say, once again trying to get the attention off me.

A smirk. *Ahh, the lovely Luke smirk.* The one that shows the small dimple on one side of his face. "You never were good with compliments." He says it as a fact.

Allowing my nihilistic view to swallow me, I say, "I'm inclined to believe I wasn't ever good at anything." I chuckle nervously in an attempt to lighten the mood.

But *was* I good at anything? I get the vague feeling deep in my chest that I've simply been falling through life. I may not remember much, but aside from my determination to save Emma, I don't feel any connection to the past when it comes to agency.

Luke's face falls, then grows serious. "M, you..."

I cut him off, not willing to hear anything more on the subject. "It was a joke."

"Ah," he sighs, nervously. "Well, you have always been very convincing as well."

I change the subject. "So how'd you get Mason to stay away from us this long?" I'm half joking. I want to keep the lightheartedness going.

Luke smirks. "Your dad is distracting him."

My heart bubbles with laughter and relief. My father is still okay. "Did you have to pay him?" I tease.

"No," Luke chuckles. "But maybe I should have."

The melody finishes and the dance floor picks up as the beat of the slow song melds into a faster pace. I do my best to open up, allowing myself to dance with not only Luke, but my father, and Mason as well. The night flies and I do my best letting go of my woes. There was nothing my father would give away for his tardiness, so I choose not to worry. Tonight is supposed to be fun.

I step off the dance floor after an indeterminate amount of time, catching my breath and cooling my slick skin. Then Lacy and Sonya finally make their way through the crowd to find me.

"There they are," I say, pulling them both in for a hug. I *do* love them. I just hope it makes me stronger because by this time tomorrow, we'll be slumming it in Undoing land. "Abby would be proud of the two of you."

Lacy backs away, petting Sarge and offering me the biggest, most understanding smile. Sonya links hands with her new wife, watching her with a smile of her own.

"Maybe one day you'll find your true love, too," Lacy returns. My eyes inadvertently flick to the dance floor where Luke, Mason, and my father are dancing, all awkward limbs and movement.

"Maybe," I say. "I think Sarge and I are going to head out. You know, big day tomorrow."

Both of them nod to me, and I hug them once more before sneaking through the heated crowd and out into the quiet of Headquarters.

We cut off in the central location, and I pray for the first time below Fortana, begging her to give me the strength I so desperately hope comes with my love for the people a few rooms away.

If I lose any of them, I'll burn the world down.

CHAPTER THIRTY-ONE ○ AMITY

THE MORNING IS CRISP AS WE FILTER TO THE SURFACE. EVERY-one is at various stages of fatigue, yet almost all of us have dark circles beneath our eyes.

The sight of General Favager waiting causes my throat to close. Will he follow through on his threat to kill Luke if he finds out who he is? Of course he would. You don't become the leader of a military organization by being passive.

My father is already standing by him, and he crosses the distance to get to me before I get close to them. "I won't be going with you today," he says, dropping a bomb on me.

"What?" I say, unable to stop my confusion. The General is watching us with smug eyes. I want to send Sarge across this field to rip him apart. Instead, I reach my fingers into his fur.

"You'll have to trust it's for the best," he says, shooting me a knowing glance. "But I want you to have this."

My eyes affix to the shiny object in his hand. Slipping it into my fingers, I rub the textured piece and study it closely. A small golden emblem of an oak tree in a circle, its roots pouring past the curvature of the bottom. Flipping it over, there's a needle poking from the back. A pin.

"It was your mother's," he says. "It kept me safe on my journey

here and gave me hope when I thought I was lost. It's yours now."
My eyes fill with tears, but they don't ever break and fall. "Bring
our little M home."

I nod to him, and he nods to me, then yanks me in for a hug so
tight I fear I may explode from the pressure.

A commotion behind me has me pulling away. Sam is at the entrance of headquarters, shouting. "I want to come, too! Wait for
me!" He's doing his best to push through the guards holding him
back, and Luke is already turning to close the distance.

I nod once again to my father before heading over to where
Sam and Luke are.

"You have to stay here," Luke demands. "It's too dangerous."

Sam scoffs. "I'm not a kid!" he argues. "I want to be with you."

My heart breaks for him. I hold up my hand, asking Luke to
pause in his instruction. Sarge and I get closer to Sam, and Sarge
gives him kiss after kiss to tell him goodbye. I lean down, whispering so no one but us can hear. "I found out my father won't be
going with us, so I need you to do something for me. Will you?"

Sam's eyes widen and he nods.

"Keep him safe. I don't have anyone I can trust here, so it's all
you. It's a very important job."

"Okay," he says, determined. "I will. You can count on me."

I offer him my hand, taking his and shaking to seal our deal.
"Thank you," I say. "And I'll keep Luke safe out there."

The boy steps back and watches us cross the field again toward
the jet-like aircraft carrier waiting for us. "What did you tell
him?" Luke questions.

"I simply gave him a job," I say, keeping my eyes forward.

When everything is packed, the group loads into the aircraft.
Nerves settle in my chest and sweat clings to my skin. Bringing
up the rear, the General reaches out and puts his hand on my arm

to stop me before I enter the machine. He releases quickly when Sarge snaps from beside me.

"Remember your objective, Miss Thorne," he warns. "Do not lead yourself astray."

Swallowing hard, I nod and everything runs in slow motion as I buckle into place. Mason looks as queasy as I feel. Lacy and Sonya are tangled on each other and my heart sours more than before. Curse them for coming along. I wish they could enjoy their marriage instead of dealing with this. They look like they haven't slept a wink, but for different reasons than why I lay awake all night.

Luke is the only one that seems at home in the chaos. His hair is tussled perfectly and his body is relaxed in his seat. I place myself across from him, pulling the restraint across my chest. Then I take the specialty one the guard handed to me outside and hook one side to Sarge, and the other to the buckle to keep him in.

His golden eyes meet mine and I instantly feel lighter. We can do this.

The trip itself is short, which offers no time to calm the rapid beating in my chest. When we touch ground, so does my heart. Lacy and Sonya rip off the craft first, dying to be on solid land once more. Mason follows closely behind, though he's not as excited to be back in the place of his nightmares. Luke is next, yet he halts by the exit, waiting for me and Sarge to follow.

There are no words when I finally make my way outside. "This is..." my voice fades. With eyes wide, I take in my surroundings. An environment that should be lifeless is filled to the brim with it. Structures are built into the sideways trees, and the boggy landscape isn't as saturated as I would've expected. The Undoing was always described as apocalyptic. This land should be uninhabitable, dead, and unsafe. Yet, it's...

"Impressive?" Mason finishes the sentence a few steps ahead of me. He glances over his shoulder, meeting my gaze.

"Yeah," I say, nodding. The camp is larger than the eye can see which is unfathomable to me at the current moment. I wouldn't even call this a camp; it's more like a makeshift town. Thousands of tiny structures expand outward from the landing pad. They get smaller as they disappear along the horizon. I hadn't realized the rebellion has this many supporters behind it.

My intrusive thoughts take over for a second, and I begin to worry if all these people have been fed a false narrative. My name and my face are behind the movement, but it is those in power like the General that are truly backing the cause. He's promised everyone a better world, one where justice for all is the mantra. What if once he gets his revenge, he simply takes the power for himself?

"M?" Luke's voice snaps me from my thoughts. I've never been so glad to hear my nickname from his lips. Everyone is moving forward, seemingly leaving me behind. Not Luke, though. "You alright?"

"Define alright," I say, stepping toward him with a grimace. Now that we're out from under the thumb of General Favager, I'm more comfortable opening up. How ironic is it that I'd actually feel more relaxed in the place we tried so desperately to run from before?

We fall into a steady pace as the leader of this camp shows us around. There's not enough room in my brain right now to catch his name as he repeats it. Almost everyone we pass looks on with awe. Sarge is loving the attention, prancing beside me as if he were the main attraction. And to be fair, he probably is.

By the time we're near the center, nearly everyone staying here has followed us. "Everybody loves the dog," Luke leans in to say after catching my anxious glances. He's trying to ease my discomfort. But it's futile. The attention is definitely on me now.

Lacy, Sonya, and Mason all stop and turn to see what I'm seeing. Hundreds of people are gathered, enclosing us in the camp's center meeting area. It's raised, and all who are around can be seen clearly.

Then, everyone in the crowd simultaneously beats their fists to their chests. "Justice for Amity," they chant. Lifting their fists to the sky, they finish, "Justice for Emma."

And suddenly everything is too much. Too loud, too bright, too dusty, muggy, overwhelming. I'm back to a place in my mind I can only assume is Omphalos. *There's a man huddled in the hallway, he's been beaten. And he's important to me.*

Those around me are young, and they complete the same ritual as the ones in this camp. Something I now realize as the symbol of the rebellion and is actually the old sign for "a" in a long extinct language. A for Amity.

It's all too much. The responsibility, it's crippling. Yet the sweet taste of power keeps me afloat. They look to me. To a nobody who is now someone in the eyes of the damned. As terrifying as this is—as heavy of a weight I need to carry—I've never felt more free.

This is *mine.* These are my people to lead, this is my rebellion. I can't say I want it, but it's not about wants right now. These people need this. Emma needs this.

The General has laid claim to my body; the Reaver, my soul. Yet it is I who command those in front of me. And together, we will conquer all.

We have to.

CHAPTER THIRTY-TWO ∘ AMITY

AS NIGHT FALLS, WE SETTLE BY THE FIRE WHILE THOSE IN THE camp tell stories. Luke is animatedly talking to two brothers he found—some that he knew from before—and his happiness lightens my mood. I can't for the life of me remember their names right now. Todd maybe? Travis? Who knows.

An aircraft touches down, pulling me from the fireside tales. What are they doing so late?

"A squad has returned from reconnaissance," a new voice says. One of the brothers, the younger one I think, has placed himself beside me.

Sarge is lying by the fire, completely unperturbed by the fact that this man has snuck up on me. I suppose this means he's trustworthy for now.

"Reconnaissance of what?" I question, curiosity flooding me.

"Part of what the Service members do here is find the spots the Headmistress has corralled everyone. Then we use that information to take out the Force and bring the Western Americans here," the man says beside me. Titus, maybe? Fuck. I wish I was paying closer attention to his introduction.

"You actively kill the members of the Force?" My brow furrows. Something about that doesn't sit well with me. It's easy to believe that anyone who joins the Force is evil, yet that would mean Luke falls into that category. My eyes flick to him sitting across the fire, his face illuminated by the flames. He meets my eye mid conversation and smiles, causing my heart to stutter.

"I don't like it either," the man says, glancing toward Luke as well. "We're told to shoot first, ask questions never." His voice is solemn.

It's believable. General Favager is becoming a bigger villain in this story. But like my father told me, the enemy of my enemy is my friend. *At least for now.* Ugh.

"Hey, Thomas!" someone shouts. "What are you doing to that poor girl over there?" The brother sitting by Luke calls over, questioning the man beside me. Ahh. Thomas.

Luke studies my face and I shake my head, letting him know I'm fine. His eyes show disbelief, so I point to Sarge, who's still lying soundlessly at my feet. Only then does Luke get back to his conversation with the other brother.

"I'm sorry," Thomas says. "Trevor is a nosey asshole." He smiles despite his words.

My lips turn up as I give him an understanding nod.

"Woah! Hey, hey!" Both Thomas and I look up, as does Sarge. Luke is holding Trevor by the shirt, keeping him from tumbling into the fire. "You do *not* want third degree burns. They're a bitch."

Trevor and Thomas both chuckle, seemingly knowing something the rest of us around the fire don't.

"Has he been burned before?" I ask Thomas.

He furrows his brow and watches me with sad eyes. Damn it. Pity. "Why don't you tell the story!" Thomas shouts across the section, directing his comment to Luke instead of saying anything to me. I'm grateful for it.

And so Luke dives in. Before getting here, we got smoked out of my old childhood home in Burns. How fitting.

Every Servicemember listens in awe, as do I. Though I was apparently there, nothing about the story brings any memories forward. Not the banging of the doors, not the twirling smoke, not the fact that I, too, had bad burns on my arms when I pulled Luke up through the sky light.

Someone asks how he looks normal, and Luke chuckles. "There are still bits and pieces to be seen in places, but it's mostly gone with help from the Service. The only reason I made it out alive was because Amity got me to an herbalist."

My breath hitches. Nan. *That's* why she had so many greens. She was an herbalist! I know he's putting me in the hero spotlight to further the plot of my figurehead duties, but it feels wrong. I don't remember getting him there and it doesn't matter anyway. Nan was the real hero.

Heads swivel to meet me and thank goodness the fire light glows red on my face to hide the embarrassment. I suppose this is what I'm here for, and while the power I hold is profound in a way I'd never thought possible, it's not strong enough to stop my intrusive thoughts telling me that I don't belong in this position.

Especially not now with the reminder of Nan. Is this what she wanted? I wish I had a more solid memory of her. Despite getting swept away at the wedding with her image, I simply can't imagine why she did the things she did. Was it for me to carry on the rebellion? Was it for me to find a chance at... love? I gulp.

Was there something she knew that I don't?

I chuckle to myself at the thought. Well, I suppose there are a lot of things she knew that I don't. I don't know anything anymore thanks to the Reaver.

Sarge sits up from his spot at my feet, placing his chin on my lap. My natural reflex is to run my fingers through the soft fur of his head, and the thick, scruffy section of his neck. I think I've had enough social time for one day.

We bid everyone goodnight. I'm adamant that Luke stays put and continues catching up with his friends. The one good thing about all of this is seeing him so relaxed, so... him. Deep in my gut, I know that's how he's supposed to be. Not the uptight, angry, stressed-out version that he's been lately.

I weave around the thrown together structures with Sarge until we find the one that was given to us. Lacy and Sonya's is two down from here, Mason's three. Luke's will be next door. There are no lanterns on in any of the huts, which means everyone else is asleep. I don't blame them. I wish sleep would claim me as well, at least then I could forget about everything that's happened in the last twenty-four hours.

But then I'd have to deal with a whole new set of issues, because, as it turns out, my mind is becoming sharper during sleep. It's terrorizing me with more and more nightmares. I haven't been telling anyone about them because I didn't want anyone to worry. And I *especially* didn't want to tell Luke because he's dealing with his own crisis.

I push open the flap, letting Sarge into the small structure first. It's not at all what I'm expecting. The entire floor is cushioned, but there's a lantern hanging from a small hook in the corner. It's also warm in here.

Though the whole town is covered by a dome to keep it hidden, the air inside still goes through a physical cycle. But at least it's not the twenties that it would be if we were truly outside. Somehow the Service has created luxury while keeping it natural.

Certain materials are easy for them to get. The odds and ends inventions around are no doubt from the brilliant mind of Cateline Pierre. I hope she's okay. Despite everything, Cateline proved to be on our side. She's the only one from the team that didn't greet us on the field when we left, though.

Sarge places himself on the cushioned floor and I file in next to him, closing the flap to block out the chill. It's small yet somewhat cozy.

Next thing I know, I'm walking through the woods with the one they call Zach. The world is calm as we walk, until all of a sudden, it's not. Knives fly through the air and sink into Zach's flesh. My mind whirs with panic and my lungs beg for air. *No! No no no.*

Zach is on the ground and he's gasping. "You did this," he coughs. "You should be the one in the ground."

My hands clamp around my ears, trying to block the echoey words as they bounce around my skull. I clench my eyes shut to stop the sight but it's still there behind the lids.

I didn't. No. I did. Did I?

When my eyes pop open, it's no longer Zach on the ground. It's Luke with red, angry skin. Heat emanates from his body, and tears soak my eyes. It's quiet around us, but the pit in my stomach is growing fast. My face inches closer to his. Is he still breathing? I need to feel the breath of Life on my cheek to be sure.

My bones rattle when he shoots out a hand, grabbing me. His eyes are wide and bloodshot. "You caused my pain," he blames. "It's all your fault!"

A scream breaks from my throat and my body lifts off the cushioned floor of the heated tent. The lantern is still on which makes it easier to get my bearings. Sarge is fervently licking my face, bringing me to reality quicker.

My skin is slick with sweat, the heat in the tent is suddenly too much to bear. *Out. I need out.*

I push through the flap and the chilled air is nice on my exposed skin. It cools the hotness of my blood. My breath turns to ice as I try to steady it.

I shouldn't be alive. I shouldn't be alive. *I shouldn't be alive.*

Right?

Maybe there's a reason I'm the one who's here today and not everyone else I've lost. But that doesn't seem right, or fair. I'm tired of shit not being fair.

I take off running and Sarge is close at my heels. Our tent structure is close to the perimeter, so we cut off into a sprint around the fallen trees near the edge. I don't want to think. I want to move. Go.

The moonlight creates pockets of darkness amidst the terrain, yet I'm not worried enough to care who might be lurking here. It isn't until Sarge is leading us back to our tent that my skin begins to crawl.

"Fancy meeting you here," a voice says from the dark, though Sarge's tail only wags. No teeth, no growl, no nothing. Luke. What's he doing away from his tent? "Everything alright?" He steps out from the shadows, and the moonlight shows his concerned expression.

"I shouldn't be alive," I say, coming to terms with it. So many times, so many instances, in which Death should have claimed me. Perhaps the world would be better for it. Perhaps not. Would the rebellion carry on without me? Would things still progress the way they have without my influence?

Luke scoffs. "Don't speak nonsense to me," he says. "You're the *only* one that should be alive."

Sarge and I settle on a sideways log on the outskirts of the town, and Luke follows. "No, I shouldn't," I argue, because I'm feeling some type of way after my nightmare. "Not only because I don't deserve it, but from every story I hear, and each little snippet of memory I gain, it's clear I just scuttled along because of others. I didn't contribute anything. Hell, even Sarge contributes more than me," I say, putting my head in my hands. Sarge sits up, lapping at my face, causing me to sputter.

Luke is silent beside me. I can't help the curiosity as I look at him. He's watching me, waiting for my eyes to meet his. When they do, he says, "So?"

I cough out a laugh. "So? Everyone is looking to me for some reason. Like I'm some hero. A brave warrior. But the truth is, all I did was love my sister and was hotheaded enough to get swept up in the idea of a revolution."

There's something to be said for the power that flows through me. But it's undeserved. My love made me strong; I know that now. But it doesn't make me deserving of this influence that I have over others.

Luke shrugs as if my words are nothing. "None of that matters," he says. "What matters is that you're here now."

Fuck. Not only do I not deserve this authority, but I also don't deserve this man. I don't deserve anything. "I'm a fraud."

"What set this off?" Luke questions.

I refuse to meet his eye, instead looking out into the vast shantytown filled with thousands of people who are all here because they believe I can make a difference. Fuck these feelings welling up inside of me.

"Was it a Zach nightmare?"

My head swivels to stare at Luke. "How did you..."

"Dreams of him usually brought out your most brutal self-hatred," he says, knowingly.

I sigh. "It seems like everything in my life has been one tragedy after another." My words flow out with a huff. "Isn't there one good thing you can tell me?"

Luke's hand finds its way to mine and Sarge places his chin on our fingers as they interlock. "I can tell you I'm not going anywhere." His voice is softer than I thought possible.

"That's supposed to be a good thing?" I joke. It's hard to contain my smile.

Luke's lips turn up as he laughs from deep in his belly. It's the most normal I've felt in a long time. I adore the fact that Playful Luke has made an appearance despite our situation.

He squeezes my hand. "M," he says. "You are the strongest person I know. You'll get through this. I've not a single doubt in my mind."

His words are sweet, but I'm worried I don't deserve them. Could I truly have been that great of a person? Surely not. The Reaver has barked such harsh words at me, and they match the terrors that are starting to fill my brain when I close my eyes to sleep. So who's right?

Am I how Luke sees me, or the Reaver? Or maybe I'm somewhere in between. I don't want to believe the negative. I'm tired of being a shell of the woman everyone is expecting. It's exhausting trying to be so many different versions of myself, like I'm at odds with all the different sides of who I've been.

"I don't want to sleep," I say, honestly.

"Neither do I," he admits. "Cateline infused the air of the tents with a new design that forces rest. Unfortunately for us, she didn't account for night terrors," he chuckles, but his brow furrows. "I'm just bumming it out here." His arms extend to show the location of his new sleeping quarters. The cushion from his tent is wedged below the sideways trunk, wrapped in the space like it's only enough for Luke to squeeze his body between the two sides. At least it's not terribly cold out here.

Curse Cateline and her smart brain. "Can't they turn that off or something?" I question. I'm sure if I ask, I can get whatever I want. Though this line of thinking only causes me to return to the top of the spiral once more. *You shouldn't be alive. You're a fraud. You don't deserve this power.*

"You're more than welcome to stay out here with me?" Luke points out.

A timid smile curves my lips only slightly. "Down in that thing?" I point to the cushion pushed into the nature around us. "It looks like it barely fits you, let alone me and Sarge, too." My nose scrunches and the air cools the inside.

"Suit yourself," he shrugs, keeping his infamous smirk. "Goodnight, M."

"Goodnight, Luke."

CHAPTER THIRTY-THREE ∘ AMITY

THE SUN RISES AND THE CAMP BUSTLES WITH ENERGY. SQUADS
of Servicemembers are gathering in the center, collecting their
breakfast and heading to their favorite spots to eat. Lacy and Sonya have been locked in their tent together since we got here, but
Mason is out and about, waiting in line for some food.

His deep blue eyes light up as Sarge and I get closer. "Hey!" he
says. "How'd you sleep?" He's well-rested. There are no signs of
any terrors eating at his mind in the night.

I force a smile onto my face. There's no reason to worry him.
Especially if he's secretly reporting back to the General. "Fine."
The word is short, but I don't dwell on it long enough for Mason
to notice. "Have you seen Lacy and Sonya this morning?"

He cocks a brow, wrinkling his nose. "No. And thank God
these tents are soundproof." His aversion to the sex life of our
newlywed friends makes me laugh.

"I suspect we won't see them for a while then," I debate. "Can
you blame them, though?" I raise an eyebrow at him.

He shakes his head, hiding his smile as he moves forward in
line. The two Servicemembers at the front hand him a small
square the color of dirt. The other hands me one, and the texture
is definitely like dirt. Mason turns to me, raising the dirt square to

clink it with mine. "Cheers." His voice is monotone and the way his face pulls in disgust as he places it on his tongue makes me want to chuck it to the ground. But then his muscles relax and he hums in satisfaction.

"What's it taste like?" I ask, not certain I can stomach the texture.

"It's..." Mason turns and quickly swallows. He points behind me. "Why don't you ask Sarge?" He chuckles. "He seems to enjoy them."

I turn to find Sarge begging for more from the Servicemembers, and they keep swatting him away unsuccessfully. My chest feels lighter as a laugh escapes me. "You're gonna have to give him your entire stock," I say to the man on the left. "Better put in a special order for your next ration."

The man doesn't know what to do with a large, drooly dog begging for food. It's hilarious. When Sarge swindles a few more from them, I finally call him off. The man's shoulders sag.

Though everyone around us seems curious about Sarge, they don't dare come any closer. It's a relief to know I won't have to be terribly social with everyone unless I want it for myself.

"So what's on the docket for today?" I ask Mason, popping the dirt square in my mouth. Flavor erupts on my tongue, my senses overloaded. Mmm. It tastes exactly like my mother's old porridge. I remember going out into the backyard with her to pick berries from the bushes that grew there. Damn, I miss her. My fingers find the pin my father gave me hidden beneath my scarf. *It will keep you safe.*

"Everyone is feeling renewed now that you're here," Mason replies. "There are two squads going out today to retrieve commoners from the Force camps. It won't be long before the Headmistress pulls away and forces everyone into the other facilities." His brow furrows.

Shivers tear through me. Not because of the Reaver potentially hiding away more civilians, but because Thomas's words are repeating in my head again, reminding me that the Service is killing without question. Without trial.

"They're killing people, you know." My voice is loud, but it feels quiet. Does Mason know? Has he known this entire time?

"What?" He stops in his tracks, halting both me and Sarge in the process.

"Thomas told me that they don't allow the Force officers a trial. They shoot first and never ask questions according to him."

Mason shakes his head, disbelief plastered on his face. "No," he says. "No. They wouldn't do that?" It comes out like a question. I, however, know all too well how believable it is. General Favager isn't the good guy here. He's the *better* one for the time being.

"They would," I say, finite. "And they are."

Sarge circles me and places himself to my right. My fingers find the soft fur of his head.

Mason's mouth opens again, but he quickly snaps it shut. His eyes droop, and they meet my greys. He nods, resigned. *So maybe he's not the mole...*

"Do you think they'd let us go?" I ask, not fully realizing how dangerous of a question I'm asking until after it's out. I'm supposed to be the figurehead. I'm supposed to be here, bolster the troops, regurgitate idiotic propaganda to the people they bring me to hope they join the cause, and that's it. Mason still believes we're operating on our old plan to locate the source. Luke and I discussed that we probably don't need to risk it. So we're developing a plan to use our knowledge of his DNA. But I don't want to sit around. I want to do something. Be useful somehow. Surely General Favager will be okay with *that*?

Mason sighs. "Why did I ever think we'd have even *one* day where you didn't try to do something dangerous?" He laughs. "There's someone here that could be discreet if necessary," he says. "But he's a bit obsessed with you, so you'll have to be the one to ask." Mason's eyebrows pop up in suggestion.

Oh, for fuck's sake.

An hour later and Luke, Mason, and I are suited and loaded up with Thomas and Trevor's squad to reclaim civilians from a small pocket of commoner camps in south Arizona. Admiral Jenkens— the man in charge of the shantytown—fawned over me for thirty minutes before finally allowing us to go. Mason wasn't kidding when he said *obsessed*. He was clearly holding back when we'd first arrived yesterday.

Luke didn't question me at all when I told him to buckle up, and the familiar power thrummed, spreading through my chest. It's holding its place even as the aircraft lifts from the ground.

It only fades once our target is seen in the distance and Luke comes to me. "Take this," he says, handing me a small device. I vaguely recall it as the same one he tried putting on me during my rescue mission. What was it called? The... "STARS," he answers my masked question.

The color drains from my face and Sarge is pressed into me in an instant. In my haste to see what was going on, I hadn't considered that I might actually have to *be* a part of it. Shit. "How will this help?" I question, my voice small. "I still don't know how to fight."

"You don't have to," he assures. "Take this, too." A gun. It feels familiar in my hands and the weight of that thought cuts deep. I've used a weapon before.

My eyes raise from the gun, skeptically looking at him.

"M," he says. "You are the smartest person I know." His hands meet my shoulders as he holds me steady. "Your execution doesn't need to be perfect, it needs to be well thought out. Keep your mind clear."

His kind words somehow find their way to my blocked heart. Luke truly does believe in me.

We touch down, and not a single person in the commoner camp reacts. They can't see us thanks to the cloaking abilities of the Chameleon Tech that Cateline designed.

"Stay cloaked," the squad leader says as the rest of us file out. What I can't fathom is if they stay cloaked, why would they ever need to kill anyone at all? "Wait." His hand extends, hitting between Luke and I, keeping me and Mason from exiting the craft. "Dog must stay here," he orders.

"Excuse me?" I say, unable to keep my tongue.

Luke turns back despite the fact that he's been allowed passage. "Shit," he says.

My eyes look past the squad leader and meet Luke's sorry hazel ones. "What?" I ask.

The squad leader speaks before Luke can. "The cloaking devices are not available for dogs, which means he'll be targeted immediately."

Mason stands up for me from behind. "The only way she's going out there is if Sarge goes with her," he argues, begging the squad leader to understand.

"Negative," the squad leader replies. "The dog is not permitted to leave the craft, for the safety of the squad. If you would like to stay with the canine, you may stay put as well." Clearly *he* is not as obsessed with me as the Admiral of the camp is. Shit.

His decision is final. I want to go, to see how the Service is doing things and actually be a part of making a difference. If I can save even one person today, I'll be able to wash some of the blood off my hands.

But without Sarge? He'd never let it happen. Not only will my soul feel the rip of us being separated, but he'll tear apart the interior just to get to me, too.

"I'll stay with him," Mason speaks up from behind me. I whip my head to meet his gaze. "You're the one who wanted to be here. You should do what you need to do." His voice is encouraging, accepting. It's also taking on a slight begging tone, which means he's been putting on a brave face this whole time and doesn't want to get in on the action here.

Sarge watches me with a steady gaze. We communicate in a language all on our own, and my mouth sets in a hard line as I think of doing anything without him. Then he sits. He plants himself down—practically on Mason's foot—and I know the decision has already been made. Sarge is okay letting me do this on my own.

His gaze flicks to Luke behind me, licking his lips, then showing his teeth for a second in warning. Okay. Never mind. He's only trusting that Luke will do what he would do. My eyes roll. Fucking *boys*.

The squad leader removes his arm from in front of me, nodding at Mason and Sarge before hitting the button to close the door of the craft. *Well, there's no going back.*

We're on the outskirts of a small, ramshackle town. There are two large tents. Both hold the Guardianship seal as well as the Force insignia on their door flaps. The one to the left is significantly larger than the other with no guards. The one on the right is guarded by two Force officers.

"That's our target," says Thomas, following behind me as we start closing the distance. Luke is in front of me, glancing back every so often, yet he's in a whole different mode. This is Officer Luke. "The guards don't let anyone in or out."

It's unnerving to walk directly toward the enemy. The guards don't bat an eyelash as we cut through the dilapidated buildings, heading straight for them. It's hard to believe that we're all invisible when the STARS allows me to see the squad of trained killers moving forward.

"This should be easy then," I argue. "We just have to knock those guards out and the..."

My words are cut short when the guards drop like dead flies. Color drains from my face immediately and from the corner of my eye, Thomas is watching me with a sorrow-filled expression.

"Ask questions never," he says, then takes off running with the rest of the crew.

Half of the squad dips into the tent on the left, and the rest veer into the right one, where the civilians are hiding. I, however, stay firmly planted where I am, unable to will my legs to move in any direction.

Somewhere in the back of my mind, the rational part of me is shouting, begging me to move, either back to Sarge and Mason, or forward toward the squad. Unfortunately, there's no time to discuss this with myself. Blood-curdling screams emanate from the tents, then the derelict town is filled with people running and bodies dropping.

Thankfully my instincts take over and I bolt, flinging my body behind a tumbled wall of rock. The air fills with dust and the stench of Death quickly, and I'm unable to see things clearly. *Luke. You have to find Luke.*

I feel Sarge's protests deep in my soul from where I am, but I've never been happier that he's not here. I don't know what I'd do if he were to get hurt... or worse.

Stop it, Amity. Focus. Shit. Okay. Someone runs by the wall and instantly hits the ground, their eyes wide as their face slams the dirt. Even through the sandy haze, it's clear that they're dead. The lifeless look of their eyes is enough for sickness to wash over me.

What happens after is what truly causes my throat to tighten and my stomach to retch. One of the Servicemembers of this squad leaps up, jamming both his feet on the dead person's skull, then backs up and kicks them again.

Thankfully the screaming buries my own cries as the Service-member spits on the desecrated body. This is *madness*. General Favager is creating monsters. How is *this* any better than what the Reaver is doing? How is this justice for all?

My heart picks up its pace as dust swirls around me and screams echo. There are no gunshots deafening my ears. Only screams, only the sound of deadweight hitting the disturbed earth. The hyper silencers created by Cateline make us an invisible enemy, and I can't begin to fathom how scared these people must be.

Where is Luke? Is he out there taking part in the unthinkable? He was supposed to stay with me, but I do my best to push the thoughts from my head. Panic will get me nowhere. Shutting down will get me nowhere. Staying on the outskirts will get me nowhere.

I need to save these people, help get them to safety, *whatever* that means these days.

My eyes squint and I force my way deeper into the town. The tents that once stood erect are now crumpled into the soil, blood-stained from unnecessary violence. How anyone can tell who is who around here is beyond me.

Thankfully, I'm relatively hidden amongst the rubble of the fallen buildings, but I clock a family off to my left through a makeshift hole in a wall. Two kids are huddled together under their mother's arms as their father blocks his wife. They push themselves into a small alcove, their outlines barely seen through the haze of filth in the air.

In a blink, there's an A.L.F. soldier standing in front of them, the blinding white of the suit camouflaged with caked on dust particles. It's hard to hear the yelling above the rest of the screams. *Move, Amity!*

Before I think to stop, my feet carry me to the family. I'm invisible right? I can take him out, do something. I don't have a clear shot of the soldier from here, but I could sneak up and hit them with the butt of the gun.

As the distance between us closes, all other sounds are drowned out by the wild beating of my heart. The sweat of my palms causes the gun to slip from my fingers, but I hold as tightly as possible and raise the weapon above my head, readying the leverage I'll need to take out someone nearly twice my size.

"What do we have here?" a voice from behind me says, startling me. It's so close, I resist the urge to turn. They can't be addressing me. I'm invisible.

Or so I thought...

An iron grip holds my wrists together, and the metal clamped against my skin bites into the softness of it. What the?

I'm whirled around, and my original target's focus is off the family now and studying me intently. At least there's that. My face meets my captor, another soldier. No one I recognize. Just one more faceless member of the Force.

"That Thorne girl!" the first soldier cheers. "You know what this means?"

The one with the iron grip grunts, not taking his eyes from me. "You'll be a nice piece of bait," he says, spitting in my face, and I cower at the harshness. "I'll be taking this," he hisses, removing the gun from my hands. "Let's move, Les."

I tug against the man's strength. "No!" Luke! Mason! Anyone, fuck. *Sarge!* "Someone help!" I cry.

But no one comes. They're all doing their own thing, they don't care what's happening when they have orders to carry out, Force members to kill. They can't hear me even if they *wanted* to help.

It's up to me.

Mercifully, the family fled in the commotion, so if this ends with me bled dry in the middle of this fucked up town, at least I helped an innocent family escape. Perhaps wherever they end up will be better than here and I at least bought them a fighting chance.

I tug again, but the second soldier has transferred my hands from above my head to behind me. He's holding them with both of his, pressing his nasty frame to my back.

If only there was something I could do. Without a gun, I'm useless. Hell, even *with* one I am. Fuck, fuck. What am I supposed to do? *Think, Amity. Think!*

That's it!

All I have to do is *think*. That's what Luke had said. Though, whether the STARS will do its job or not is a different story entirely. I was supposed to be invisible, too, and I'm not. The tech is not to be trusted so it's a long shot, but if I could rear my head and hit him in the...

The back of my skull connects with the second soldier's face with a loud *crack*.

"Fuck!" he shouts, momentarily letting go to grab his gushing nose. He twists in pain, giving me a short reprieve. Yet, the first soldier, Les, turns, assessing the scene around me. Les jumps into action, lifting a hand to grab me while his partner is down, and I want to dodge it. I think about it so badly that somehow my body maneuvers exactly the way it's supposed to. Fuck yes!

While dipped away from him, I raise my fist and uppercut

him square in the jaw, countering his blunder. He reels, shaking his head in disbelief as he stretches his mouth in response to the strike.

Before Les has a chance to recover, I aim for the low blow, kicking him straight in the balls. It's a coward's shot but who cares. He drops to his knees, cupping his gonads. Then warning bells are ringing in my head and somehow, I know the second soldier with a gushing nose is about to grab me.

My body spins, but not before his blood-covered hands grip my hair, and I shout in response to the force of the tug. "You fucking bitch," he sneers. His fingers rip at my skin, and we scuffle to the ground as I struggle to pull away. Something deep inside me claws out, like I've been here before—like I've *done* this before—and my mind shuts down. Shit, shit, *shit*. No!

Think, damn it. Think! *Don't shut down, Amity. You* can't.

My eyes close; I clear my mind. The pain of his fingernails scraping my skin attempts to pull me from my peace, but I focus on calmness. On Sarge. He's here in my mind, and he's waiting for me to return to him. I won't give up. I just *won't*.

My eyes fly open with the warning bells, and Les is back, crawling toward us. His face twisted with anguish, but I kick him again, despite the hold the second soldier has on my neck.

"Fuck the bait," Les says, keeled over. "Just fucking kill her."

"The fuck you think I'm doing?" the second one spits, tightening his grip on my airway, and my vision blurs at the edges. It feels like my eyes are going to pop out of my skull with the pressure.

His hands are still slick with his own blood. If I can move fast enough, I might be able to get him to slip. All I need is a second. His legs are twisted beneath me, so I flip my body around, going feet over head, making sure I kick Les a third time in the process. The second soldier's hands tighten further until they slip, and I'm upright, straddling his chest, my thighs holding his arms at his sides.

My lungs expand as air floods them, and I gasp, but not before I punch the second soldier in his jewels as well. He bucks me like a bull, but I hold on and do it again. Then he leans forward, sinking his teeth into my lower back.

"Shit!" I seethe, flying off him. He rolls to the side, his body curling into a fetal position. Blood drips from a perfect bite mark in the fatty flesh above my hip. Seeing both the soldiers writhing on the ground surges me with a familiar power. *You did this, Amity. You put them in their place.*

The feeling carries me even further once I locate a thick brick with jagged edges on one side. Red is all I see as I lift the stone, slamming it into Les's head, and his body goes limp with one blow. But I don't stop there. My steps are slow, closing the distance between Les and the one that choked me out. His eyes widen as I lift my weapon.

"M!" Luke calls from somewhere to the right. I don't take my eyes from the soldier in front of me though.

The brick slams into the side of his head quickly, then once again with extra force.

I only stop when he's completely unrecognizable on the dusty ground.

"Fuck, M," Luke says, beside me now. "Are you hurt?" He drinks me in, his gaze scouring every inch, trying to determine if any of the blood caking my skin is mine. The truth is, I don't know.

I take two steps toward him, then promptly empty the contents of my stomach on his shoes.

CHAPTER THIRTY-FOUR ○ AMITY

Night descends on the camp and the quiet eats away my soul. Sarge and I stay far from our tent. I refuse to let him out of my sight. His fur is always in one hand. In the other, my thumb caresses the tree pin my father gave me.

The entire way back from our mission earlier, everyone kept their distance. Whether from Sarge's extra protectiveness, or Luke's murderous rage, I couldn't tell. Nor did I care. All of their voices sounded underwater anyway. Mostly the ramblings from Luke made it through. He yelled at Mason, he yelled at the squad leader, at everyone. Apparently I was given faulty cloaking and communication.

Not only was I not invisible, there was supposed to be communication in the STARS as well. Communication I did not have. It's why Luke couldn't find me and why he's still probably cursing everyone despite it being hours since the event happened. Yet nothing uttered from my lips. All I did was sit there, keeping my fingers twisted deep into my best friend's fur, ignoring everything.

We sit at the edge of the dome's protection. Dinner was an easy refusal because I didn't want it coming up again. I saved a family, at least. I hope, anyway. I haven't asked if they were within any recovered bodies or on the list for staying here. A part of me doesn't want to know.

"Hey," a gentle voice says, causing me to jump from my thoughts back to reality.

I relax—only slightly—at the realization of who is now beside me. "Hey," I say. "Didn't think I'd see you or your other half out of that tent ever again." Sonya offers me an understanding smile as I do my best impression of a Luke smirk, pushing away the nervousness that skitters around in my chest.

"Soreness does put a damper on marital activities," she says, sighing. "Besides, I heard you had a rough day today. Figured maybe it would be nice to talk."

I scoff, tightening my grip on Sarge. He scoots into the opening between my legs, pressing himself as close as possible. I don't want to *talk*. I want... shit. I don't know what I want. But I know if I was going to talk, it wouldn't be to Sonya. She doesn't know anything, least of all me.

"What do you think happens when we die?" she questions, changing direction.

I avert my gaze, staring at the grass gently blowing in the artificial breeze. I've been wondering that since I caved that soldier's skull in. He's dead. I... *killed* him. What fate did I send him to?

No. That feeling needs to be shoved deep. At least the man wasn't innocent. He was going to hurt me. But if that's really true, then why do I feel so guilty?

Sighing, I shake my head. Sonya wants to know what happens when we die, but I'm still trying to figure out what it means to be alive. Maybe Death is better overall? The suffering ends, and the pain is gone. Would it really be so bad? Maybe I did that soldier a favor... he would've been killed anyway; I was only doing the inevitable...

"You're bargaining," Sonya says, pointedly.

My neck snaps in her direction. "What?"

"You took a life today," she says. "You're not a trained mercenary, you're just an ordinary person."

I look at her now. Really look at her. My eyes study her, probing deep into her soul, before widening. Oh, shit. "You've killed someone, too?"

Sonya sighs. "Lots of us have," she points out. "But it's... different for you and me. A lot heavier, somehow."

My mouth pops open to say something, but I quickly close it. Sonya is a mystery to me. I thought she knew nothing of me, but the truth is, it's me that knows nothing of her. *Maybe give her a chance, Amity...*

"Have you ever gone cliff jumping?" Sonya asks, catching me off guard.

My eyes meet hers as they soften. Any anger I felt before melts from my icy heart. Sonya doesn't deserve my misplaced emotions. She's not the one I'm angry with. I shake my head.

"Imagine you're staring at the dark waters from a high cliff. It's... exhilarating, yet frightening. What do you do?" Sarge's weight pushes into me further, calming me once again.

I stay quiet, not sure if this is meant to be rhetorical or not.

"You jump," she argues. "You jump exactly at the moment you realize how scary it is because life is too short to hesitate—to tremble in fear. Zach taught me that." She smiles fondly. "I think he may have taught you that, too."

My mouth pops open. Zach. The man from my nightmares. The one whose garbled words terrorize me; the one who died for me.

"I'm sorry you don't remember much," Sonya continues. "But that doesn't make you any less brave. It doesn't make you any *less* in general."

My knuckles tense. Do I think I'm less? No. I don't. I...

I flick my greys to meet her blues. I *do* think I'm less. It's why I felt the need to go on the mission; to do something, *anything*, to prove that I'm not a fraud. I tear my gaze from hers, wanting to avoid their knowing expression.

"I have these nightmares," I say, gulping, remembering the tortured look on Zach's face, on Luke's. "It's my fault everyone is dead and now..." My voice fades into the din of the night. "Now, I think it might really be true." I was a monster today. I was the very thing I abhorred. I ended a life. I *chose* to end a life in my anger. Fuck...

Though my eyes don't lift from the ground, I sense Sonya's watchful gaze on me. Sarge is cuddled deep into my chest, and I hug him closer, tightening my grasp.

"You can't save them all," Sonya says, shrugging. "Just remember that." She offers me an apologetic smile. "I miss Zach every day, but I'm not mad at you for it. And you shouldn't be either."

My mouth dries, a sob forming in my throat. How can she say it with such certainty? Though she's talking about Zach, I have a feeling she's extending it to my victim from today as well.

"Anyway, you know how everyone is, always *worrying* and whatnot." Her hand slices through the air in a dismissive manner. "I'll tell 'em you're doing alright, and if you're ever ready to talk, know I'm always here." She places her hand on my thigh, giving me a reassuring squeeze and smile.

I nod. Sonya leaves us, but before she gets too far, I call out to her. "Thank you."

Through the darkness, her hand raises above her head in a thumbs up and the soft wind carries her chuckle. Then it's just Sarge cuddled between my legs. We're surrounded by silence once more.

I should get some rest, but I don't want to close my eyes. I don't want to see whatever nightmares will plague me this time. I shudder, pulling Sarge closer to my chest, sinking my fingers deep into his fur.

This is wrong. It's *all* wrong. How am I any better than the H.P.S.? Than the A.L.F.? There's so much Death, and somehow, I find myself contributing to it.

A gargled scream escapes my throat and my fists ball into Sarge's softness. His hot tongue finds my face, instantly trying to calm me. How did this happen? How did we get here?

I'm not a hero; I'm not a leader. I'm a... a *monster*.

I don't want to be this way. These people are killing in *my* name, and I somehow descended into the madness as well. No one should ever feel this way. I slump backward, leaning against the shrubs that line the outer edge of the town. Sarge leaps next to me, pushing us further into the branches. How am I supposed to go on? How can I be the leader they need? I wanted to prove to myself that I wasn't a fraud, but only proved how much of one I truly am.

"Ugh," I spit out into the nighttime quiet.

Next thing I know, I'm walking through the woods with Zach and a familiar fear creeps beneath my skin. "Stop!" I cry.

He looks at me with confusion. Tears spring to my eyes.

"We have to stop," I repeat. "You're going to die if we go on." My tone is tinged with distress and my fingers lock into his shirt.

"Slugger," he says, relaxing his shoulders. "We have to be brave."

The tears roll down my face now, I can't help it. "I don't..." My lungs expand and expand but they never seem to get air into them. "Don't..."

"Listen to me." Zach holds me at arm's length, bringing his eyes in line with mine. "Bravery is when we feel these fears—these terrorizing thoughts—and still push forward. If you aren't afraid, you can't be brave."

My eyes scan his, and I sniffle. I don't want to be brave; I want him to *live*.

Zach continues, slowly leading me further into the woods, the pit in my stomach deepening. "The fact that you are fighting day in and day out despite what you're feeling proves how strong and brave you are. Make no question about it." His smile is peaceful despite the anxiety growing in me.

Am I brave?

I don't feel it...

"We have to stop," I say again, this time pulling him backward with me. "You don't have to die! We just have to go back."

Zach shakes his head, chuckling. "We can't change what has happened, we can only decide how we're going to continue." And with his next step, he spins directly into a knife.

"No!" I scream, dropping to my knees. "Zach!"

"Keep going, Slugger," he says, garbled around the blood pooling in his mouth. It drips down his chin and I gag. "You can do it. Keep going."

Sweat clings to my skin, drenching my hairline, as I shoot up from the bushes. Sarge is already licking me profusely. Shit.

I can't escape the nightmares no matter where I sleep. But maybe Zach is right. Sonya said as much, too. I can't be stuck in my feelings when there are people looking to me for change. I need to be brave; I need to push on.

But this isn't the way it's supposed to be, and if we're going to keep going, things are going to have to be different.

CHAPTER THIRTY-FIVE ∘ AMITY

MASON AND LUKE WALK UP TO THE CROWD FORMING WITH furrowed brows. I do my best to ignore their probing gazes. The fact that they're together is alarming enough, but I shove the nerves down.

After my nightmare, I realized things need to shift. Just because we can take control in such a violent way, doesn't mean we should. Things may be scary, but we can be brave and keep going. Our methods have to change because killing is not the answer. It will only lead us down the road the Reaver has already paved.

The people of the shantytown are congregating in droves, waiting to hear what their figurehead has to say. Sarge and I spent the rest of our early morning leaving notes on everyone's tent, telling them to gather at breakfast.

When I can barely see the faces of those at the back of the crowd, I begin. "As the Guardianship's true nature comes to light, the Reaver heads into her endgame for the hope of saving Humanity," I call. "But that doesn't mean we retaliate with hate. If we answer her call with the same methods that she founded herself on, we're only continuing the violence."

The voices thin out. Everyone stares on with more confusion than before. Shit, I need to be better at this.

"Right now, the members of this group are partaking in hei-nous acts of killing in the name of justice," I say, rethinking my words. "Just because the people of the American Liberation Force seem different than us, doesn't mean we should take their lives. Don't they deserve trials? Don't they deserve our mercy?" My fin-gers find their way to Sarge's fur. Thankfully, his presence keeps everyone from closing in on us too tightly.

"The Force members deserve to rot!" someone calls.

My mouth pops open in shock.

The unruly crowd-goer gives confidence to others. "They de-serve to burn for carrying out her plans!"

Hoping it would be that easy is a fool's wish. I lift my hands to signal everyone to quiet. "I know it may seem scary to change the way things are, but we can be brave, and we can transform the future," I say, hoping they see the vision. "One where we embrace our differences and work together to create something wonderful for *everyone*, not just those we deem Exceptional, or better."

The sea of people murmurs loudly, whispering amongst them-selves in general disgust. No one is happy with this, and it dawns on me that these people may be too far gone. The General has woven his own evil in the name of the people—in my name—and they're eating it up. They've idolized me, idolized their sense of justice for all, and it's beyond fixing now. It's all twisted. This is how the Reaver took over. She radicalized simple things, rooting them deep into the people, and before they knew it, they'd con-tributed to their own division and downfall. It's killing me that they can't see what's so plainly right in front of their faces. We are repeating history.

"This can't be the same girl that stormed Omphalos," someone in the front says. "She must've hit her head a bit too hard." Their friends beside them laugh and heat flushes in my cheeks.

Anger surges forward, my fists tighten at my sides. "*You* will be the one to burn in hell for your actions, right alongside those of the Force that truly believe killing is the only way." I take a step closer as the rage builds inside. Sarge keeps himself against me. "You are no better than the people you spit on."

The person in the front comes back with, "Word in town is that you enjoyed killing as well." They scoff. "You're a hypocrite!"

Red. All I see is red. My heartbeat pulses in my ear. Sarge snarls beside me, baring teeth to the loudmouth. "We may win the battles with this cowardice, but we will not win a *war*," I spit. "The Reaver is but one of many evils, and if we cannot learn to accept one another and live in peace, then the cycle will continue."

My body is radiating heat. The person of the crowd is within arm's reach now. They look to me, and then down at Sarge still snarling at my side. Their hands go up in surrender. "The only coward I see here is you." And with that, the crowd disperses.

They break off in sections and discuss amongst themselves what they'd all just witnessed. My fingers fist into Sarge's fur and I keep my breaths as even as possible to avoid making myself look even more foolish. Just like that, I've lost my influence. My chest deflates with powerlessness.

Are they truly so far gone that peace is a foreign, unachievable concept?

Mason and Luke enter my space methodically. "What was all that about?" Mason questions.

My knees hit the ground; my head falls to my hands. Sarge pushes into my side. Mason and Luke stand in front of me, blocking the scene from others. Two more sets of shoes stand behind me. Probably Lacy and Sonya.

"The way they do things here is nightmarish," I say, not taking my hands from my face. As the words leave my lips, it's clear how pathetic they sound. *And* how hypocritical I am. Damn it. I don't want to see the pity in everyone's eyes.

Lacy drops to sit behind me, wrapping her arms around my shoulders. "That certainly wasn't the welcome we'd received when we first got here," she says in my ear. Her cheek rests on the back of my head.

"It was brave of you to stand up here and try, anyway," Sonya adds, slinking down next to her wife, wrapping one arm behind her love, and the other around Sarge beside me. His tail wags, beating lightly against the dirt.

"We have to leave."

My eyes shoot up to the source of the sound. Luke is standing directly in front of me still, with Mason beside him. The latter is nervously rubbing the back of his neck, while the former stands with his arms crossed.

"What?" I ask.

"Maybe we discuss this out of the way of prying eyes?" Mason suggests, his eyes bouncing between me and Luke.

Luke's gaze is hardened on me, but after a few seconds, he peers toward Mason and nods.

Then, our little group travels to the edge of the town, the place where Luke made his own camp.

"What's all this about? We just got here," Lacy points out once we're all settled. I'm right there with her. Sure, their methods are demented, but leaving? How would we even do that? It won't be us against the Reaver. It'll be us against all. And that worries me. Because too many innocent lives are at stake.

"Staying won't suit us. Not for long, anyway," Luke says, his brow furrowed.

What else has Luke discovered? We were supposed to hang out here for a while until we could figure out a new plan, one that could replace our "finding the source" idea, while also keeping Luke's identity a secret. Does he believe leaving is the answer? *Does he know the General is looking for him?*

"If we cut away from the H.P.S. then we'll have two enemies on our tail. We'll be outlaws no matter where we go. Is that really the better method?" I question.

"We have two enemies regardless," Luke replies. "You remember your faulty tech?"

I nod, gulping. A reminder of the misdeed creeps into the back of my brain but I shove it down. Sarge snuggles into my thigh and my fingers find familiar comfort in his fur.

"That was on purpose." Luke's voice is dark, his expression hard. His muscles ripple with tension beneath his shirt. *What?* "Think about it. What's the only other most effective way you could help win this war? A way in which you won't be such a thorn in Favager's side."

Mason is a ticking time bomb of nerves. Lacy and Sonya are whispering amongst themselves as usual.

"No," Lacy says, realization dawning. "You think so?"

I glance between her and Luke, confusion contorting my features. What am I missing?

"I do," Luke nods. "And I've convinced chucklehead here of it as well, so it must be solid." His thumb jabs through the air, indicating Mason.

"What's going on?" I ask, done with the games. My brain is too mushy. Someone is going to tell me what the answer to this question is right now.

Luke's hazels meet mine and they soften. "Dying," he says. "That's the answer."

I can't help the sharp intake of breath at this news. Dying? I was given faulty tech in hopes I would perish?

"This whole assignment was set up with you in mind," Luke continues. "Favager knew you'd go off and try to do shit on your own. He's been pulling the strings this whole time. He doesn't just want you to *be* here. He wants you to *die* here."

Fuck. We've gotta get out of this camp.

o   o   o

BY THE TIME night falls, I'm tired of pacing, but I'm sure Sarge is having a blast. Lacy and Sonya are dizzy watching me. They stopped trying to get me to sit hours ago. We're really going to leave here. Mason and Luke are working on stealing us a craft to fly on out of this little town. How ridiculous!

I'm a ball of nerves and restless energy. "This isn't going to work," I say once again, pacing the length of a fallen log. "What are we even going to do out in the wilderness with nothing?" I want to rip my hair out.

"Woah, hey," Lacy says. "We did pretty good the last time we were roughing it." Oh, right. When Abby and Zach died. My eyes roll.

"Last time was a disaster if I remember correctly, and that's only with *half* of my memories," I say, sighing. Shit. I plop myself on the log, causing Sarge to run into my legs at the quick motion. Then he weasels his way close to me, his tail rubbing a line into the dirt from its wagging. My head rests in my hands.

"Just jump," Sonya says, sitting beside me.

I scoff. She wants me to jump off the cliff with every ounce of courage in my heart. "I don't want to. This is becoming too much."

"Becoming?" Lacy chuckles, taking the other side of me, petting Sarge mindlessly. "We're all in this together," she says. "Don't ever forget that."

My shoulders tense. That's the problem, isn't it? If it were just my life on the line like it is here, maybe I could get behind it. But once we leave, I'm putting all of the people I care about in danger as well. We'll be fugitives from both sides. There will be no one to help us but ourselves, and it'll be extremely dangerous around every turn. Damn it! *This is exactly why you shouldn't get close to people, Amity. It only makes things harder.*

"You should all stay," I say. "If I must go, I can do so by myself. Then you won't be in any danger."

"Hell no!" Lacy says, cutting into the quiet of the night. "We're going with you. You're not doing this alone."

"Ugh!" I cry. "I'm going to get you all killed." The words fall out of my mouth in a whisper. Just like Abby, just like Zach, like Nan, and... the soldier. They will all die because of me. I feel the spiral taking me before I can stop.

My vision darkens around the edges, it's hard to get air into my lungs. Then there's earth beneath my knees and palms. I'm not on the log anymore.

"Hey!" a voice in the distance calls. "Hello! Amity?"

When I come to, Sarge is staring at me from above, as are Sonya and Lacy. Sarge lies down, placing his chin in the crook of my neck, pressing himself into my skin.

"Welcome back," Sonya says, smiling. "Everything's alright." Her calm tone is reassuring, but my mind is still whirring with panic.

Lacy flops onto her back, lying next to me. Sonya does the same. They both reach for my hands simultaneously and my fingers flex in their grip. The three of us sit like this, with Sarge above us, staring at the stars.

When my heartbeat finally calms, I say, "Thank you."

"No problemo," Lacy says, offering a squeeze of her fingers.

"Listen," Sonya says. "*You* are not going to get us killed. We're all adults capable of making our own decisions, and we've decided we're doing this with you. There will be no blaming you for anything that happens. Do you understand?"

Her hand tugs on mine and my lip quivers. When did I become deserving of friends like this? I sniffle, then nod slowly.

"Good," Sonya replies. "Now let's all jump together."

CHAPTER THIRTY-SIX ○ AMITY

LACY SHAKES ME AWAKE AND I'M MORE DISORIENTED THAN I'D like to admit. "What?" I question, coming to. "What's going on?"

Of course, the one time I actually get a decent rest. I stifle an eye roll.

"They're ready for us," Lacy says. "We have to go now."

My heart picks up its pace and Sarge taps his feet beside me as I sit up. We're on the outskirts of the shantytown. *Oh, right.* We were waiting for Mason and Luke to secure us an aircraft to escape when I had a panic attack. I must have been more wiped out than I thought, because I don't remember succumbing to sleep...

"Come on, they're waiting." Sonya backtracks to her wife, telling us we need to move. This is it. It's really happening.

Lacy helps me the rest of the way up and we follow Sonya, slinking along the outer edge, using the cover of dark to keep us as hidden as possible. Though it's still pretty early in the morning, there are a few stragglers around that are thankfully too engrossed in their own lives to detect us. We need to be long gone before anyone notices that we're not present.

Luke is standing in the doorway of a *mostly* invisible aircraft. Even from this distance, his weighted expression is clear. When his eyes finally observe me, his shoulders sag with relief. The dangers of what's about to come hit me full force. We're really doing this.

Sonya is the first to board—about a hundred feet ahead—and she disappears around the corner once inside the craft's cloaking. Lacy is just about there when someone shouts, "Hey!" and her head whips toward the sound, as does mine and Luke's. Shit. We've been compromised!

"Let's go!" Luke shouts, motioning for Lacy to quicken her pace.

Dirt ricochets to the left of me, then again slightly behind, and my eyes widen. My heart beats wildly in my chest as Sarge and I take off into a run. Lacy jumps in the aircraft, disappearing the same as her wife. *Thank goodness she's safe.*

"Stop!" someone calls. "We don't want to hurt you!" More bullet holes plague the ground beneath my feet. Don't want to hurt me, my ass. They're *trying* to hit us!

Luke shouts something into the void of the craft, and it fires up, ready to take off. "Sarge!" he calls, urging Sarge to go ahead.

Sarge offers a sideways glance to me. I tell him to go. Maybe if he's a safe distance from me, the Service won't accidently hit him if I'm the target.

My four-legged companion pushes on, breaking away. The craft lifts from the ground and Sarge dives, making it in before it's too far up. I'm still a bit away. The panic in my chest is tightening, making it hard to breathe. *Am I going to make it?*

As the thought materializes in my brain, a burning sensation radiates from my calf, then the ground rushes up to meet my face. Shit.

I scramble to my knees, my gaze watching the aircraft elevate faster now. Luke leaps out, tumbling to the ground and running toward me all in one swift movement. The shower of bullets around me slows a bit as Servicemembers scramble to catch up now that I've fallen. It's then that I glance back and notice the wound on my leg. Color drains from my face.

"Luke!" I shout, reaching forward as if it might help him get to me faster. *Get up, Amity! Go!*

Pushing through the pain, my body lifts and I sprint, stumbling every time my right leg thumps the ground. I ignore the bodies that are coming from behind me, only focusing on the man in my view. Thankfully, Luke's hand finally grasps mine. He tugs me forward, hauling me against his chest. It's a split second before we're moving again and a rope tumbles down from above. The craft is directly over us.

"Hang on," Luke instructs, then he leaps. My arm feels like it's being torn from its socket as I'm ripped from the ground with him. He's holding the rope with one hand, me with the other. *Don't look down, don't look down!*

I grit my teeth and reach my other hand up, locking both around his wrist. We're above the tree line now. A fall from this distance would likely mean dozens of broken bones... or worse. Luke is doing his best to muscle me up despite the bullet fire around us. His grunts are drowned out by my beating heart, but eventually he gets me against his chest, and I lock my arms around his neck in a Death grip. My legs wrap around his midsection just the same. My eyes clench shut in fear, in relief, in... whatever. Who cares? I'm not on the ground, I'm not dead. Everyone is safe in the craft.

"M," Luke says after an indeterminate amount of time. One eye pops open and I realize we're in the aircraft. "You can let go now." His chest bounces beneath me with a chuckle.

When my feet hit the floor, Sarge circles around me and my fingers find his fur subconsciously. Lacy grips me in her arms, hugging me tightly to her.

"Thank goodness you're okay!" she cries.

My heart is still unable to slow, but I take in my surroundings once Lacy releases me. Sonya is beside her wife, consoling her more than she's worried about me, which is exactly how it should be. Mason is working his way toward me, medical bag in hand.

Shit, that's right.

As the adrenaline wanes, a deep, throbbing ache spreads through my calf. My balance shifts and I find myself using Sarge as a brace to keep myself upright.

"Sit," Mason says, pointing to the seat off to my left. I do.

Dizziness runs rampant through my brain. Everyone is beside me, watching, but my eyes don't focus on anything in particular.

Sarge's tongue finds my cheek. It helps root me in reality.

Who's driving this thing?

"Hold her leg up," Mason instructs to someone, possibly Luke. "This is going to hurt."

A scream rises in my throat as Mason pokes and prods my leg. My fingers rip at Sarge's fur, and darkness swims at the edge of my vision. Sweat drips from my hairline, my shirt sticks to my back. At some point, Lacy wipes my forehead with a cold rag and I welcome the cooling sensation.

"There," Mason says, standing back to admire his work. His gloved hands are covered in red and sweat clings to him just as it does me.

"M," Luke says, gently setting my leg down. "How are you doing?" The concern etched across his face causes my heart to constrict.

"Fine," I say, but it comes out barbaric and grunty. My throat is dry. "Who's driving?"

A smirk curls on Luke's lips. "Trevor," he says.

Trevor? Does that mean Thomas is here, too?

As if he's heard my silent question, Thomas makes his presence known. "Now that they know we're gone, we're not going to get very far," he says, addressing Luke. "Trevor says if we don't touch down soon, our controls will be disabled."

Mason has gone to clean himself up, Lacy is gripping my hand so tightly I think my fingers may fall off. Luke stands up, making himself level with Thomas. His crinkled expression has a heavy weight spreading through my body. Did I ever think we'd be safe?

"Tell Trevor to do whatever he thinks is best. We'll have to gather up our supplies and travel on foot." Luke's voice is commanding. He's hot when he's in charge. *Shit, Amity. Did you really just think that right now?*

Color flares in my cheeks.

"You think they would risk killing us all?" Lacy questions beside me.

"It's possible," Luke replies. "They could spin whatever story they wanted to."

I pull Sarge closer to me, holding him tightly. How stupid would it be if we did all this work to escape only to barely make it outside of the dome?

"M?" Luke is directly in front of me now. "You should rest if you can."

My head shakes without much thought. "No," I say. "I'm not resting while everyone else does something to further this mission. Give me a job to do so we can be ready."

Luke's eyes widen, but then he purses his lips, nodding. "Fine," he says. "I'm going to check in with Trevor, then we'll make a plan. Wait here for now," he says.

He doesn't make it far before we start plummeting from the sky.

CHAPTER THIRTY-SEVEN ∘ LUKE

GRAVITY SHIFTS AND MY EYES NATURALLY FLICK TO M. HER eyes are as wide as saucers and my heart nosedives into my stomach faster than the hovercraft is headed toward the ground. My only concern is getting her out alive.

Mason runs in from the washroom and clocks the situation. As much as I hate him, it's best if he stays with M while I convene with Trevor to figure out a plan. We're not going to have much longer before the earth is upon us.

"Stay," I say to Mason, pointing to the woman I love. He nods, immediately understanding my command.

There's hardly any time between the word leaving my lips and me spinning away to find the cockpit. Trevor is working hard on the controls, shouting orders at Thomas behind him. "We need to release the slats!"

"What else do you need?" I ask, closing the distance. My eyes roam the large map to my left to see where we are. We're somewhere within old Utah. Running through multiple scenarios in my head, my mind keeps coming to only one possible way we make it out of this alive.

"To live," Trevor responds, not taking his eyes from the windshield.

"Our best bet is to land in this lake here," I say, pointing, hating the idea even more out loud despite it making the most sense. "These things become submarines, don't they?"

Cateline once shared with me all the crazy designs she'd come up with. The hovercraft isn't one thing, it's multiple. Land, air, or sea, it's capable of traversing a wide range of terrain, and it should keep us safe until we can figure something out.

"Not with the controls disabled," Trevor says, bursting my idea before it ever really blooms.

Fuck. "How deep is it?" Maybe there's something we can do. It'll be the softest landing, though I hate to think we'll be encased in a watery tomb for any period of time, let alone possibly until we die.

"One hundred feet at its max, on average it's about eighty, though," Trevor answers. "We'll all suffocate within two hours, less if we hit the deepest part, and we won't be able to open the doors or move." He's still furiously pressing buttons and levers around him to see if anything at all will work. "We can't deploy any of our safety measures, either." His mouth is set in a hard line when he finally looks at me.

"We're not giving up," I say, more like a reminder than a command. The woman I love is on this flying Death trap. There will be no stopping until we succeed. Failure is not an option.

Trevor fondles his chin with his fingers, a comical way to think in a time like this. Though it's Thomas who steps forward now.

"There's got to be a better way," he says, practically begging. "What if we manually inflate the flotation devices? Sure, we won't be able to move, but at least the craft will float?" His voice is hopeful, causing my heart to flip. It could work, but we have about three minutes max before we're above the lake, and Trevor will have to put us into a nosedive to hit our target.

"Even if we're successful in any sort of landing, the Service will be right on our trail," I point out. "What then?" Sinking us may be the best bet, at least they'll think we're dead. Hopefully. I share this line of thinking with the brothers. "They can use M as a martyr. It also gets one enemy off our ass." I pour my focus back on Trevor. "Is there *anything* we can do once we're at the bottom? Anything? What if we do the flotation devices once we're sunk?"

"Shit!" Trevor shouts. "I forgot! Every aircraft features a crash bubble. It's a manual pull string. We could, in theory, use it to shoot back to the surface."

"Is it strong enough to raise us from the depths?" I question. I don't dare allow myself to get too hopeful, but we're quickly running out of options.

Trevor decides that in theory it would work, but it's never been tested before. "If we do, in fact, make it back to the surface, we'll be faced with a whole new set of problems, but we don't have time to discuss it. If we're doing this, we have to do it now."

My shoulders sag with the news and I clench my teeth. Is it worth potentially dying over an unknown theory? Shit. My eyes bounce between the brothers. Ah, fuck it. "Let's do it."

"We'll have to hit on the nose perfectly or we risk cracking the windshield," Trevor says. "Hold on tight," he warns, then lifts the steering to drop us into a nosedive.

My arm shoots out, fingers tense, white-knuckled on a random lever sticking out of the side wall. My body is fighting the change in gravity. I hope M is safe where she is. If she's not—and we survive this—Mason's head will be on a platter.

The lake gets closer in the windshield, my body tenses when we make contact. A loud cracking sound reverberates through my skull as we slice the surface. Then, everything is dark, and gravity shifts once more. There's an odd sense of floating before the plunge in my stomach returns. Everything groans around us as the pressure drops.

After a minute or so, the emergency lights kick on, casting an eerie glow on everything. Thank the stars they still work. Trevor is no longer frantically pressing buttons, and Thomas is as still as a statue, eyes wide. A part of me wants to drop and race to wherever M is, but I know it'll be safer where I am until we hit bottom.

"What's that noise?" Thomas asks, pulling me from my thoughts.

"It's the rush of us dropping," Trevor answers. "No need to worry." He rolls his eyes, spinning in his chair. He's dismissing his brother as he always does, but I hear it too. It's almost like...

"Uh, are you sure?" Thomas points as my eyes catch the scene. Water gushes in from the windshield all the way to the right, pouring over the control panel from the seam. Shit!

Trevor's eyes widen and his palms meet his temples. "Think," he says, hunched over, trying to pull an idea from his head physically. If we don't patch this up, we won't survive long at all. "We could bust an air tank to equalize the pressure, but we'll be using up oxygen faster than I'd like."

The craft continues to sway as it drops further into the lake's depths. "We're going to have to deploy the crash bubble," Thomas says. "It'll block more water from coming in."

"No!" I shout, "It's too early. We can't surface yet." This whole water crash will have been for nothing if we shoot to the surface prematurely.

"Well, if we don't do something fast, we're all going to drown!" Trevor yells. As if he's already decided, he continues with, "Thomas, it's over there. Remove the panel. Boss, grab that metal bar in the corner. Put it through the loop that falls and both you and Thomas will be able to hang on it at once. It's going to take a lot of pressure."

Shit. I know we need to stop the water, but the Service will no doubt be waiting for us at the top. Another crack sound pulls me from my thoughts. Water floods in faster now as the windshield separates from the seam further. Fuck, we're out of time.

Despite the feeling building in my chest, I rush to grab the piece. Thomas already has the panel open by the time I turn around with the bar. Trevor is frantically trying to strengthen the seal and slow the stream of water pouring into the captain's room. Water sloshes at my ankles now, drenching my shoes. I quickly slide the bar through the looped rope and grab one side while Thomas grabs the other. We look at each other for a split second before nodding. Then, we both jump, and our dead weight moves the rope only halfway. Shit!

We try again. Nothing.

"Trev!" Thomas shouts.

"Fuck," he seethes, turning to us. He returns his gaze to the window and then back in our direction, contemplating what to do next. "Fuck it," he says, releasing the pressure on the windshield. The second he does, it splits further. Water pours in even faster now, the whooshing sound growing louder. "We've got about forty seconds to get this or we're going to have a lot less air than I initially explained." He's already grabbing in between Thomas and I on the bar by the time he finishes his lecture, and the level of water really starts to take its toll. Without someone holding back the water, it'll quickly be at our knees.

"1... 2..." I start. "3!"

We all jump, our full weight coming down. But it's still not enough. Damn it!

"Baines get your ass in here!" I shout, and we jump again, water splashing beneath us.

The water is shin-level as Mason trudges through the door. Without any explanation needed, he grabs where he can. We all jump together.

Finally, as the water reaches knee height, there's a loud *pop*, and through the windshield, the protective bubble surrounds us. The water slows now that there's a dam between the lake and us, but it doesn't completely stop. Whatever is within the bubble will still work its way through the opening in the seam.

My arms burn from exhaustion and all of us drop to the floor at nearly the same time, sloshing water around us. Trevor, Thomas, and Mason take a moment to catch their breath, but the minute my feet hit the floor, I'm running toward M.

Supplies litter the ground, floating in the water, and I almost trip on more than one occasion getting to the girls. They're all thankfully buckled in, not a single one hurt. I release the air from my lungs. M clings to Sarge, holding him close, and I put myself right in front of her in an instant. Even though physically she appears fine, I need to hear her say it.

"M," I whisper. She's staring at me blankly. My fingers reach out to swipe the loose hair from her face, but before they make contact, she recoils. Ouch. "Are you okay?" I ask, clenching a fist at my side.

Her eyes focus on mine. It takes her a few seconds, but eventually she nods.

"Did we really just plummet into a lake?" Lacy questions, one arm hooked onto Sonya and the other onto M.

"Yes," Trevor says off to my right, entering the passenger section. "Hope everyone's okay because we have to get moving *now*."

"What do we even do?" Mason questions. I hate that I agree with him. What the fuck happens now?

Lacy and Sonya have already worked themselves out of their restraints and are helping M and Sarge out of theirs. I stand, facing Trevor, the cold water numbing my shins.

"Are we suspended?" I question. As much as I didn't want to risk surfacing too soon with the Service tracking us, potentially being stuck underwater without a way up is no better.

It makes sense that the Service would tear us down to drag us right back to their camp. As much as we're prisoners in Western America, it seems that's just as true with the Service. M knows as much as anyone that we're not safe wherever we go now, and both players are willing to kill to win. But I'd only wanted to convince them we were dead, not *actually* die.

Trevor nods. "I think so. Fucking lake is pitch black so it's hard to tell, but it doesn't seem we're moving at all." His mouth is set in a hard line. Shit. I was really hoping this escape would be easier. What a foolish thought.

"There's a simple way out, right?" Sonya asks. You would think with the craft being equipped with an emergency impact bubble for when all controls fail, then there would have to be an easy way to break out. But even if that were the case, we're still stuck at an undetermined depth, surrounded by water.

"Unfortunately, no," Trevor says, shaking his head. "The only thing it has is an Emergency Signaling Beacon to alert other members of your location so they can rescue you."

"Fuck," Mason and I say at the same time beneath our breath.

"This wasn't meant for fugitives," Trevor points out, shrugging. "Nor was it meant for... whatever this is."

This is ridiculous. The Service locked us out and gave us a choice. Either crash and burn or deploy the bubble and alert them right to us. Fuck. Evil bastards. Smart, I'll give them that. But still.

I'm acutely aware of M behind me, but I keep most of my focus on the task at hand. I owe it to her to get us out of here as safely as possible. They won't get us.

"What are the odds the H.P.S. will save us down here?" M questions. It's a valid point. This whole plan was meant for them to think we're dead, but since we deployed the bubble, they're being alerted to our location at this very moment. Will they do something to get to us?

"They risk everyone, including their own, if they cut the bubble open," Thomas points out.

Trevor's brow tightens, as does mine. If we can somehow find a way out of here, we may be able to further lead the Service off our trail.

"Wait," Mason says. "Don't they have all types of emergency gear in here?"

Trevor's eyes widen with realization. "Yes," he confirms. "There are airlock masks and emergency wrist floats. That's it!"

Thomas cuts in now. "Why didn't we think of that before?" His palm slaps his forehead. "We'll be able to climb to the surface and swim to shore."

We're going to cut our way out of here and escape that way. It's a good plan, except...

"What about Sarge?" M asks, worry dripping from her tone. Sarge won't fit the masks, nor will putting the wrist flotations on him work because it will carry him to the surface upside down, probably drowning him in the process.

Trevor's mouth hardens into a line. "We'll figure it out, but for now, everyone work on gathering supplies that we can use on the run and I'll gather the emergency gear."

My eyes meet M and she swallows hard. Think, Warin. Think! What are we going to do?

CHAPTER THIRTY-EIGHT ○ AMITY

WHY DID WE EVER DECIDE TO LEAVE CAMP? EVERYONE IS scrambling, finding supplies and packing them into bags, but I'm just sitting here wondering how the hell I'm going to get my best friend out of this alive.

"M," Luke says, closing the distance. "We need to get you a supplies bag."

Pfft. I fight the urge to roll my eyes, my fingers tightening in Sarge's fur. "What I *need* is a solid plan. Fuck the supplies. If Sarge dies, nothing matters." A white-knuckled fist is pressed to my side, muscles tensed. The thought is almost too much to bear, but Luke must understand.

His shoulders sag as he takes a somber breath. "You think I'd let that happen?" he says. "Never."

I want to believe him, but that's how we got into this mess in the first place. We should've taken our chances with the H.P.S.. I shake my head. "We don't even know how deep we are," I argue. "Unless you can rig something for Sarge to breathe, I don't see how you're so sure." My mouth sets into a hard line. There may be a way to get Sarge safely to the surface without a mask, but if we don't figure out how deep we are, we won't know if he'll even be able to hold his breath that long. What's the point of getting him up there if he suffocates anyway?

The thought makes me gag. My chest tightens and I feel like throwing up right into the water that's causing a creeping chill to sweep through my body. The level is above my knees and it's hard to walk in.

"I know what you're thinking," Luke says, scoffing to himself, turning toward the others scurrying through the water like flopping fish.

My eyes scan over his face. There's a sadness to it. "What am I thinking?" I ask.

He sighs. "You think we should've stayed at camp," he replies. Shit, that *is* what I was thinking. "But if we did that, there would be a one hundred percent chance you'd be killed, and probably Sarge, too." His eyes meet mine now. "After that I'd do something to get myself killed as well, because a life without you isn't one worth living."

I can't help the sharp intake of breath that cuts my lungs. How does he say things like this so casually?

"Our chances for survival aren't great," he starts again, turning once more to study the others, "but it's better than zero, which we both know would've been the outcome if we stayed."

Another chill sends a twitch through my muscles, the cold aching deep, especially in the wound on my leg. Then, I nod. Luke is right. It's a constant fight for survival and we have to choose the route with the best odds, no matter how difficult it may be.

Luke nods in return. "Good," he says. "Now go gather supplies with everyone. I'll try to figure out our depth and look at the gear we have available." He scans my face before twisting and trudging away into the captain's room.

Once he disappears, my gaze falls to Sarge standing next to me. His mouth pops open in a smile as his tongue flops out. The water is up to his chest, but he doesn't seem bothered at all. Luke better come up with a plan, or Trevor, or anyone really, because I'm way out of my league here. The only thing I know for sure is that I'm not leaving this underwater tomb if Sarge can't.

I join the others in gathering supplies, trying my best to ignore the sweeping chill of my muscles that are covered by water. Sarge holds the pack in his mouth as I load in everything we could possibly think to need while on the run.

By the time Luke and Trevor return, my legs are numb, as are my fingers from grabbing saturated supplies in the cool flood. The longer we're below the surface, the more the worry weighs me down. If there's no sensation in my toes, is Sarge going to be okay? If we can't figure out how to save him, how will this end? If we resurface, and everything goes well, do we risk being captured anyway?

Luke's expression as he walks up helps to relax my shoulders. I hadn't realized I'd grown so tense. Sarge nudges his head beneath my hand, and I grip his fur without taking my eyes from the men trudging toward us.

"Good news is, we have a plan. Bad news is..." Trevor starts, causing me to hold my breath in anticipation, "there are risks."

The air blows out from my lungs in an exasperated sigh. Of course there are risks. But is the plan worth it?

Lacy, Sonya, and Mason surround us now, joining in on the meeting as Thomas comes up from behind his brother carrying a large instrument of some kind.

"Thankfully, there are enough airlock masks for all of us," Trevor begins again. "Not so thankfully, we are sitting at roughly seventy-two feet."

"What's wrong with that?" Lacy questions, and despite the fact that I don't fully know myself, I can imagine it's not great for

Sarge.

"A controlled ascent is essential for preventing decompression sickness," Thomas chimes in now, handing off the tool to his brother. "About thirty feet per minute is recommended for safety. That's about two and a half minutes at its quickest before we reach the surface."

"So?" Mason asks. "The airlock masks aren't great, but they can handle a few minutes for sure."

"What do you mean not great?" Sonya probes, tightening her grip on Lacy's hand. Too much is happening at once and my heartbeat picks up speed.

Trevor closes his eyes in frustration. Luke sends a murderous glare in Mason's direction.

"One question at a time," Luke says. "For one, you're forgetting about Sarge," he grits at Mason, who cowers, turning ghost white. "That's been our problem all along. We have a plan that will help him not intake water, but he'll have to somehow get three minutes' worth of oxygen from nowhere." The heat radiating from Luke seems like it could boil the water beneath him. I'm surprised Mason forgot about Sarge, but it's been one fight after another since we left camp, and I don't blame him for getting caught up in it.

"As for the masks," Trevor says, "they're fine in emergency situations such as these." He assures the group but mostly directs it to Sonya. "Airlock masks work like gills, but the concentration of oxygen in the water isn't enough to fully sustain a human, so they can't keep up with the demand for long. There won't be any joy-diving through the lake today, but they'll suffice in getting us up to the surface."

Sonya relaxes against her wife, and Lacy pulls her closer in a sideways hug.

"But Sarge is still the problem," I say aloud, my soul ripping from my body as the weight of what I'm saying takes hold. "You said you have a plan?" I ask Luke.

He nods. "We can rig something up to give him limited oxygen," he says, though I don't allow myself to be hopeful yet. Then he continues. "The problem is, we don't know how much oxygen he'll utilize or if it will hold under the pressure." Luke's mouth sets in a hard line. It's clear he's torn with wanting to deliver the news straight but also keeping me from falling into panic. It's too late. My palms start to sweat, my body heats up. *You're a mess, Amity.*

"How are we going to get out of here ourselves?" Mason asks. He sounds far away. Trevor responds, though I clip in and out of the conversation, putting all my energy into keeping myself upright rather than focusing.

He's going to cut a hole in the floor and equalize the pressure somehow, and we're jumping through the hole. Or so I think. *Is that what he said?*

"Amity?" Everyone is looking at me with worried glances while I come back to reality.

My eyes scan through the group until they land on Luke. "What's up?" It's better to pretend nothing is wrong, so that's what I do.

"You're going to be tied to Sarge by a rope. You'll have to use it to locate him in the blackness of the water," Trevor says.

"Okay..." I say, my voice trailing off.

"You'll wrap your body around him so you become as close to one entity as you can, then you'll inflate your wrist devices to carry you *both.*"

My eyes flick between the brothers again, avoiding Luke. After what feels like a century, I'm able to nod.

Trevor goes over everything with everyone else, but Luke pulls

Sarge and I away to talk separately. "M," he says, once there's distance between us and the group. "Are you okay?"

What a stupid question.

"Okay," he says, "don't answer that." *Shit.* I have to get better at controlling my facial expressions. "Just listen to me. This *will* work." He grabs my shoulders, gripping tightly as he makes himself eye level. "You're going to want to get up there as fast as possible—I know you. But you have to fight the urge. The panic *cannot* win, do you understand?"

The insistence of his tone causes everything inside me to tense. The way he's holding onto me makes it nearly impossible to look away, but I steal a glance at Sarge. His eyes meet mine and, somehow, I know things will be okay.

My gaze finds Luke again. I nod.

"Good," he says, releasing me. "We can't risk you or Sarge getting decompression sickness."

"Hey, Boss," Trevor calls, interrupting us. Luke glances his way with curiosity. "You remember the plan?"

Luke nods, his brow furrowed, wondering where this is going.

"Good, you're on the K bottle. Thomas is about to cut."

Luke ushers us all into the captain's room to be safe, then he's off. Thomas is cutting the hole, Luke is manually adjusting the cabin pressure to equalize, and Trevor is communicating what's needed between the two to make sure we stay stable.

My heart beats up into my throat, but there's almost no sign that anything is happening outside the walls of the captain's room. I trudge through the water to stare out the windshield into the dark abyss. Sarge is sitting up to his chest in water, but he rubs his head into my hip, begging for attention. The numbness of my legs is making it nearly impossible to stand, but thankfully I can't really feel the wound much anymore.

"You okay?" Mason plods through the flood to reach us. I don't take my eyes from Sarge.

"Sure," I say, casually. "If you mean absolutely, utterly panicking internally, then yes."

"Ha," Mason chuckles nervously, reaching his palm to the back of his neck. "Yeah," he says, his voice fading. "Listen, I'm sorry I sort of forgot about Sarge earlier."

I hold a hand up to stop him, shaking my head. "Stop it," I say. "This whole thing has been one crazy hell scene after another. Sarge is my responsibility. Not yours."

Mason opens his mouth to speak, his eyes searching mine, but then it closes and he nods, resigned.

"Do we think the H.P.S. will be waiting for us at the surface?" Lacy asks, open to anyone in the room. Both Mason and I turn to find her and Sonya in a sweet embrace.

Mason is the one who answers. "From what Luke explained, the hope is they think we're dead down here."

My head spins to study Mason, to see if this is true. He seems to believe it, and it makes sense. But could it truly be that simple to evade the Service?

"Time," Luke says, peeking his head in. Lacy and Sonya break off their intimacy and Mason and I look at each other with uncertainty. Then we head out to find Thomas and Trevor with gear, standing next to a hole in the bottom of the craft at least five by five.

The brothers hand the gear out as they explain how to use each piece of equipment, while also giving us a line up for escape.

Thomas is first in line so we can follow his ascent timeline. Lacy and Sonya have chosen to go together, holding hands the whole way, so they'll be next. Mason follows behind the girls, and Luke is after him. Then Sarge and I follow behind. Trevor will be the last one up.

"This is the most reasonable method. You'll have Mason and Luke on the surface already to help you with Sarge in the event something goes..."

"Stop," I say, cutting Trevor off. "Don't say it."

His eyes study me, then he nods. "Okay, let's do this."

Watching everyone jump to a potential Death is not something for the faint of heart. By the time Luke is up, my heart beats wildly. He pulls his mask over his head but doesn't fully secure it. He turns to me, reaching out his hand to grip mine. A gentle, reassuring squeeze is all he offers before pulling away, fastening his mask, and jumping in.

"Remember," Trevor says, pulling a rope out and handing me one end. "Don't go too fast, but don't go too slow."

He tightens the rope around Sarge while I affix the other end to my waist. My eyes roll. "Huh," I sigh. "That it?"

Trevor smiles. "Don't die," he says. "I don't want to get beat up by your boyfriend." Ignoring him, I position myself in front of the hole, Sarge next to me.

This is it.

My eyes find the golden orbs of my best friend and he smiles at me. *I'll see you on the other side.*

I quickly push the makeshift mask onto his snout. It cups him, latching behind his head like a muzzle. Then I secure my own before we plunge into the darkness together.

Despite being used to the temperature of the water up to my knees, being completely encased sends my body into shock. My muscles tighten, but I have to push on. Though I can't see, I know Sarge is swimming beside me. The rope that tethers us is swishing from his movements.

Ten strong pulls later, we should be out from under the craft.

Light isn't a luxury we have, but it's time to deploy the floats. Hopefully. My breath is loud in my ears as I tread, but I take a moment to relax. One breath... two. Okay. Let's do this.

My hands feel along the rope until they make contact with Sarge. Then, I wrap my legs and arms around him like we discussed. When he's securely attached to me, I rip the cords for the wrist floats, and next thing I know, we're shooting up.

The sloshing of the water is all I hear as we're tugged upward, and my grip tightens around Sarge as if my life depends on it. His head rests in the crook of my neck, his snout over my shoulder like a hug. *Please be okay, please be okay.*

Adjusting the air of the floats, I work diligently on a controlled ascent. It's not long before the surroundings lighten, and I know this means we're almost to the top. *Just a little more, that's it.* We can do this.

My ears start to pop and everything tightens around Sarge. His body grows heavy and it's getting harder to keep him close. My gut screams at me, warning me that something is wrong. My heart beats violently in my chest, so harshly that I fear it's pushing outward and creating waves with its power.

When we breach the surface, I rip off my mask and gulp the fresh air. Sarge is limp in my arms. Keeping myself afloat is hard. I make quick work of his mask too, only to realize he's still not moving. *Oh no. No!*

The world slows around me. I hear nothing but my own breath. Then, Sarge hacks and his legs take over. His tongue laps at my face, my heart flips in my chest. A sigh of relief escapes me. *We made it! He's okay!*

My hand instinctively finds the golden pin my father gave me and I thank everyone possible for the luck we've had with this.

Once I'm certain Sarge is safe and swimming well, I take a moment to look around. Everyone else is working their way toward the shore, so I direct Sarge to do the same. Though I still can't shake the feeling that something is wrong. Trevor should be up by now, assuming he jumped at the same interval that the rest of us did.

I slip my mask back on and dip my head below the surface to see if Trevor is on his way. At first, there's nothing to see. But then, out of the corner of my eye, I catch what looks like a body floating. *Shit!*

"Sarge," I say, popping above the waterline once more. "I'm going to untie you, please get to shore." At first it seems like he doesn't understand, but once the rope is loose, he spins and heads toward the others.

Pushing aside the panic, I clear my head as best I can. *Think, Amity, think!*

Diving down, I pull through the water fast to reach Trevor. His arms are suspended above him from the floats, but he hangs as though gravity still pulls at his body. If I adjust his floats, I can at least get him closer to the surface and his head above water.

I hold on tightly to his torso and make quick work of the dials that control the air in the floats. Thankfully we start to rise, but there will be a whole new set of challenges once we reach the surface. I'm not going to be able to keep him above water for long, so I start there. If I use the rope to tie the flotation devices behind his head and at his chest, it should keep him upright and make it easier for me to pull him to shore. There's no time to debate with myself. When we breach, I push forward with the plan.

I do my best to yank him up so his head is above water. It's then that I notice his mask is filled. *Damn.*

After ripping the mask off and deflating the floats to make them easier to work with, I run the rope across his chest, below his shoulders, and around the back to secure one float to hold his head from lulling back and another to the front to keep him stable. Both the floats inflate and thankfully, it seems to hold. My body sags with relief. There's no time to waste, though.

Some of the others are on shore, yet Luke is already making his way toward me. Seeing Sarge on his own must have set him into a panic. I keep moving, pulling Trevor behind me with the rope. I've never been a strong swimmer, but I rapidly pull my arms to catch up to the others and get to shore as fast as possible.

"Help," I shout, getting closer. Almost everyone but Luke and Sarge are on shore. "We need help!"

Warning bells rush into my skull. *It's too late, it's been too long! He's gone. We lost him!*

Pushing the damning thoughts from my brain, I make it to shore with Luke, Mason, and Thomas rushing to our aid. They lift Trevor out of the water, laying him flat on the ground. Thomas and Luke work quickly on removing my makeshift life preserver, and Mason fumbles around, checking for a heartbeat.

Mine, however, is clearly way too fast and I should sit down. I stumble, falling to my knees, but I can't remove my eyes from Trevor's lifeless body on the ground. *Not another Death,* I think. *Please, there can't be any more Death.*

Lacy and Sonya are beside me in no time, holding me upright, though their faces hold their own worried expressions.

"There's a pulse, but it's weak," Mason says. Nervous energy spikes through the air but I won't let it get to me. This could have been Sarge, and I can't imagine how Thomas must feel right now. *There can't be any more Death.*

Mason starts pushing on Trevor's chest, hoping to strengthen the beat of his heart.

Luke tells Mason to get Trevor on his side to allow the water a way out. After a few more compressions, they waste no time in maneuvering the body. The seconds seem to stretch, and we all watch on in silence until finally, Trevor sputters, water cascading from his mouth in a sharp cough.

Soft, involuntary cheers sound from each of us in the group. Sarge wags his tail happily. We're all thankful that Trevor is okay.

"Trev!" Thomas says, squeezing his brother's arm to help him sit up. "Don't ever do that again."

Trevor laughs, coughing when the pressure is too much on his lungs. "That's definitely a one-time-only thing, I swear." He smiles.

"What happened?" Luke asks. He's standing off my right in front of me but staying far enough back from Trevor to give him space.

It's a question we're all wondering. Trevor was the most experienced of all of us, so how did his ascension end up so terribly wrong?

We all wait for Trevor as he situates himself, getting more comfortable. "I noticed a crack in one of the masks and there weren't enough good ones for all of us," he says. "Someone was going to have to use it, and I figured that someone would be me." Trevor shrugs, seemingly unaffected by his decision.

Thomas can't help but speak. "You were just going to die? We could have figured something out! Done something different!" Thomas is hysterical, understandably so. "You do some crazy shit, Trev, but this is one of the stupidest, most ridiculous..."

Thomas stops speaking, and he looks at Trevor for a moment before leaning forward to hug him. The brothers stay there for a while. Their relationship leads my mind to Emma. There's something special about sibling love. Something that brings out a certain level of insanity.

I'm clinging to the hope that my theory about Emma being alive is correct. Apparently I've already lost her once, and I can't imagine it being forever. That's how Thomas must have felt.

"Typical," Luke mutters, whispering to me. "This is just like Trevor." He chuckles, smiling to himself in disbelief. "He made us all go first so we'd be safe."

"Are we safe?" I question. "I don't see any Servicemembers, but that means nothing."

Luke's brow is furrowed as his eyes scan our surroundings. "We'll give Trevor a few to recover, then we'll get out of here. No point hanging around to find out."

The wind picks up, reminding me how cold I am from the water. Now that the adrenaline is wearing off, the numbness of my extremities is growing more apparent. We'll have to settle and set up a heat source sooner rather than later if we're all suffering the effects. I have a feeling this is only the beginning of a long, rough, road.

CHAPTER THIRTY-NINE ○ AMITY

WALKING THIS MUCH IS STUPID. MY FEET HURT, MY BACK hurts. Everything hurts. Last night we took cover in a small patch of trees and warmed up by a nice fire. But the ground is hard. Slumming it out here is nothing like the posh shantytown of the H.P.S.. At least I have Sarge to cuddle for warmth. Having my memories would have served me well here—then I could've been prepared for what we're up against.

"Do you really think the Service believes we're dead?" Sonya asks. Her and Lacy are walking at the back of the group, hand in hand, meandering as if this were another walk in the park. I get that this is technically their honeymoon, but how are they so calm?

Mason responds from the front, "I sure hope so. Having one entity after us is hard enough."

"The Guardianship is hardly the issue these days," I point out, before realizing what I've done. My eyes widen involuntarily and my fingers stuff themselves into Sarge's fur, who's been glued to me nonstop since the lake.

"What do you mean?" Lacy asks from behind. Everyone in the group stops walking.

Heat raises beneath my cheeks, turning them red. My fingers

tighten. "I... well, I don't..." I'm not sure what I meant by the saying. The Reaver is horrible, and her hold on everyone is enough to put us all in danger. But she wouldn't hurt Luke, right? Nor would she take someone he cares about for fear of losing him forever. Relatively speaking, General Favager is our group's bigger threat at the moment. "I just meant that the Reaver could have killed us all multiple times but hasn't. The General actively wants to."

Sonya sighs. "The good news is, we can locate that source you were after, right?" Her voice is hopeful, yet my heart hammers in my chest. Luke and I haven't said a word about our knowledge to anyone. They still believe we're here to find the Reaver's son. And it would make sense that we would need him now more than ever, since we don't have any alliance anymore.

Luke finds my gaze and we stare at each other, allowing the silence to overtake the group for longer than it should. Then he says, "I'm the son we're looking for," without taking his eyes from mine.

Shit. My heart plummets in my chest. I know, out of anyone, this group of misfits is the most trustworthy. But knowing this information puts them in danger.

Collective gasps filter through the woods as the news settles into everyone's brains. "General Favager can't find out. Ever," I say, nearly begging. His words play through my skull like a loud warning. Luke will be killed if General Favager gets involved. "Not only will it put Luke in danger, but all of you as well if he finds out you all knew."

The group starts asking questions, naturally. How do we know Luke is truly her son? Why is Luke in danger if the General finds out? When did we gain this knowledge? I ignore Luke's expression from my earlier admission.

"We'll explain as we keep moving," Luke says, handling this much better than I expected.

After the initial, heavy news of Luke's identity, the rest of the day goes by with lighthearted conversation, most of which I don't partake in.

My mind is too heavy with what's to come. What happens if Emma is really gone? What happens if all of this was for nothing? What if we can't get the Reaver and we have to live the rest of our lives on the run from two evil dictators? What about Luke and his lineage? Ugh. It's all too much right now.

As if Sonya has read my mind, she asks, "Not to end this on a dark note, but what happens when we return? Is the Service not going to be furious that we ran, destroying equipment?" We're coming to a place for camp, and everyone is giddy to rest after a long day of travel. But that doesn't change the fact that we're still in danger. Rest doesn't truly mean relaxation in these parts.

Luke sighs. "Hopefully once Ren is defeated, it won't matter *how* we did it, only that we did."

A fire is set up quickly, and the group surrounds it, laughing as if they're all one big family. And I suppose they are. *We* are. Bile rises in my throat at the thought. *Just more people to lose...*

"I'm going to take Sarge out for a walk," I announce to the others. Most don't question, but their knowing looks eat at me. "He's a bit restless," I say, hoping to convince them I'm okay.

"Mind if I join you?" Luke asks at the last second before I fully turn away.

A part of me wants to say no. Some space to clear my head will be good for me. But there's another part that's craving alone time with Luke, and it's a part of me I'm curious to explore.

So I shake my head. "Not at all."

Despite the ache in my calves, there's an unfamiliar pep in my step. That is, until we get far enough away from the fire and Luke finally starts to talk.

"Earlier you said I'd be in danger if Favager found out about me," he says. "What do you know?"

His probing eyes cause guilt to flood up through my chest. I kept the General's threat to myself, but maybe I shouldn't have. Sarge stops his gallivanting and returns to my side. My mouth pops open, ready to speak, but no sound comes out. How am I supposed to tell this man that he's got a bounty on his head simply because of his DNA?

"General Favager has a vendetta against the Reaver," I say, averting my eyes from Luke and keeping them on Sarge to hold myself steady. Then I add, "*And* anyone with her DNA."

Luke is silent, so I look back at him. His brow is furrowed and although his eyes are on me, he's somewhere else entirely in his mind. "That's unfortunate," he finally says, shrugging.

"Yeah," I reply, scoff-laughing. How is he so uncaring? "Before the wedding, he said I wasn't allowed to look for the Reaver's son anymore. That he would take over the operation and 'snuff him out' of existence."

"Ahh," he says, kicking a rock out of the path as we walk. "So that's why you were all weird at the wedding." He smirks, and I can't believe how calm he is with all of this.

I smack him lightly. "No," I answer. "That was because this dude I like escorted me there." My cheeks flare red at the boldness. *Did I really just say that?* I peek up through my lashes and catch Luke's expression. He's doing his best to keep a straight face.

"Did you say this *dude*?" He chuckles, smirking.

I nod, defending my choice of words, giggling back.

The world closes off, and somehow our lips get closer. We're both leaning, but then we startle when Sarge barks. I'd almost forgotten he was here, somehow, but he's making himself known now.

Luke and I desperately search the area around us, knowing that Sarge doesn't bark without reason. After a few minutes of nothing, I question whether maybe he simply didn't want Luke and I to be so close. I can't believe I almost crossed that line. *Stupid, Amity.*

But then there's a rustle from a few feet away. Sonya bursts out from behind a cluster of trees, nearly running directly into us. She falls into Luke's arms and lifts her head to meet his eye.

"Luke?" she says it like a question, her face frozen in an expression of confusion. She's dirty, her clothes are a bit torn up. Sarge's nose is in the air, smelling wildly. *What happened while we were gone?*

Nerves shake me to my core. My gut knows something is amiss, and it's not something small. "What's going on?"

Sonya breaks her gaze from Luke, relief settling on her face. "We thought you were hurt," Sonya says. "We... they..." She's out of breath. Luke helps her to the ground, tells her to breathe.

My scalp prickles. I don't know what's bothering me more: the fact that Sarge is as restless as I am, or that something bad is happening and I have no idea what it is. Why would Sonya think I was hurt?

Once she catches her breath, Sonya starts fresh. "Luke came back to the camp and started tying us all up," she says, taking shallow, fast breaths between each word. "He kept asking where Amity was. We figured something bad must have happened." Her eyes flick between the two of us, and a sideways glance in Luke's direction shows me he's as unsettled as I am.

There's only one person who has the ability to make direct copies of a human being.

"Fuck!" Luke shouts, running his fingers through his hair. The loud outburst startles me, and Sarge puts himself between the two of us.

"What are we going to do?" I ask. Luke is ruthless. He's been able to take on every opponent thus far, but facing himself? This could end catastrophically. For him, for the group. For all of us.

"*We* are doing nothing," he says, becoming Officer Luke in an instant. "You will stay here with Sonya. I will go kill the son of a bitch." His determination is admirable, but his stubbornness is going to get him hurt... or worse.

Anger floods my veins. "I will not sit here and do nothing," I argue. "How are you going to fight yourself? He knows all your moves, all your special techniques."

Luke's frustration is building. "You think I don't know my own weaknesses?" he counters. "I'll be fine."

I can't let him go off on his own. "That means he will know them, too!" Ugh. This is frustrating. Sarge and I could help him, but he's being stubborn. "Are you that dense?"

"You are staying here!" he yells. His chest is flared outward, but then Sarge's eerie snarl causes Luke to back off. He takes a deep breath, seemingly counting in his head, before he speaks again. "I'm sorry," Luke says, his teeth grit as if he were in pain. "Look, you may not remember, but I was a *ruthless* Force officer. *That's* the version of me back at camp. You don't need to be anywhere near him."

My shoulders sag. *He's worried about what I'll think?* "None of that matters!" I argue. "Our friends are in trouble. We need to go. Now!" I ignore Luke, ordering Sarge to lead me back to camp. Then we take off running.

Luke's feet thump behind us, catching up quicker than I expect. When I realize he's carrying Sonya in his arms, I slow. Shit. Should

I have listened to Luke? Sonya was finally safe, and we're bringing her right back into danger. Why didn't he leave her there? She would've been alone, but out of harm's way.

I wipe the thoughts from my mind. There's no need to think like this when my other friends are being tortured. I'm not sure what Luke is going to try, but from what little information Sonya gave us, the subcopy is looking for me. If I present myself, perhaps he'll leave the others alone.

Sarge stops short, slowing his speed. We must be close to camp. Luke sets Sonya down, then puts a finger to his lips. Shouts sound off in the distance. We all get low, following Sarge's lead to crawl.

Hiding behind the small bushes that litter the terrain, we work to get as close as possible without being noticed.

The scene is an obvious one. Horrific. The fear plastered on the faces of our friends is real, as well as the mixture of confusion. To them, it's our Luke doing this, hurting everyone. To them, someone they care about has hit them with a major betrayal.

Before Luke has a chance to stop me, I step forward out of the bushes, Sarge standing tall at my side. The subcopy is facing away from me, holding Thomas by the collar of his shirt. I ignore the harsh whispers behind me.

"Luke," I say, addressing the imposter as if he were the true person. "What are you doing?" I don't have to fully feign confusion, thankfully—I've been told I'm a terrible liar. *Have I?* Stop it. Doesn't matter. I truly haven't a single clue what this man was sent here to do.

The man turns, dropping Thomas like he's a sack of potatoes. I fight the urge to wince as his body hits the ground. Though he's conscious, he doesn't fight. His legs and feet are bound tightly, and his cheek rests against the earth, tears streaming from his eyes. "Amity," the man says.

Looking at this subcopy is different than when I looked at my own. It was easier to separate from the ones that were supposed to be me, because it *wasn't* me. And even though I know that the person in front of me isn't the Luke I've come to know, it's hard to tell my brain at this moment.

Sarge twists, putting himself in front of my legs to create a barrier between me and the stranger. The subcopy's eyes stay flat with no emotion, though I catch him watching my best friend. "Stop hurting them," I order.

The Luke subcopy chuckles, causing goosebumps to raise on my skin. "It's what I do," he says, not taking his eyes from mine. He reaches behind him, gripping at Thomas again. "This was the order I was given. I don't question; I just do." Thomas' eyes widen with panic as the subcopy grips his head with both hands. Sarge takes off without warning, but it's too late.

"No!" I shout, then force my eyes away when he snaps Thomas' neck.

"You son of a bitch!" the real Luke races from behind me, screaming, in the same second. "I'll fucking kill you!"

I don't dare look at the rest of the group, though. Especially not Trevor. And *definitely* not Thomas, whose body is more than likely in a lifeless pile.

Sarge snarls, leaping toward the stranger, teeth out. The imposter is expecting it and side steps quickly, almost inhumanly fast, but Sarge recovers quickly. Luke catches his twin in the motion, using the momentum to haul the subcopy away from the others. In that same moment, Sarge crouches behind him, tripping the fake Luke so his ass hits the ground, hard.

I snap myself out of the shock, moving to the others now that there's a bit of distance between them and the evil that the Reaver sent to us. Mason is on the end of the line, so he's the first one I reach. His eyes show relief when I get closer. The rope around his hands is tied tightly. I struggle to undo it, but then it frees and he lifts them to remove the gag from his mouth.

"Go," he says. "Start on Lacy."

I nod, leaving him to work his legs free on his own. Getting to Lacy, I focus on her ropes, ignoring the fight going on. My gaze is locked in front of me, hoping to tune out the peripheral of Thomas a few feet away.

By the time Lacy's hands are free, Mason is already starting to work on Trevor beside us. There's only a few times Lacy has been speechless—that I can remember anyway—and this is one of them.

"Sonya is safe," I say, whispering in her ear. "She's in the bushes. Go to her."

Lacy hugs me quickly, her body tensing, before she runs off.

"Get back here!" The fake Luke shouts, forcing me to watch the scene in front of me. It appears as if he and the real Luke have been in an intense hand to hand combat fight, and Sarge is circling, gnashing his teeth every so often to aid. If he has a gun, why isn't he using it? A voice from deep in my mind says, *"Where's the fun in that?"* and I shudder. *Is he enjoying this?*

The stranger takes off after Lacy, somehow freeing himself from the real Luke, but thankfully Sarge launches into the man's shoulder, pulling him roughly to the dirt.

"It's me you're after!" I call. "Let them go!" No one was supposed to get hurt. I was supposed to come here, save my friends, and figure the rest out after. But that went to shit the second Thomas... fuck. I swallow hard.

Sarge is shoved off, but he lands on his feet. My eyes meet hazels. "I will kill every last one of them," the stranger says, his words staccato. Chills erupt through my body. It's hard to witness a familiar face with such evil intentions.

His neck ripples, blood dripping from the tooth holes in the fleshy part that meets his shoulder. Sarge launches into another attack, but the man jams his foot directly at Sarge's throat, causing him to hack.

"Sarge!" I cry. He shakes off the jab but doesn't go in for more. His lip raises above his teeth, the snarls harshly loud despite the commotion. The real Luke is next to me now, but he quickly grabs at my body, holding me in a headlock. It hurts to breathe.

"Don't come any closer or I'll kill her," he says, and the stranger in front of us somehow melds into the man standing beside me. Why is he doing this? My eyes widen. There's no stopping the tears from slowly dripping down my cheeks. *Someone should have done this a long time ago, Amity. It's better off if you're dead.*

The fake Luke cackles. "Don't cry, sweetheart. This is who he is at his core." He takes a step closer, and Luke's grip tightens, causing me to wince. "Is this who you want to be with? A monster like this?"

Luke's hold on me slackens, his mirror image getting to him. Something isn't right here. The subcopy doesn't seem affected by my potential death. Maybe this has nothing to do with me at all. My subcopies were a taunt, but perhaps it wasn't meant for me. Maybe they were intended for the Reaver's *son*.

I use the opportunity of Luke's inner turmoil to slam my head back into his chin, spinning from his hold and stealing the weapon he keeps hidden in his waistband. If it weren't *my* Luke, I don't think I'd have been able to do it so seamlessly. His hands go up and he lowers himself onto his knees. The look on his face breaks my heart.

"I will kill *him* if you don't tell us what the hell you're doing here!" I push the barrel of the gun into Luke's forehead, staring daggers at his doppelgänger. The man's face remains impassive, but his feet stay firmly planted where he is.

"For a stupid, vile girl, you're actually pretty smart," he says. "But it won't work. This ends only one way." The mischief in his expression is oddly familiar, and my eyes dart around to think of something else. That's when I notice Trevor in the bushes. They have a plan; I just have to stall.

"No," I say, shrugging. "Maybe not."

At my signal, Mason and Trevor bolt out from hiding, each holding a rope in their hands. Sarge finally sinks his snarling teeth into the man's back, sending him forward. Then the boy's each grab an arm, tying the subcopy's wrists quickly and expertly.

By the time it's over, the fake Luke is on his knees, with his wrists bound, pulled away from his body. Sarge removes himself and sits, watching, red teeth still showing.

Ignoring the real Luke, I walk up to the fake one, demanding answers.

"You already know," he seethes.

So I put a bullet between his eyes.

CHAPTER FORTY ∘ AMITY

Sᴀʀɢᴇ ʀᴇᴛᴜʀɴs ᴛᴏ ᴍʏ sɪᴅᴇ ᴀs I ᴄʟᴏsᴇ ᴛʜᴇ ᴅɪsᴛᴀɴᴄᴇ ʙᴇᴛᴡᴇᴇɴ me and the real Luke. He's not moved from his spot. His weapon feels heavy in my hand as I pass it to him.

There's a silence that stretches as we stare into one another's soul. It's only broken when Lacy finds her voice, returning from the bushes with her wife. "What the actual fuck was *that*?"

When I turn, Trevor is on the ground, holding his brother, but I block it out. I can't...

Thankfully, Luke is up from his knees and taking the lead once again. "The Nameless Soldier project. AKA Plan Z. Ren made a copy of my memories, and she was going to implant them into every able-bodied citizen she needed to create a massive army. She never mentioned making them look like me, though, so there's more to it than that." His brow furrows. Perhaps coming face to face with himself has messed with him more than I thought.

"This makes no sense," Lacy says. "She knows where we are, so why send another subcopy? Err. I mean... Nameless Soldier?" My head is reeling just as Lacy's must be. Sonya is cuddled beside her, clinging to her love. "We were wrong. The Reaver doesn't care if we're alive this time around."

Mason agrees. "Why the parlor tricks, though?"

"It probably has something to do with Amity, as per usual," Trevor says, lifting his eyes to meet mine. "Thomas deserved better." His words cut my heart. I want to argue. *It's not about me. It's Luke!* But that's not going to get us anywhere. The worst part is that he's right. Thomas believed in the cause—the real one—and deserved to see the outcome.

"Hey," Mason says, "We're all sorry about Thomas, but none of us are the enemy here."

The muscles in Trevor's neck tense, but he nods.

We agree to dig a hole and have a small ceremony for Thomas. In the moment, we decide it might be worth it to have a grave for the Nameless Soldier as well. Whomever he had been before deserves the honor of a resting place.

The sun is nearly setting by the time we're done. Everyone is mourning in their own way, but once again we're in agreement when it comes to staying here for the night. No one wants to travel after everything that's happened today.

Everyone except me.

Personally, I want to be as far as possible from the scene of the crime. The area is plagued and so am I. It's better to keep busy, so I tell everyone I'm going to find firewood. Most don't question me despite the fact that we have a decent sized pile already and the dry tumbleweeds around us would be great kindling. Though I'm told to stay close.

If I stop moving, I know the thoughts will come. If I stop moving, I'll have to admit my role in all of this. If I stop moving...

I do.

My knees buckle and my face hits the dirt. Sarge licks at my cheeks rapidly, trying to stave off the demons spinning around me. But it's no use.

My vision darkens and my lungs quickly expand as I hyperventilate. I... killed. No. I killed... *again*. And Thomas is added to the long list of people that are dead because I wanted to go after my sister. It's all unfair.

"Why now? I was fine. Things were *fine*," I argue aloud to the wind, the scattered trees, myself, but I don't truly believe it. *Were things okay?*

Sarge barks from somewhere beside me, though he sounds miles away and the thought deepens the sadness. The passage of time isn't clear, so I don't know how long I lay like this, but I come to and stare directly into hazel eyes.

My heartrate picks up and a scream escapes me before I think to stop it. He's here to haunt me, I killed him. He's a monster. *I'm* a monster.

"M," he says, "hey. Hey!" His solid muscles encircle me. He pulls me close to his hard chest. I squirm, getting nowhere. Where is Sarge? Why isn't he here to save me?

"Sarge!" I call. "Help me!"

Sarge is here. His tongue is hot on my skin. There's no attacking, because he knows I'm not in danger, which means...

"Luke," I sigh, relaxing my tired muscles. The *real* one. He holds me as the panic subsides. Sweat clings to my skin, the wind is cool as it whistles around me. My lungs inflate with a large breath. "Okay," I say, when the episode finally passes.

The man with the same face as my victim releases me, and I shimmy beside him, allowing room for Sarge to crawl into my lap. The pressure is nice. My fingers instinctively reach for the soft fur of his head. Luke said I'd wandered too far and he was coming after me.

"I'm sorry I'm not who you want," I say after an eternity of silence. I'm not who *anybody* wants. They were all expecting someone different, but instead they got... me—a sad excuse for a leader and an even worse pinnacle of Humanity. I've... *killed*. I've gotten others killed. *Maybe the Reaver has been right all along?*

Luke stiffens beside me. "You are everything I want," he replies, shrugging, as if he didn't just say the sweetest thing.

I blush. The Reaver led me to face my demons. See what a monster I really am, and I succumbed. I did whatever I needed to help myself. And Luke doesn't deserve that. Not after everything he's been through. Not after being there for me in ways I couldn't begin to thank him for. "But I'm not the person you were expecting. And I've been so selfish in my endeavors that I hadn't considered everything you've been going through." He deserves better than me. I suspect he always has. "What *everyone* has been going through." Lacy and Sonya followed me to this hellscape for their *honeymoon*. Mason is confronting his past in a personal way and he's all alone.

Luke's eyebrows pull in as my words ruminate.

"I wish I could be what you want of me," I say. I wish I could be what *everyone* is expecting of me. "I'd give anything for things to be normal again." Who am I, really? A no one? The face of a rebellion? A killer? All of the above, somehow none of it at all?

Luke chuckles. "Nothing was *ever* normal. But quit it." He sighs. "I already told you I'm not like Ren." He watches me carefully. "Memory or not, you're stuck with me." He shrugs once again.

I laugh. "You're nicer than I am," I deliberate. "I shut everyone out when I'm going through shit." I mean, hell, I escaped so I didn't have to face the group.

"I know." He laughs as if it were funny. Then, in an instant, he's completely serious. "M, I'd go to the ends of the earth for you. There's no stipulation on that. You don't have to be a certain way." He pauses, hesitating, then continues. "I love you, and I'm starting to think it'll be like this forever. No matter what." His eyes soften and I find myself averting my gaze. *What is happening?*

"Doesn't love just suck?" I joke, trying to keep the mood light. Sarge stirs in my lap. I'm anything but light. I'm heavy with an unknown emotion. Luke admitted he loves me. Were things that serious between us? *Are they that serious now?* Shit. I... I can't...

"Sometimes love doesn't make any sense," he agrees, and it's familiar. It's *all* familiar, suddenly.

"Love is reckless." I scoff, trying to convince myself more than Luke. I don't deserve his love. Why isn't that clear to him? I killed like it was nothing. *I'm damaged.*

"That it is." He chuckles. "Good thing reckless is my middle name." He smirks, revealing the dimple on his right cheek. Oh, hell.

I meet his eyes, my greys to his hazels, and a warmth spreads through me. All at once, I wish I could remember everything between us. Much better than seeing him and seeing the face of my victim. *Maybe there's hope?*

This feels like a whisper of another life. Like I've been here before, felt this pain dulled by the safety of a man who believes *he's* the monster.

That line of thinking can be dangerous, so I curb it, heading in a different direction. "Do you need to talk about what happened earlier?" I ask. Not that I necessarily want to drudge up those particular memories. But I *have* to stop being selfish. "I know a few things about what it's like coming face to face with yourself." I do my best impression of a Luke style smirk and he shakes his head.

"No," he says. "I'm just sorry you're going through this. If she wants her son back so badly, why is she going through you to do it?"

"I think everything thus far has been about you, actually," I point out. Something clicked in my brain earlier, when my death was inconsequential. Everything is seemingly tailored with me in mind, but it's deeper.

Luke stares at me blankly.

"We've had this whole thing wrong. There's *something about me,* sure. But I'm just a means to an end. *Your* weakness. Everything since Emma has been about getting *you* back." It's a tough pill to swallow. Crazy to think none of this would have happened if Luke and I never met. "We need to flip everything we've been thinking on its head."

Luke agrees. We go over everything from start to finish with the knowledge that we have, looking at it from the perspective of a distraught mother going after her son. It dawns on us both.

"She needs me to make the decision myself," Luke says, realization sparking in his expression. "She thinks you're the reason I haven't returned, but she knows if she forces me, it won't be real. That's all she's ever wanted," he muses. "Something real." Luke clicks his tongue, scoffing, before a light flickers behind his eyes. "So that's what I'll do."

Fear slams into me, making it hard to breathe. Sarge cuddles close in the moonlight, helping me stay as calm as possible. "What are you saying?" I ask, though deep down I know what he's about to suggest.

"Ren said you wouldn't trade her son for Emma," he says. "But that's exactly what's going to happen."

CHAPTER FORTY-ONE ∘ AMITY

"WHAT?" LACY SCREAMS. SHE CAN'T BELIEVE LUKE WOULD WALK headfirst into Death. He made it clear he was doing the plan with or without my consent, but I agree with Lacy here. This is madness. Though, so is everything else that's happened. We can only hope that *this* piece of madness will actually work.

"Amity so smartly figured out that Ren is targeting her because she's *my* only weakness," Luke replies. "I'll be able to do far more damage from within, while you guys work on the Guardianship from the outside."

Mason tosses a twig onto the fire. It's early morning and the chill of the air is still present. Everyone but Trevor is huddled around for warmth. "What makes you think she'll believe that you're not playing an angle?"

Hm. It's a valid argument. One I'm sure Luke has thought about yet secretly hope he hasn't. The truth is, I don't want him to go. My hand keeps its hold in Sarge's fur, ignoring the urge to beg Luke to reconsider.

"People see what they want to see," Luke argues, shrugging. *That's it?*

Sarge shimmies onto my lap. I snake my arms around his neck and hug tightly, resting my head against him. It's an impossible choice. Let Luke go for the *chance* to get Emma, or keep Luke here where we know he's safe.

"Since we're on the discussion of crazy plans," Trevor says, stepping into the circle of us by the fire, "I'm heading back to the H.P.S.."

We all gasp collectively, my head shooting from its resting spot. Even Sarge gets up, sitting beside me in bewilderment. Everyone except for Luke, I realize.

Sonya is the first to speak. "You can't... they'll..."

"What, kill me?" He cuts her off. Trevor's chest is flared. The air of his tone is chilled. I'm familiar with the resigned indignation. "So be it," he says, his eyes full of fury. "Thomas is gone."

My heart shatters for him. Something deep within me ignites, and I'm in his shoes. A sibling lost is a forever wound, an emptiness unmatched. My palms begin to sweat, causing Sarge to scoot closer.

"I don't need the pity," he scoffs, scanning us. "That bitch is going to burn for what she's done. If my kill order isn't initiated, I'm hoping I can rally, securing you back up for whatever plan you come up with once you're inside." His gaze is focused on Luke now, but the muscles in his neck are tense. Does he see his old friend? Perhaps he sees the face of his brother's killer, instead.

"When?" I ask, my throat dry. This is my fault. I rushed in when Luke told me to stay away. I got Trevor's only living blood killed. If I could shrink away and disappear, I would.

"Now's as good a time as any," Trevor says. "My job here is done. You've survived a trek like this once before without me, and you'll do it again."

The silence is deafening, only broken by the crackling of the fire beside me. Luke is the first to acknowledge Trevor. They shake hands, then Luke pulls him in for a hug, slapping his back supportively, yet Trevor is anything but at ease. Whispers are passed between them though it's too quiet for me to make out the words.

We take turns saying goodbye. It's uncomfortable, and sad. Knowing that we'll have to do this all over again with Luke is rough. When everyone else has had their turn, I stow away with Trevor to say mine.

"Your boyfriend's a crazy son of a bitch, isn't he?" Trevor says, bending to grab the supplies he must have already packed for himself.

Sarge nudges into my leg. I wipe my sweat covered palms in his fur, chuckling nervously. "So I've heard."

Trevor slings the bag up over his shoulder, turning around to look me in the eye. "I'll keep his secret," he says, exhaling. *Does he sense my nerves?* "It dies with me."

"Thank you," I say with a sigh. There shouldn't have been any doubt in my mind that Trevor would keep Luke's DNA link a secret, still sometimes I can't help the worry that overtakes me. "But don't die," I order him, like he did me what somehow feels like eons ago. "I already have enough people on my beat-up list." I offer him a small smile and he returns it, though it doesn't seem genuine.

"No promises," he says. "That General Favager guy is a real tool." Trevor chuckles, as if our entire future isn't growing more uncertain by the minute. It's a mask; something I know all too well.

My mouth pops open, but no words come out. How did this become our reality? Luke is leaving, Trevor too. Thomas is... gone. I gulp, snaking my fingers away from Sarge, then back again.

Should I give Trevor more information? Maybe blackmail can save him. If there's even a slim chance it'll give him an edge, it's worth it. "Hey," I say. "The Reaver is General Favager's niece by marriage. Use that if it helps." His eyes flare mildly. I glance away from him, not sure how it can help, just hoping that it does.

"This *will* work." He's adamant. A renewed sense of hope filters through him. "It has to. For Thomas."

My eyes flick to his once more and I understand. This is his version of an apology. He doesn't blame me for his brother's tragedy, not like he did in the heat of the moment. He knows we have a common enemy. We're going to take her down, one way or another. I nod.

"We all have a path to walk," Trevor says as he turns to leave. Sarge rubs himself against Trevor's leg, and his eyes close when Trevor's hand pats his head. "May you travel with certainty."

Then he's off.

Sarge plops himself back beside me and our eyes meet. His tongue flaps, laying to the side of his mouth. *May we travel with certainty.* My fingers trail through his fur as we head toward the group.

This is a mess. I can't lose anyone else. Maybe Sonya and Lacy should catch up to Trevor. They might be safer that way. Hell, Mason too. They still have a chance.

My heart and brain war with each other. I don't want anyone to leave, yet I want them all to go. I want to make sure they're safe, but I'm also utterly terrified of being alone...

Shit. What should I do?

Sarge and I traipse up to the fire. The pressure he puts on my thigh is comforting, giving me strength to say, "Anyone else want to go with Trevor?"

I'm met with confused expressions. "Why would we leave?" Lacy asks, her brow scrunched.

I glance around, flicking my gaze between the four of them. "I... well," I stutter. Lacy stands, leaving Sonya behind, warming by the flames. Mason and Luke keep to themselves, but it's clear Luke wants to speak. "You have Sonya to think about," I say to Lacy as she gets closer.

"I am," she says, her hands resting on my shoulders. Her eyes meet mine, and though I want to shrink away, I hold steady. "We told you we're with you. We're not backing out."

My lip quivers. How much could I possibly be willing to lose? I should order them away; tell them I don't want them here. But my heart swells instead, bursting open at the support they've given me thus far. I melt into Lacy's arms, hugging her tightly, letting the stress of the last few days out. Tears stream down my face. My arms cling to Lacy as if my life depends on it, my body racking with sobs. She squeezes back, trying to keep all my pieces from falling apart around us. Sarge nudges between our bodies, causing us both to laugh, despite my sadness.

"Thank you," I say, meeting Lacy's eyes once more.

She nods. *Man, I miss Grace.*

"We need a plan, then," I say, wiping the tears from my cheek with my fingers. A chill sweeps through me and I move closer to the fire, Sarge sitting beside me. Lacy takes her place near her wife, and Mason and Luke slide in as well.

Everyone looks to me. The familiar singe of power bubbles through my veins. *Can we really do this?* We have no choice but to succeed. For everyone we love. *For Thomas...*

For the next hour or so, we go over possible scenarios and battle plans, soaking up the warmth of the fire. Despite the topic of conversation, I'm more relaxed than I've been in a while, here in the woods, far removed from what's about to come. There's a tiny slice of normalcy we've achieved here. It's only tainted when my eyes drift to the area of freshly lifted dirt, where Thomas' body lay beneath the surface.

I suggest to everyone that we pack up, hoping to leave the environment of yesterday's woes. Though it's a reminder of my mistakes, it serves as a warning, too. Something I can't ignore. If I keep going down this path—the one where Death is justifiable— it will be those I care about six feet under. Death is not particular; it takes anyone. If I'm not careful, if we're *all* not careful, we're just one wrong move away from being another Ren Keres.

As we travel, everyone is light, full of jokes. It feels like family, like old nights in Burns when my mother and father would put on puppet shows for a toddling Emma. Her giggles would carry, making us forget the brutal world because we had our own little slice of heaven wrapped within the rickety four walls of the house I grew up in.

This will all be worth it if I see my little M again. Though our mother is gone, our father waits for us at Creyke Point. If we make it out of this, we'll be a family again. *We can be whole again.*

But in order to do that, I have to say goodbye to Luke. The muscles of my face tense in worry. Why does every choice have to be an impossible one? I long for the days where the toughest choice I make is what to have for breakfast.

"Everything okay?" Luke slows to match my pace. I've fallen behind the others.

I nod, removing my fingers from Sarge's thick neck fur. He licks my hand. "I was thinking of Emma," I admit. "And... you." My ears burn red, my cheeks flare. Embarrassment is not a good look. Memories can be taken away, but some feelings are rooted deeper than experiences.

A smirk slides its way onto his face. "All good things?"

My heart beats a million miles a minute. *Why does he make me feel this way?* When there are so many other things to worry about, this should be the last on the list. But faced with the impending goodbye, it simply won't stay pushed down.

"Of course," I say, fluttering my gaze up through my lashes. "Is there even anything bad?"

Luke's demeanor changes like the flip of a switch. His smirk falls from his lips, creasing his features into a frown. My stomach drops to the floor and Sarge nudges my palm, which I graciously accept. *Did I say something wrong?*

"There's plenty of bad," he says. "I'm sorry."

He walks faster ahead leaving me winded.

○ ○ ○

THE SUN SETS and we push forward long after the chill seeps into our bones. My toes are completely numb by the time we stop. We don't really know where we're going or what we're doing, just that we need to find a good place to hide.

A small dwelling in the vast open landscape pulls our attention. There's hardly any cover here, so finding shelter is a miracle.

"Let's start a fire and check out the cottage over there," I say, pointing. It's hard to see without the sun's rays, but after everyone squints, they cheer me on for noticing it.

Sonya and Lacy gather up some sticks, Mason pulls the fire starter from his pack. Luke follows me and Sarge to the cottage. It's made of stacked stone. Dried lichen covers each nook and cranny. Vines wrap around the roof, draping over the cracking, wooden door.

The hinges creak as I push it open. Cobwebs rip from the corners. I think it's safe to say no one has stayed here in a long while. From the inside, we can see that the vines from the roof stream down through a hole in the ceiling, unnoticeable from the outside. It's one big room with a wood stove in the far left. There's a singular bed to the right, and a table directly in front of us in the center. Dust covers every inch, silken webs tie corners together, and it's drafty, but cute. It's small, yet it reminds me of home, and suddenly my chest aches for something that I don't even know exists anymore.

"I miss home," I say, wrapping an arm around Sarge's neck, pulling him into my side. He leans his snout across my midsection to return the hug.

Luke inhales deeply beside me but doesn't say a word.

We head back outside to find the rest of our group cuddled by the fire. The flames call to me, my body begging for the warmth they'll provide. Sarge and I plop down between Lacy and Mason, and Luke finds a place on the other side of Sonya.

"I think this would be a cute place to stay for a bit," I put out there. "At least until we formulate a solid plan."

No one argues. That sizzle I've come to know flows through me again. It pays to be in charge.

"You and Sarge should take the cottage," Sonya suggests.

I was hoping someone else would jump at the chance for a roof and a bed. Someone more deserving, someone who may actually sleep. But Lacy and Mason agree that it should be me.

"I'm surprised you and Sonya don't want the bed for yourselves," Luke jokes, raising a brow.

"Sonya likes Ruffian Lacy more," Lacy says, lifting her arms to flex her muscles. "There's nothing like doing it beneath the stars." She smiles, pulling Sonya in for a quick kiss.

Mason rolls his eyes, and I stifle my chuckle. "I suppose if staying in the cottage will help your marriage, I can't really refuse, can I?" I smile, genuinely, for what feels like the first time since we returned to Western America.

We talk around the fire of things that used to be, of what's to come. Lacy shares that she was adopted. Her mother—the one who shared her bold sense of style—was actually a kind woman who found Lacy stumbling around the streets at three years old. Age sequencing helped Trina Barnett find a birthday, but that's where science stopped for her. Lacy wasn't part of any database, so if she had family, Trina couldn't help. Shortly after she took Lacy in, the Undoing happened, and any chance of reuniting her with her blood was forgotten. Every day after that was spent raising Lacy to be a symbol of the good times.

Lacy and Sonya want to adopt for this reason: to give a chance to another forgotten child. It's cute, really. I hope for their sake that the Reaver falls and society rebuilds. My heart aches for them, deeply wishing that they're blessed with as many children as they want. They deserve it.

Mason's going to follow in his father's footsteps. He wants to be a part of a new leadership that will undoubtedly form. The blanks of my memory make it difficult to follow, but from what I gather, his father was never found like mine was. Mason's the only surviving member of his family. It's heartbreaking. I realize how lucky I might actually be, reuniting with my father and potentially getting Emma back as well.

"I want to be normal," I say, adding my two cents. When everyone, except Luke, stares at me as if I've sprung a second head, I elaborate. "You know, maybe this life is entirely more normal than I'm expecting, but I've only known destruction," I admit. "I was too young to remember before the Undoing. I want to know a *normal* world. One where you can actually exist without worrying you or someone you love will be targeted because of an arbitrary thing some person decided was a flaw."

"Amen to that," Lacy says, raising her fist, pulling Sonya closer to her with her spare arm.

"What about you?" Sonya questions Luke. He's been adding quips here or there, but mostly he's kept to himself. I figured that was nothing out of the ordinary. But the truth is, I want to know what he imagines for the future as well. Is it something elaborate? Something simple? Impossible?

His eyes glaze over as he stares into the fire. I hold my breath, not wanting to miss whatever he says if he decides to speak. "I don't want my past to catch up to me," he says, nearly a whisper. "The longer we have to fight to survive, the quicker it sneaks up." His gaze never leaves the flames. No one dares speak. My heart ignites like the fire in front of us.

"It's a good thing we'll be living soon," I say. He lifts his hazels to my grays across the bright blaze; the fire dances in his pupils. "Simply surviving is no longer an option."

CHAPTER FORTY-TWO ∘ AMITY

THE BED IS A HARD LUMP BENEATH ME, BUT SARGE HUDDLES close, and anything is better than the ground so I can't complain. The crackling of the branches in the wood stove is peaceful, though still not enough to lull me to sleep.

Somewhere outside, the people I care about are scattered around. We agreed it would be safer to keep space between everyone. I'd always thought there was safety in numbers, but Mason and Luke explained that it may protect us if someone were to sneak up again. It's better we catch whomever by surprise, thinking they've stumbled on an easy target.

The hours stretch. The line between late night and early morning blurs. Everything passes uneventfully, allowing my thoughts to run rampant throughout my brain, until a soft knock on the door alerts me and Sarge of a visitor. The door creaks open, scraping against the wooden floor. Through the vines covering the hole in the ceiling, the moonlight streams in. It's still dark, but it helps me see that Luke has entered the dwelling.

I sit up, as does Sarge. His tail beats against the covers, causing dust to puff into the air. "Everything okay?" I ask. He kept to himself after his confession for the desired future. He slinked off without so much as a glance in my direction when it was time for bed. "Did something happen to the others?"

My palms grow slick with sweat as worry fills my chest. Would he be this calm if the others were hurt? Surely no. He'd only be this way if they were okay, or... dead. I swallow hard.

"Couldn't sleep," he admits. "That's it." He shrugs. The bed dips beneath his weight when he sits at the foot of it.

Sarge relaxes into me as my shoulders sag with relief. "Me either," I admit. "Overthrowing an all-powerful leader requires a plan, and my mind is struggling to come up with one. Therefore, no sleep," I say, shrugging in return.

Luke chuckles. It's a sound I hadn't realized my ears were craving. "All the best leaders question their own actions. It shows they aren't for themselves. It also creates insomniacs."

His words surge something in me. I want to do the right thing. The fact that I'm in charge still baffles me, but I like the way it feels. Power can be dangerous though, my father used to say. I don't want to be the type of leader that hurts, bullies... kills. I want to be the type of leader that shows others kindness, that doesn't do anything for personal gain. Which is why I'm now fully realizing the reason I'm struggling with a plan.

"Can I be honest?" I ask. My fingers fumble over the dusty covers to find Sarge's fur as per usual.

"Always," Luke replies, twisting to fully face me on the edge of the rickety bed.

"I can't morally agree to a trade," I admit. "We don't even know for certain if Emma is alive." It sucks to admit this out loud, but it's the truth. This whole trip may be based on a whim, but I won't let Luke turn himself in over one.

His brow furrows as my words sink in. It's hard to think of him leaving, but it's even worse to reduce him to a bartering chip. That's not who I want to be, so it won't be. We'll get Emma another way.

"I have to go," he finally says, looking me dead in the eye. "It's the only way I can ensure you stay safe."

The urge to roll my eyes is strong, yet I somehow avoid it. "You can't guarantee my safety, but I'll tell you I'm definitely a whole hell of a lot safer with you by my side." My heart flutters when his lips twitch.

"As much as I love hearing you say that, I still have to go. At the very least, I'll buy you some time." His eyes soften in the moonlight, and an emptiness spreads through me. It's hard for me to admit how much I want him here. He weaseled his way in, though I suppose he was always there beneath the surface; I just can't remember. "Ren is in the dark about what I know," he says. "I'll have to get her attention, but maybe I let her believe I want to come back? Gain her trust."

"That could work," I ponder aloud. It's the best I can do while trying to be supportive. He could find out if Emma is alive once he's inside and we can work on a plan to break him out. They did it with me once before, right? "We don't have much time, though. How would you get her to trust you within days, maybe weeks, when normally that takes months or years?" A part of me is still hoping he'll back out, stay with me.

"I learned a thing or two about psychology being around her. People see what they want to see," he says, repeating his sentiment from earlier, lifting a shoulder in a half shrug. "If she thinks I'm coming back on my own, she'll hopefully assume I've succumbed to one of her many attempts and be blinded by her pride."

The worst part is that all of this makes complete sense. If we can play her at her own game, we may get an edge. The problem is, "I just don't want you to go." Shit. *Did I say that out loud?*

Heat flushes beneath my cheeks. Sarge nuzzles into my lap, so I drop my gaze to him instead of the man in front of me.

"M," Luke says, his voice low and soft. He's closer somehow, now, and the warmth radiating from him doesn't help my nerves. "We can't lose any more of this little family," he says. "Thomas was a wake-up call. She won't ever stop."

The mention of Thomas has bile rising in my throat. If Trevor could have left his brother, but it meant Thomas would stay alive, he would have. I know that I would do the same for anyone I care about, Two told me as much. I just don't like it. "Can I ask you something?"

"Anything," he says, not missing a beat.

"I saw a side of you that's dark; the side the Reaver wanted me to see. But you had to face yourself and your past," I say. "You didn't suggest the trade because you think you deserve to be punished?"

He shakes his head. "No," he declares, though I'm not fully convinced. "I'm doing it to hopefully get Emma back and to keep you safe. We'll figure the rest out later."

The silence swallows us once more. Luke stares into the wood stove's flames as if they're hypnotizing him.

"Find the balance," I say.

"Hm?" His gaze flicks to mine and, in the firelight, the small flecks of green in his irises are hard to see. The shadows cascading from the hole in the ceiling accentuate his troubled expression.

"We are not our past," I say. "If we were, you would've forgotten about me."

His reply is instant. "I could never."

"Exactly." I nod, holding out my hand. "So move forward. You aren't a monster. From what I've seen, you're the exact opposite— only letting that side of you out when you know it's deserved." Unlike me, who, without my memories, seems to be stumbling down a dark path. I don't want to be that way. *We are not our past.* We are everchanging. That's what the Reaver doesn't understand.

"Sometimes." Luke smiles.

"We are not our past," I repeat. "And we can move forward despite the weight it holds." I'm saying it more for myself, but the way Luke's shoulders dip with a deep breath, I know it means something to him as well. "So let it catch up. It won't overtake you. You are stronger than that."

At some point our bodies grow closer, and I'm acutely aware of my face in proximity to his. Warmth pools in places I'm not used to. All I want is for those smirky lips to be on mine.

Time slows; the world disappears. I don't feel like I'm in the middle of the desert in a cottage that's falling apart; with original inhabitants who probably have some tragic backstory. My eyes close as Luke leans in. Our lips barely brush.

"Is this wrong?" Luke says, pulling away. I don't know how something like this could be wrong. Tomorrow is never certain. He was right. Thomas was here and gone in the blink of an eye, and though I don't want to imagine the same fate for Luke, it's a horrific reality we must all face. The sun may rise, but we may not, so why not take what we can while we can?

"Feels right to me," I whisper against his lips. "Maybe this *is* normal." I chuckle, smiling.

"It's the only normal I could ever dream of," he says. His lips meet mine and everything melts away.

CHAPTER FORTY-THREE ∘ LUKE

T HE MOON IS NEARLY FULL, BRIGHTENING THE SURROUNDINGS when all I want is to be coated in darkness. Sure, it helps me avoid the sticks and debris—anything loud to alert the others of my whereabouts—but it offers no coverage as I go.

M will wake without me beside her. The ache in my chest is almost enough to have me turning around, but I know I won't survive it. I swore to myself she would never leave my sight again after disappearing into the clutches of my bitch mother, yet somehow, we're right back where we were before. Only this time, it's me walking away.

It's for the best. At least, that's what I have to tell myself to go through with it. The last few hours spent with M—her tiny breaths, her body wriggling beneath me—has been nothing short of heaven on earth. She is my everything. And that's precisely why I must protect her.

Sneaking by Sarge was the hardest, but I begged him. Thankfully, he understood. He simply watched as I left. The rest of the group will be easy.

Lacy and Sonya are mangled in a pile of limbs. Despite the moonlight, I'm unable to differentiate which belongs to whom. One of them snorts as I sneak by. I'm going to miss this. *The nor-*

malcy, as M says.

Mason is passed out with his back against a sporadic tree further up in my path, his head lulled back casting shadows across the trunk. I'll even miss... no. Fuck that guy.

I'm almost out of sight from them all when a hand grips my arm. I whirl around holding back a fist, half expecting small orbs of grey to be staring up at me, but also preparing for another ghost of my past sent by Ren. Instead, it's Mason's round, punchable face I find. I scoff. "Don't you know not to grab at me in the dark?" I whisper, harsh.

At first, I think he's going to try to stop me. Then I think better and believe maybe he'll actually tell me he's glad I decided to leave sooner than expected. But he surprises me when he says, "Here," while thrusting a case in my direction. "Take one."

The case is familiar in my palm. I don't have to study it to know what it is. "WICS," I say.

He nods. "Cateline removed the locators in them. Figured they might be helpful at some point in our journey." Mason shrugs. "I'll give the other to Amity."

Why is he being so kind? Does he pity me after finding out that I have basically the worst mother in history? Ugh. That's awful if it's true. I can handle a lot of things, but Mason Baines feeling bad for me? No.

"Thank you," I say, removing a WICS and placing it on my skin. Hopefully Ren doesn't have any tech detection. This should keep us all together no matter how far we may get from each other. I hand the case back to him, hoping he stays true to his word.

"Not for you," he points out. "Amity loves you. This is for her." Dick.

I can't really be mad when he's doing this, though. I nod. "Take care of her." Then: "All of them," because even though M is my main priority, I've let Sonya and Lacy in all the same.

"Yeah, yeah. You'll kick my ass if anything happens to them, I know," Mason says. He pauses, rubbing his palm to his neck. "Goodbye and good luck." He doesn't wait for a response before returning to his place on the tree.

There's no time to unpack whatever that was, or how it affects me. Deep down, I'm terrified that I won't return to M, that Mason will be there to swoop in. But another part, the fighter, squashes it, saying there's no way in hell that M and I don't meet again. That part will do it strictly out of spite to make sure Mason Baines never takes my place. Is that shitty?

Who knows. Who cares.

I walk for what feels like eternity. The desert is vast and ridiculous. The sunrise comes and passes. It's midday before I reach a town with Force tents built. Unfortunately for me, they're abandoned. Ren must have already evacuated this section. Either that, or the Service did. Fucking war.

I keep moving. My brain torments me with thoughts of M. What's she doing? How did she react when she woke up and I wasn't there? Did it break her heart?

The next town I stumble on thankfully has Force officers posted outside the tents. It takes only a few seconds to shrug into Officer Luke persona, preparing myself for anything and everything. Stay cool, calm, collected. My body is relaxed as I walk up, even as they shout at me to get on the ground. They threaten to beat me, shoot me, but they don't know who they're dealing with. Lucas Warin is no match for them. Never has been and never will be.

"Your Headmistress is going to want me alive," I say, raising my hands in surrender. "Better be careful with those."

Lowering their weapons slightly in hesitation, a smirk crawls onto my face. Pussies.

In one swift movement, I knock both guns away. The weapons fly, hitting the dirt. I grip the man on the left—Donnings—by the wrist, then spin him so his arm is pinned behind his back. He'll be a good shield since the other one is currently scrambling for his gun.

When he turns, it's clear he's frustrated. I taunt him. His name tag reads Artelle. "Go ahead, shoot. I dare you." Artelle grunts, tossing the weapon before rushing us.

How cute. When his friend gets close, Donnings wriggles in my arm like a drying worm. His goal isn't fully clear, but if I had to guess, he wants to flip me to gain the upper hand. His form is messy; his techniques are garbage. I could hold him like this all day without tiring.

Artelle hesitates, wondering what to do now that his Force mate is still between us. Whoever is training the Force now that I'm gone is a loser. They should be ashamed of the product they're releasing. He skids to a stop, his eyes widening.

There's no way he's having this reaction from me, and I know, somehow, the person who gave birth to me is somewhere behind us. I flip around, keeping the officer in front of me still.

Meakly Marcus Giles stands awkwardly behind Ren Keres, watching the scene. She clicks her tongue. "You've always been such a troublemaker."

"The apple doesn't fall far," I spit back, releasing my hold on the startled officer beside me and clocking him right in the jaw. He goes down like a sack of bricks.

Ren smirks at me. "I knew you'd figure it out." She turns, Giles at her heels. I know to follow. "Naturally, we'll search you first," she explains, waving her hand around. "Some other housekeeping duties are in order as well." We're headed toward a Force car. Not as fast as the O Train, but who knows if that's even still operational. They've either made some upgrades to the system, or she was close by. There's no way she got here this fast otherwise.

"Interesting options for a family reunion," I say, scoff-laughing.

"Mistress, are we going to ignore the clear lack of insubordination that Mr. Warin has..." Giles doesn't even finish his sentence before his knees hit the ground. Hello?

Ren's thumb is on a device she's pulled from her pocket. Giles backtracks, apologizing like a good little boy. Idiot. Like a dog with a shock collar.

"Have you not learned since the last time you questioned my authority?" Ren's tone is menacing, but her body is calm. I see where I get it from. Shit.

She releases the button, causing Giles to fall forward onto the balls of his hands. The shock must've taken a lot out of him. Ren shakes her head, dismissing the weakling at her feet, and keeps walking. I follow.

I spit on the ground next to Giles when I pass. He shoots daggers at me with his eyes, but it's pointless. He knows I'm untouchable.

"Come over here to get your tracker," Ren orders, pulling my focus away from the man on the ground. I'm no stranger to pain, but I certainly don't want to give Ren any more control over me than she already has in this situation.

"What," I say, smirking, "you don't trust me?" The words come out nonchalant, but my heartbeat gives me away, I'm sure. Screw the shocking. Mason told me she melted a guy from the inside out using these trackers. There are so many moving parts to getting out of here alive—to seeing M again—that adding this into the mix is a hurdle I don't want to deal with. Do I believe she'll blow me sky high? No. Ren Keres would not have gone through all this trouble to get me if she just wanted to kill me. But if things go south...

"I know you may think many things of me, but a fool, I am not," she says, lifting a brow. "Come."

I step forward, placing myself beside her as a random, faceless woman places the needle to my arm. It stings pushing into my flesh, but the features of my face remain steady. The woman gets into a secondary car I hadn't noticed originally, disappearing as insignificantly as she came.

A Master Sergeant approaches. His reflection in the car window isn't clear enough for me to identify him. Once he speaks, I know it's Dean Carovak behind me. I roll my eyes. Pompous ass.

"Officer Donnings is conscious. Everyone from inside the tent enjoyed the show, Madame." His tone is smug. It takes everything in me not to spin around and plant a fist on *his* face.

"I suppose that means you knew I was coming?" I ask, though I know the answer already. She's had eyes on us for a while.

Ren smiles mischievously, then thanks Carovak for his help. Giles is back on his feet now, waiting patiently for his perfect *Headmistress* to give him the order to get in the car. Putting her back to me, she waves him off. Like a lost puppy, he retreats to the car with the nameless woman.

Ren's unprotected with her back to me. I could end it all, right now, if I could just grab my...

"Your gun, please." Her hand is out, waiting for me to drop my weapon into it.

I need to be smart. I also can't ruin my chance at getting answers. If she's been watching us, that means she knows M is without my protection. My compliance is going to be M's greatest safety net. This is exactly why I didn't remove all my weapons from my person. Ren would never have believed I left on my own with no gun.

I chuckle, placing the cool metal into her palm. "I've always been better with fists anyway," I say.

She smirks again, turning my stomach. "That's what these are for." From behind her back, she pulls out a pair of handcuffs. Shit. I hate those. They dig into my wrists.

"Am I a prisoner?" I question. "Or am I your son?" That last part gags me, but thankfully the words come out without a hitch. Her face flashes with a momentary blip of something unrecognizable, but it's washed away in under five seconds. The goal is to get her to trust me, let her guard down. I can't do that if I don't at least address my lineage in a straightforward way. My earlier comments were beating around the bush, but now the cat's out of the bag, fully. No question.

The gun is placed atop the car. Ren turns to me, her eyes softening further than I've ever seen. "Oh, Lucas," she says, putting her bony, skeletal hand to my cheek. It takes everything in me not to slam my head into her. "Right now, you are both."

o o o

RIDING IN A car beside the woman who carried me in her womb is something I never thought I'd do. I also never thought I'd hate every second of it, but that's true as well. Little Lucas Warin would have done anything to see his birth mother again; give anything to remember her face that was simply a blurred mess in his memories. Sometimes you get *exactly* what you wish for.

This is the woman who's keeping me from love. Who killed my father, probably my stepmother and sister, too. She's a monster in every sense of the word. I hate her.

"I'll show you to your room once we're there, Lucas," she says as we pull into a shabby parking lot in center city Los Angeles. With Omphalos buried, she's resorted to the second biggest hub: Deutereon.

M's bad habit of eye rolling has transferred to me. Thankfully, Ren doesn't see. Or if she does, she ignores it. "Can you agree to treat me like an adult?"

She studies me with her calculated gaze. I hate her, I'm going to kill her. "I'm not sure I know what you mean, dear," she says. Though she uses the moniker for most, it makes my skin crawl now.

"I don't want to be monitored like a freak in a cage," I say. "We both know I'll whack out the sound of the camera and somehow find the blind spots. Please allow me some privacy when I'm in my room. I'm not four." Which is coincidentally the last time she was my mother before she abandoned me and my father.

I hold her gaze. The handcuffs have been digging into my wrists for the last few hours. If I have to agree to keep these on in order to get some true privacy, I'll do it. Anything to be alone with M.

"You haven't even asked me why I'm here," I say, changing direction. Some nameless officer opens the door. I lift myself out despite being cuffed. Ren circles the car, placing herself at my side again.

"Miss Thorne's sibling, is it not? A trade for a trade?" She chuckles. I guess that means Emma is alive? "One look at who you truly are and she tossed you out like garbage. Isn't that right?"

"No," I reply. Here it goes. "You reminded me of the good old days with that Nameless Soldier." The lie falls effortlessly from my tongue. I lay it on thick. "Nice touch making him look like me."

There's a moment of shock that flashes across her face, but it's gone quickly. Her lips curve into a wicked smile. "My hope was that the vile girl would see who you truly were and leave you, but this is better." The pride in her voice curdles my stomach, creating a deep ache in my chest. "I knew you would come around, though I admit I thought there would be a few more steps in between. Oh, how wonderful." Her wrinkly hands clasp together in front of her with excitement. What kind of mother gets happy when her son tells her he likes being a monster? Yours, Warin. Get fucked.

Two soldiers fall behind to keep me in line while Ren leads, with Marcus somewhere trailing behind like the pitiful shadow he is. It's all formality, really. Ren knows I could take them all out with one swift movement, but if I did that, we could potentially lose Emma forever.

Deutereon is much like Omphalos, but rather than being built up, it's built out. It spans a few hundred miles. Rehabilitation in one part, Force quarters and training in another. Higher ranking officials also have a section, which is where we're currently going.

The maze of hallways is one of the harder things for Force officers to learn. Everything looks the same in stark white, and it's easy to get turned around. Learning Ren's direction system was easy for me. Finding all the hidden spots was the challenge.

We come to the location of locked doors. Only those with a code past this point. Ren steps aside, smiling, waving her hand in the direction of the keypad.

She's giving the honors to me. I raise my hands, locked together by the cuffs. "Kind of hard being locked up," I say, smirking back.

Ren waves Giles over. He begrudgingly takes the key from his pocket, unlocking the cuffs while muttering under his breath.

"Your code entered by your DNA will take you directly to your room once in the transporter. It will require permission for you to leave, but you will be completely isolated once you are in there. Is that to your satisfaction?" Her eyes are alight with wonder, like she truly cares. Like she's trying her best to honor my wishes. I long for the day her brain is splattered out the back of her skull.

I nod, pushing forth the most appreciative smile I can muster.

"Wonderful," she says. "Your code is today's date." Her eyes study me. She's so full of herself, so stuck in her misguided ways. I know exactly what she wants to hear.

"The day I came home," I muse, though I'm sick to my stomach.

"Precisely." She smiles. "This is the start of our legacy," she says, putting a hand to my cheek. This type of contact is jarring—especially when I remember her as my leader during my Force days—but I choke back the disdain.

The door slides open when I step next to it, revealing a small room with mirrors on all sides. Ren's narcissism knows no bounds. She likes any excuse to gaze at her own reflection. I, on the other hand, have always hated it. The man in my reflection is not me. He never has been. He's someone I don't recognize, a monster creeping up.

Swallowing the resentment, I step into the transporter. The door closes behind me and I spin, staring at the keypad that lights up in the glass. Today's date.

Once the code is entered, the center of gravity shifts, and I know I'm in motion. Since Deutereon only expands out and not up, the transporters here do the same. It's about a seven second trip, then the door opens into a plush room of deep mahogany and neutral greens.

This was specifically set aside for me. Ren is all clinical lighting and blinding white perfection. This is more my style and she knows it. I hate that she knows it.

The room is a large studio, with one small adjoining room for a bathroom. Everything I could possibly need is in here, like it's meant to distract me from the fact that, however cushy, I'm still a prisoner.

Despite the exhaustion that plagues my body, I spend the next two hours thoroughly scouring for any hidden surveillance. Ren may act altruistic, but her issues run deep. When I'm satisfied that I've combed every aspect, I collapse onto the bed with a huff.

Finally alone, I slide the WICS from its place on my arm and put it on my temple. When it registers, M's faint voice filters through my mind. Its slightly desperate tone breaks my heart. "Hello? Luke? Hello?"

"M," I croak.

"Luke!" she cries. "I've been trying to reach you for hours." Damn, I'm an asshole. I left her, kept her guessing. She must have been worried sick.

"It's good to hear your voice," I say, latching on to the good rather than the bad.

She sighs. "Yours too."

The silence stretches, but it doesn't matter. There's something in the knowledge of knowing I'm not alone; that at any point, my mind can reach out and M will be there. I wish she had this the first time we were separated.

"How could you leave like that?" she questions, her whispered voice cracking. "No goodbye."

"Are you mad?" I ask. It's a dumb question. Of course she is. I would be. I'd be pissed, hurt. Hell, I'd have burned the world down to get her back. I almost *did*.

Another sigh escapes her. "No," she admits. Then she laughs, but it's uncomfortable. "I understand why you did it."

All words are lost on me. I've always known I didn't deserve M, but the closer I get to my... Ren, the more I realize how true of a statement that is. Somehow Ren believes loving M will taint me, but it's almost certainly the other way around.

"Where are you?" she asks, pulling me from the intrusive thoughts.

"Old Los Angeles. A rehabilitation facility called Deutereon." I can't help but think about M's time as a prisoner of the Guardianship. She didn't have trust, nor a room tailored to her style. She was alone—truly alone—and tortured. How could Ren believe I would forgive her for that?

"Omphalos is gone, then?" she asks. Does she remember anything about her time there? Or only the bits and pieces that Two shared with her?

"Mhm. It was buried after the rock collapsed on..." I gulp. What is the matter with you, Warin?

"It's okay," she says. "Just be careful, alright? Don't get caught up in this. We're going to find a way to get you out. One that doesn't involve crumbling rock." She's smirking, it's in her voice. Is she mocking me? I can't help but smile.

"You think it's that easy, huh?" I joke, chuckling.

"You did it once before," she teases. "Can't be that hard, right?" Her tone is tinged with sadness, but I appreciate her trying to make light of our shitty situation.

Soon enough, Ren will pay for pulling us apart. And for every Death that's happened from her maliciousness, she will get twice as many lashings in Hell.

CHAPTER FORTY-FOUR ○ REN

"LUCAS WILL LOVE HIS HOMECOMING PRESENT," I SAY, RUFFLING the bow atop the Cryopod. Lily Warin is a perfect, porcelain doll in her package.

This will be something for him to work toward. When trust is fully restored, Lucas can have his half-blood back. Out of stasis, returned to the program, she should be a lovely addition. Left to the devices of her former parents, she would have lost the qualities that make her Exceptional. They would have almost certainly tainted her beyond repair. But with my help, Lucas will raise her beautifully.

Marcus groans from behind me. Surprisingly, too, because he knows better than to question my work. But not even he can get to me today. My son is here. Paul would be rolling in his grave. It makes my heart leap with joy. "Can you not see that he's using you?" Marcus argues. "Mr. Warin is not as happy to be here as he says."

"Do *not* call him that," I spit, then think better and cool my features. "This is new for all of us, but there is good reason to feel optimistic." I fluff the bow again, turning toward the sour face of Marcus Giles.

He scoffs, folding his arms across his chest.

"Oh, seriously, Marcus. Jealousy does not suit you." I wave him away with my hand and he stalks out of the room without much protest. He's mad because he knows my sweet Lucas will soon be his superior in the American Liberation Force. You'd think he'd want to suck up instead of act out, but men are fickle.

Not my Lucas, though. He's no bullshit. It's one of the many qualities that make him Exceptional. Paul could never see the vision; he was only going to hold him back. Of course, I expect Lucas to have questions. Maybe about his father, maybe about the endgame of the Guardianship. I will meet my son with transparency, unlike what my ex had done.

Punctuality is important to me, but I want to let my sweet Lucas rest. He hasn't asked to come out yet. It's important that we start our journey on the *right* foot this time.

By noon, I'm slightly irritated, so I send Marcus to retrieve him. The office has been blocked off for hours while Lily takes up space. Lucas will forgive my intrusion when he sees his gift. I know it.

It's not long before he's here. Marcus Giles stands at the door, apathetic. Lucas I can't quite get a read on, but he's like his father in that way. He's studying the pod, carefully stepping closer until he's face to face with its occupant, only separated by glass.

My eyes scan over him quickly. His pulse quickens, the vein in his neck bulges as he tenses. These are all signs of anger, disdain, not happiness. Why isn't he happy?

"Do you like it, dear?" I ask, stepping closer, placing a hand on his back to steady him.

Marcus scoffs from the door. "You know he doesn't, Madame. He's never been grateful for anything you've given him."

My fingers are on the device in my pocket faster than the last word passes his lips. Marcus crunches down, shockwaves pouring through his body. How dare he say such a thing. How dare he speak up. I should cut out his tongue for this.

Yet, it's my Lucas that places a hand over mine. His eyes beg me to stop. Is he so weak now? No. Maybe a little compassion on today of all days would be okay.

"What is Lily doing here?" he asks. For once, my throat closes, and I don't have the words to speak. "Forget Marcus, he's garbage. There are things we need to discuss. I won't be bothered by his trivial attitude."

A smile snakes onto my face. My son. He's a natural born leader, taking charge, making decisions in the heat of the moment. I love it.

Marcus is sent away with a tail between his legs, left to lick his wounds on his own time. My sweet Lucas is right. This is *our* time. We don't need to sully it with other things.

Lucas sits on a plush chair and leans forward, clasping his hands in front of him, resting his forearms on his knees. His brow is tense, no doubt a side effect from all of the questions he must have swirling around in his head.

He is curious. It's only natural. He wants to know all the things I've kept from him. Including why his half-blood is iced over in a Cryopod. "The Reserves house special cases. Mostly perfect candidates for Nameless Soldiers, but sometimes there are others. I'm short a body since you took out the man I sent. We could have reused him, you know." I offer this information up willingly, so he doesn't have to ask. I take my place in the seat next to him, still studying him. I want Lucas to know we are in this together, which means there is nothing to hide any more. His father is gone; there is nothing standing in the way of us taking over the world. Except for maybe one thing... but we'll deal with that when we come to it.

"What were you waiting for?" he questions.

Lucas is familiar with the Impetus Method. The plan B for saving Humanity. People making their own changes has proven better than any other method. It's important. "Organically fixing Humanity was always the goal, but it's clear that we're too broken. This was always the plan for when things went too far. I've been cleaning house, finding good candidates for Nameless Soldiers as well as more Exceptionals for breeding."

His eyes flick to mine and I hate to admit how unnerving they are. They are a direct copy of his sperm donor's. "So why is Lily here?" he repeats his question from earlier.

"Lily is an Exceptional, but it was too risky to run her through the program. I was saving her for the right time. She will come out of stasis for you when you have proven your loyalty to me."

His voice is soft, taking me off guard. "Can I talk to her? Will she hear me in there?"

Oh, my sweet boy. He's always had a caring heart. I'm so glad my supposed death helped give him a tough exterior to house it. "Those in stasis are very deep in sleep. She may believe it to be a dream, but I don't see why not?" I offer him a smile. Surely he sees how generous I am. How much his presence here means.

"Can I see the Reserves?" he asks. "If we're moving into the Impetus Method, I'd like to meet the army that you've built."

Something unfamiliar tingles down my spine. "In due time," I say, resting a hand on his knee. "In the meantime, enjoy Miss Warin for a bit. Talk with her. Do what you must. I will be here when you're done."

I leave my son alone with the half-blood. Why do my palms sweat so much? If he learns some of the others that I have in the Reserves, will he still be a willing participant? I must move them around, keep only the Nameless Soldiers in one place so I may

Some knowledge is simply not ready to be shared.

CHAPTER FORTY-FIVE ○ AMITY

Sitting around the fire feels disingenuous. No one is asking me questions. Perhaps they're used to walking on eggshells around me. I don't know whether that makes me feel good or the opposite.

Sarge found us a rabbit for breakfast. Those dirt squares from the H.P.S. just weren't doing it anymore. They're good for emergencies, but we all need something real right now.

Yesterday was hell. The hours passed achingly slow. Each passing minute ripped dreaded visions from deep within my mind. Images of torturous pods, bloody children, and the face that's destroyed everything. It hurt to think Luke might have been seeing the same things. Each hour, new memories would surface. New *horrid* memories. No matter how much I tried to remember the good over the last few years of my life, only the bad resurfaced. Each memory caused the pit in my stomach to deepen. *You're guilty of it all, Amity. You always were.*

The worst one being Emma's death.

I see it now, how I could be so blind. Every time I close my eyes, it's there. It's hazy, but crisp, and it has me questioning everything. Was this trip all for nothing? Is Emma truly just... gone?

Lacy knocked a lot, attempting to get me to leave the cottage, but I refused. Mason gave me the WICS to talk to Luke and I didn't want to miss anything from him somehow.

It wasn't until late into the night that I finally got something. But no one is asking about it. Why?

"Luke is in," I say between small bites of crispy flesh. "It's our job to somehow get him out."

Sonya laughs, giggling with Lacy. "Déjà vu," she says.

"Y'all are exactly the same," Lacy comments. She's happy I've finally come out of the cottage.

My eyes dart around to all of them until they land on the deep blues of Mason. He's been quiet, not sure how I'll react since I yelled at him before. He knew Luke was going and didn't try to stop him, nor did he wake me to let me know. My gaze prompts a response from him. "Last time there was an extraction mission, we had a whole heck of a lot more tech." His mouth settles into a frown.

"You're talking about me?" I question. Extraction attempts seem rare. So many kids have been suffering for so long, yet General Favager only sanctioned a run when *I* was a potential prize. The thought has me holding back gags. It's not much to conclude that the General won't feel the same desire for rescuing Luke.

Mason nods. I groan, rolling my eyes.

"To be fair, we did it for your sister with just sheer guts," Lacy says, making her argument.

She doesn't get far with it before her claim is countered. "I *really* hate to say this, but we had Luke both times," Mason points out.

A sigh escapes me. We have to look at this in a new way. "What was the reason the General never ordered another raid to take her out?" I question. "My extraction saved a decent amount of displaced commoner children in the process, but why not get the

Reaver then? Why not now?"

It's a question I've asked before but never truly understood the answer, which seems stupid when I think about it. After seeing the army he's built within the Undoing land, there's no reason to believe they couldn't handle any dissenters. It seems unlikely his worry of another civil war is the true reason. So what's he waiting for? Is there something more we've all been missing?

No one speaks. Collectively, we can't think of anything besides a threat. And what would have General Favager so intent on staying away from his main goal?

The afternoon is used to workshop, as I call it. Luke has been gone for almost thirty-six hours. *It's only been that long?* It's pathetic how much I miss him. I can't help it. I'm hoping if I sit here with no distractions, I'll somehow come up with a foolproof plan to get him back and rescue my sister. *If there's still a sister to rescue...*

I'm completely taken off guard when there's more than one person in my head.

"M?" Luke's voice is hoarse. *How is he talking to me during the day?* My chest tightens. Something must be wrong.

"I'm here," I say, immediately focusing. "What's wrong?" My head shoots off Sarge. He watches me with worried eyes, splayed out at the foot of the bed.

Luke sighs. Or maybe it's something else entirely. It's hard to talk to someone you can't see.

"What's happened?" I repeat. Nervous energy radiates around me. It must be something terrible to have him so worked up. Sarge shifts, nuzzling closer to me. I wrap my arms around him, tightly hugging him to my body.

"My sister... she..."

Oh no. Lily. *She's dead, isn't she?* The Reaver found her before

Mason could. Shit. I grip my fingers into Sarge. I'm starting to understand exactly how that feels. I hate that I can't be there with him in his time of...

"She's frozen."

Excuse me? *Did he just say...?*

"Ren has a section called the Reserves. I'm currently staring at my sister in an icy glass tube. Cryogenics. Why didn't I think of that?" He chuckles in disbelief, as if this is the most ridiculous thing that's happened to us so far. Maybe it is. "There must be records somewhere of the people who are in there. That's the best bet for where Emma is. Ren all but admitted she was alive."

My mouth forms an O shape, but no sound comes out. Emma. *Is it still possible?* The memory of her death filters back to the forefront of my mind. Is that what really happened? Or was my drained memory fog paving the way to the truth?

"That, or she's hidden in some off location of the rehabilitation schools," Luke continues, bringing me back to reality. My head swims with the possibility. *Emma? Alive?*

The memory of her death pops up again, curbing my hope.

"Your sister," I say. "Lily, right?" He's so focused on my sister, that I want to circle back to his. He hasn't talked about her much since that one night when he learned his proper family tree. I need to talk about someone else.

"Yeah," he replies. "She's in stasis. It's taking everything in me not to break the glass right here and strangle Ren with my bare hands." Luke is seething, barking through his teeth. I understand the anger. Now that I remember the moment before that nurse injected the needle into Emma's tiny arm, it's easier to empathize. I was ready to burn everyone in the room to get to her.

"I'm so sorry," I say. "You shouldn't have to do this." Though he made the choice to go on his own, I feel as though I may have been a driving force.

His scoff rings through my skull. "If I complete the reason I came originally, there's a good chance we *both* come out of this with our sisters."

I can't help the words that escape my mouth. "Do you truly believe that?" My brain circles back to my little M.

With the slow return of some memories, I'm finding it impossible to separate. It's hard to believe that I was once so adamant that Emma was alive. Two had been right all those weeks ago. She wasn't convinced because she had the memory. *But Luke had said the Reaver admitted it, right?*

"Ren's running a tight ship here," Luke admits. "It'll take some smart thinking on our end, but yes. I do believe it. I have to."

The determination in his voice gives me strength. If Luke still believes we can do this in the face of evil, then perhaps we truly can. "Do you know what the Reaver has on General Favager?" I ask. "We know of their relation. She's his niece by marriage. But that isn't enough of a reason for him to stay away from her. She must've threatened him somehow, with something." I fill Luke in on our discussion from earlier.

"That would make sense," Luke says, without committing fully. "She likes to even the playing field usually."

My brow furrows. "If we could figure out what she's got, maybe we could use it for ourselves, too." It's a plan—or a semblance of one—at least. It's more than I've had this whole time, so it's worth exploring a bit.

Luke tells me all about the Reaver and her history. John Collins, the Senator, wanted to keep his perfect image squeaky clean, so he married Donna Lee Favager, the sister of Victorian Premier Olivier Favager. They had a beautiful daughter—one to replace the crackhead's offspring he left behind.

When the Reaver took over, she tried to wipe the memory of her own father, hoping to create a new relationship for them. But when that failed, she killed him, forcing Donna and their daughter to watch.

As far as Luke knows, they've been killed too. His words are rushed, I know there's not much time. Yet the parallel between what she's done and what she'd asked of Luke sticks out. "She asked me to kill my father in front of Lily and Janet. If Lily is alive, there might be something with the daughter."

If there's some connection to General Favager, perhaps we have a way to get him to work with us despite our insolence.

The cogs of my brain turn as the possibilities swirl. There's one more confirmation I request before Luke disappears. "Do you think you could get more information on all that? There's got to be something we can use."

"I'll see what I can do."

CHAPTER FORTY-SIX ∘ AMITY

LIKE EVERY MORNING SINCE LUKE LEFT, THIS ONE STARTS WITH walking Sarge around to find a nice breakfast that isn't a Service dirt cube. But unlike the others, my hair stands on end. Sarge's hackles raise, which doesn't help the ominous feeling that's thrumming through my chest.

Mason never lets me leave the area without one of the guns Luke left behind. It sits heavy in the waistband of my pants, and the thought of using it makes my throat close, but I slyly reach behind to grab it.

Maybe I'm on edge because I still haven't heard from Luke. Something must be terribly wrong. It's been too long. We'd been cut off the last time we spoke, when he was getting into the mainframe to find more on the General's family. Unfortunately, I never got to learn what, or if, he found.

But since his rushed exit from my mind, so much has run through me. We're no closer to figuring out how to get him out, take down the Reaver, and rescue both of our sisters, all while somehow getting back into the General's good graces. I've been struggling with keeping the anxiety tamped down.

Were we always this way? Flying by the seat of our pants and hoping it works? It's exhausting.

Sarge's golden eyes meet mine for a second before he whips around, his teeth gnashing in the direction of nothing. Or... is it nothing?

Clamping down on a figment my eyes don't place, Sarge appears to be wrestling with the air. His growls carry across the plain. The gun in my hand is pointed, but I don't know what I'm aiming at.

"Show yourself," I shout, the gun steady in front of me.

Sarge's gnashing gets worse. He pulls; whatever he's latched onto is big. What could possibly be invisible like this? Oh!

I imagine a human shape, as best I can given what information I have, and shoot at what I hope is the arm or shoulder.

"Fuck!" a voice shouts, then a body materializes. "Can you get your mutt off of me?" the man says.

He's a Serviceman. Alone? That's odd.

"Are you going to go invisible again?" I ask, raising a brow. The gun stays trained on him, as do my eyes.

Sarge is clamped onto the man's right wrist, holding him steady. The man's left hand is grasping at his ear with blood dripping through his fingers.

The man scoffs. "I'm not promising you anything." He cries out when Sarge grips him harder, another growl ripping through. "Okay, okay."

Scrutinizing the man for another moment, I order Sarge to release. Blood drips from both sides now that Sarge's teeth are pulled from his arm.

"Get down on your knees," I order, the gun used as a pointer. I'll shoot again if I have to, though I'd rather not. My heart pumps heavily, racing in my chest. How am I in this situation again?

Sweat beads on my face, dampening my hairline. *Please don't make me shoot.*

Thankfully, the man lowers. It's awkward with his injuries, but eventually he gets on his knees, raising his hands in surrender. Sarge sits directly next to him, his teeth peeking from his lip in reminder for the man not to try anything.

Satisfied that he's going nowhere, I stash the gun in my waistband again and shrug out of my sweater. Using the sleeves, I bind the man's hands tightly behind his back. The fabric swirls around, over and under, to ensure he's locked in.

"Stand up," I say, lifting the tether. "Let's go."

Blood still weeps from his ear, but his wrist is covered by my sweater. I realize I don't know the man's name. I swivel around, clocking his name badge. Gagnon.

Giving myself the time to truly study him, I notice he's not much older than Luke. Late twenties maybe? There's a gnarly mark below his left eye, freshly red and puckered. It's a symbol of some kind. His hair is tussled. It hangs over one eye, but is buzzed on the sides. *He's another human, Amity. Remember that. He is not the enemy.*

Sarge nips at Gagnon's heels like it's his job. Keeping him in line and at a steady pace.

"They'll come after me," Gagnon says, after walking for a bit. "They know where I am."

His tone is projecting malice, warning, but it's an empty threat. Why would a Servicemember be alone? Without his own weapon, no less. If they knew where he was, they would've gotten him already. Mason will understand more about what's going on.

Lacy and Sonya have their backs to us as we approach, but Mason is wide-eyed, already privy to my find for the morning.

"Guess we'll be eating good this time," I say, smacking Gagnon's back, pushing him down by the fire in front of the others. His eyes widen, but he refuses to move. Sarge is still hot on his heels, ready to strike at a moment's notice. "All jokes of course," I whisper.

"They'll come for me," he breathes, repeating himself, his eyes downcast.

"No, they won't," I say. "Right?" My gaze clocks Mason. He knows what this man is doing all alone. His expression as we walked up told me as much.

Mason's mouth settles into a straight line. "Dernier."

"Excuse me?" Lacy says, not truly following what's happening around her.

"He's on his last mission," Mason explains. "This is a punishment. If he survives and offers something useful, he gets back in the graces of the Human Protective Service. If he doesn't? Well…"

"General Favager does that?" Sonya gasps. Honestly, someone could tell me the General boils children and eats them and I'd believe it at this point. He and Ren are cut from the same cloth, yet somehow, he thinks *he* deserves all the glory. It's ego. It's sick.

But all of this gives me an idea.

Circling Gagnon, I lower myself to his level. "Seems like we could help each other out," I say, hoping to appeal to his survival instinct. "We need you to contact your friend. And you need us in order to get back in the Service."

Gagnon side-eyes me, his lip pulled up in a snarl. Sticky saliva splatters my cheek. Okay, so apparently I'm not as good at this as I hoped. I glide my palm across my face, sliding the spit away while I stand.

Sarge is laying, ready to pounce, his nose touching Gagnon. Lacy and Sonya watch on with horror at what's happening, and Mason is giving me the courtesy of trust.

What should we do? I know this man will be useful in contacting the General. Maybe he senses my lack of conviction? We still don't have a plan, and Luke is still M.I.A.. My eyes dart around the group, hoping something will pop into my brain if I look hard enough.

"Mason," I say, after a few thoughtful moments. "Take Gagnon into the cottage, check his wounds, and tie him up there. We'll figure out what to do with him later."

Mason nods. I glance at Sarge, sending him off to follow with the tilt of my head. Then it's just Lacy and Sonya with me, watching with some sort of emotion that I can't place.

"What?" I question, slumping down to the ground next to them. "Too harsh?"

Sonya chuckles, Lacy smiles. "I was thinking how absolutely smoking *hot* you are when you take charge," Lacy jokes, laughing.

o o o

THIS IS IT. My heart beats in my chest rapidly. Luke contacted me earlier in the day, thankfully. My heart nearly shot out of my chest. It was good to know he's okay. And it's all clear now: if I can convince Gagnon to contact General Favager, we may actually have a solid plan.

Luke's research yielded a name from within the Reserves; frozen until someone can set them free. The person in question? General Favager's niece. Luke had hoped for the General's sister as well, but hopefully a niece will do. He'd been right, though, of course. The Reaver created a parallel between her situation and the one she put her son in.

If we can promise a safe return for the General's blood, perhaps he'll send us the backup we require.

"One more time, Gagnon," I say, sighing. My eyes tumble in my head while I pace back and forth in front of him. Mason bound his wrists behind the wood stove. Gagnon sits in an awkward position to keep his shoulders from dislocating. "You contact General Favager so we can discuss things with him, and we appeal for your reinstatement."

Sweat clings to Gagnon's skin. Whatever he did to become a Dernier, it's bad. He needs something fool proof to get himself back in. He's terrified that somehow this won't be enough. *What does the General have on him?*

"I already told you," he spits through clenched teeth, "if I contact the Service with some type of joke information, General Favager will have me killed."

Mason is watching from behind the veil of vines. "What makes you think it's joke information?" He stands up now, walking closer to where I'm pacing. Sarge's gaze is still trained on our prisoner.

Gagnon scoffs out a laugh. "If I was calling with news of your death? Sure. But I'll be the laughingstock of the Service when they find out I was bested by... *you.*" He squints, sending daggers at me through his eyes. Ahh. So that's what this is about. More ego. Of course.

"Would it be better if you mention finding us and realizing that we are better alive?" It's an olive branch I hope he'll take. We've been at this for hours already and time is wasting.

Gagnon's eyes roll. "Are you truly this foolish?"

Mason runs his fingers through his hair. "How could there possibly be an issue with that?" he asks. "General Favager may be a scary individual, but he can be reasonable. We are appealing to his ego here. It's *family*." Mason's hands are pressed in front of him in mock prayer, hoping Gagnon will accept.

"I will be mocked for falling for your lies!" Gagnon cries. "Do not tell me of the General's grace. He has none." Gagnon's eyes fall once more to his feet. There's real pain here. Whatever the

General has on him is more than Death. It's more personal. More detrimental somehow.

Stooping closer to him, I place my fingers gently on his chin to lift his gaze to mine. I soften my voice, keeping everything low and quiet. "What has he done to you?" I ask.

Gagnon is a human being. Gagnon is not the enemy. It's hard to remember that when anger gets the best of us, but it's exactly the type of shit our real enemies hope for. Distraction, letting us do their dirty work. I lost sight of that for a second because I'd been blinded by my eagerness to save Luke.

Gagnon's pupils dilate with fear. It's familiar.

There are so many different scenes that plow through my brain. *A man in a bright white uniform that stands outside a door, pleading with me about his daughter. Hands that close around my throat with the hope of selling information for a loved one's freedom. Nan holding her own in front of a platoon of Force officers to give us time to escape.*

"Who does he have?" I ask this time.

Gagnon's mouth pops open with shock, fear, anger. So many emotions flick through his irises at once. They settle on defeat. "My daughter." His voice cracks.

Every level we pull back from the General, there's another layer of filth we uncover. My father had said there were two enemies, but it grows increasingly more clear with each passing day how true it is.

Does the suffering cease with the Reaver's end? *That's a problem for another day.*

Pushing the thoughts from my mind, I retrieve a knife from my pocket. "Will your daughter be safe if you're dead?" I ask. Gagnon's eyes widen, nervous energy radiating from him. Shit. This looks bad. "We won't actually kill you," I clarify. "If we contact him claiming we found your body, will that save her until we can guarantee her safety?"

Gagnon thinks about it momentarily. The fact that he's even considering this offer over the others means that there might be something to it.

I raise the knife once more, cutting away the rope around Gagnon's hands.

Mason watches with a tense gaze but, thankfully, keeps to himself.

The rope releases, Gagnon's hands fall in front of him. He rubs at his wrists and rotates his shoulders, stretching them now that they're not in such an uncomfortable position. I'm not worried about him attacking me. Sarge is still pointed in his direction, waiting.

"We are not the enemy," I say. "I'm sorry we acted like one." The knife is stashed safely in my pocket once more and I raise my palm to shake in agreement.

Gagnon stares at my outstretched hand, hesitating. He meets my eye after a few seconds then places his palm in mine.

We're going to save Luke!

CHAPTER FORTY-SEVEN ∘ AMITY

MASON SUCCESSFULLY PULLED THE TRANSMITTER FROM Gagnon's suit. It's set up in the cottage. Lacy and Sonya sit on the bed whispering to themselves. I love that they have each other in all of this chaos.

Sarge sits at my feet, his body contorted between the legs of the chair and table. Gagnon is outside. At least, I hope. Transmission scans surrounding areas, logging bodies and structures. We're hoping by sitting inside, General Favager will only know of what we want him to.

Thinking of the General has my throat tightening. Will this work? Do all rebel leaders feel this way before they're about to do something they can't take back?

"That should do it," Mason says, backing away from the camera. It's a small speck, barely noticeable. Hard to believe it will scan everyone and everything nearby before sending the information thousands of miles away. "Get ready."

A lump settles in my stomach as the line holds a solid tone. Then a small screen projects. There's someone I don't recognize within the frame.

"Hello, it's Amity Thorne. I'm reaching out for correspondence with General Olivier Favager." My intro is formal. I'd rehearsed it in my head multiple times, praying my nerves stay tamped with the stress of the situation.

"Miss Thorne," the Servicemember says, equally scripted and formulaic. "Where is Dernier three four six?" Their hair is slicked behind them, accentuating the concern etched into their eyebrows. Does this person truly care about Gagnon?

I gulp, remembering my speech. Gagnon explained what would happen when we reached out. "I'm not sure what that means, but if you're talking about the Serviceman this camera was attached to, he's dead. I need to speak with General Favager."

The Servicemember notates my response. "One moment please."

My heartrate spikes. Sarge lifts himself from the ground, placing his chin on my lap. The hologram turns a staticky blue. One second, two. *Maybe they hung up?*

Three seconds, four.

Time slows, though my heartrate doesn't. My fingers flow rhythmically through Sarge's fur, breathing in time with it. Waiting.

Five, six, seven.

Heat flushes in my skin. It's over, isn't it? There are so many people counting on me, yet I've failed. Maybe the General already has the information he needs to take us all out. Maybe these are our last moments on earth.

A few more seconds pass and the hologram blinks. General Favager is in the frame, pompous in his office.

Sarge's throat rumbles from my lap, though the rest of the room falls away, and it's just us.

"You've requested correspondence?" the General asks. "I notice you're one person short." His eyebrow raises with smug satisfaction. He thinks he knows everything, which means Trevor made it and only told him about his own journey, not ours.

"We are requesting back up forces," I say, my voice as even as possible. There's a bit of a shake to it. I hate how much this man unnerves me.

He contemplates my plea. His fingers fiddle in front of him, clasped together. "You've abandoned your post, and broke every promise you've made to the Service." The General is calm on the exterior, but anger flashes in his eyes. "Mr. Warin goes missing and now you demand help?"

Rage tightens my hands into fists. Sarge nudges them with his nose, hoping I relax. *This self-righteous asshole.*

I plaster on my best impression of a Luke Warin smirk. "We found where your family is," I sneer. His face flickers with a blip of surprise. I don't stop. "The man you detest so much has infiltrated Madame Keres' mainframe. If you give us the support we need to take her down, we'll rescue them for you." At some point, I leaned forward in the chair, pushing myself closer to the camera. Now I sit back, relaxed. My arms cross my chest, and Sarge lifts his head from my lap, sitting proudly beside me. There, that should show him.

"How cute," he says. "Don't you know there's a reason your father wasn't allowed to follow you?" He chuckles and my veins turn to ice, cooling me. "What about the boy. Sam, is it?"

It takes everything in me to keep my emotions from showing on my face. Deep down, I knew something was wrong when my father was staying behind, but I hadn't realized it was this bad. And Sam? How dare he utter his name. I suppose it's confirmed that General Favager isn't above using kids. Isn't that exactly what happened with Gagnon, anyway?

Taking a deep breath, I play my hand. It's all I have, and it's hopefully enough to win. "Seems like we each have loved one's worth saving. You'll get yours back if mine are okay. Otherwise, we'll both have funerals to plan I guess." I shrug, hoping the nonchalance shows despite my fear. Will he believe that we truly have his family? Is bartering with the lives of my loved ones really the right call?

Then: "One condition," General Favager says. "Ren Keres is delivered to me. *Alive.*"

The feed goes blank, and that's that.

Mason, Lacy, and Sonya tell me how great I've done. It doesn't feel that way. They locate Gagnon, then leave me alone.

I lay on the dusty floor, Sarge at my side, staring into the open hole of the ceiling out toward the sky. The clouds roll by, and it bothers me how unaffected everything else can be when my own life is experiencing inner turmoil.

After a few hours, there's a loud rumble from somewhere outside. Sarge leaps from the noise, jumping to his feet quickly. *What the hell was that?*

"Amity!" Lacy shouts from outside the cottage. "Come quick!"

Sarge and I bound through the creaky door to an H.P.S. craft landing in the dry field a few hundred feet away.

When the door lowers, a familiar face is the first to descend the ramp. He shouts, "Anyone order back-up?"

"Trevor!" I run to him, leaping into his arms. He catches me with ease, and Sarge prances around happily.

After a few moments, Trevor sets me down. His smile isn't as full as it once was, but it's not the same hollow husk it was when he left us. "I'm glad you've survived, or rescuing your boyfriend would have been a Death sentence for all of us."

"It ain't over yet," I say, nudging him. "There's much to discuss."

○ ○ ○

"GOOD NEWS," I say as Luke settles into my brain for the night. "We're getting you out."

He chuckles. "Damn, I was starting to like it here."

The smile that spreads across my face is involuntary. I miss him. It's undeniable, though I tried to keep him at arm's length. "I can call off the plans if you're pleased as it is?"

The happiness in our moods is leached away as fast as it comes. "What's changed?" he asks, serious now. *Always like the flip of a switch...*

"I sort of, maybe, threatened the General..." My fingers lace into Sarge's fur as he snuggles close. We're playing with fire here, but in order to burn the Reaver down, we knew we'd have to.

Luke is silent for a few moments. "You what?" he asks. "Just clarifying I heard you correctly."

I nod, even though he can't see me from where he is. "Yes. I told General Favager we'd get his family to him if he helped, otherwise we'd leave them where they were forever." I leave out the threats to Sam and my father. There's no point to worrying him when there's enough of that coming from me as is.

He's silent again but then he laughs. It's a true belly laugh. My smile spreads once more. "Damn, M. You really know how to grab a guy by the gonads, huh?" He chuckles.

"Damn straight," I say, puffing my chest. "You best remember that."

"I never once forgot," he says, softly. Then the sadness returns.

"Trevor is here." It's a decent hope that this news will lift Luke's spirits. "He's leading the extraction."

"That's good," he says. "But what about you, miss Face-of-the-

Rebellion? What's your job?" The smile is back in his voice. Such a roller coaster of emotions. "Or were you just the threatener?" I gulp, knowing what I say next will upset him. But he needs to understand.

"I'm the bait." The words come out in a whisper.

There's a sharp intake of breath, something he must have meant to block out, yet maybe not. "No," he argues. "Absolutely not. Put Trevor on the WICS right now, I'll kill him."

I cut him off. "It was my idea. I'm the only one that can rile her. Well, besides you. But this *is* going to work."

It's hard to imagine what's going through his head. The rest of the Servicemembers will be cloaked. I will be the one dangling in front of her. Will she believe I've come on my own? Who knows. The General is going to release a statement that I'm a fugitive of the law. We're hoping she'll see it and assume I'm coming for a second chance. Or third... Fourth?

I've lost count.

"You are going to be the end of me," he finally says, sighing. "Who taught you to walk headfirst into Death?"

"A very wise man," I say, giggling. "The last step is to come out holding it by the neck."

CHAPTER FORTY-EIGHT ○ LUKE

Ren's urgency is never good. Punctuality? Sure. But an *as soon as humanely possible* invitation? Last time she did that it was about my father.

"Have you enjoyed your time here?" she asks when the door clicks behind me. I've barely been in the room for a second and she's already bombarding me with questions.

I've never relished lying, but I do it flawlessly these days. "Of course," I say, nodding.

Her snake eyes study me. I hate it when they do that. "And you'd like to keep staying here?"

My chest tightens. Something deep in my brain is telling me I know where this is going, and I don't want to hear it. There are many things I can pretend about these days, but if this is what I think, I know this is the end. M's plan be damned.

"Is this an ultimatum?" I press. Whatever she's getting at, it's big and she knows it. My fingers tense at my sides, but I keep my face plain. A lot of lives depend on my ability to stay cool, calm, and collected.

Ren scoffs, which has always been a weird sound coming from someone so poised. "It shouldn't even be a question," she elaborates. "It's a... simple request, really." She casually rests against her desk, crossing her legs in front of her. It's disgustingly clear where I got my ability to turn off my emotions from.

"Get on with it," I spit. If I'm too eager, she'll know it's all a charade. If I'm not eager enough, she'll undoubtedly use it as reason to punish someone I love.

"You said you wanted to make me proud, once upon a time," she starts, stalling. She's always with the theatrics.

"Sure," I say, nodding. "So?"

Silence stretches for a moment before the hammer drops when Ren says, "So kill Miss Thorne."

The vein in my neck bulges and my fists are clenched at my sides. I knew it. This is exactly like the loyalty test with my father. She wants me to show that I will do anything she asks; that no matter who or what gets in the way, I will take care of it without question. Of course she's been watching M. She knows she's on her way. Was this part of M's plan?

"It's dad all over again. Wasn't me coming back enough?" It's not. Nothing will ever be good enough for her. She takes and takes, never giving a damn about anyone but herself. I fucking hate her.

"You can right a past wrong," she argues. "I understand how hard it is to kill your own father. But this is some bitch who opened her legs for you." The attempt at empathy is almost too much. It takes everything in me to hold back the cackle of disbelief. Yet it's the dismissive attitude that causes rage to grow quickly. How dare she reduce everything M is to *some bitch*. Her eyes morph from excitement to disappointment. Shit. "Oh, Lucas, darling." She shakes her head, draping her bony fingers off either side of the desk. "Please do not have me admit that Marcus Giles of all people was correct."

Fuck. I let her under my skin. Damn it, Warin. Can I keep the charade alive long enough for M to get here? Who knows. But I have to try. "It's hard to believe that man could be right about anything, but you're the all-knowing *Headmistress*." I roll my eyes, falling into the sofa on the right that's opposite her desk. Then I look directly into her eyes, challenging her. "You tell me."

Ren squints her eyes, scrutinizing me. She lifts herself from the edge of the desk, moving closer. "Honestly, dear. I didn't want to have to do this, but if you won't, you know what happens to your precious Lily." Her gaze darkens as she steps toward me. Lily gets her plug pulled if I don't kill M. Or at least agree to killing her. "A half blood is still blood. Don't tell me your little pet means more than that?"

If I don't do something, Lily is as good as dead, and probably so is M. Something's got to give. And perhaps it's something for my soul alone to bear.

"We're a few minutes out," M says into my head. Just a few minutes more. Her voice is everything to me right now.

A new plan hatches inside my brain. If I insult Ren, keep her talking, she'll have no choice but to explain herself. She justifies what she does every day, but she needs others to see it too. Especially those she deems worthy enough to get close. Everyone else she blows sky high or melts them from the inside out. But me? She'll want me to understand. It's the long con we've been working toward. She'll do everything she can until she gets cornered. At that point, I only hope the bullet is aimed at me and not M.

"Using fear tactics on me isn't very motherly," I point out, keeping eye contact. We stare at each other for a moment, contemplating each other's next moves. Then I say the unthinkable. "It's also unnecessary. I'll do it."

Ren's composure is solid while she finishes her assessment of me. Am I telling the truth? She's wondering, but this is the test.

Does she trust me?

She clasps her hands together, excitedly cheering like a child would cheer for a new toy. It's unlike anything I've ever seen from her. She's carried away about future plans, rattling them off like she were reading a shopping list.

The commotion provides a good cover for me to do what needs to be done. "Goodbye," I say, beneath my breath, sending the signal through my synapses and the WICS carries it to M. "I love you. Just remember who I am." Sometimes plans change; I hope she understands.

"Luke? What?" M's frantic voice filters through. "Luke! Luke, please. Answer me!" I slyly remove the WICS so I don't have to hear it anymore. I will hear her voice, calling to me, in every version of my Hell. Yet, she can't know what's coming or Ren will figure out there's more at play here and we'll lose our trust.

Ren loops behind her desk, pressing a button to summon Marcus Giles. Fuck that guy.

"One condition," I say, keeping myself firmly planted where I am. I will not remove myself from this spot willingly. Not without my condition being met. I need her to keep talking.

Ren grows quiet, the happiness of her expression draining away in a millisecond. She gets up from her desk again, circling around once more. "For you, Lucas, I will consider. What is it you demand?" Her eyes darken as the final word escapes her lips.

"Answer me this. Do I deserve to have a family of my own?" My aspirations for life have changed significantly since I've met M. I didn't think having a family was possible. I didn't think something so mundane would work for me. Now, I put all that anger into my question. How shitty to have my eyes opened to the possibilities of love, only to have it ripped away.

"*We* are family," Ren replies, sitting beside me now. One press of the button on her device and I could be melted from the inside out. Blown to bits if she wants. Though, her choice to be next to me is telling. It's a good sign. "You will also have Lily when it's all said and done. But there's nothing like loving a child that spawns directly from your own DNA." She smiles at me. She *actually* shows her teeth in a smile that I'd describe as... reverence. Is that possible? "You must do it with a more... agreeable suitor. That's all," she says, flippantly. Her bony finger rests on my knee and my skin crawls. Fuck her.

I rip my leg away. "Before I do this, you *must* understand that Amity is the only person I've ever loved, and the only person I see myself with."

Her hand is held in the air, frozen with the sudden burst of anger from me. Then she rests it back into her own lap. "I know you're smarter than this. You truly believe she left my facility without sterilization?" Ren leans her back against the couch, more relaxed than I'd like.

My anger comes out before I can reign it in. "You didn't..." My voice fades. "You sent her to the chambers?" Damn it! I should've known. Ren doesn't take chances. Though M and I never discussed children, it should be *her* choice. That choice has been ripped away, like so many others.

"Oh, dear. You're so behind the times. These days it's more time efficient. Her doses were during the pods. It was all her own doing, really. The more trips she needed, the more doses she received." She swings her hand to the side, dismissively.

"Does it ever end?" I ask, meeting her eyes once more.

Her eyes squint. "Excuse me?"

"Do your asinine justifications ever end?" I clarify. "If we're going to do this, you will have to take my input seriously. People can be *good*."

Ren is back to her scrutinizing self. "I've satisfied your one condition," she plays. "It *ends* with a bullet in Miss Thorne's brain. After that, we'll talk." Her voice lilts in promise as her fingers caress my chin. She walks back to her desk, ruffling through the drawers. Then she sets my Beretta on the blackened top. I wonder if she recognizes it from my father's collection. Surely she wouldn't let me use it if she did.

"One more thing," I add, just to piss her off.

She breathes out harshly, exasperated at my impertinence. "Yes?"

"If Favager has truly ousted Amity as a traitor, she may be coming to appeal to you. If there is anything that you have that she could use for him, I recommend stowing it away." The suggestive tone of my voice is enough to get my message across. Ren regards me with praise.

"Ah, look at you. Blossoming already." She smirks. "Though, there's no need to worry. Miss Thorne will not live to tell any more tales." The sinister expression that unfolds from her features is enough to open the pit in my stomach once more.

Marcus enters the room now. "They're here."

The walk from the office out into the courtyard of Deutereon feels like a walk to the gallows. Giddy energy emanates from Ren. I do my best to keep the rigidness from my step, but I'm more than likely failing at that. M will be with me soon, and I will have to look into her eyes while I hold the metal of a gun to her. If Hell on earth existed, I know I'd be parading straight into it with this.

The sun scorches me as we exit. M is standing solitary in the middle, her head held high. Sarge is behind her, which I find strange. Usually he'll put himself in between M and the threat. Then I realize he's seeing me. He doesn't expect me to be the threat I am.

There are six guards surrounding the perimeter. I clocked them the second we stepped foot on the grass. Giles stands in front of Ren. She doesn't fully trust me. With good reason. These are my safeguards. If I don't take her out, they will.

"What, no hello?" Ren toys from behind me. When M doesn't speak, she clacks her tongue and sighs. "Still no manners."

M sees me with gun in hand, the muscles in my arm as tense as can be. Her eyes soften with pity. I don't like it. I step closer to her, Marcus and Ren following behind, but not too close.

"On your knees," I shout, putting every ounce of harshness I can muster into my tone.

"Wha... what?" M hesitates, not knowing whether to raise her hands in surrender or flip me off.

I gulp. "You heard me. Knees. Now."

I'm so close. Sarge circles her, a growl from deep within him carrying toward me. His teeth are sharp; his lip is pulled back in a snarl. Shit. M's face falls with the realization of what's happening. She drops to her knees, Sarge places himself on the ground beside her.

It takes everything in me to keep the gun from rattling in my palm as I lift it to her forehead. Sarge leaps with a snap of his jaw, but I don't flinch. He doesn't bite me, either. I swap the gun's trajectory to him and he backs off.

"Oh, dear," Ren says. "We can utilize him. He'll make a great guard for us. Only one bullet needs to be used today." The sadistic grin is clear from her voice. One bullet with her name on it, maybe.

The barrel returns to M's forehead and sweat drips down the back of my neck. Does she know it's me, or does she think I'm another subcopy being used to torture her? Fuck it. It doesn't matter.

"Any last words?" I say to the love of my life, hoping she understands. This was the only way.

Her grey eyes meet mine, red-rimmed. My heart is breaking more than I ever thought possible. Even though I know this is the only way, even though I love her, it's too much.

"What are you waiting for, Mr. Warin?" Marcus goads. "Do it! Your Headmistress demands it!"

I rotate, glancing behind me, and put the gun under my opposite arm. The bullet lands cleanly between Marcus Giles' eyes. He hits the ground with a satisfying thud. Oh, how I wish it were that simple for Ren herself.

Her arms go up, halting her men from taking me out. The gun is already pointed back at M, anyway. "Thank God," Ren says, scoffing, unaffected by the splatter of blood on her fresh jacket. "Should've done that myself ages ago." Her pointed shoe taps Giles away, nudging his lifeless body from her vicinity. She gets closer to us. "Go ahead, dear."

"The memory loss backfired," M says, drawing my attention back to her. What? Her tone is rushed.

"Excuse me?" Ren says.

"Thanks to you, I'm able to see past your trick. Without the memory draining, I would've lost Emma forever. You lose."

Ren chuckles, stepping closer again. "Lucas is here with me. Your sister is irrelevant." Her body leans in with a menacing smirk. "I never lose."

In the commotion, M slams forward, ripping the gun from my hands, spinning it to Ren's temple, hiding herself behind my body. Sarge presses her close, keeping M sandwiched in between us for safety. Ren knows I can get out of this, but if I had to guess, she's also banking on M not having the guts to pull the trigger.

The other Force members around the perimeter are motionless, but Ren doesn't seem to notice. Her intense gaze is plastered onto the scene in front of her.

"Shoot me," she says, goading M. "Go ahead." Ren's arms are crossed, and a smug smirk sits on her face. I can't see the expression on M's face, but my lungs deflate.

"The gun doesn't work for her," I say aloud, realization hitting. "You figured this would happen?"

Ren shrugs. "I took a calculated risk. You're still a bit soft," she argues. She pulls another gun from her waistband, pointing it back at M.

"You never trusted me?" An unfamiliar feeling sweeps through my chest. Though my intention was never to shoot M, the fact that I've been played causes a deep ache. Why does it bother me? It shouldn't.

Anger surges through me. How is Ren Goddamn Keres always one step ahead? I will kill her. She's practically within reach. I lunge forward, ripping the gun from her and taking the controller from her pocket in my other hand.

My arm goes around her neck, keeping her in place, pressing the metal to her forehead. "I will blow us all if you hurt her," I shout. "Don't fucking tempt me." I'm using her body to block mine, ensuring no one will shoot. This is dangerous, because M is left unprotected, but then I'll blow us all anyway. Even if there wasn't something greater at play, Ren knows that.

"Stand down," she commands. "I am the Headmistress. Not you."

"No problem," M says, and as if she's pressed a button herself, all the officers drop to the ground. Ahh. The Service is around. They must be cloaked.

Ren's temperature plummets as blood drains from her face. "There is still time to make this right," she says. Desperation doesn't suit her.

"You can, and absolutely should, shut the fuck up," I say, gripping tighter. Her body against mine makes my skin crawl. I want to wash every instance of her from my life. She's a joke, a killer, a monster. It's hard to see anything else when all I see is red.

"Through everything, you still choose her," Ren says. It's an empty statement, one that doesn't fit into the scene. Yet after everything that's happened, I feel the need to defend M.

"You're damn right!" I yell. "Because that's what friends are for." I offer a sideways glance to M, smirking, and her eyes soften, melting my heart. She played the bait perfectly.

"Why?" Ren asks. The age-old question. This is something she couldn't crack. She doesn't understand why she's always the one left behind, but I don't care. "Why won't you ever choose me?" Her voice breaks.

"That's what this is about? The fact that I don't love *you*?" The harsh spit of my words momentarily stuns her. Her features smooth out after a few seconds, and she's back to a cool, calm, collected demeanor despite having a gun pressed to her head.

"Human nature intrigues me," she starts. "I want to know why people leave or stay. Love or hate. Why do some people fight while others run? Miss Thorne was a neat little gift to show up unexpectedly that held the key to it all. I needed to dissect her for the mission of the Guardianship, and the very essence of my being." The words pop out of her mouth like a script she's rehearsed for years. Her justifications for heinous acts run deep. I'm actually glad I got away when I did or I know I'd have fallen down the same path. It's what my father had been trying to keep me from.

"I should've shot you a long time ago," I spit, tightening my hold on her.

"Lucas," she chides. "Is that any way to speak to your mother?" There's a vein popping out in her forehead. "Honestly. You said I should treat you like an adult. Why is it that you insist on acting like a child?"

I roll my eyes, furthering the childish act. Sometimes she surprises even me with her ability to be so detached from reality.

She scoffs, then sighs. "Look. I didn't kill her, Lucas. I wouldn't do that to you. Don't you see the lengths I'd go to for you? She's been nothing but trouble for me." She's placating. She can go to Hell.

I scoff. "No, instead you'd ask *me* to do it. Does that sound like me? Do you even know me at all?"

"Of course I do..." she argues. "You're my s..."

I press the metal to her forehead more harshly, indenting the skin with the barrel. I don't want to hear her say the words. I am *nothing* like her. "I am *not* yours."

She sighs. "I should've known it was too good to be true."

Her voice is too much for me. Everything wrong that has ever happened has been her fault. My father, Lily, Janet, M, Emma, Zach, Trixie, Abby, Sam, Nan, Thomas. The list is never-ending and rolls continuously through my head. How is she still so calm? How, in the face of Death, can she not see the error of her ways? Humanity has a chance if she's as far beneath the earth as she can possibly be.

I take my other hand, clamping it around her throat. Her eyes bulge, and the panicked expression of her eyes drives me further. This bitch is going to die. We'll deal with the consequences later.

"Luke," a whisper carries across the way. My eyes lift to see M's terrified expression, and the anger dims a bit. The world slows, time stretching. Only the sound of Ren's gagging fills my ears. Until: "This isn't the way." M is begging me, calling me back to her.

It takes a lot to push the monster down, but I count to five, relaxing slightly, allowing Ren to breathe a bit more air.

"Do you suppose you got the idea to carry multiple weapons from your father?" Ren croaks.

In that same moment, the hand I haven't got a hold of reaches behind her to grab a gun I didn't see. It's pointed at M before my brain can process.

"No!" I shout, shoving, but not before the trigger is pulled.

M screams, and I quickly render Ren unconscious with a blow to the head. I hate that I can't just kill Ren now and get it over with, but Favager wants her alive. She's our ticket back into the Service. Besides, I need to check on M.

Please don't be dead. Please don't be dead.

Time slows as I turn to find M crumpled on the ground. But it's not her that's been shot.

It's Sarge.

CHAPTER FORTY-NINE ∘ AMITY

I DON'T KNOW WHAT'S WORSE, THE FACT THAT SARGE IS THE one on the ground, or the fact that I wish it were me.

"He... he jumped in front of me," I cry to no one in particular. "He pushed me out of the way."

"Mason, we need medical. Now!" Luke says from somewhere far away. *Or is he close?*

There's blood. There's so much blood. *No, no, no!*

"Is he breathing?" Luke is shouting. To me? I can't formulate a response. "Damn it, Amity! Is he breathing?" Yes, to me.

Through blurry vision, I focus on the rise and fall of Sarge's chest. It's shallow and fast. I nod, hoping Luke sees, too, as he rushes up on us.

My fingers trail through Sarge's fur, caked with blood. In my head plays a thousand memories of us together. Memories I thought were long gone from the Reaver's evil. Finding him in the woods, all those nights at home with Emma, traipsing through lakes. So many memories I'd lost but now are rushing back. *Please let us make more.*

Mason arrives carrying a med bag. "I got this," he says to Luke, but I'm far away in my mind and it's hard to hear. "Radio the Service. Tell them we've got her. Go find Emma."

Luke is torn. He glances to me, Sarge, and back to Mason before nodding. Then he's off.

My fingers fumble under my jacket to the golden pin. Pulling it from its place, I press it into Sarge's fur, uttering a quick prayer as I do. *Please, please, protect him. Make him whole.*

"Do you know what you're doing?" I ask, with scratchy voice and sniffles. I back away from my best friend, giving him a wider space. Mason fixed my bullet wound, but there wasn't nearly this much blood.

Mason doesn't look at me. "After I lost Abby, I swore never again. I demanded advanced medical training." His brow is furrowed, sweat clinging to it. "I'll do everything I can."

The commotion around us threatens to draw my attention from my best friend. Thanks to Trevor, the Service was able to clear out every Force member at once while I kept the Reaver distracted. Now they are circling back to take care of the civilians. Yet my eyes can't remove themselves from Sarge. He's panting heavily now. I don't know if that's a good sign or not and I'm too afraid to ask.

It's not long before people of all ages take to the field. We did it. The Reaver is down, our fellow citizens are free. Not everyone knows it yet, but soon, we'll enter into a sweet peace. *Hopefully...*

After enough people pass us by, my eyes inadvertently scan the crowd, looking for a familiar face. Mason is working hard on Sarge still. Though a part of me wants to watch every second of it, I need to keep myself busy.

Will I recognize her? Will she recognize me? Maybe we've both changed so much we'll pass each other without a second glance. Maybe she's not here... maybe the Reaver got to her before we did.

Then:

"Sarge?" Emma says looking past me. She's so beautiful. Her caramel locks sit perfectly below her shoulders. Her blue eyes sparkle in the sun. It takes everything in me to pull my eyes away from the face I've longed to see for so long, yet I whirl around to catch a glimpse at what she's looking at. Sarge is up, wagging his tail. *He's okay!* My heart skips a beat.

"Sarge, stop moving!" Mason chastises.

I flip my gaze back to Emma. The connection clicks on her face, realizing that Sarge and I are one; we're always together. She peers at me expectantly. "M!" She leaps forward, nearly jumping to where I am, and wraps her arms tightly around my body.

It feels like home.

My mind is in shock. *It's her. It's really her.* She's here. "Little M," I breathe, sighing. My arms tighten as my shoulders relax. She's so big. I have no memory of her since she was four. A smile works its way onto my face, yet tears threaten to fall.

Mason continues to yell at Sarge, who is circling around us, happily twirling between me and Emma. Out of my peripheral, Luke makes his way toward us with a young girl next to him, but he stays back. I pull away from my sister, kneeling down to her eye level. "There's so much we have to do, but will you keep an eye on Sarge while I go take care of something?"

Emma smiles, nodding excitedly.

She's my everything, my little M, but there's room in my heart for Luke, too. And I'm so glad he's okay. I run to where he's standing and slam into his chest, wrapping my arms around his torso. My tears can no longer hold themselves back.

Luke squeezes me to him. We slowly spin until Emma and Sarge are within my view. "You were right," he says. I don't have to see him to know he's watching the same scene that I am. It's my family. *Family.*

"About what?" I question, not removing myself from his hold and keeping my eyes on Emma.

"You believed Emma was alive, and you were right," he clarifies.

My eyes still refuse to look away. Yet, Luke pulls my gaze to his by gently pressing his tough fingers against my chin. Then it's my greys to his hazels.

"You *deserved* to be right."

My bottom lip quivers, fighting my muscles from the involuntary spasm of emotion.

"Ahem!" the girl beside him says. "Ick." Yet she's smiling. Luke pulls her to his side, mussing her hair. My face flushes red with embarrassment and I wipe the pooling tears.

Her eyes are not the same hazel that her father and brother have, yet they're still striking all the same. She has long brunette hair that falls in thick waves down her back.

"You must be Lily," I say, sniffling. "It's nice to finally meet you."

We make our way back to Emma, Sarge, and Mason. I can't tell if this is all scary or exciting to Emma and Lily. So much of their life has been hidden away while they were stuck in stasis. I know I'm feeling a mix of both right now. There's excitement for the future, yet a scary anticipation for it all the same. They'll have questions; they'll need patience. We all will.

Mason monitors Sarge while Luke, Lily, Emma, and I hang around, waiting for the crowd to clear. Once he knows Sarge is stable, he takes off to help medical with anything that may arise. The Service has sent hovercrafts for extraction, but I'm in no rush to return. Lacy and Sonya are getting their hands dirty somewhere, helping extricate some of the children from the facility. Everything I could ever want is right here.

Emma finds the golden pin in the dirt, shot from Sarge's fur when he jumped up in excitement. "Look!" She cries. "Look what

I found!"

I smile at her. "Wow," I say with awe. "You're very lucky. That's beautiful."

Her eyes sparkle as much as the pin does in the light. *There it is. My reason. Why I never gave up.*

"Where is the Headmistress?" she asks. "I have to thank her." She drops her hands, the pin a forgotten heirloom barely a few seconds in.

My head whips to my love, studying the downturn of her lips and the tenseness of her brow.

Emma returns her gaze to me. "She's not as bad as you and Daddy thought, I promise." Her voice portrays a certain level of desperation that my head can't wrap around.

"Little M," I say. "She's done very, very bad things," I argue, but fail.

"No," she replies, shaking her head. "No! She made me a promise and she kept it. She's not all bad. People make mistakes, right?"

I study Emma for a long time before nodding, resigned. I pull her to my side, sliding my arm behind her back. "Okay," I start. "How about this? You tell me everything that happened to you on our way back to Creyke Point."

She nods in return, enthused. My heart breaks, but if Emma has somehow been shielded from all of the horror, then for that, I'm thankful.

I reach for the pin in her fingers. She hands it over without much protest. Carefully, I fasten it to her shirt, and she beams at me with the brightest smile I've ever seen. *My light is back.*

Sarge takes one side of my little M, I take the other, running my fingers through her shoulder length curls. Tears spring into my eyes once more. I wrap my arm around her and she leans into me as we walk. Luke places himself at my right side, with Lily beside him. I take his hand in mine. Without looking, I know he's tense but happy. His lips twitch in a hidden smile as our fingers interlock. What do we do now that the Reaver is captured? Does the General turn on us? Where do we go?

The fight isn't over yet, but it seems like we're getting closer to the light at the end of the tunnel.

CHAPTER FIFTY ∘ AMITY

I SHOULD'VE KNOWN WE'D BE MET WITH DISDAIN. GENERAL Favager is waiting amidst a crowd of Servicemembers as we land on the field above H.P.S. Headquarters. We'll either take one step out and never touch ground alive, or we'll be immediately apprehended as the criminals we are.

Trevor assures us that the General was amiable when he returned, but I'm not so sure it'll be the same for us. I did threaten him after all...

I order Sarge with a swing of my hand to guard Emma, keeping her behind my back. Luke stands off to one side, Mason the other. Trevor behind. I'm the face in the front, ready to accept my penance for all I've done. Yet, as the distance closes, the more I realize this is less of an execution and more of a celebration. Everyone on the field claps and cheers as we exit.

"This is surely a warm welcome," I say, skeptically. If the General is upset about our disappearance—or my threats—he's not making it known at present. *Perhaps the hammer will fall later...*

He nods, giving a self-assured smile that chills me right to my bones. "I wanted to personally thank you for your participation in achieving our goal," he addresses our misfit group. I can't help but pull Emma tighter to my back. Sarge has already put himself in front of us as a barrier. "In three days' time, we will fulfill our Cleansing Ceremony."

"Your what?" I ask, blurting before I can stop myself.

The General tenses his jaw but then answers my question diplomatically. "It is the celebration of our success." He nods again, bidding farewell, leaving without another word.

"Why do I feel as though he's being intentionally vague?" I question so only Luke hears me.

"Maybe he knows who I am..."

"Luke! Amity, Sarge!" Sam is bulleting through the field of Servicemembers as if his life depends on it. He slams into Luke for a giant bear hug. The sight makes me smile. But if Sam is here, then where is...

"Dad!" I say, relieved. He's meandering through the crowd at a much slower pace than Sam. His eyes widen, his knees wobble, when Emma peeks out from behind me. Her face lights up and she takes off running, meeting him before he has a chance to register what's going on.

The scene is something to behold, for sure. Now we can start healing.

The day passes in a blur. So much happens, it all feels fake. I'm waiting for the shoe to drop; for the dream to end and I wake up in a dusty bed in the middle of nowhere. But it doesn't come.

Lily, Sam, and Emma are passed out on the couch, all limbs and snores. Today has been tiring and exciting. Emotions have been all over the place. I envy their ability to sleep. Luke is inside watching them, but I'm outside with my father. It's the first time we're able to catch up. I've missed him.

"How have you been?" he asks.

I study him, working in my head if this is a real question or not. How have I been? I've been through the wringer. I've been tested emotionally and physically. Morally, even. Luke says all the best leaders go through it. I think maybe he's full of shit.

"I've..." I start, yet the words die on my tongue. "I've missed my family," I admit, sinking into him, resting my cheek on his chest. Sarge is on my lap, getting in the way of me fully hugging my father, but it still feels like heaven. My family is whole. At least, as whole as it can be. I know mom is looking down on us with a proud smile.

I pull away. "How have *you* been?" I question. The General held my father here, using him to lure me back; keep me in line. I'm thankful it's all worked out how it's supposed to.

"General Favager made me stay here as collateral for you, though I've won his favor," my father admits, sharing what I already know. "I can be quite useful." He winks at me, and I smile.

My father has always been crafty. It's why I ultimately felt comfortable with taking the risk of threatening the General. He had no idea he was playing the game on both fronts. Thorne's are everywhere, and they're sharp.

"So you know what this Cleansing Ceremony is then?" I ask. It's been bothering me all day. It's not hard to imagine what it could possibly be, but I'm afraid the answer will scare me. General Favager told me he'd extinguish the life of anyone with the Reaver's DNA, including—unknowingly to him—Luke, the Reaver's son. So what will he do with the true object of his aggression?

My father clears his throat. "It's basically a public execution. More barbaric, though. And he will demand her son's identity so he can do the same to him." His eyes meet mine in warning.

I quietly listen as my father explains, in detail, what the General has in store. The Reaver will be dragged into the center of the field above Headquarters, strung up for all to see. She will get each phalange removed, slowly, to signify each year we lost to her terroristic reign. She will get no last words, no fair trial. She will die a gruesome Death at the hands of another tyrant in front of thousands, but only *after* she gives up her son. Until then? Torture.

Fitting? Maybe. But humane? Certainly not.

And what do we do with her sympathizers? With those that were high in the Force, doing her bidding? Where do we draw the line?

What's the point of taking the Reaver down if we pick up where she left off?

We're supposed to be better. Why is it that we clear one hurdle and another gets in the way? I don't want to kill, hurt, lie... *survive*. I want to live and be the best person I can be in this life. That's what I want for everyone. For Emma. Reaver be damned.

If the General wants his family back, he's going to have to earn them through kindness.

o   o   o

I STORM THE General's office, shouting at everyone to let me through. No one can stop me. Thanks to Sarge, not a single guard is willing to put their hands on me. Growling fills the air and flashes of teeth snap around me, but I enter the room unscathed.

"She deserves the choice of redemption," I argue, not giving the General a moment to process my advance.

The General places his hands in front of him, resting on his desk, seemingly annoyed. It's early in the morning. The stench of coffee with something stronger swirls my nose. He's only just woken up. The crumbs of a pastry hastily eaten are still sprinkled around his desk.

Finally, wiping his mouth, he sighs. "Miss Thorne, she is the face of evil," he argues. "The figurehead of Humanity's downfall. Does she not deserve to pay for the crimes she's committed?" The General is letting his need to avenge drive him. He thinks I don't understand, but I do. And I also know what it's like to let those emotions take control. It wasn't until my memories were gone that I truly saw the full picture and was able to push forward, shedding the need for revenge. It wasn't until I've known personal forgiveness that I was able to look forward for others as well.

"She can atone," I argue. "Why does payment equate to Death?" I know I sound absolutely mad. Completely brain fogged. Yet Emma's words whisper in the back of my mind. The Reaver is a person and she deserves a chance.

General Favager shouts, shooting from the desk. "She is the very abomination to society she tried to rid. *She's* the Tainted one!"

I'm struggling to find words. I expected push back for my argument, but not such an uncontrolled outburst from the leader of the Service. The General stares angrily, but I don't shrink away. "We have *all* killed, burned, cried. We have torn apart ourselves and others in the name of something bigger. It *has* to stop!"

"You of all people should know of her depravity." His voice is a sweetened tone, dipped in the acrid scent of manipulation. I almost smell it on his breath from here.

I don't know what to say, so I stay silent.

"And you have yet to tell me where my family is. I've been patient in giving you rest with *yours*. Shall we get them in here for retribution?" He lifts a brow in sly contempt. He's threatening my family again.

I cross my arms. "Luke is the only one who knows where your niece is. The *better* one, anyway." I roll my eyes and he squints, studying me.

"Is that supposed to mean something?" he grates. "I have one niece. She is all that's left of my sister since that evil monster killed her." Spit flies from his mouth. He's angry. Does he not know of the relation or is he simply in denial? Disowning the Reaver is certainly something he'd be capable of.

With the wave of his hand, the General sends someone after Luke.

"You may think you're a leader, but you're being pulled by revenge. Only your best interest is at heart, not the world's. Not Humanity's."

Luke enters, stopping the General from a response, though I hadn't missed the flare of anger within his eyes. I'm surprised, however, when my father enters as well.

"M," my father says, worry wrinkling his face. He's crossed the room and puts himself beside me. "What's going on?"

My mouth is set in a hard line. He's upset? "The Cleansing Ceremony cannot happen."

"Your mother died because of that woman, you suffered... I suffered." He's begging me. Or is he? The General believes him to be on his side after all of this.

My voice is lost for another minute or so. Then: "I know," I sigh. "But Emma believes her to be capable of good, and what would we do if she found out I killed her?"

The pain in my father's eyes is enough to shrivel my heart. *Is this real? It's so hard to tell.*

I now address Luke. "I know it sounds stupid, but if we don't at least give her a fair trial, we'd be no different than she is."

"M..." my father starts, attempting to cut me off.

"Mark my words, I'll pull that trigger if she proves it necessary, but if there's any outcome where she can change, why wouldn't we try?" Luke's arms are crossed and his expression is dark.

"People don't change," he says, completely still as a statue. I'm mildly surprised he's been silent up until now.

"You did," I say, reaching out to put my hand on his chest. "And so have I."

His features soften slightly, then harden again with new resolve. "No. I'm still the monster I've always been, and so is she."

He spins away, storming out of the office, yet he's stopped before he gets away. The General still requires information from him.

My heart aches, but I can't focus on that. Emma believes in the good of people. We need to do this fairly. I spin back to the General, who's been watching the scene with mild amusement.

He cackles, uncharacteristic and scary.

"Is something funny?" I ask, puffing my chest with defiance, hoping to make myself appear more confident than I really am.

"Yes." He smiles, his lips pulling back over his sharp teeth. "The fact that you believe you can storm in here making demands after your insubordination." At this, he slams his palms down on the desk, pushing himself up from his chair. "I may not be able to kill you without risking disorder in my Service, but that does not mean you will get whatever you want."

Sarge puts himself in front of me, baring his teeth in warning. We all stare at one another for a few tense seconds, until an idea pops into my head.

"When I lost my memory, there was a moment of clarity. I didn't feel any pain until I started to remember again," I explain. "At least give her the option. If we could make the Reaver forget—give her new, nicer memories—I think we could bring out her better qualities."

The General's eyes widen, but he quickly covers his shock. "On the inside, maybe. But to everyone else?"

My father speaks up again. "You sure you don't want to complete the Cleansing Ceremony after everything she's done?" I hope that my father is on my side, but he's feeling the pressure of being back under General Favager's thumb. He has to play the part. Especially now that the General's true feelings are out.

I shake my head. "No," I say. "I don't. That would continue the cycle. It ends. Now." I swivel my head to glare at General Favager once more. "There's no world that survives if we meet hatred with more hatred."

Sarge and I storm away without another word.

CHAPTER FIFTY-ONE ∘ AMITY

FUCK THE GENERAL AND HIS BACKWARDS WAY OF THINKING. He's no better than the Reaver. He hides behind a sense of misguided moral superiority. I'll convince him yet, but I'm more worried of Luke's response to all of this. He'd said that people don't change, but we decided that our past was not our future. What happened to that? *What happened to* him?

I circle to the VIP section, checking in on the children. Lacy is sitting outside the door and Sarge takes off to smother her with wet kisses. "What are you doing here?" She was reading, her back to the structure. She folds the book with one finger to mark her page.

Sarge backs off, returning to my side. "Luke summoned me when he left. Wanted to make sure the kids were good," she replies.

I slump down, placing myself next to her. Sarge lays in front of both of us, like a protective wall. "This whole thing is a mess." My head falls into my hands. One problem taken care of, yet another one arises. Should I put it all behind me and let General Favager complete his Cleansing Ceremony? Will the Reaver give up Luke after his rejection of her?

"Usually is where politics are concerned," Lacy mutters, setting the book beside her. "Though, maybe it's just us humans over-all." She shrugs.

"After everything she's done, would you be mad if the Reaver lives?" It's a genuine question. Maybe without my memories, I'm too blinded. From curse, to blessing, to curse all over again. Without the loss, I wouldn't have gotten my little M back. But with it, I seem to be way too forgiving for some.

Perhaps that's more the new experiences. Placed in a new environment without the lessons I'd learned over the last six years, I started to fall into a difficult pattern. If it's true what Luke has told me about the Reaver, maybe it's not entirely her fault? Ugh.

Lacy considers the question. It was dumb to ask, I know. Yet she surprises me when she says, "I don't think so."

My mouth pops open in shock. Everyone else had seemed so mad about my stance. "I wish kindness and forgiveness could win over hatred," I muse out loud. The Reaver deserves some kind of consequences for her actions, but why does it have to be a gruesome, public Death?

"Why can't it?" Lacy argues. "This is *your* show. Not the General's, not Mason's, or your father's. Not Luke's. Amity Thorne is a badass," she says smiling. "And Amity Thorne is the only one that knows what to do."

I chuckle. "That's a beautiful sentiment, but General Favager is a real piece of work." Air rushes from my lungs in an exasperated sigh.

Lacy places a hand on my knee, gently squeezing, and my eyes meet hers. "I think you'd be surprised how many people are behind *you*."

No more words are passed between us, she simply gets up, heading to Mason's VIP suite. She and Sonya must be staying there for the night.

With Lacy's absence, Sarge shimmies to the empty space next to me. His chin rests on his usual spot in my lap and I stroke the soft fur of his head. It's nice to know that some things will always be the same.

My wayward thoughts are only stopped by Luke. He lumbers up to me after some time of sitting alone. His face is no-nonsense; his body is tense. I can't imagine what he's been through. I can't imagine how my views of the situation must make him feel.

"Where's my father?" I ask, growing wary. Thankfully I know that Sam, Emma, and Lily are still safely tucked behind the walls of my suite, asleep. But my father? Did the General do something to him?

Luke drops in front of me, opting to sit instead of pace the way I would. Most of the important VIPs have left for their day already, getting an early start for whatever misguided deed they're tasked to complete. "Said he had some business to take care of."

"Did you tell him where she was?" I ask, cautiously. Luke is the only one who knew where General Favager's niece was being held. He must be in a terrible position right now, but I need to know.

He sighs. "Yeah."

I don't blame him. There will be another way we can work out something with the General. We'll make it happen.

The silence stretches for only a few seconds before he says, "I want to understand you. How could you not want Ren dead?"

The tone of his voice is enough to crack my heart. Deep down, Luke is hurting. He finds out his birth mother isn't actually dead, but instead this harbinger of Death. She killed his father, tortured the person he loves, took his sister. It's hard to see past the hurt. I don't want to lead with his safety because, the truth is, it needs to be for a better, more altruistic, reason.

My fingers delve deeper into Sarge's fur. "What if Lily had said to you what Emma had said to me?" I plead, hoping he'll see it from my perspective. "Those that follow after us are innocent. We cannot perpetuate hatred with more hatred. Consequences exist, yes. But does this end justify the means? We cannot repeat history when it's hardly even history."

"She shot Sarge," he says, his face contorted in confusion. "She almost killed you." There's so much more behind his eyes. The Reaver has a laundry list of evil that follows her around like a shadow. "I've always stood beside you, but this? She's a menace to society. How could you think I would ever forgive such a horrible devil like her?" He's begging me. My chest is hollow, aching. Luke deserves to have someone in his corner after all that he's been through. But I don't want to abandon myself. There has to be a middle ground.

"I'm not saying you forgive her," I clarify. "I'm just saying maybe be gentle."

"She doesn't deserve *gentle*," Luke spits. "She deserves every punishment known to man."

I sigh. "Are all monsters born? Or do they morph later on?" I want to make sense of it all. My head spins faster than ever before.

If John Collins really did choose a different family over the Reaver, I understand her frustration and anger. It even helps me see the flaws of Humanity she's trying to change.

She grew up in poverty, her father was making six figures. She only ever wanted to be loved, yet her mother chose drugs, leaving no one left. Then, the father of her child abandoned her, too. I'm not saying what she's done is right, by any means. A lot of people have difficult childhoods and they don't become sadistic overlords that kill hundreds on a daily basis. But it does help me understand. She's a monster now, but was she always? Maybe she started out as simply misguided. What if there was a way to change all of that?

Maybe there's a way out of this without more Death.

"If you want, they can target the memories of her having a baby and she could forget you even exist," I suggest to Luke.

Realistically, it should be his decision to kill or not, to pardon or condemn, but I'm scared that deep down, her being his mother won't be enough. The cycle has to end.

"But," I add, "maybe in time, her memories of you could be altered. You could mend your relationship with her. She could be a *real* mother."

This isn't something Luke wants. It seems necessary to suggest it anyway. Everyone deserves the chance at a good life. That's truly how we'll advance Humanity. Kindness and understanding. Forgiveness. Giving help to those who need it. We must be willing to grow and heal our wounds.

"But she wasn't!" he shouts, slapping the ground with his palm, startling both me and Sarge. "You can erase hers, but will you erase mine?" His eyes meet my greys once more and the hollowness of my heart deepens.

"Do you really believe you're still a monster?" I swap tactics. I thought we'd gotten through this before, but it must be rushing back to him. "You *have* changed. We all have the capability to. Including her." I say the words but even I know that it's far-fetched. I owe it to Emma—to all the girls like her who can grow up with happiness and love in their hearts instead of bitterness and constant animosity. We can set the tone for the new world.

Luke's muscles tense, his fists clench. Instead of opening his mouth to argue, he shoots up from his spot. He turns, and that's that. It's pointless to tell him that his identity will be forced from her and he'll share the same fate. At this rate, I'm not entirely sure he wouldn't accept it for himself.

I want him to come around for the right reasons. For Sam, and for Lily. I know with time he'll see the same things I do.

But first, the Cleansing Ceremony must be stopped. With or without his consent.

Emma, Lily, and Sam wake up shortly after. They join the other kids for the day. Those that were liberated from the Reaver's program, and those that have been in the Service's watch for some time already. If it weren't for Lacy and Sonya being a part of it, I'd have never let the kids out of my sight. She assured me that they will be safe. I'm not sure how she could possibly know that. But it gets me thinking that maybe she's been right all along. Perhaps there are more people in my corner than I initially thought.

o o o

EMMA SLEEPS SOUNDLY beside me. Her head rests on my lap in the place Sarge's normally would. I run my fingers through her hair. She's an angel in my grasp. Sarge is at my feet, pressed against the sofa. It's like those nights after mom died, when Emma didn't want to be alone, and honestly, neither did I.

In this moment, I know that I will do anything to keep her safe. I will do whatever it takes to leave her with a life worth living. A life of happiness, love, and hope.

Luke hasn't returned to me at all since our talk. He needs the space and I'm happy to give it. After everything we've been through, I'm not one to talk about demanding his presence. I've learned that love is funny sometimes, but when it's real, it's real. I don't fully understand how I got here, I just know that I have.

Sam and Lily never returned either. After the kids had their

time out and about, having fun for the first time in probably forever for some of them, it was only my little M that Lacy dropped
back at my doorstep.

In the early morning hours, blaring sirens wake us abruptly.
There's to be an emergency meeting in the celebration hall. Everyone filters from their rooms in orderly fashion. Emma clings
to my side, Sarge clings to hers, knowing that by protecting her,
he's helping me.

Mason shuffles into the ocean of people beside us.

"Any idea what this is?" I ask, giving him a sideways glance.

These people don't seem concerned. They aren't used to the
things that Emma and I were used to. Sirens often meant something bad around the Slums. Sirens meant Death.

"What's going on?" Lacy and Sonya find us as we get closer.
The only person missing now is Luke. My father should already
be here, yet I can't find him.

A man I recognize as General Favager's lead Serviceman, the
Second in Command, stands at the front of the audience. His face
gives nothing away. Once we're all in place, he begins speaking.

The General is dead.

CHAPTER FIFTY-TWO ○ AMITY

THE HUMAN PROTECTIVE SERVICE IS ABUZZ WITH RUMORS AND questions and anxiety. What happens now? Who takes over the Service? How did General Favager die?

Naturally, I'm looked at as an answer, or excuse, to all of these questions.

General Favager's Second in Command has summoned me into a meeting which is where I'm being escorted now. Lacy and Sonya agreed to watch Emma, and Luke is still not talking to me. I have no idea where my father is. This morning has been utter chaos for us all.

Sarge and I enter the office of the General. The smell of chemicals breaches my nostrils the second the door opens. I'm half expecting to see General Olivier Favager sitting at his desk, like it's all a joke. I'm, instead, surprised to find that my father is here with the Second in Command.

"Welcome," he says, his face friendly and inviting. The tone doesn't match the memories of this room. "Please sit."

Hesitantly, Sarge and I walk to the front of the room where my father is already sitting. There's life in his eyes where I once remember seeing a dulled light.

"Jonah and I were discussing the future," my father says.

I plop into the plush chair beside my father and Sarge takes his place at my feet. "Anything good?" I ask, apprehensively.

Jonah replies, "Life as we know it is about to change. Surely there is good in that?"

Heat creeps beneath my skin. This *is* good. I can't shake the feeling that my father has had something to do with this. "May I ask what happened to the General?" I ask, innocently. It may appear that Jonah has been in on this all along, though I can't be sure.

My father answers. "Rumor has it, his favorite Danish in the morning had been poisoned. Could have been anyone." He shrugs. Our eyes meet in understanding. "Formal investigations will be taking place soon." His lips purse.

"Your father and I think it might be best to have you be the face of the Human Protective Service now. While there may be some unrest, you already have people following your lead." Jonah stares at me expectantly. Just like that, I'm promoted? *How has my father weaseled his way in this deep?* My brain recalls our conversation from before. He'd mentioned falling into General Favager's good graces. I'd only tossed some ideas my father's way, like removing General Favager from power somehow, yet I dismissed most of them for being too senseless. We never discussed much of what we would do after any of those plans hypothetically came true.

Power thrums through my veins. Could I truly lead the way they want me to? I barely made it out of all this without losing my head.

I glance between Jonah and my father, an idea popping into my head. "If the people follow me, wouldn't it be safe to assume they would trust who I appoint?" My eyebrows raise in questioning. I realize there's someone much better suited for the position, someone who will do the job with their entire soul. They were practically born for it.

My father smiles, knowingly.

Jonah studies me with silent approval. "Who did you have in mind?"

Mason Baines is walking into the office shortly after. "Me?" he says, his face turning red. His palm clings to the back of his neck. "Are you sure?"

Jonah and my father stand behind me. They watch on with reverence. "Never been more sure in my life," I say, smiling. Sarge sits proudly beside me, looking at the leader of the new world the same way that I am.

"Please, take your place at the desk, sir," Jonah says, satisfied. Mason glances around the room, nervous energy radiating from him. He may be wondering if this is joke, but it's the farthest thing from.

Mason places himself behind the desk, sitting in the plush chair, running his palms over the polished wood. His mouth morphs from a straight line into a small curve, then his teeth show in a full-fledged grin.

"You can make sure that Abby lives on forever in your policies. She always knew the kind of man you were, and though it took me some time to relearn with my hazy memory, I know it, too," I say, returning the smile. "Lead on, General Baines."

I leave him behind to have breakfast with Emma. Her eyes widen at the sight of the food here. "There's so much!"

I pile a plate for Sarge and laugh when Emma's is just as high.

People in the room whisper, glancing at us. I ignore it all despite the heat creeping into my ears. Mason will lead us well. I know the right decision has been made.

The day passes by with ease. Sarge, Emma, and I play in the field above Headquarters. We have a picnic which, despite being a part of, I can't believe it's actually happening. Am I the only one who feels the air is fresher somehow?

When we return to the room, I'm summoned away again. Then I'm in Mason's office for the second time today.

"General Mason Baines," Lacy says. "Can you believe this?" Her arm is around her wife, and we're awaiting Mason's opener. He'd called more than just me in to touch base after nonstop meetings all morning. What's one more, right?

Sonya nuzzles into Lacy. "Who would've thought we'd be here?"

I watch them and peace spreads throughout my body. A new world is beginning. Now we just have to figure out where to go from here.

My father is already in the room, Jonah too. We're waiting on Luke. He's certainly not happy with me already, and I can't believe the news of Mason's new career will bring him any closer to contentment.

Yet he walks in, all confident and unbothered. His moods send me in circles sometimes. When his eyes meet mine, they ignite with a fire that makes my heart beat wildly.

"Alright, now that everyone is here, let's get started," Mason says, sitting at *his* desk.

Lacy coughs, saying, "Try hard," with a smile. Everyone giggles. Mason shakes his head, but his lips flip up at the edges.

"You'll be happy to know that I've sent for Gagnon. His daughter is safe. They will be reunited soon."

Lacy and Sonya cheer. Luke is stoic. My father and Jonah are content the way I am. Gagnon was an integral part of our plan, but he had to be hidden away, perceived as dead in order for his daughter to live. I'm so glad that they'll be together once more.

"But there is an important matter to address," Mason says, his face growing serious. My heart drops. "Everyone is asking what will happen with Madame Keres. I've decided to leave it up to you, Amity. We will do whatever you think is right." Everyone turns their head to look at me. The heat rises in my cheeks. Though I've grown used to the power I hold, it's unnerving when I know everyone is torn about my thoughts.

Luke's gaze is intense, his jaw ticks. He's in the back of the room, leaning against the door frame, arms crossed.

My throat is tight as my eyes flick away to Lacy. She offers me an encouraging nod.

Taking a deep breath, I ready myself to speak. My brain recalls Lacy's words. This isn't anyone else's decision. It's mine.

Mason's patiently awaiting my response. "I'd like us to choose forgiveness. Call the Cleansing Ceremony off." Though the Ceremony could remain without jeopardizing Luke's safety now that the General is dead, it still doesn't feel right to go on. Those in attendance will not be satiated. More blood will always be expected. And how much must be spilled until the revenge is cleared? We have to start fresh.

The expressions in the room are mixed. Mason doesn't give away his stance. He simply nods. "And after that?"

Shit. I'm bad with plans, which is exactly why I left being in charge to Mason. I haven't thought of something that will be fair, only that the Cleansing Ceremony is barbaric and a horrible perpetuation of hatred. "I figured a trial would be best?" I say it like a question, my face scrunching. My voice raises a few octaves.

Mason purses his lips, his fingers rubbing his chin in thought. Everyone listens with bated breath. "Jonah, let's call a meeting to make the announcement. The sooner the better."

"Of course, General," Jonah replies.

The room is dismissed, but Mason keeps me and my father behind. Sarge shuffles beside me, feeling my restlessness. I was hoping to catch Luke before he snuck out.

"I'd like you both to stay hidden until we figure out what we're doing," Mason says. "Emma will be safe with Lacy and Sonya in the meantime. The Thorne name is regarded as royalty, mostly, but there will certainly be discourse after our announcement." His brows are knit together with unease. "There are other matters I must address, but Jonah will fetch you when the meeting is to take place."

With that, Mason is up and out the door before we have anything else to say.

"How are you feeling, kiddo?" my father asks, drawing me from my thoughts once we're alone. I latch my arm around Sarge to pull him close.

"Suppose I could ask you the same thing?" I raise a brow.

"I'm proud," he says. "And I think your mother would be as well." He smiles, tears catching at the corners of his eyes.

I race to him and hug him, not caring what happens after this, only that we're all together again. His arms envelop me, and Sarge wraps himself around the both of us.

"Everybody better remember to watch out for Thornes," I say, sniffling. "They can be sharp." I smile, chuckling through the tears. I remember when my father first said that to me. It made me giggle then, as it does now. I love him.

A few hours pass and Jonah fetches us. He explains that Mason would like my father within view. He's not sure about me.

When we get through the halls, Sarge and I are directed to hide behind the stage. Both my father and Mason agreed that having me visible might still be too much for some. My father will take the brunt of whatever there is to take. I can't help but question whether I've made the right call. Will we start another war if retribution isn't met?

I peek out from behind the curtain, extra careful that both Sarge and I stay concealed within the shadows. The sea of people is darkened from here, but the restlessness is clear. The chatter silences once the new General takes the stage.

"Keeping transparency in mind, it is of the utmost importance that I share with all of you our immediate plans for Ren Keres," Mason says, starting his lengthy monologue script. "I believe it reasonable to allow the figurehead of the rebellion and capturer of evil—Amity Thorne—the sole responsibility of deciding our prisoner's fate."

Unenthused murmurs carry through the crowd of disgruntled Servicemembers. This is certainly not what they were hoping for. My arm pulls Sarge closer to me for comfort.

"It has been decided that a trial shall be held. There is much to determine yet, so while we do not have a firm plan of action at this moment, it is certain that the original Cleansing Ceremony that my predecessor, General Olivier Favager—may he rest in peace— had in place, will be cancelled."

The people of the hall sling curses, shouting obscenities about the unfairness of it all. But what really is fair? The General was the Reaver in different skin. Anyone has the capability of being her, and some are closer to it than others. There needs to be a reminder that hatred is not the default setting of Humanity. Why should anyone get to deem another unworthy? It's all messy, but it's something we can clean up in time.

A voice in the sea of angry Servicemembers carries above the rest. I recognize it immediately. Gagnon.

He gives his praise and shares of my blessing. Mason allows him on the stage. Where the old General cast Gagnon aside, using his daughter as collateral in a war she never had any part in, Amity

Thorne had stepped up and chose forgiveness.

I am the one that brought his family back together. His and so many others.

But maybe everyone is right? Perhaps I'm not qualified to make this decision. Maybe it should be Luke who decides, since the Reaver is his mother. Or maybe a vote should be held so the majority of those that have suffered may feel they're receiving justice. Yet I've come too far for us to fall back into old patterns. Watching all of this unfold, I'm set in my resolve.

This whole thing started with me, and now I will end it.

CHAPTER FIFTY-THREE ∘ LUKE

THIS IS A SHIT IDEA. M DOESN'T FULLY UNDERSTAND THE MONster she's up against, but I do. It's a mirror image, unfortunately.

"What do you think?" she says, hopeful that we'll all go easy on her.

M wants to *talk* to Ren before her trial. As if that's ever worked before. She wants to push for the choice to have her memories wiped, the same as Ren had done to her, but only if she surrenders and agrees. M needs something to take back to the judge—something to vote for—and then it's up to the jury from there.

"Take a gun," I say.

"What?" Her eyes flick to mine. No one else has said a word. I wouldn't expect them to. They know this is between me and M at this point.

"Show her you're not messing around." M swallows hard once I make my next words crystal clear. "Kill her once you realize she'll never change. Fuck the trial." As much as this decision pisses me off, I can't stay mad at M. I've let her know that I'll follow her to the end.

After an eternity, she nods. Her fingers are thick into Sarge's fur and he clings to her side like they were born that way. Though there are others in the room, they disappear into the background.

I reach behind me, pulling my father's beretta from the waistband of my pants. She transfers it into hers, wordlessly.

"I'll have Jonah escort you both to the Oubliette," Mason says, acquiescing to the plan. "I will publicly back whatever happens." His hand rests on M's shoulder, yet for the first time I don't want to pummel him to the ground. Maybe just a slap this time?

Mark Thorne is surprisingly calm knowing that not one, but *both* of his daughters want to give the woman who nearly took everything from him a chance. He won't meet my eye. Yet, there's a sense of pride that swells inside him when he looks at his eldest.

Trevor nods at me as we pass. Mason made him the Head of Military Operations for the Service. Thomas would be happy for him, which is another reason Ren Keres needs to absolutely fuck off and die. Thomas should *be* here. Yet, Trevor shows only understanding about M's plan. He's a better man than I am.

Jonah leads us through Headquarters until we get to a room with nothing in it but a rusty trap door. He muscles the thick metal up, waving his hand to signal our way down the ladder. M descends first; I follow. Sarge lays, waiting, with his paws folded over the edge.

The air is dank, the smell of mildew permeating my nostrils almost immediately. It takes a moment for my eyes to adjust to the dim lighting. M is in front of me, already processing our surroundings. Then I lock my gaze on Ren.

"What a pleasant surprise," she muses. Her neck is latched to the wall behind her, the rest of her body is free. She can easily slide up or down, giving her the ability to sit or stand at leisure, but her neck is clamped, so she can't lay. Sleeping must have been a bitch. Good.

"That makes one of us," M says, revealing the gun in her hand. Ren doesn't react. Her eyes flick lazily over the weapon, then settle back to me for a moment before returning to M.

"You're here to shoot me, then?" Ren questions, annoyed. I hate her with every fiber of my being. The room is only about eight feet tall from ceiling to hard cement floor, though it stretches horizontally for quite a bit. Yet, there are no other prisoners. Either General Favager had been a forgiving man, or everyone was cleared out for Ren's stay. "Should have done it on the field," she sneers.

M scoffs. "You may have gotten free of the Cleansing Ceremony General Favager had planned, but the only reason I haven't shot you is because Emma believes you're good."

Ren doesn't say anything, but her eyes flick, past M, to where I'm standing behind, stoically.

"He wants you dead as well. If you can convince him you deserve to live, that's your ticket out of here."

M says this hinges on me, but it's a falsehood. The choice was never mine. If it were, Ren's skull would have been crushed ages ago. She wouldn't have made it out of Deutereon alive.

"The whispers were true then?" Ren starts. "Olivier is dead?" Her eyes light up with amusement, as if somehow this news is the best she could hear.

"Poison," M spits. From where I stand, M's face isn't clear in my view, but I know she's narrowing her eyes. Was it Ren that poisoned him? Did she think she could ever escape this place alive?

"Glad you came to your senses," Ren commends. "Perhaps you have learned some things after all." The smugness of her tone makes me want to pull the shackles around her neck tighter. She doesn't deserve to breathe.

M laughs, tilting her head to the side and rolling her eyes. "Is that supposed to make me feel something for you?" she asks. "Do you believe you were a better leader?"

Ren clicks her tongue. "Is this what you came to discuss?"

My jaw ticks with disdain. M has taken the reins completely, which is good, because if I were going to speak, I don't know that I'd be able to keep a handle on my anger.

"We're here with a peace offering," M shares. "Convince us you deserve another chance, and we will have your trial vote on wiping your memories, giving you the opportunity to forge a new path."

A smirk plasters itself on Ren's face and I want to smear it. I don't think I'll ever smirk again. "How does it feel to be on top?" she toys, her teeth clacking on the final syllable. Even now, on Death row, she won't stop. Would erasing her memories truly help? I'm inclined to believe she's a monster straight down to her DNA.

"It's over," M says. "You either convince us you deserve a second chance, or there's a bullet with your name on it." M lifts the gun, pointing it square at her target. My heartbeat picks up. Will she do it? After all this time, will she abandon this stupid trial and send Ren where she belongs?

A hard cackle falls from Ren's throat. "Power is a privilege. Olivier didn't understand that. And neither do you, vile girl."

That's it. "Privilege?" I burst in, the anger getting the best of me. "You don't know the meaning of the word. You had the power to *do* something, and how did you use it? By killing innocent people! You toyed with everyone's lives as if they were your personal puppets." Ren's eyes narrow and the shackle clanks at her neck when she shifts in her spot, getting a better angle to look at me. Digging under her skin is exhilarating. "You thought your privilege with power made you a God—gave you the ability to be judge, jury, and executioner—but you were nothing more than a devil in disguise. *You* are the disease that has plagued us. Not the so-called flaws you detest so much." Sweat clings to my upper lip. I realize at some point I've put myself closer to the monster chained to the prison wall. My chest rises and falls in jagged motions of heavy breaths. She's everything wrong with the world. She's everything wrong with *me*.

The room is cold. When Ren opens her mouth to speak, a small cloud escapes. "I wanted this to be ours," she says. "I wanted you by my side as we molded Humanity into a better future. I have maybe cared too much about a rotten son." She snarls at the word rotten. It makes me want to reach out and choke her all over again. It's M's voice that stops me in my tracks.

"You don't know anything about family," she argues. "Family isn't marked by blood, but by those you'd bleed for. You've only ever cared about yourself," M barks. The gun is still raised, held out a foot from Ren's forehead. Will she kill Ren, here and now? How much more of her scrutiny must we endure before M can pull the trigger?

A drop of sweat beads down Ren's hairline. It's unlike her to be so unnerved. She meets my eye and they soften, as if to say, *I would bleed for you.*

My skin crawls. The veins in my neck bulge with a tough swallow. There's a momentary flash of pain in her expression, but within a few seconds, it's gone. Her features relax and she speaks as though she's reciting from something; emotionless and stiff.

"I needed to stay focused, but Lucas—you were my downfall." My nostrils flare, though only slightly. I won't give her the satisfaction of a response. She continues. "Perhaps you are right. Maybe *I* was the fault. Perhaps I, too, have succumbed to the flaws of Humanity."

This is too calculated, too calm. There's something off about these words. I can't put my finger on it. My mind scans through years of memories, trying to pinpoint exactly what she's playing at. Ren loves a good competition. We may have changed the game, but she will surely do her best to play her hand.

Ren has let us think we were ahead from the very beginning, only to tear us down at the last second every time. Then it hits me. Her words are a goodbye...

"Wait!" I surge forward but it's too late. The gun is ripped from Amity's hands before either of us process what to do, though I don't worry she'll aim it at M this time.

The barrel flips in her unchained hands and presses beneath her chin. Then Ren's brains splatter against the walls of the prison.

CHAPTER FIFTY-FOUR ○ AMITY

IT'S BEEN A MONTH SINCE WE'VE STEPPED FOOT ON THIS SOIL.
A month since the Reaver rid herself from this world. Sometimes
I wish it were different, but then I remember that everything hap-
pens for a reason.

Life is finding a new balance. People are rebuilding. Most everyone has accepted Mason Baines as their new figurehead. Mason!
I know he's going to lead with kindness. We all would. And even
though it was my decision, it's still a crazy thought to wrap my
head around.

"Be nice," I say, stepping into the underground headquarters of
the H.P.S.. Mason is eagerly awaiting us. Sarge takes off from my
side, racing to say hello. It's been too long.

"Hey, we took down two other leaders before," Luke says,
shrugging. "I'll take Mason down, too, no questions asked." Now
that time has passed, he knows the truth. My father was one of the
many behind poisoning General Favager. He knew that I would
always have a target on my back as long as that man was alive.
Though I wish my father hadn't taken a life. I swore to myself
there would be no more Death. Not from my hand, nor my family's.

"Luke!" I chuckle, smacking him playfully in the chest.

"Alright, alright. He's not that bad," he says, laughing along with me. "But don't tell him I said that." Luke insisted on coming with me. I wouldn't want it any other way. Though, I can't imagine how being here must feel for him. It's his first time back since the Death of his birth mother as well.

He's been keeping it all inside, but I know it hurts. Luke wanted the Reaver dead as much as anyone, yet he jumped to stop her before the gun went off. Maybe it was because he didn't want her to be in control of it, or maybe it's because, in that moment, he knew he was truly losing his mother. Either way, there are so many emotions we still have to explore.

We've been staying in my old house back in Burns. My father is there now with Sam, Emma, and Lily. He went from believing his whole family was gone to having a house bursting at the seams with us all. They're patiently awaiting our return, hoping this time that when we split, we'll always come back together.

"Are you ready?" Mason asks as we close the distance. Pushing everything else from my mind, I focus on the here and now. Today is the day I get my memories back. Mason sent a team on information recovery. They found all sorts of things, but among the spoils was a copy of my memories.

I nod toward Mason, feeling happy for the first in a long time. Things are finally looking up. We're out of the tunnel and into the light. All that's left is to fill in the gaps of my memories. I'm ready to replace my lost time. I need to deal with my past so I may continue to move forward.

Lacy and Sonya hurry to us from wherever they've been hiding out lately. Our last correspondence said they adopted a pair of siblings. One a few months old, the other, three years. My heart swells when I see them. Yet, once again, it's Sarge that races forward to get his hello pets first.

"We can't stay long," Lacy says, pulling me into a hug. "Gotta get back to the kiddos." Her face is glowing. I've never been happier for her. She deserves this. They both do.

"Of course," I say. "How are y'all fairing?" Luke has told me I can't have children. I've never had that unexplainable desire for a child—and I don't think I'll ever feel safe enough to bring one into our world—but something inside of me feels empty somehow. Like a piece of my womanhood is stolen away.

Sonya beams. "It's magical," she says. "Especially doing it alongside my best friend." Lacy is pulled into the arms of her wife. Then we say our goodbyes as quickly as our hellos.

"Do you think we'll ever be as happy as them?" I ask, keeping my voice low so only Luke hears.

I receive no verbal response; he just reaches toward me with his fingers and interlocks with mine.

Mason leads us into Cateline's lab. It's been a long time since we've been in here. My eyes flicker to the back of the room where Two used to stay, but the makeshift walls of the rooms have been removed. There's nothing left of her here, only what we carry within us.

"Luke!" Cateline says, smiling. "Miss Thorne. Welcome back!"

I've never been particularly close to the brains behind the entire H.P.S., but I leave Luke to do all the catching up. I do, however, raise a brow at Mason when Cateline brushes her fingers across his shoulder. His face flushes a deep red and I stifle a giggle. *I guess her crush on Luke is gone...*

Cateline hooks me up to her memory machine, new and improved since the last one she worked on. But before she presses the button, I stop her.

"Are you sure you're ready for this?" I ask Luke.

"You're about to get all of your memories back and you're questioning if *I'm* ready?" He chuckles.

I suppose it seems ridiculous. There are a lot of traumas that I'll have to overcome. Traumas he was lucky enough to avoid the first time. "I may be... different," I say. Maybe I'm just nervous. Like he'll finally see my true self and decide I'm not worthy. Perhaps I'm still stuck in survival mode.

Luke smiles, pulling me in to kiss my forehead. "I'll have you in any version, in each universe, in every timeline." His hazel eyes are so intense when he pulls away, I nearly melt from their gaze, let alone his words. "This love cannot be squandered. I think every test up until this point has proven that." The smirk is my final undoing, and I liquify.

I chuckle. "Until the next time we have to take down a government, of course." A smile spreads across my face. Luke grabs my hand, gently squeezing. "Okay," I direct my words to Cateline. "Let's do this."

She nods, getting straight to work. At first, there's really nothing. It's slow, and wispy; almost non-existent. But then, moments hit me. The good. Oh, how sweet the good is. Finding Sarge in the woods, all those nights with Emma in our house. Mason, Lacy, Abby, Zach. Luke. Everyone is here.

The bad comes, too. Scenes return fully shaped, not just the mismatched pieces that came through in my nightmares. But it's not sad. It's bittersweet.

We've come so far.

We've been beaten down, pushed around. We've come out on top each time. We broke a damn regime! The Reaver was a formidable opponent because she was willing to die for the cause. But so were we. We were never afraid to die if it meant others could live in a better world. That means we're the most alive we've ever been.

It's in this moment—with all of my memories filtering back—that I realize why.

Something I tried so hard to fight has been the true cause of our success this entire time. Above all else, when it's all said and done, with every trial and tribulation: love is lurking in each test. And boy did we love hard.

And in the end, love prevails.

EPILOGUE ∘ SARGE

TODAY IS A JOYOUS DAY. EVERY YEAR, PEOPLE GATHER IN OUR home. The small ones run around, giddy with the idea of visitors. I used to run along with them, but today I'm tired.

First to arrive is Mason and Cateline. Her belly is full, though they haven't eaten anything yet. They all take turns touching it, which is strange. There's a new smell about her, one that's exciting.

Then Lacy and Sonya come in. Zachery and Abigail follow, though it's always been confusing to me. They share the names of some other people I used to know, but they don't look or smell the same. These ones are small people, always joining us with Lacy and Sonya. They must be connected. Like me and Amity. Abigail gives great hugs even though her arms hardly reach around my body. Zachery pulls my ears sometimes, but I still like him.

Those that come in make their way around saying hello. I want to greet them at the door, but the bed Amity got me is so comfy these days. Sometimes I don't want to get up from it.

Mark is resting in his chair, watching the hustle and bustle the way I am. He's happy, I feel it. There is happiness everywhere, really. I like it that way. There's less work for me to do.

As the day goes on, everyone gathers around the table, and love fills the air. I know what that feels like because anytime Amity pops into my head, I feel her in my heart too. That's love I think.

She's happy. She's secure.

Despite the commotion, she glances over and our eyes meet. My tail thumps lightly against the ground, though it's tiresome on my bones. She gives me a wink and returns her focus to the table; to her family.

Amity is finally safe. I made sure that every step of the way she would never be alone. That she would have someone by her side, as she had done for me when I was lost and alone. Now I know that she will always be surrounded by others who love her and will keep her safe the way that I did.

The night grows long, but the laughter filters through. Amity places herself at my bedside and helps me lift my chin onto her lap. This is home. Her fingers trail through the fur of my head and my eyes close.

This is my forever.

ACKNOWLEDGEMENTS

THIS JOURNEY HAS BEEN FULFILLING IN SO MANY WAYS, AND I couldn't have done any of it without the continued support I received. So with that comes a new set of acknowledgements for the extra special people in my life who have always been there for me throughout this process.

To Morgan, because she deserves a special shout out. It was a ritual that no book would be released without her stamp of approval, and it certainly wouldn't be seen by any other eyes before hers. However, this book is different. While I really struggled to get the words on the page, she was struggling in real life. So much has happened, and I love her dearly. I knew fairly early that she wouldn't be able to read it before anyone else this time, and while this makes me sad, I just appreciate her in general anyway. She is my very best friend, and she will hold a special place in my acknowledgements every time simply for having that title alone. I love you, girl. Thank you for everything.

To Liz, for being the best writing buddy, event partner, and dragon friend. I'm so happy we met and have forged this amazing friendship together. I hope for many more years of our senseless antics as we both grow in our craft. You outshine everyone in the rooms you're in and I'm just happy to be able to cast a shadow.

Thank you, MJ, for helping me in so many ways. I've learned so much since you've come into my life and have felt a sense of support that's like no other. Our mutual love for each other's books is wonderful and it keeps me going on hard days, as I hope it does for you.

To C.C. and Kleigh, for being the best writing partners. I love our days where we would meet up and workshop. I think y'all are at least 50% of the reason I was able to get this third book done before the universe is destroyed. Our friendship means the world to me, and I can't wait to watch both of you flourish with your own books someday. Until then, I'll keep on enjoying our writing days.

Thanks to Squee, for letting me bounce ideas off him so I'm able to work out my thoughts. Your help with the summary and plot checking is invaluable.

Thank you, Stephanie, for once again creating a beautiful interior and helping me with anything I might need. I'm lucky to have you and am so thankful that these pieces of my heart are laced with your touch as well. It makes them all the more special!

Thanks to my mom, Amy, for her support and for always being proud to tell everyone that her daughter wrote these books. Now you can say your daughter has a completed series!

Thanks to my dad, Marty, for always giving me grace in my schedule to allow for inspiration to flow. I'm so thankful I was gifted your creativity. I hope these books make you proud.

To my grandmother, Lori, who I've chosen to dedicate this final installment to. She has been there, pushing me, day in and day out. It was my biggest motivator. I hope the ending is everything and more for her. Thank you.

Thank you, Matthew, for reminding me that I'm an award-winning writer when the imposter syndrome gets to me. It's always the right pick-me-up when I'm feeling down. This means more to me than you will ever know.

To GetCovers, for once again putting together and refining all of my images in another beautiful cover.

I CAN'T BELIEVE I HAVE A COMPLETED TRILOGY!

AUTHOR INFO

KATI KIRSTEN IS A NORTHEAST PENNSYLVANIA RESIDENT FOR life. On her off time, you can catch her with one of her many animals whether furry, scaley, or somewhere in between. She loves to read, listen to music, and basically do anything she can creatively.

Follow her socials or check out her website to keep up on future projects!

Instagram: @katikirstenwrites
Facebook: Author Kati Kirsten
Website: www.katikirsten.com
TikTok: @katikirstenwrites